OUBLIÉ

A TIMELESSNESS NOVEL

Susana Imaginário

ISBN: 978-1-7398202-5-1 (paperback)
ISBN: 978-1-7398202-4-4 (ebook)

Also by Susana Imaginário

Timelessness
Wyrd Gods
The Dharkan
Nephilim's Hex
Anachrony
Anamnesis

Asterius
Daemons

To Gracinda and Tucha for their unconditional love and life lessons.

You are not forgotten.

Note from the Author

Oublié was originally written as a sequel to *Wyrd Gods* (back when *Wyrd Gods* covered the events of what is now the Timelessness series).

Turning a sequel into a standalone novel was not an easy feat. I spent most of 2023 working through the mother of all revisions, trying to untangle and simplify plot lines so that the bulk of the narrative made sense while still leaving enough connections to the main series in order to (hopefully) trigger the reader's curiosity about the previous books.

Time, and I guess you, the reader, will tell if I've succeeded or not.

Personally, I am happy with the result. *Oublié* is now a much better book than it was when I first wrote it, and it has become a lot more than just a sequel.

Think of it as a monochromatic Bifröst between series.

Thank you for reading.
Susana Imaginário

PART I

*In the beginning, there was darkness and peace
in the Universe.
Then Time wrought light and changed it
forever.*

– Memory on Record

CHAPTER 1

The State of Affairs

*I am the echo of everything, everyone, and
every place that ever was. I am memory.
Nothing more.*

– Memory on Record

The moon was in a bad mood. Seismic waves shook walls and souls alike. Rubble fell from the ever-widening fissures along the tunnels of the ancient structure with each rumble, adding dust to stale air, making it hard to see and even harder to breathe.

Prometheans and Narrum, both descendants of humankind and as averse to each other as they were dissimilar from their ancestors, suffered the tremors with the resigned apathy of those caught in torrential rain with no shelter in sight. After years cramped together underground, they no longer feared being buried alive, at least not half as much as they feared being murdered in their sleep, that is. But for once, the disgruntled dwellers of this primordial ruin had something else to worry about besides each other, the integrity of the walls around them or the moon's moods. Their minds and tongues were kept occupied by the news that had trickled down from the surface in whispers, already exaggerated beyond truth or coherence so that little being said actually made sense. Disagreements abounded, some teetering on the verge of violence, especially amongst those for whom a different opinion was often perceived as an attack. One thing they all agreed upon, though: something had happened. For the Prometheans this meant an opportunity to learn and change, while the Narrum saw it as another excuse to complain and remain still.

Lyam was a Promethean and a man always in a hurry to get somewhere, trapped in a place with very few destinations. He never stopped worrying about the claustrophobic burrows dug deep below the craggy moon's surface by something as ancient as it was forgotten, nor the temperamental celestial body into which they'd been carved, for he better than most knew how much they were unwelcome there. Why the moon hadn't smothered them all yet was anyone's guess. Although this sure felt like a final warning – or, as his sister would put it, a desperate plea.

"Let me through," he said curtly for the fourth time to an equal number of idle Narrum standing in his path. They complied, with the usual mixture of suspicion and contempt reserved for his kind, before resuming their hushed conversations, leaning against the uneven rock walls as if to brace them. Lyam strode past each one with purpose, powered by an irritation forged out of years of forced confinement, and stormed into the captain's private quarters, determined to have his way.

"Eloin, is it true that – oh!"

Eloin – or captain, as she was now commonly referred to for leadership effect – sat on a crate, her worn-out shirt open, pale breasts exposed under the dim light. Jolyan stood at her side, bent over with one ear pressed against her chest, straining to listen.

"Now is not a good time, Lyam," Eloin told him matter-of-factly.

Lyam cursed under his breath. "There hasn't been a good time to talk to you since you assumed command," he pointed out sternly, immediately regretting the words as well as his tone upon seeing the anguish on Eloin's ashen face.

Jolyan frowned at him reproachfully. The deep wrinkles along her brow – carved by age and expressions such as this, he was sure – displayed a magnitude of disapproval that she'd never been able to express with mere words. The crone claimed to have once been a medicine woman, which amongst the Narrum meant she mostly concocted foul poultices from psychotropic herbs to keep the sick docile or chanted around her patients to scare the ailments away. Unfortunately, that still made her the closest thing to a doctor in the colony. To her credit, she was devoted to both her craft and her patients, and she did her best – everyone did under the circumstances – but with no medical supplies or equipment, her best often fell short of saving lives. And by the look of things, this would be one of those times.

Lyam lowered his gaze. His eyes met the lavish quilt Eloin used as a rug. The centrepiece of the otherwise stark and unadorned space always aggravated him. Not only was the fabric wasted on the floor, it proved Eloin cared more about decorating the room than leaving it.

She claimed ostentation was as much a part of being a leader as empathy and ruthlessness. They'd bickered about it often enough. As they did about pretty much anything.

He had no time for petty quarrels, so he swallowed his irritation, peeled his gaze from the floor and took a deep breath to collect his thoughts before speaking again.

"Just tell me if it's true."

"If Thoth says it's true, then it must be true. What do I know? I rarely leave this room," Eloin said bitterly, buttoning her shirt with unsteady hands.

"And whose fault is that?" Again, he spoke in anger. Eloin hadn't chosen their situation any more than she'd chosen her illness or rank in their makeshift society. What was to happen next, however, would be her choice, and he was determined to make her choose correctly.

Eloin's scowl revealed her awareness of this. "What does it matter, Lyam? True or false, it makes no difference to us."

"Of course it does! How can you say that?" He strode across the room to crouch at her eye level. "This is it. This is what we've been waiting for. I can feel it," he added in a whisper.

"Don't," Eloin warned. Her eyes darted from his to Jolyan's, but the elderly woman showed no interest whatsoever in what Lyam said or felt.

"I'm sorry. I know I shouldn't talk about it, but I believe I'm right," he insisted.

"That's not a good enough reason," she hissed. Even like this, pain stricken and frail, her hair thin, the body thinner, eyes sunken in dark circles, Eloin's temper and intelligence shone through her gaze, sharper and brighter than anyone he'd ever known. It was the reason she was the one in charge. That and the fact no one else wanted to be – except him.

"Well, I disagree," he said stubbornly.

They glared at each other for two, three heartbeats.

"Thank you, Jolyan. That will be all." Eloin addressed the elderly woman politely but firmly. Jolyan's bent back stiffened, and she spared Lyam another reproachful frown before leaving the room without a word.

"You should never have taken this responsibility," Lyam said through clenched teeth. "Not in your condition. I should have been the one to –"

Eloin huffed loudly. "Yes, brother, you've made your opinion on the subject perfectly clear on many occasions. The irony is, if it wasn't for you, I wouldn't have to be captain. And without me, you would be dead. Or have you forgotten that?" She pressed her lips in an effort to not let the conversation digress into old grievances. Her body could no longer take the strain of conflict and aggravation. Her mind, on the other hand, still seemed to thrive on it. "Seriously, Lyam, what possessed you to reveal your ability to the Narrum?"

Our ability, Lyam almost said. All Prometheans had telepathy, for all the good that did them.

"Did you actually expect they'd be happy to learn that you can read their thoughts, let alone put you in charge?"

He did. After all, wasn't that what common people wanted? Someone who understood them, who knew what they wanted without them having to ask or explain. Then again, to his eyes, Narrum were not exactly people.

"Besides, you're a man. Men are not cut out to lead." Eloin summed up her little tirade, already out of breath.

"According to women," he grumbled teasingly.

It was true that men were not allowed to govern in Promethean society, an archaic rule decreed by the Matron in another time and on another world. It had no purpose here, in his opinion. Especially when most of the population were Narrum, and they had a completely different perspective regarding gender roles. That had been the reason Lyam figured he'd had a chance. But as it turned out, to Narrum, all Prometheans were meat. And meat isn't supposed to rule either.

Eloin, reading his thoughts, shot him an admonishing look, and Lyam had to fight the overwhelming maelstrom of anger, jealousy, devotion, concern, shame, and pity he always felt in her presence. Added to the struggle were her own mixed feelings of grudging irritation, grief, love, determination, disappointment and pride, both in herself and – even if reluctantly – in him. And pain, of course. So much pain he could hardly breathe.

"Oh, for fuck's sake, stop wincing, Lyam."

"I'm sorry," he said without thinking. Empathy was not something you could just turn off or shut down, like an annoying routine in a Nephilim's artificial mind.

She clicked her tongue. "Stop being sorry, too. It's not your fault."

They were brother and sister; or at least they thought they were. They looked alike. Both had fair skin, light brown hair prone to unruly curls, and large blue eyes. And they could read each other's minds better than anyone else's. It was said post-humans always gestated in pairs to enhance the telepathic abilities between siblings. Their purpose – for there had to have been one at some point – was unknown and no longer particularly useful in this society, such as it was. He'd discovered the hard way that any telepathic ability was more of a hindrance than an advantage in such close quarters, especially when most of those around him lacked any telepathic ability at all, or empathy, for that matter.

Lyam clenched his jaw, determined to get his way. If Eloin still had the strength to appear cold and resolute, then so would he. "Is it true?" he asked again earnestly.

Eloin shook her head wearily. "It appears so. The Nephilim have vanished from the surface of the moon. How or where they went, I honestly don't know. They're not down here, that much is certain."

"They can't have left the moon. Their ship was as much a wreck as ours. There's no way they could have fixed it. Could they?"

Eloin shrugged. "Not even the gods know the extent of what the Nephilim can or cannot do. They are resourceful machines who don't need to eat or sleep. They don't age and they rarely break. Besides, they wouldn't need to fix the entire ship, only the comms, then send a message to another ship to come for rescue." Her eyes widened exaggeratedly. "Or maybe they set off on an expedition to the burning side of the moon and are now partying with the cairn builders. What difference does it make?"

Lyam wanted to scream. Eloin was not prone to bad

jests or speculation. She was being deliberately glib, and for the life of him, he could not figure out why. "You need to send a party to the surface to find out what really happened."

She raised her eyebrows at his suggestion. "What for? It's not like we can follow or contact them, and they would only take us along as cargo. I, for one, am glad that they're gone. It's one less thing to worry about." She glanced at the cracked ceiling as she spoke. The tremors had subsided a bit, but the stillness wouldn't last, she knew.

"For Olympus' sake, Eloin! We need answers. What if they return with reinforcements to storm the temple?" It was a valid concern.

She laughed – a bitter, hopeless sound. "Then there's really nothing we can do about it, Lyam. But if that was their intention, they'd have done it a long time ago. They had the numbers and the means to do it. There's nothing here they want. Not even us. We are not important to them."

"We were, or we wouldn't be stuck here where – everyone agrees, except me – it is safe."

"Safer, yes."

"From what? You just said the Nephilim don't care about us."

"And we shouldn't care about them either!" Eloin strained for patience. "Just because they left us alone all this time doesn't mean they will continue to do so if they suspect we're attacking them. We may never know what really happened that day. But whatever significance we might have had to them, we don't anymore." She touched his cheek tenderly and looked him in the eyes.

"That is a good thing, Lyam. And if they have indeed left this cursed moon, I need you to help me forge a way out as well. Alive," she added as an obscure afterthought.

He snorted at that. They'd tried many things since the crash; leaving had never been one of them. Sure, everyone talked about it and planned for it, but when it came to actually making it happen, no one did anything, not even him. There was always something else more pressing to do, some other task to complete, another tunnel to dig and explore, another problem, another conflict to solve. The years went by, and all they'd achieved was to dig themselves deeper into that hole. "Maybe it's the temple that is cursed, not the moon," he mused. "We are stuck, Eloin. Like insects trapped in cosmic amber. This place…" He trailed off, grimacing at the slaty walls. "It's not natural. We don't even know what it is. What it's made of. Who built it or why it was built. There has to be a reason for us to have been drawn here."

"There was – survival." Eloin indulged him curtly.

"And look how well that turned out for us," he retorted sarcastically. As far as he could tell, they'd lost more people to petty fights, cave-ins, disease and depression since the crash than in the actual battle or crash itself. The elders and most of his people's brightest minds were amongst the first to perish under the cruelty of the resentful Narrum, who'd blamed the Prometheans for their misfortune. Years later, even after the two factions of humanity had resigned themselves to cohabit and work together, things had not improved overly much, and life no longer resembled anything they remembered – as little as that might be. Most of their memories had been lost in the crash, along with pretty much everything else that had once made Prometheans the most advanced – and most respected – post-human race in the Universe. Lyam believed the Nephilim had had something to do with it. And if they were gone, then so were his hopes of ever recovering his memories, let alone regaining control over his life.

"Lyam…" Eloin sounded drained. "I can't have this conversation again. Not now. The Nephilim are not the ones responsible for our amnesia."

"And how would you know? Did Thoth tell you that as well?" he sneered.

Eloin exhaled. "For the last time: I don't need a god to tell me what to think. And the Nephilim have no need of our memories. You must trust me on that."

He felt how deeply she believed it to be true. And that troubled him.

He remained silent for a moment, pondering the best course of action, then asked, "What exactly did Thoth say?"

Eloin closed her eyes and sighed, aware of the consequences an honest answer would have, but decided to give it nonetheless. "He said that he couldn't Reach the Nephilim anymore. That an old curse had taken them to oblivion." She blew out her cheeks. "I'm not even paraphrasing. You know how cryptic he is and how seriously gods take their curses." Like any pragmatic mortal, she gave little importance to the magical or supernatural. But gods lived by means and rules as alien to mortals as the deities were themselves.

Lyam, too, was well aware of the gods' whimsical interpretation of reality and their role in balancing the forces governing the Universe. What happened in their worlds and metaphysical realms was of no consequence to him. To most beings alive, only one reality mattered. "Do you trust him?"

She made a helpless gesture. "As much as I trust any god, I suppose. He keeps to himself and his records. And he's done nothing to harm us," she reminded him.

"That we're aware of," Lyam countered. "What if he's the one responsible for the flaws in our memory, huh?" Another hypothesis they'd explored over the years with no means of testing.

"It's not his talent."

"So he claims. But what if he's the one keeping us here? What if he was already here when we arrived? No one remembers him being on board. And frankly, I can't think of a reason for him to be on the Eagle in the first place."

She clicked her tongue. "Now you're contradicting yourself. If Thoth wasn't travelling with us, then how would he have sabotaged our memory bank?"

"He is a god! Gods have powers we can't even name."

The usual frustration that came whenever they discussed Thoth threatened to get the better of him. But Eloin was right. He could not afford to go off topic. This was about the Nephilim, not gods. He took a deep breath and dropped the argument.

Eloin, however, picked it right back up. "If not for Thoth, we'd not remember anything at all; we wouldn't have a plan or a schedule. We wouldn't even have light, for fuck's sake!" She pinched the bridge of her nose, annoyed that she was repeating herself again.

Besides, it wasn't like Thoth needed her to defend him. He was a god, as Lyam so often liked to point out. The only one that would help her. And she owed him everything.

"Lyam, I understand you're suspicious. We all are. Paranoia is our greatest enemy. Not the moon, nor a curse, and certainly not some bookish deity from a bygone pantheon no one has even prayed to or worshipped for millennia. Let it go. Hey, are you listening to me?"

Lyam wasn't listening, lost as he was in his own chain of thought. Eloin had a point, though. Convenient as it was to blame a god for their troubles, it was also contrived. Not to mention primitive. That was the Narrum's way of dealing with problems. He had to do better than them. Thousands of years of evolution, learning and independent thinking had to come up with a better hypothesis than 'it's the gods' fault'. Still, the simplest explanation is often the most likely… He shook his head in an attempt to dismiss this persistent idea and focused back on the issue at hand. The Nephilim's disappearance was far more important than Thoth's presence. Sure, perhaps they had left – somehow. After all, why wouldn't they? But then why was the moon so upset?

And why did it all feel so wrong?

These arguments got them nowhere. On top of everything, he was now exhausted and depressed, a combination of both his and Eloin's emotions. They held their hands in a silent truce.

"What happened to us, Eloin? The Nephilim might have forced us to crash here, but what's become of us since is our fault. We gave up. You gave up," he amended. "You'd rather we all remain ignorant than risk learning something we don't like."

She shot him a warning look, having learnt from Jolyan that sometimes they work better than words. "You know perfectly well not everyone here is able to deal with the things they don't like. It's all I can do to keep us civilised."

"Perhaps you should do more, then. Civilisation only works when everyone agrees on what it stands for."

Eloin hung her head, already regretting what she would do next.

"Help me up," she said, then took his arm. "Walk with me."

Chapter 2

The Colony

To dwell on me is to miss out on
everything else.

– Memory on Record

"Are you sure you don't want me to fetch one of the twins to carry you?" asked Lyam.

"I am still perfectly capable of walking by myself, thank you," Eloin said petulantly while leaning heavily on his arm. Her weight didn't bother him, only her pace. Each step was performed in agonisingly slow motion, as if to mock his urgency. She could walk faster, but then everyone would see how much even that little exercise cost her, and so they ambled leisurely down the crowded tunnels, seemingly without a care as the walls shook, littering their path and their heads with debris.

Walking down the crowded tunnels next to Eloin was a completely different experience for Lyam. Not just because of their speed but because most of the Narrum loitering about didn't snarl; some actually smiled, in fact – even if half-heartedly – as they flattened themselves against the narrow walkways to let them pass.

There was something about Eloin that, despite being female and frail, she still held their admiration and respect, as if Narrum would only follow someone they were confident they would easily overtake.

Maybe that was his problem, Lyam reflected. He just walked too fast.

They crossed paths with few other Prometheans, which in itself wasn't strange. The Narrum outnumbered them almost twenty to one. Still, something was amiss.

'Where's our people?' Lyam asked her telepathically, keeping his expression locked in a neutral smile.

'Digging,' Eloin replied in the same fashion, waving back at a pudgy child clutching at the dirty skirts of her begrudging mother. 'Where you, too, should be, by the way. We need to lead by example, show the Narrum that we can't stop digging every time the moon has a fit.' 'Perhaps we should,' Lyam said. And he meant it.

She bristled. 'That's not the point. They like to use superstition as an excuse for laziness and discontent. I can't have that.'

'They are lazy, and they use everything as an excuse for discontent.'

'Be that as it may, whatever little work they do helps us.'

A bulbous specimen stood further ahead, one hand scratching his crotch. Another sat beside him, picking at his nose. Little, indeed, Lyam thought with revulsion as he stepped over the man's outstretched legs, all but carrying her along with him. 'Honestly, Eloin. When will you accept that working, and especially working with us, does not agree with these creatures?'

The mystery of the Narrum's presence amongst them was one even greater than Thoth's or the selective amnesia. But at least no one contested that they'd crashed together. There had been plenty of corpses left in the wreckage, and many still wore the coverall uniforms reserved for the lowest-ranking members of a crew. 'I'd love to know how we ended up on the same ship. I mean, they couldn't all have been part of the crew. They are too lazy and dumb to accomplish most tasks. And too ugly to be pets,' he added mockingly.

Eloin kept a straight face, her thoughts neutral.

They had discussed this at length before and narrowed the mystery down to two possibilities: either the Narrum were part of an army, of sorts – for if there was one thing Prometheans were not good at, it was physical confrontation, something the Narrum excelled at, especially en masse – or they had been slaves, which explained their instinctive resentment and mistrust towards Prometheans. Neither option sat well with Lyam, though. The need for an army implied a war. He remembered their ideological strife well enough.

Prometheans despised slavery. They could not bring themselves to enslave machines, let alone other living beings. Not due to any sense of morality, mind, they just didn't trust any work carried out through directives or coercion. To them, only merit and the deep sense of personal accomplishment that came with it mattered. That, in fact, had been the final tear in the schism between Prometheans and Lokians, the Nephilim's creators.

This was not a memory, just something Lyam knew it in his bones to be true.

He realised Eloin had been quiet for too long, her thoughts shielded.

She felt Lyam probing gently at her mind, like one trying to assess if another's asleep. 'We share the same ancestors,' she told him in a tone that implied there was little more to say on the subject.

He had to force himself not to scoff. 'And now we're not even the same species. Be honest, how long do you think this community of ours is going to last?'

'As long as it takes.' Eloin stopped to kiss the forehead of a grotesque baby cradled in its father's arms as she thought this, ostensibly beaming with delight.

She's right, Lyam thought. He was not cut out to be a leader, for he could never be as deceptive as she was towards them. Or to anyone else, for that matter. Say one thing for Eloin: she sure was able to deal with the things she didn't like. If only those Narrum knew the reason they hadn't been expelled to the surface was because she needed every single hand available to dig through the rubble.

∞

They headed down towards the core, the site of Eloin's pet project, where she'd put all of her and everyone else's hopes.

The room that haunted Lyam's nightmares.

On the way, they passed another group of Narrum kneeling in a circle, hands clasped beneath their chins, mouthing prayers to the gods. Brother and sister shared a judgemental glance, in agreement, for a change.

"The imbeciles still rely on prayers," Lyam muttered in disapproval, earning him a sharp pinch on his side from Eloin. Words like those had the potential to start riots amongst such crowds.

Prometheans had long abandoned religion in favour of more pragmatic and useful pursuits. It wasn't that they didn't believe in gods. Quite the contrary. Their criticism of prayer wasn't about belief, but sense. They knew gods were real. They'd often met, traded and even worked together throughout history – or at least they had until the Lokians created the Nephilim, who in turn had decided to enslave the gods. Now few gods remained free, and even fewer cared to deal with post-humans. To them, there was little difference between Prometheans and Lokians, which, to Lyam's mind, was mightily unjust. Prometheans were the descendants of the many who had been against the creation of artificial intelligence, defending the integrity and potential of the human mind. A mind that, when combined with its soul, would always be superior to a soulless sentient machine. But alas, all post-humans looked alike in the eyes of gods. Even the Narrum.

'They would rather do anything but work.' Lyam carried on telepathically, words laden with disgust. 'What are they praying for, anyway?' He avoided Reaching into Narrum minds, for it often felt akin to dipping his hands in shit.

'Some pray for salvation and remembrance, others for destruction and vengeance. It keeps them busy.'

'I thought digging kept them busy.'

'This keeps them busy and happy,' Eloin elaborated scornfully. 'Don't worry. Thoth says most gods are too concerned with themselves and the Nephilim to pay attention to prayers. If any are listening, it's only to laugh at our misfortune. From their perspective, no descendants of humankind are worthy of salvation, nor even vindication. We're rightly harvesting the doom our ancestors sowed.'

Lyam was almost inclined to agree with the accursed gods. Their human ancestors had had it all, but they'd still wanted more. Striving for the improvement of the species was all well and good, but creating the Nephilim as the next step in human evolution towards immortality had been a catastrophe of such a magnitude only truly appreciable in hindsight. Because of it, humanity was now all but extinct. Still… praying was a new low, even for the Narrum, who strove for nothing but the satisfaction of their immediate subhuman needs.

Further down the tunnel, a Promethean couple dragged a tarp loaded with debris; their statuesque bodies bent with the effort, their handsome faces covered in dirt, their once delicate hands calloused and bleeding. Both inclined their heads to Eloin in respect without pausing their task. They tried to keep their thoughts and emotions hidden, but Lyam could tell they, too, had been praying. The realisation revolted him further. 'We were scientists, for fuck's sake. The best humanity had to offer in every field.'

'We still are,' Eloin said firmly.

'Are we? All I see is brilliant minds wasted digging through rock.'

It was an overstatement. The minds may have once been brilliant, yes, and the intelligence was still definitely there in most cases, but the knowledge, the life experience, that was as scattered as the dust in the air.

'Minds without identity, without memory,' Eloin

confirmed. 'At least digging gives us purpose, a goal, much like prayer gives them hope. It's harmless.' An affirmation to herself rather than a statement of surety.

Lyam disagreed. The mind needed more than mere occupation; the soul more than a goal. And he didn't need full access to his memories to know praying was a huge mistake. Gods didn't deal in hope.

You should never let a god learn your deepest desires. It was one of those things he was sure of but unable to explain why. Much of everyone's knowledge was like this: based on intuition or feelings rather than facts. And people having different feelings about similar facts with no way to actually explain, test or prove them was why they'd fought each other and probably why they now prayed as well.

And to think, the reason they'd stored their memories during long voyages was to preserve them, to make sure they remained intact in case of some catastrophe during stasis. Idiots.

They kept walking downwards, faster now, taking advantage of the steep decline. Eloin let go of his arm to walk on her own. She would have to be carried up the slope on the way back, but for now, she relished this small reprieve from her dependence on the strength of others.

"Does Thoth give you hope?" Lyam asked cautiously once they were out of anyone's earshot.

She was taken aback by his question. It almost sounded as if he was jealous of the god, which made no sense for so many reasons. "I don't pray to him. I talk to him."

"And he listens, I'm sure," Lyam teased, trailing a short distance behind, ready to catch her in case she fell or fainted. "Still, that's not what I asked."

She pressed her lips in annoyance. She saw exactly what he was getting at. "Yes, he gives me hope. Thoth's not like the other gods. He's neutral in all this."

"Neutral. Right," Lyam scoffed. Neutrality was not a god's forte. Nor was it something that placated the Nephilim's power lust. If anything, they preferred neutral deities, for they had fewer allies and didn't put up much of a fight. Besides, no sane creature would remain neutral when their survival, their very existence, was at stake.

"Thoth's hiding like the rest of us," Eloin said in the god's defence. "He could have left us up there in the heat or let us all freeze to death here in the dark. He didn't. He cares for our survival. We're in this together, whether we like it or not."

"He definitely cares for something," Lyam agreed.

The thing that most disturbed him about gods wasn't their aspects, or their powers, nor the talents they used to bend matter and reality to their whims. It was how alien their minds and motivations were. After all, to understand an action, one first had to understand the motivation behind it.

"Fine," Eloin said tersely, coming to a halt. "You want my opinion? I think he's lonely and bored and we helpless little mortals keep him entertained. And whatever else he might be, he is a god. So don't piss him off. You won't win that contest, and I can't protect you from him."

He smiled. Well, at least Eloin wasn't blinded by Thoth's divinity, and she was probably a much better judge of character than Lyam would ever be. Still, he wasn't convinced. They might be helpless against a god, but they were not stupid, nor that gullible. Lyam had perceived enough glimpses of Thoth's mind to know he was wary of something. If not them or the Nephilim, then what?

CHAPTER 3

The Temple

To live and to exist are two different things.
Life began with Gaea so Kali had something to
kill. I was aware long before I became alive.

– Memory on Record

They'd arrived at the temple – what everyone called the huge pyramidal chamber at the heart of the underground labyrinth. In truth, no one was sure if the cavern was indeed a temple. They only called it a temple because it sounded better than any other alternative.

When the survivors of the crash had first encountered the intricate network of tunnels, they'd figured it had once been a mine, but the lack of any visible mineral deposits or mining equipment quickly dismissed that hypothesis. Then they'd found entire storerooms filled with nectar – a nutrient-rich paste with a sweet aftertaste, named so after the fabled food of the gods in Olympus. Without it, they'd be dead from starvation; with it, they were simply dying from many other causes.

This discovery, combined with the small number of

cells along the main tunnels, most furnished with beds carved into the walls, some still covered by dusty old tattered blankets, suggested they had once been used as a bunker or – as some, such as Lyam, believed – a prison. There were no signs of prisoners, though. Or of anyone else, for that matter. Dead or alive. They had no clue why the tunnels had been dug in the first place or how any of the stuff got there. And they didn't really care. At least not at first, when their primary concern was each other and an enemy capable of wiping out all their other concerns. They sure cared now.

But those oddities were far from the only mysteries surrounding the temple. For example, there was no running water; they had to collect it manually by container from a well. However, there were waste disposal facilities in several cells. Why not in all, and where did the waste go? No one had cared enough to find out. Most were just glad they existed and were in working order. There was no power either. Every light source was either organic or divine. The glowing moss growing along the walls and luminescent ant-like critters crawling over them defied any attempt at biological classification or ecological comprehension.

And the greatest mystery of all: how the massive subterranean pyramid had been precisely carved from a single block of obsidian-like stone and then filled with rubble had become a source of endless speculation, not to mention the near illegible symbols decorating its walls. The truth was, no one knew where they were. The moon and the eerie planet it orbited featured in none of their databases – that much the elders had gathered before the crash. And the prospect of exploring more of the alien structure – especially the parts that had been clearly sealed on purpose – worried Lyam no end.

The large room was awash with the light of a tiny and flameless white sun conjured forth by the will of Thoth and set floating high up close to the apex. On the ground the outlines of a huge round hatch were now visible after months of digging. The thing that puzzled Lyam the most, and should at least concern Eloin a bit more, was that the rubble had come not from the ceiling or walls of the room itself – for they were perfectly intact – but from other areas of the temple purposely destroyed to fill in this one, and all tunnels giving access into the pyramid had been collapsed in as well.

They'd been living there for months before they'd even stumbled upon this chamber, thanks to the Narrum's relentless search for food and treasure. When questioned about it, Thoth revealed that yes, of course he'd been aware of its existence – for a god's senses reach far beyond a mortal's – but he'd remained circumspect about its purpose, claiming that the obstruction occurred long before they'd arrived and that he had no record of the event or the reason for it.

It was a lie. It had to be. All gods were liars. He'd been the one who guided the crew there after the crash in the first place. But if Thoth wanted them to dig that chamber out, why wait until they'd found it to tell them about it? And why not uncover it himself? Any god can move rock, it is known. Sure, some gods refrain from interfering in the affairs of mortals, but somehow, Lyam believed Thoth was not one of them.

The god in question stood in the middle of the room, close to the rim of the hatch, supervising the work, gilded pen in one hand, black book in the other as usual. He wore nothing but a shendyt and a large ankh that seemed to have been tattooed with liquid sunlight on his chest. His bronze skin glowed with a radiance all its own, patterned by veiny tendrils of gold spreading from the ankh along his chest, arms and back, down his legs and up his temples. He was a scion of Ra, which apparently meant he had some special affinity with light, in addition to the usual powers common to most gods. The moment the siblings arrived, he turned his bright gaze in their direction and smiled deliberately, letting them know he knew they were there and, of course, that they'd been talking about him.

That was precisely why Lyam would never trust a god. No being with so much power could remain uncorrupted or neutral.

They locked gazes in mutual understanding.

"I don't care what you say, Eloin. That one is a lot more than a scribe or an extravagant lamp."

"Shhh! He can hear you."

"I know."

"The fact that he lets you get away with those childish remarks speaks volumes about his character," she said.

On that, Lyam could agree. He just wished he had a better understanding of the language in which the volumes were written.

Eloin nodded in Thoth's direction. "Go ahead. Ask him yourself if the rumours of the Nephilim disappearance are true."

"I already have," Lyam said truthfully. He'd prayed

the question directly to Thoth the moment their eyes had met. It wasn't much different from asking a question telepathically of another empath. You just had to put a bit more conviction into the words. The answer had been the same given to Eloin, likely in the same calm and enigmatic manner, too. This time, however, Thoth had questions of his own. He opened his mind to Lyam, and Lyam promptly closed his mind to him. He had no intention of picking a god's brain, let alone having his brain picked in turn. He'd got the answer he needed. It was true that the Nephilim had vanished from the moon's surface, and that was enough for him – for now.

Lyam's attention shifted from Thoth to the hatch on the floor.

Both the pyramidal core and its buried hatch, crafted out of a type of unknown metal not found anywhere else in the tunnels, were a source of constant unease amongst Prometheans and a powerful motivation for him to leave. Even more so than the Nephilim's supposed disappearance. Unfortunately, it was Eloin's ambition to get that hatch open at all costs, and he – if he was being honest with himself – really didn't want to be down there when she did. Just looking at the thing made him sick. The insignia of a snake eating its own tail had the same effect on him as a radioactivity warning.

"Don't be silly," Eloin had said to his unshielded thoughts after the Ouroboros first became discernible. "Snakes have always been associated with healing and rebirth." She'd used that argument to convince the others. And slowly, by knife, chisel, tooth and nail when it came to that, they'd been digging and scratching around its edge under Thoth's illuminating eye.

"Why doesn't he help?" Gods were prideful beings for sure, but few were actually lazy. "All he does is stand there, scribbling. Is he afraid of breaking a nail or something? And what is he writing, anyway?"

Eloin took a deep breath. "Writing is one of his talents. He can't help himself, you know that. As to helping, Thoth claims he's powerless inside the temple. That it was designed that way; a place of judgement and execution for both mortals and gods."

"It's no wonder they buried it, then," Lyam snorted. "Explain to me again, why are you so determined to unearth it?"

"Because it's important," she replied tautly.

"To whom?! Eloin, just what do you expect to find under there? Tell me the truth, please."

Her posture slackened slightly. The walk had taken its toll. She struggled to stand now, he noticed. "I don't know. I just…" – she took a moment to make sure no one was listening as she spoke the taboo word – "I feel that it needs to be done."

"That's not what I feel at all," Lyam said in all seriousness.

She eyed him askance. "Be more specific."

"I hate it. It makes me anxious. Someone went to great lengths to bury it. I, for one, don't want to find out why."

"I believe it's a door," Eloin said.

"Tsk. If it was a door, it would be vertical. A trapdoor, maybe. And that seal…" He paused, also measuring his next words. "Sometimes I feel the pull of whatever is under it, like it wants to suck me in," he admitted.

She smiled. "Precisely. It calls to us."

He blinked at her. That was close enough to the truth, all right. But how could she not sense it as a threat? "It's a lure, Eloin. Not a call. Whatever is under there, it's evil."

She tilted her head in its direction, as if listening. "Not evil... just... angry and misunderstood."

For the first time, Lyam questioned just how much his sister's illness affected her reasoning.

They believed their affinity with the moon was a consequence of their gift. The problem, as always, was not what they felt but how they interpreted the feeling. One of them had to be wrong. And Lyam didn't think it was him.

"Please, let me go to the surface," he whispered. "If the Nephilim are truly gone, we may finally be able to leave this place. Not the moon itself, perhaps, but maybe we can find somewhere less claustrophobic, less crowded and a lot more civilised." He spared a glance at a Narrum doing the minimum amount of work with maximum grudge, and he sighed. "Eloin, I know you're doing what you think is best for everyone, but digging is only making them more disgruntled and putting our people in more danger. You won't be able to control them for long, not even with Thoth's help – yes, I know you two have been glamouring their thoughts. We share a mind, remember? And I approve. But we need more options. We may not survive another uprising."

She winced, remembering the last time the Narrum had tried to assert their needs. There were only five things they were good at: eating, looting, killing, fighting, and breeding. There was nothing to loot, no conditions to breed – not that that stopped them, mind – nothing to fight over, only against, and even though nectar provided more than enough nourishment, their primal urges demanded meat. To a Promethean it was like cohabiting with rabid and resentful flesh-eating beetles.

"Come on, don't you want to see starlight again before…" Lyam trailed off. It was a cheap shot, he realised, and didn't care.

Her jaw tensed. She was livid, but too tired to express her anger properly. Her heart fluttered painfully in her chest, and she had to force herself to breathe normally. "We're too close to a breakthrough." She'd been saying that for months. She desperately wanted to be right this time.

"Close to an even deeper hole, you mean," Lyam snorted derisively. "It's not just the Narrum who are on edge. The deeper we dig, the more displeased the moon gets. The way to salvation is up, not down, sister." It was an old adage from the time humanity had divided into Narrum and post-human, the latter having left their home planet to explore other worlds and evolve, the former remaining attached to gravity and their old ways.

She scowled at him. He scowled back, mimicking her expression in a way only a sibling could.

"Come on! We can't remember our lives, can't be true to ourselves, can't build anything that works, can't even raise children properly. We dig and eat the same shit every day, and we haven't seen a sky in years!" Lyam's wail called too much attention to them. He lowered his voice. "There's only a handful of us left. We may be the last of our kind for all we know. And we are wasting ourselves buried alive in this hole. Please, Eloin!"

"Things will soon change, you'll see." Eloin spoke like a mother soothing her distressed child. How he hated when she patronized him in front of the others. She would not embarrass him into submission this time.

He pulled her closer. "Things may have already changed. That's the point. Let me take a small party up. Six, maybe seven of us. The twins said it's safe enough to travel in small groups. They'll take us to the nearest cairn and then –"

"Absolutely not. It's too dangerous up there. Besides, I need the twins to remain here for protection. And the moon's unpleased as it is!" Eloin broke free of his grip with surprising ease and started towards Thoth.

"No shit," he said, going after her.

As if on cue, another rumble shook the gloomy cavern. They both stopped in their tracks and turned to stare at each other. For a moment he glimpsed the Eloin she'd been before she'd got sick. Ruthless, unyielding, and uncompromising. She still was all those things, but now he also felt the echo of her doubt, followed by desperation caused by intense fear and pain.

'Why are you doing this, Eloin? Is it to punish me for trying to take leadership, or are you trying to teach me something?'

She closed her eyes and only spoke when the moon had settled again. "I can feel it – as you do – the doom. We don't have much time. Someone needs to keep the Narrum calm, so it too remains calm, understand?"

"Calm as we dig into it?" The question was rhetorical. They both knew that wouldn't happen.

'Please, Lyam, this needs to be done. I need it to be done,' she pleaded telepathically.

'Why?'

'I just do.'

'And I need to know what really happened up there.' He pointed to the ceiling.

It grated on him that he had to ask, let alone beg her permission for something he knew to be the right thing to do.

She frowned at him, unable to understand how her own brother, almost as gifted as she was, could be so clueless, so wrong about this.

He thought the exact same thing about her.

Everyone was watching them now, seemingly just standing there, staring at each other like star-crossed lovers. Lyam took her hand, hanging limp, almost forgotten by her side. It was cold. Her skin had an unhealthy tinge of grey, as if blood no longer ran through her veins. He really could not fathom what possessed her to waste so much of her limited time and energy on this course of action. And she did with the fervour to rival a zealot. 'What are you not telling me, Eloin?'

'Why can't you just respect the wishes of a dying woman?'

He shook his head before he spoke, for words sometimes carry more weight aloud. "If you die, you know what will happen to me next. To the rest of our people. The Narrum can't bear the sight of us, let alone the idea that we can read their minds. They hate us more than they hate the Nephilim. Please, let me do this. Half a dozen workers won't affect progress that much, and if we don't succeed... Well, a minor delay is still a small sacrifice for a chance to learn some answers, no?"

"Don't talk to me about sacrifice!" Her voice broke

as pain assaulted her again. She squeezed his hand until he bit out a curse. Not because of her feeble grip; it was the echo of the pain she felt that made him want to yelp.

She shut her eyes and groaned. "Two."

"What?"

"You'll take no more than two others to the surface: Rai and Audric," Eloin said through gritted teeth.

Lyam opened his mouth to argue, but her tone left no room for arguments and, fearing she might change her mind altogether if he objected to her choices, he remained silent.

"And if," she added in the same manner, "at any point, you encounter one of them, return immediately. Do not engage in any way. I mean it!"

"All right." He was surprised at how convincing he sounded.

"And only go as far as the river. I don't want you getting lost on top of everything else. Learn what you can; enjoy the hot air," she sneered. "You have three shifts."

"Three? That's not enough. It will take at least one shift to reach the river, then another to –"

"Three! Not a moment longer," Eloin said adamantly. "After three shifts, I'm blocking the passageway. I need to put the safety of the temple and our people first. And I'm only agreeing to this because I'm tired of arguing and I know you'll not let it go. But whatever has happened to the Nephilim, we need to make sure it won't happen to us next. Understand?"

"I –"

"Say it!"

"I understand."

She held both his hands in hers, avoiding his gaze. "Promise me you'll return."

He hesitated, for he'd rather not make promises. Promises were for gods and liars, but all things considered… "I promise," he said.

She smiled wanly. "Then go, before I change my mind."

Eloin pushed him away feebly. He spared her one last glance, then another at Thoth in his line of sight behind her and, close to bursting with emotion, turned on his heels to leave.

"Lyam," Eloin called.

Please don't change your mind, he prayed to himself. "Yes?"

"Good luck," she said with tears in her eyes. It was a strange thing to say, for there's no such thing as luck. Unless you count Tyche, the goddess of fortune, and she's not known to be good. But in that moment, Lyam saw that, more than anything, Eloin wanted to go with him.

Pity cut through his soul again. He vowed to himself to find out what had happened to the Nephilim and, in doing so, save her and what remained of their people from that cursed pit.

"Thank you, sister. I will not let you down."

CHAPTER 4

The Party

*To remember is to live – or so they say. I
don't know why. Life is in the present, and
I am the past.*

– Memory on Record

"She wants me dead, is that it?" Rai stood in the middle of her room, hands on her hips, tapping a foot vigorously. Convincing her to join the party had turned out to be much harder than Lyam had estimated.

"What? No. It was my idea." Well, at least the going up to the surface had been. He wondered if he would have included Rai in the party had he been given the choice and realised, not without surprise, that he probably wouldn't have. She might be his lover, the most suitable person for the task, in fact, since she'd been to the surface before, but he did not trust the woman. To say her presence would complicate things was an understatement. They hadn't even left yet, and already it was complicated. He shook his head, grasping at straws to convince her. "I'm going too. Eloin wouldn't send me if it wasn't safe. You know how much she likes me."

Rai eyed him narrowly. "I know how much she dislikes me."

That was not too far from the truth, actually. He puffed his cheeks and tried again. "Come on, don't you want to see the world above?"

"I've seen it."

Damnation… "Again. Don't you want to see it – again?"

"Not really."

He rubbed his forehead. "Curse you, Rai, why do you have to be so difficult?"

She smiled coquettishly. "Difficult, me? I'm already packed." She tilted her chin towards a bag on the floor next to the door. "I'd never sit this one out, darling. It just annoys me that now I'm doing Her Majesty's bidding. It's half the fun and twice as dangerous."

Of course, he should have guessed. A rebel to the bone, Rai was, with her wild red hair cropped short and tomboyish attitude. She always did what she wanted with no regard for permission or need for company. It was one of the things he both admired and disapproved of about her. Always contrary, the best way to stop her from doing something was to command her to do it. Eloin must have relied on that particular trait to hinder his excursion. And the fact that Rai still agreed to go regardless of the command meant more trouble for him.

She picked up her backpack and pecked him on the lips. "I'll be waiting by the passageway. Don't take too long or I'll leave without you."

It wasn't a jest. She definitely would. With no time to lose and no desire to lose it, Lyam stuffed a towel and a change of clothes into his bag along with a few rations of nectar and a sparse collection of items that he figured might be of use, then ran down into the depths of the temple to fetch the second member of Eloin's chosen party.

∞

Audric, unlike most dwelling in the improvised colony, lived alone. Privacy in a place with so few actual living spaces was a luxury, not to mention dangerous, for the Narrum despised privilege almost as much as seclusion and individuality and would take any opportunity to start an uneven fight. But since he'd shown nothing but cold indifference to any potential roommate – not that many volunteered, mind – and made even the most belligerent Narrum anxious, he'd been allowed his own private space: an alcove barely large enough for a man his height to stand or stretch out in, behind the remotest of storerooms.

Whenever Audric wasn't working in the tunnels, he was either drawing or reading. He now sat where he slept, seemingly fixated on sketches of the hieroglyphic symbols found on the pyramid's walls, studying them under the light cast by hundreds of luminescent ants. The ants loved nectar, and Lyam wondered how much of his rations he'd had to use to feed so many of the hungry bugs. And why did he? Moss gave less light, true, but at least it stayed in one place, consumed only water and wouldn't try to eat you while you slept. Still, those were problems Audric didn't seem to have. The ants were all gathered in one spot on the ceiling just above his head, almost as if they were reading together, and there were never any bite marks on him. Lyam would like to learn how to tame the little critters to this level of servitude one day, but he'd sooner ask Thoth for illumination than Audric for advice.

∞

Audric heard Lyam approach and didn't even bother to glance in his direction. This complete disregard for others was one of the many reasons people shunned him. The main one being that he didn't quite look or behave like everyone else either, Promethean or Narrum. On top of that, small accidents often happened whenever he was around. Those had more to do with how others reacted in his presence, forgetting their ongoing tasks to stare or gossip. Nevertheless, it had gained him a reputation of being an ill omen of sorts in the community. It came as no surprise that Eloin wanted him out before they opened the damned hatch – just in case – and Lyam had given her the perfect excuse, while simultaneously encumbering himself with the two most insubordinate, stubborn and hard-to-deal-with people in the colony. Clever Eloin. Well, he'd prove to her how he too could be stubborn.

As usual, when he Reached for Audric's thoughts, it was like shouting into an abyss. He heard nothing but his own echoing query. Not even Thoth's mind was this well guarded.

Lyam took a fortifying breath.

"We're going up," he said matter-of-factly from behind the pile of crates that marked the room's threshold. There was no reply. Audric just kept staring at the page, silent, motionless, apparently oblivious to his presence.

Bristling with annoyance, Lyam forced himself to enter the room. Upon closer observation, he noticed Audric was actually looking at the likeness of a woman, not some cryptic text. She resembled Audric in a superficial way, with the same alabaster skin and jet-black hair. She could be his mother, or more likely, his sister. Whoever she was, she wasn't amongst the survivors, of that Lyam was sure. He opened his mouth to ask about her identity but thought better of it. There was no time, and it really wasn't his business, so he repeated himself instead. A little louder this time.

Audric glanced up at him then, the slightest of queries in his deep red eyes.

"To the surface, yes," Lyam elaborated unnecessarily, before clearing his throat. He felt himself blush, as if he'd done something wrong just by standing there, telling him what to do, let alone prying into his affairs. The truth was, he hated how much Audric intimidated him. He had no rational reason for it beyond the fact that the man was always so quiet and he looked weird, like the brooding blood-sucking villain of a young girl's erotic novel from ages past. Just, well… scarier. His black hair seemed almost blue in the ants' light, and his skin was so pale Lyam could actually see the purple veins underneath it. None of those things should matter, of course, although a different, more accessible personality would have gone a long way to minimise the damage caused by his looks.

The fact that Audric never even made an effort to improve anyone's opinion of him was at odds with Lyam's own approach to social conduct in crowded spaces. Still, this aversion was absurd. The man had never harmed anybody who didn't deserve it, nor had Lyam ever sensed any intention to, not even during the Narrum's riots when he'd bashed in the skulls of a couple of instigators against the rock, without a word or bead of sweat, practically putting an end to the uproar then and there. If only others had followed his example, Lyam mused, remembering the fated event that had claimed so many lives. But that was exactly it, he realised. A mentally sound Promethean would never engage in melee, let alone kill with their bare hands. And no one's that serene. Not after going through what they had. Not while living the way they did. Lyam had never even sensed any genuine emotion from Audric. Everyone felt something. That's why empaths like him had to hide their ability. But not Audric. Now that Lyam thought about it, he didn't remember ever seeing the man laugh, or cry, for that matter. Then again, everyone's memories were fragmented and unreliable, to say the least, so just because you didn't remember witnessing something didn't mean it hadn't happened. Audric may have laughed a thousand times for all Lyam knew. Though, staring at his stern face, clean of expression lines, he very much doubted it.

Please don't make me say it again. It was closer to a prayer than a thought. The silence – and the stare – threatened to break his confidence.

"Does Eloin know about this?" Audric eventually asked in a deadpan tone.

"Of course! She commanded it, in fact." Lyam reinforced the blithe tone with a grin.

The quiet man nodded once slowly, placed the crumpled paper on a pile with others, picked up a satchel, strapped it across his shoulders, and walked past Lyam, heading up the tunnels in long, elegant strides.

Was he packed already, too? Lyam tried not to dwell on the implications of this, glad that at least he didn't have to convince him. He wasn't sure what he would have said to persuade the strange man otherwise.

His gaze drifted back to the woman's likeness, discarded atop the pile. He picked it up and stared at it for a moment, then without quite knowing why, he put it inside his bag and followed suit.

∞

"Finally!" Rai exclaimed when Lyam turned the corner to the entrance of the narrow passageway leading up to the moon's surface.

The self-appointed and almost indistinguishable guardians of the passage, Nenhum and Ninguém, stood at her side, exchanging whispers with identical smirks on their lips. Sharing a private joke at my expense, no doubt, Lyam thought in irritation. The twins possessed an exceptionally enhanced anatomy but a mind not much more complex than a Narrum's, thriving on derogative and coarse humour. Virtually inseparable and incapable of forming a meaningful connection with anyone else, they were a prime example of the genetic achievements of post-humanity as well as of their downfalls. Whenever Lyam saw them smiling at each other like that, he was reminded of Narcissus who fell in love with own reflection.

Their mirth vanished when their eyes met Audric.

"He's coming too?" More a protest than a question from Rai.

Audric spared her a condescending look, not bothering with an answer.

"Eloin's orders," said Lyam.

"The fuck it is. Everyone knows he's Thoth's pet."

Lyam didn't. He thought Eloin had that role. Come to think of it, he couldn't even remember ever seeing the two together, which now raised a few concerns. He'd lost sight of the man right after he left his alcove, walking with a speed and purpose to put Lyam's own hurried steps to shame.

Audric seemed annoyed by the remark; then again, that might have been Lyam's annoyance projected onto the blank man.

"So… just you three, then?" Nenhum asked as he helped his brother pull the intricate yet primitive assembly of cogs and pulleys necessary to move the round stone slab blocking the exit.

"For now," Lyam spoke loudly, hoping to inspire the small crowd gathered there for their departure to at least consider the option. "Eloin fears a trap," he explained in a much lower tone for diplomacy's sake.

"You need bait for a trap." Ninguém chuckled.

"But the captain's right: expendables first," his twin added.

Lyam, Rai and Audric exchanged glances.

"Just open the damned thing," said Lyam, rubbing his forehead. His head had started to throb.

As formidable specimens as the twins were with their towering height and overdeveloped muscles there was little need to guard the passage. Few shared Lyam's burning determination to leave the temple, even fewer his desire to.

If Eloin's soothing empathic abilities and the circumstances that prompted an entire crew of spacefaring people to hide underground hadn't been deterrent enough, years of accumulated rumours and horror stories painting the world above as a nightmarish place of blinding light and eternal suffering combined with their memory – and subsequently intellectual – deterioration created a growing affinity with dark, dull places to the point most Prometheans had become quite content with their surroundings if not their lives. It was one of the reasons Lyam was so intent on bringing them out of those cursed tunnels before they all turned into troglodytes.

"Let's go," Lyam said, taking the lead.

The moment he was about to step through the opening, he felt something push back, as if he'd slammed against a very heavy curtain or a thick membrane, and he had to fight the instinct to lift his hands and push it away. Considering there was nothing there, that would have made him look pretty foolish.

Must show no hesitation, no weakness. Lyam set his jaw and forced his way through it – whatever it was – almost falling over when the resistance sud-denly ceased. It was as if something had been ripped out of him and left behind. The urge to turn back around became overwhelming, and he had to brace himself against the wall so as not to give in to what he was now sure had to be some kind of curse or shield surrounding the place.

Must stay strong. Must keep going. Even if I'm alone. I must –

A hand fell on his shoulder. "Are you all right?" Rai asked, genuine concern in her voice. Audric loomed behind her, red eyes seemingly black in the moss's dim light.

Not alone. Lyam released the breath he knew he'd been holding and smiled reassuringly at her. "I am now."

∞

"So tell me, why did you two agree to join me?" Lyam asked to keep his mind off the dull ache building in his legs and shoulders. The tunnel leading to the surface was much narrower, longer and steeper than he remembered, and he already regretted half the things he'd packed. The weight wore him down – as did the silence.

"I go wherever you go, darling," was Rai's glib reply.

"That's very sweet," he said sarcastically, glad it wasn't true. She liked him well enough, and they were well matched as lovers, but they would never have become a couple without the demographic constraints of their situation. If they could indeed be called as such. A couple of horny strangers, more like, he mused, for the truth was he barely knew the woman. Her personality was quite the challenge, her mind and emotions a chaotic jumble of deceit. He supposed the challenge had been part of the attraction in the beginning. Now it was merely a source of frustration. That being said, she was uncharacteristically candid right now: radiating excitement, eagerness and apprehension – all understandable under the circumstances. But there was something else in her mind he could not quite figure out. A concern, not for herself exactly. If he didn't know any better, he'd say she was concerned with someone's feelings about herself, which, coming from Rai, made absolutely no sense. She never cared what anyone thought, let alone what they felt. Then the idea that she might be considering taking off on her own at the first opportunity occurred to him. Maybe that was what Eloin was counting on. He cursed inwardly and promised himself that if that was the case, he would not waste his three shifts chasing after her. No, he would not.

He prompted Audric for an answer.

"I'm not afraid of the light." Audric's voice echoed solemnly in the dark. By Prometheus, however uncomfortable Audric made others with his silence, it was much worse when he spoke. The planet's light, yes, Lyam remembered it well – too well. He'd tried not to think about it, for he refused to let that grim recollection deter him from his goal. And now, thanks to Audric, he was sore, exhausted, irritated, and anxious. Curse the man.

"Good for you, red eyes." Rai spoke crossly, sharing Lyam's feelings.

They trudged on in a heavier silence than before, which was just as well. The path turned steeper with each step, and the direction the conversation was going didn't exactly inspire the effort required to climb it.

CHAPTER 5

The Record

They also say life is pain. And that is why they chose to forget.

– Memory on Record

Eloin had to stifle a sob when she sensed Lyam vanish from her Reach. She had not realised how much she'd been relying on his presence, and she clearly had not been prepared for the pain of his absence, like the sudden realisation of having forgotten something vitally important. Her heart ached, her stomach sank, while her eyes filled with tears and her mind with doubts.

She looked up at Thoth, writing furiously in his weighty tome. He claimed the black leather-bound volume held an account of every soul he'd assessed, and no matter how much he wrote, the pages never ran out. She believed him. The book itself appeared and disappeared from existence at his will, much like the conjured ball of light above them. Not by magic, not exactly, just one of his many godly perks. To gods, another realm was much like another room. A room to which only they had the key.

Gods are the most privileged beings in the Universe, she decided; they didn't even need to carry their stuff around with them. She wondered what she would store in her private realm, if she were a goddess, and immediately chastised herself for such a stupid reflection. She was no goddess, never would be, and she no longer had anything worth storing either. All she'd ever owned had been destroyed in the crash, including her most precious possession, her health. *And now, my brother is gone as well.*

"Have I done the right thing?" she asked the god. Eloin always preferred to use words to communicate with Thoth. Not only was his telepathy so strong it gave her headaches, it was always safer to talk rather than to pray to a god. Fewer opportunities for misunderstandings, as words were easier to control than thoughts. Still, she suspected he knew what was on her mind, whether or not she voiced it.

His answer came almost before she finished the question. "Yes. The boy won't rest until he sees it for himself. He'd just be a nuisance and a liability to our efforts, staying here."

"And what will he find up there?"

"Nothing," Thoth replied straightforwardly. "There is nothing to find."

Eloin pressed her lips. "Let's hope nothing finds him, either."

Thoth chuckled and kept writing. She'd tried to read a page once. It was all pictographs and strange symbols she did not recognise. She'd asked him to teach her to read it once, he'd said that the language of reckoning could only be understood by gods.

"Why is that?" she'd demanded, offended. "Are gods that much smarter than Prometheans?"

The god had laughed then. The first and only time she'd heard him laugh. It was a roaring, vicious sound. She had no wish to hear it again. And the answer had haunted her since.

"No, Eloin. Intelligence is not what makes a god. I reckon your kind is more intelligent than most gods, by now. But much like the machines, you simply lack the ability to perceive beyond what's in front of you. It's not your fault. For beings with such limited senses and lifespans, you are actually quite remarkable."

Thoth always had a way of using honesty as one uses a cudgel, each word a blow aimed at breaking your spirit.

Time, she knew, is what separated mortals from gods. It didn't matter how much they learned or developed, how well they perfected themselves. When the body died, so did the mind and all it had accomplished. Why had Prometheus created them this way? Why gift ingenuity, self-reflection and willpower to humans without giving them a chance to overcome their own mortality? He wouldn't have. Prometheans like her believed the Titan had given them all the tools they needed to overcome that challenge. And yet here they were, on the brink of extinction.

Here I am, about to be fed to the ants, or worse, the Narrum.

She closed her hands into fists. It wasn't fair. "What is it like knowing you cannot die?" she asked.

Thoth's bright pupils slid from the page to scrutinise her. "Gods can die," said he.

"Not really. You just go to another realm like the Underworld. Or turn into something else, as Ra did. It's more a break from reality than an actual death."

The god stopped writing and closed the book. "You are mistaken. We can and do die – permanently. The Nephilim have killed many gods without even having to chain their souls to their power sources. We die whenever we're forgotten or when we no longer wish to live."

"Is that even possible?" For a dying woman, the notion of not wanting to live was absurd.

"Of course. Even gods have their limits. And we are extremely resistant to change. Adaptation to new environments, new circumstances is not our forte. Many would rather cease to exist than be anything else than what they once were." A shadow crossed his distinguishably handsome features. "One day, even this Universe will die. I look forward to recording the event."

"For what purpose? No one's going to be around to read it."

He blinked at her, his perfect composure momentarily disturbed, then brought forth more light, opened the book and resumed his writing.

"So you're counting on that book to last longer than you, then? Longer than the Universe?"

"Absolutely. What was never alive cannot die."

"Huh, by that reasoning, the Nephilim will outlast us all."

He gave her one of those infuriatingly cryptic but also reassuring smiles only gods can pull off. Her heart began fluttering again. She felt light-headed and wanted to sit down, but there was nothing to sit on and she couldn't afford to appear weak. She focused on the hatch as if drawing strength from it.

"Thoth…" she whispered.

"Yes?" He kept his eyes on the page, but his mind was on hers. She could sense it, a pressure behind her eyes like the prelude to a migraine, mixed with the drum of the moon's heartbeat almost as fast and irregular as hers.

"What's really down there? And please, no cryptic answers, no vague explanations. Give me an answer that I, a mere mortal, can understand."

He nodded and said, "A gateway."

She frowned. Not quite the answer she expected. "To where?"

"That depends. This sort of gateway can lead to many places and many outcomes according to the will of those who enter it."

"So, if my will is to go to heaven –"

"– Cats! Why would you will that?" He sounded genuinely appalled. Now, so was she.

"Why? Does heaven actually exist?"

"Of course it does. And it's a very dull, very grim place." An aversion close to horror radiated from him in waves. "The only way to leave is to make an angel laugh." He spoke as if the task itself was ludicrous.

"Oh…" she said, coming to terms with the idea that angels existed and might not be the beings she had in mind. Then again, neither were gods.

"Dreadful things, angels," Thoth continued. "Rarer than Elysian horses and completely humourless. You'd have a better chance of coaxing a kiss from a cat. Ra knows I tried…"

"Right…" said Eloin, who frankly couldn't care less about angels or cats, or heaven for that matter. Conversations just had a way of getting out of hand with Thoth, and they often ended with him ranting about cats. "Forget I mentioned it. You once told me some wills are stronger than others and that a god's will is the strongest of all. What is your will, then?"

He cupped her chin, a gesture as tender as it was possessive, and for a moment, all the exhaustion, pain and worry just melted away from her. She felt weightless, healthy, and completely carefree.

'I want to know how it all ends so I can make sure the worthy will triumph.' His voice boomed inside her mind, the very definition of a ring of truth. "I want the balance restored and justice served," he said. "Do not lose faith in me now, Eloin. You alone know the truth. I have not lied to you, nor will I betray the trust you put in me. Death will not be your fate. You have my promise."

"But what we're about to do is…"

"Necessary."

She nodded despite herself. How could she not? Gods were bound to their promises, after all.

"Now, are you prepared to do what is required of you once it's open?"

"Yes," she said, and this time, she actually meant it.

CHAPTER 6

The Unexpected

*Oblivion is my gift as well as my curse because
I cannot gift it to myself.*

– Memory on Record

"We've made it," Lyam said after what seemed like an eternity, a great distance from their starting point. Or at least he hoped they had, for they were no longer inside a tunnel but in some sort of chamber. Its surroundings and dimensions were impossible to discern in the gloom.

"I swear, it feels longer every time I climb it," Rai said, catching her breath.

How many times have you climbed it? Lyam wondered but then decided he probably didn't want to know.

"Maybe it is," Audric told her.

Questions about to be raised were forgotten by the light – actual firelight from the lantern he pulled out from his bag. None had seen real fire since the crash, and they all moved closer, mesmerised by the flame.

"Beautiful." Rai's fingertips reached for the flame, driven by childish wonderment. "Ouch! It's real."

Audric smirked at her. "As opposed to what?"

"Thoth's conjured beacons," she said absently.

"How did you…?" Lyam trailed off, glancing at the pitiful light provided by his glass jar filled with glowing moss in jealous dismay. Eloin would be livid if she learned about this, he thought. Fire was not allowed inside the colony – a place with limited oxygen, no proper ventilation and many flammable tempers. Not that they needed it, mind. They had enough warmth, plenty of light, and nectar didn't require cooking.

"Thoth gave it to me," Audric said, all but daring Rai to question him. But her attention was still on the flame.

"Of course he did," Lyam sneered. Bloody god. So that's where you went off ahead of me. He didn't understand why the realisation made him even more jealous and annoyed. He should be grateful. After all, light, especially firelight, could be very useful, and he didn't even have to be the one carrying it.

Audric lifted the lantern high above his head so all could take a good look at their surroundings. They'd arrived at another pyramidal chamber, similar to the one at the core of the temple except in size. This one was much smaller, though extensively decorated with tapestries, cushions and actual furniture, not hollows dug out of the walls or carved from the stony floor. Piles of rubbish salvaged from the Eagle lay against the walls and an assortment of skeletal body parts from the Nephilim's Faithful, the basic constructs programmed to defend their sentient masters, were arranged on the floor, like a madman's attempt to assemble a jigsaw puzzle of artificial anatomy.

"What is this place?" Lyam asked no one in particular, his mouth slightly agape. There was even a bed, complete with pillows and covered with a quilt fancier than Eloin's rug.

"You're in my room." Answered a low, gruff voice from right behind them. The three turned at different speeds: Lyam being the fastest, nearly jumping in place as he did so, Audric the slowest, moving more as a formality to face the speaker rather than a reflex.

Barely four feet tall, the man addressing them was two-thirds the size of a normal human, his bone structure disproportionately deformed. The legs too short for the torso, the head – of normal size – too big for the body. He had long coarse hair and an even longer and coarser beard complemented by a smooth and well-groomed moustache. He wore leather overalls and a metal helmet, a light fixed to it.

Lyam had heard of the existence of these creatures, often featured in fantastical stories told to entertain young children, usually involving a helpless princess and a prince with nothing better to do but rescue her. His ancestors had long ago fixed the human genome to avoid such mishaps, even amongst the Narrum. Lyam never imagined he'd live to see one, certainly not here of all places.

"Berdnard!" Rai bent to hug the creature as if it were a child. "It's so good to see you again!"

Lyam could only stare, his mind struggling to come to terms with his senses. He glanced at Audric and got an insouciant shrug in reply.

"Yes, good to see you too, lass. Them, not so much." Berdnard's voice sounded like it came straight from the depths of his barrelled chest. The dissatisfied curve of his mouth was enhanced by the thick moustache, beady eyes glaring suspiciously at the two taller men. "You said you'd bring the twins. Those two aren't even brothers."

"Circumstances changed," Rai said. "I had to make do with these two. One rarely speaks and the other talks too much, but they won't be too much trouble. Will you?" she asked defiantly.

Audric gave her a thumbs up and went about picking at random stuff in the room.

"You two are acquainted?" Lyam asked unnecessarily. The idea still confused and appalled him in equal amounts.

"He likes stating the obvious, huh?" The short man snorted, one bushy eyebrow raised towards Rai.

"Give him a moment to adjust," she said charitably.

Lyam needed a lot more than a moment to make sense of this development. "You live here?"

Berdnard sneered at his incredulity. "The perks of exclusion, my boy. I'm too offensive, even for the Narrum."

Lyam had no arguments there. "How? I mean, what do you eat? Drink?"

"The same as you, Promethean. Use your superior intellect to figure out how," Berdnard replied gruffly.

"The twins, of course," Lyam realised. "But… why?"

"Someone needs to keep an eye on the Nephilim," the dwarf said.

"That's Thoth's job," Lyam protested, not sure why.

Berdnard frowned, giving him a truly savage look. "Thoth, bah. Don't ever trust a god."

Again, no argument from Lyam on that observation, only confusion. Words failed him. His mouth was unable to keep up with the many questions running through his mind, but he did not dare ask them telepathically in case Berdnard, like all Narrum, took it as a personal assault.

"And I thought the twins were thick," said Berdnard. "You people really favour height over wit, don't you?" He spared another suspicious glare at Audric, now towering above him with the intent a predator would show its prey. "Or manners. What are looking at?"

The pale man smiled wolfishly. "Berdnard. The name suits you. Did you pick it yourself?"

The creases on the short man's forehead put Jolyan's to shame. "Well, aren't you tall and witty. Mind your own business or I'll take you down a notch!"

"Ignore Audric," Rai said. "He likes to make others uncomfortable. It's his talent." She shot him a warning glance, then whistled approvingly at the bed. "I should have pissed off Her Majesty a lot more. Maybe she'd have exiled me too," she said wistfully, stretching herself on top of it. "You're living the life up here, little man."

"Careful with your adjectives, lassie. I've killed men for less."

Rai grinned mischievously. "Ah, but you don't kill women, not while they're in your bed, surely."

"Keep your boots off my pillow or I might make an exception!"

This was when Lyam noticed the massive axe strapped to the short man's back – another perk of exclusion? Weapons were not allowed in the colony, where so many Narrum would gladly cut a slice or two out of you. Eloin had made everyone throw pretty much anything that could be used as a weapon, even tools, down the well after the massacres in the first few days, when the Narrum realised they might be stranded there forever and feared there would not be enough food for everyone. That knowledge, added to the general state of paranoia and frustration caused by the crash and memory loss, led to a regression in social behaviour of such magnitude that it halved the number of survivors. Only when the nectar stores were found was the animosity, much like the initial incident, willingly and collectively forgotten. For the most part, anyway. It was no secret to the post-humans that many of the carnivorous subhumans cohabiting with them would gladly eat steak instead of nectar. Still, it was amazing how less homicidal Narrum got when they had to use their bare hands and look their victims in the eye before slaughtering them.

The gut-wrenching realisation that Lyam had nothing to defend himself with in case the angry little man decided to use his axe on him forced him to take a step back. He glanced appealingly at Audric, who had lost interest in Berdnard, his attention now on a tapestry hanging on the opposite wall. It featured a diagram of sorts. His momentary levity towards the dwarf had already been replaced by the usual mental and emotional vacuum.

"This one's a bit small for me," Rai was saying about the bed.

"More like you're too large, perhaps," Berdnard replied.

Lyam had had enough. "Stop the mindless banter, you two. Rai, who is this man and where the fuck are we?"

"I told you who I am already! We are in a room, under a mountain. I live here, and I'll be your guide to the river. Good enough?"

Lyam turned to Rai. "Does Eloin know he's here?"

"Of course she does. Who do you think banished me in the first place?" Berdnard replied.

"And the twins know it too…"

"Obviously."

Suddenly, much of their joking and behaviour around him started to make sense. No wonder they mocked him. Eloin had kept him ignorant on purpose. How did she even manage to keep something this big a secret from him? And why?

"Who else knows?" Lyam's gaze fell accusatorially on Audric, now shaking some sort of cubic container close to his ear, straining to listen.

"Only us," Rai said. "It's our secret, a backup plan, if you will. In case we have to abandon the temple for some reason, like say, for example, its collapse due to us messing with its foundations. Or something worse."

"Like what?!" Right then, to Lyam, nothing could possibly be worse than this revelation, this betrayal.

Rai propped herself up on the bed. "I don't know. But it can always get worse. I know that much. To expect otherwise is a failure of the imagination." She paused,

musing to herself. "I wonder who said that. Anyway, it was Eloin's idea. She's obsessed, not stupid."

Lyam's imagination had failed for sure. Of all the things he imagined finding on the surface, this had not even come close.

"A backup plan," he muttered ruefully. Yes, if there was one thing Eloin liked, it was backup plans, since she herself had been one. In hindsight, some of Eloin's irrational decisions regarding the exploration of the surface, as well as her enmity with Rai, started to make sense. But how could both women in his life keep Berdnard a secret from him for this long? And for what reason? She would have a world of explaining to do when he returned.

"Why didn't she tell me?" Lyam whispered to himself in dismay.

Rai snorted a chuckle. "Are you joking? You can't keep a secret."

"What? Of course I can! How can you say that? The shit I Reach daily from everyone's mind. When have I ever shared any of that? Even with you!"

"Oh sure, you can keep other people's secrets well enough. Just not your own."

He blinked a few times.

"Come on! You're an open book, an emotion dispenser to anyone but a Narrum. And even they can probably sense something when you're in a particular mood. You're honest and passionate. Two of the things I like about you." She winked.

Honest?! All these years he'd done nothing but deceive: he'd lied about his feelings, his ideas, his plans – his dreams. Had he failed miserably, or had he

been too successful? Either way, he burst out laughing. But honestly, he wanted to hit something.

"What's this?" Audric asked, holding up an extravagant piece of arm jewellery with several embedded gemstones.

Berdnard gave Audric a shrewd look. "I found it the other day by one of the cairns."

"Can I take it?"

"If you like. It's too flamboyant for my tastes. But if it turns out to have value, I expect some compensation."

"Agreed."

Lyam had stopped laughing and was back to trying to make sense of it all – one odd and cruel revelation at the time. He squinted at the walls again.

"I don't remember this room."

"That's because you were probably too busy looking over your shoulder the first time you ran through it," Berdnard said. "It was empty back then. Likely you thought it was just part of the tunnel."

Lyam summoned the fragmented memories of that fated day. They'd run after they crashed. They'd had to. The Eagle was burning, about to explode. The Nephilim's Faithful chased after them, closing in. The planet's light glared oppressively from above, and there was nothing but rock and ash in every direction. Then Thoth had lighted their way and guided them to the base of a sheer cliff face. He remembered the half-concealed opening between two massive boulders clearly. He, Eloin and the few surviving elders had cleared the entrance of small rocks and sandy ash with their bare hands while Audric and the twins deftly moved the heavier stones

almost as if they'd done it many times before. Then the Narrum swarmed on the Nephilim's Faithful like ants, tearing them apart with their bare hands. He glanced at the proof of it scattered on the floor. The remaining survivors made it through the aftermath to join them. They'd run straight into a downwards tunnel. There'd been no rooms in between. He would swear on it. Those memories had been etched with enough adrenaline to make them unforgettable, visceral. And as far as he knew, there was only one way in and out of the temple. The tunnel might have seemed longer this time, but it had been as straightforward then as it was now. So how in Prometheus' name had they got here?

"Do any of the cairns have access to the temple?" Rai asked, as if reading his thoughts. Maybe she was. He really had to do something about his alleged transparency. Either that or use it to his advantage.

"If they did, you'd have known about it by now," Berdnard said. "Nah… This is the only access as far as I can tell. Maybe Eloin's mysterious door will lead to others…" He trailed off, chuckling to himself as if at a private joke. "I guess we'll find out soon enough."

Something in his tone triggered Lyam's senses. But unlike most Narrum, Berdnard kept his mind well guarded – the word buried came to mind – and all his emotions tempered with curmudgeonly and highly aggravating to read.

"You took these from their ship?" Audric asked of a length of tapestry depicting what looked like a woman in a radiant suit of armour bursting from a bearded man's head.

"Most of what you see here came from the crash," Berdnard replied. "And no, that one you can't have. I like it."

"I can't believe this…" Lyam moaned to himself, unsure of how to deal with this turn of events and completely lost about what to do next.

"You want to take a cushion, have a rest, moan about my existence and your cunning sibling a bit more, or do you want to go outside and look for the Nephilim?"

The half man had a point. This exasperation led nowhere. Lyam had been deceived. He felt hurt and confounded, and too tired to deal with either emotion. He would stick to his plan.

"Where's the exit?" he demanded, making no effort to disguise how much he wanted to be out of that room and away from those who he was beginning to consider strangers if not enemies. You have a goal to accomplish, he told himself and held on to that thought, for time was running out. He would find out what happened to the Nephilim. Then deal with these bizarre developments afterwards.

Berdnard pointed to the opposite wall where another stone slab stood blocking the exit. Lyam ran to it, tried to push it aside, and failed. He tried again, powered by pride, fear and frustration. Failed again. It always took at least two people to slide the enormous stones. And the twins were giants compared to him. "Can one of you give me a hand?" Lyam grunted, face pressed against the immovable object, muscles and patience almost depleted.

Rai remained sitting on the bed, sucking on a bulb of nectar. Audric kept studying the tapestry.

"We are wasting time here!"

Berdnard put on a coat. "Hasty, isn't he?"

"Very." Rai's tone implied more than one meaning.

The short man moved to unlock the mechanism. "Normally I wouldn't lock it," Berdnard explained, turning the lock, "but I didn't want to risk leaving it open this time, in case you people are right and this vanishing act is part of some desperate attack plan."

"Sensible," Audric said, rejoining the group. "And what will you do if the Nephilim are waiting for us right outside, ready to barge in the moment the barricade is removed?"

Berdnard strained his neck to glare at the tall man. "I'm sending you ahead."

Audric smiled genuinely this time and, with little effort, pushed the stone aside, then stepped through the gap without hesitation.

"Humph," the short human grumbled in his wake, then turned to Lyam. "You two go next. Tall folks first."

"Aren't you supposed to be our guide?" Rai asked mockingly.

"Yes. I'm guiding you out."

Lyam didn't need to be told twice.

CHAPTER 7

The Moon

There's no such thing as collective memory.
Only collective agreement – or delusion.

– Memory on Record

The passage was another Lyam didn't remember crossing. Then again, they were all starting to look the same, like psychic wormholes. He kept his eyes on Audric's lantern ahead to make sure there were no branching paths or detours. Rai's footsteps sounded sure and steady behind him, followed by Berdnard's more rushed ones.

This is wrong, he decided, unsure if it was even real. They had not taken this route the first time. He would bet his life on it. My life, he mused. My wasted life playing second fiddle to a woman who clearly didn't consider me fit to keep a secret. Oh, Eloin, why do this to me? I deserved better…

"Stop feeling sorry for yourself. You're making me sad," Rai said mockingly.

Damnation, am I really that obvious? Not for the first time, he cursed his gift, wishing he had no empathic ability, like the Narrum. Or Audric. He glared at the back of the tall man's head. How come he had not taken offence at being lied to, nor showed even the slightest concern about the turn of events? He always acted like nothing was out of the ordinary. And sure, no one even knew what ordinary meant anymore. Still, the way he bargained with the dwarf as if he was a customer talking to a merchant at a market stall, without even raising an eyebrow at his existence – not to mention appearance – or where he'd got all his junk to begin with was a bit too casual, too nonchalant for someone kept in the dark. He had to have known something, suspected it somehow. Either that, or he really didn't care either way about anyone or anything. Lyam wasn't sure which option concerned him the most.

"Now you're making me frustrated…" Rai sighed.

He turned on her. "Well, deal with it! You've done a fine job ignoring my feelings all the time we've been together. Why change now?" By the gods, he was so angry he could have kicked her. In the back of his mind, he felt the moon shudder and, in a pique of irritation, stomped the ground instead.

"Actually no," Rai said.

"Huh?"

"I never ignored your feelings. I just… Well, they never bothered me before. Now they are pretty damn loud. Tone them down a bit, will you?"

If only it were that simple, he thought bitterly.

Her own feelings of annoyance exacerbated his, and the longer they stood there arguing, the worse the tremors seemed to get. "Can you feel the moon too?" he had to ask.

She stiffened. "No. I want nothing to do with the moon's feelings. Why?"

"Nothing. Let's move on."

Lyam found himself suddenly pinned down by the spotlight on Berdnard's helmet. It moved from him to Rai.

"Got anything to share, lass? The only moon I feel is the one under my boots." The disgruntled suspicion on his face was magnified by the light halo above it.

"Empath's superstition," she said dismissively. "Ignore him."

So, it appears I'm not the only deceived party in the group. How women loved to make fools of men.

He turned back around, savouring this new morsel of information, and nearly bumped into Audric. His gaunt face, half-concealed by shadow, betrayed nothing, and the way the lantern's light reflected in his eyes made them burn like hot coals set in a skull. "Yikes!" The exclamation was out of his mouth before he could close it.

"Now he's afraid," Rai chirped.

"Shut up, Rai," Lyam snapped over his shoulder. "Keep my feelings to yourself until this is over. Agreed?"

She poked her tongue at him in the gloom.

They kept going. Slowly, light began to filter through a gap up ahead, brighter and warmer than the one inside the temple. A harsh and uninviting light. Its purple hue, so different from the moss and ants' soft white luminescence they were used to, and even more so from Thoth's tiny stars or any actual flame, appeared unnatural and punishing to their eyes. They kept on towards it, regardless. And Audric stepped into it unhesitant and unafraid, as he'd said he would be. The rest of the group slowed their steps unconsciously and approached the threshold between shadow and light as if it were a physical barrier, an obstacle they had to jump through.

"Welcome to the real world," Berdnard said. Several interjections and grunts followed. "There's no shame in crying. Everyone does when they first see the light, like a newborn babe!"

This wasn't the first time any of them had seen the planet's light, of course, but their memories were like their eyes, unaccustomed to the experience.

"Don't look straight at it unless –" Berdnard continued, but it was too late. They all had their faces turned to the angry ball of multicoloured swirls taking up most of the sky. To the left of the tempestuous maelstrom of clouds surrounding the gas giant around which the moon orbited, a white star shone shyly and alone against a dark canvas of emptiness. The star, a yellow dwarf roughly the size of Midgard's sun, was the smallest of two in this system. Lyam remembered that much, for some reason.

"Ah! Mother Earth!" Rai exclaimed.

"Now, now. Don't insult Mother Moon by calling out to another," Berdnard chided.

"Celestial bodies are not gods; they know nothing of jealousy," she told him.

He laughed. "Want to bet your life on it, lass?"

Lyam cursed, for he certainly wouldn't. The moon orbited a lot closer to the planet than he remembered. Her black shadow taking up almost a quarter of its diameter, a stark void amidst the glaring light. It then occurred to him that perhaps the reason Mother Moon was in a bad mood wasn't because of them, but the fact she was stuck with such an ugly planet.

"Our discomfort amuses you, old man?" Audric asked sternly. He might not be afraid of the light, but he certainly was not comfortable under it, either.

Berdnard sobered a moment, then beamed back at him. "Oh, it does, very much so."

That's a point, Lyam thought. Berdnard was not only the shortest man he'd ever seen, he also seemed to be one of the oldest. His best guess put him over half a standard century, like an elder, while most in the temple seemed between twenty and thirty-five years of age – an estimate, for no one knew exactly how old they were. Their relative youth, much like their fragmented memories, was a taboo subject, especially around Jolyan, who had to be well over seventy. Of course, the only reason Lyam was thinking about it now was to distract himself from the pain in his optical nerves.

He narrowed his eyes to focus, both out of disdain and necessity. The damn light was indeed too bright. And the heat wasn't helping matters either. He could already feel the sweat soaking the thick fabric of his shirt. Right then, the reason the crew retreated underground seemed pretty obvious indeed.

"If you think it's bad now, wait until the red sun's shining directly upon it," Berdnard said.

"It gets worse?" Lyam almost squeaked.

"Yes," Rai said miserably. She'd succeeded in keeping her emotions contained, but her body language showed how oppressed and uncomfortable she felt. Two states never before witnessed in the woman. "This is nighttime."

"Eh?" Lyam squinted up again. It never got dark

on the moon, but nothing this bright should ever be called night.

"Does it look bigger to you?" Rai asked Berdnard, shielding her eyes from the sky.

They'd never got around to measuring the planet, the moon or their orbit properly. "Too erratic," Eloin had said. She'd been working on it before she found out she was sick, and other more pertinent things had been on her mind since.

Berdnard frowned at the planetshine until his eyes started watering. "Hmm. It is particularly bright today," he conceded with a hint of annoyance, even if neither temperature nor brightness seemed to affect him overly much. "Better to leave nothing exposed."

Lyam was about to ask what Berdnard meant when Rai took out of her pack a large hat made out of what had once been a thermal blanket. From his own pack, Audric took out a long black cloak with a wide hood.

"Yes, very good. It's always wise to carry your own shade up here," Berdnard told them.

Lyam could have cried. The only thing he'd packed that might provide some sort of shade over his head was a towel.

"Where did you get that?" he asked of Audric's striking cloak. Something about it put him in mind of clerics and secret societies.

"My pack," the man replied curtly.

"And before that?"

"Who knows?"

Lyam wondered what would happen if he punched Audric in his stoic face but got distracted by Rai, who had begun taking off her clothes.

"I wouldn't do that if I were you," Berdnard warned. "It's too hot!"

"You'll get used to it."

"I don't remember it being this hot," she insisted.

He shrugged. "That's because your memory sucks."

He said it as a joke, but it wasn't funny, of course. Everyone's memory sucked. Or had been sucked into the ship's computer, where it remained, out of reach forever. No one remembered their childhood, their family, their life before this. Only flashes of particularly traumatic events, a few random names, the odd mantra or task that had been learnt through rote. Even keeping track of time required a chronicler. Between that and the monotony of their tasks, the days just blended in together in the underground. No one knew for certain when anything had happened in relation to any other event. Life before the temple was like a dream, the experience fading with each waking moment, leaving only a feeling, the imprint of a memory to build upon.

These few minutes spent on the surface, on the other hand, already felt like a never-ending nightmare. Something their bodies would definitely remember, if not their minds.

Lyam wrapped the towel around his head and considered hanging a shirt under it as a veil, but he didn't want to mess up his spare one. By how much he was sweating, he would need it soon enough.

"I believe in learning from experience. Experience is better than memory," Berdnard offered as a means of apology, staring up at them. "After this sunburn, you'll never forget to bring a hat when you come back here."

"If I'm ever coming back," Lyam grumbled. Frankly, he was starting to forget why he'd wanted to come up so badly in the first place. Nothing so far had gone according to plan, or sense, for that matter. I'm such a fool, he thought. Then he realised something. Had he not been feeling so sorry for himself, he might have realised it sooner. The moon had gone silent. There were no emotional echoes or tremors in his Reach, only the roar of the mighty celestial body above. He looked at it again and could almost swear he sensed it looking back.

Behind them, an enormous mountain of a rock jutted from the ground. It was rather too cylindrical in shape for a mountain and the only geological formation for miles in every direction. Lyam reckoned it was the remains of some ancient alien volcano. And it had to be at least part of the reason the temple had been built underneath it.

Far ahead the wreckage of the Eagle could still be seen covered in ash.

"What happened to the bodies?" Lyam asked, realising he'd never really cared to before. "I remember seeing bodies everywhere." I remember running over them, he added to himself.

"Buried," Berdnard said. "The Twins took care of it, after the elders perished. I helped. The moon did the rest. Nothing remains now.

"Are you coming or what?" Berdnard called, already a fair distance away with the others.

Lyam had not noticed the group leaving his side, and he had to run to catch up with them.

CHAPTER 8

The Planet

I've lived countless lives through the memories of others. I enjoyed them better than my own.

– Memory on Record

Compared to the kaleidoscopic planet up in the sky, the moon couldn't be more achromatic. There was little more than ash and rock in every shade of anthracite as far as they could see. Cairns, the only signs of civilisation on the surface, were few and far between, and almost all of them were in ruins. Named so after their resemblance to prehistoric memorial tombs in ancient Midgard, they comprised small domed structures erected by piling up the eroded stone strewn about the moon's surface. Much like the network of tunnels under the mountain, no one knew who had built them or for what purpose. Their overall dimensions suggested the builders had to have been roughly the same height and build as humans, but even the largest ones wouldn't have sheltered more than three or four people and none had any of the common features found in early human dwellings: no hearth, no tools, no waste or remains of any kind in those that had been searched. They could be decorative for all anyone knew. When asked about it, Thoth only said that they were old, very, very old. And that was saying something, coming from a god.

Walking through ash was hard. The worn-out and inadequate footwear, designed for the flat decks of ships, made it even harder. And the effort, along with the heat, the light, and the alien moonscape, left Lyam dizzy. He breathed heavily, which made him even dizzier until he was forced to brace himself on Audric's sturdy shoulder following a particularly badly placed step. Something about the cloak's fabric under his fingertips triggered a memory.

"I've felt this before," he said.

"Maybe you had one too," said Audric.

"Maybe I did…" It was a fine cloak, and he liked fine things, after all. Now he really was jealous of the man's attire and the cover it provided. His improvised turban did little to protect his eyes from the noxious light. However, there was something else beneath this practical covetousness he couldn't quite place a finger on. An indistinct crowd wearing identical cloaks appeared in his mind's eye. They were chanting – No, wait – His ears were ringing. He was about to faint.

"Apologies, I'm a bit lightheaded," he admitted, leaning heavier on the taller man. Audric had an unusual physiology, to say the least. Prometheans had been genetically selected and enhanced to reflect the Olympian ideals of beauty. Their bodies were meant to be looked at and admired, and as such, they possessed the aesthetic perfection of a marble statue: beautiful, imposing and utterly rigid. Audric didn't quite fit this standard. Taller and thinner than most, he had the body of a dancer: strong and lithe in equal amounts. He still looks like a bloodsucking corpse, though, Lyam thought pettily.

"The dizziness is normal. It will pass in a few days," Berdnard said matter-of-factly.

"You mean shifts," Rai corrected him.

"No. I mean days. You're on the surface now, lass."

"Days… That's great," Lyam mumbled to himself.

No one cared to comment. They all waited for him – again. How was he the one dragging behind? It wasn't fair. Without him, they would not have come. Would they?

Damnation. He had no time to speculate, to doubt. No time to be this weak. He took a sip of water and another bite of nectar, both fuelling his body and perking his mind almost instantly. Under normal circumstances, he rarely needed to drink. Nectar alone was enough to sustain a living body, but in this heat, his small supply of water was dwindling alarmingly fast. They'd better reach the river soon.

Lyam straightened himself, reinvigorated. "Thanks. I feel better now."

Audric acknowledged his gratitude, then left his side to pick up something a few paces away that had caught his eye – a brooch. It was dark grey, like the ash and the stone that made up the moon, about three inches in diameter and a snake devouring its own tail.

"Well spotted, red eyes," Rai said while looking around in case there were more artifacts to be found. "I always figured you saw things on a different spectrum."

"I saw a glimmer," Audric offered as an explanation. He sounded far away, like his gaze.

"May I see it?" Lyam took it from the man's palm without waiting for an answer. The metal looked dull and aged. It reflected little but the snake, exactly like the one on the hatch Eloin so desperately wanted to open. "What do you think it means?"

"Means it's mine." Audric took the brooch back and pinned it to his cloak.

"You're a strange man," Rai said, squinting up at him.

He winked at her.

"We'll never reach the river if you keep stopping for snacks, banter and trinkets," Berdnard huffed.

They resumed walking.

Lyam occupied his mind, wondering about rocks. The whole moon seemed to be composed of ash, dust, and stone. Sadly, all he knew about geology would fit on one page, even before the memory loss. These rocks were similar enough to what the temple had been carved from, just a lot more worn somehow. They sort of looked and felt like granite, but they were much harder and lighter – even if still too heavy for him, Lyam thought grudgingly, remembering his struggles back in the dwarf's den. In truth, he couldn't care less about rocks. He was just trying to avoid giving much thought to the things he did care about, which now also involved snakes and cloaks, apparently.

"So, when did it happen?" Lyam asked, making a tremendous effort to keep his mind on his quest.

"Hmmm... two, maybe three days ago, I guess," Berdnard replied.

"You guess?"

The short man scowled up at Lyam over his shoulder. "Yes. I guess. Whatever happened must have happened during daytime – when the planetlight is at its brightest. I always spend the days inside the rock. That cursed light bothers me sometimes. It makes you see things…" he added gloomily, smoothing his moustache and pulling the rim of his helmet down past his eyebrows. It was both reassuring and worrying to know that even Berdnard, a man of naturally low sensitivity, actually feared something. The vulnerable state didn't last long, though. "And it's not like I saw them every day; they rarely leave their cairns."

"If you rarely saw them. How can you be sure they're gone?" Lyam insisted.

"Their pets."

"Pardon?"

"They were roaming the hills, looking for their owners."

Pet was a kindly term for the reptilian monsters and daemon hounds engineered in the likeness of some mythological creature or other that the Nephilim employed to guard the cairns they used as shelter. The idea of them loose on their path without their masters was a pretty alarming one.

"They let them out?" Rai said in disbelief.

Berdnard shrugged, a motion largely lost under his heavy coat, backpack and axe. "Either that or they let themselves out. The cairns are wide open."

Rai turned to Lyam and said what they were both thinking. "It does sound like a trap."

Berdnard tutted. "You only set traps when you

want to catch something. And a few dozen predators on the loose doesn't exactly encourage the prey – if that's how you see yourselves. Besides, that's not how the Nephilim think. They're not hunters. They've always been aware of our location, and if they wanted the temple, they'd have taken it by now. We are of no consequence to them anymore – if indeed we ever were. Rai, remember what happened when you let yourself be spotted by that Nephilim atop the ridge?"

"Yeah…"

"What happened?" Lyam asked sternly, for this was news to him. Rai had hardly ever mentioned her excursions to the surface, let alone an encounter with the Nephilim. They'd been sharing the same room – the same bed! – for years. Oh, he knew she kept secrets. Everyone did. He just never imagined there'd be this many, or that they'd be this big. Rai and Eloin, the two women in his life – who supposedly hated each other – shared more secrets between them than he'd ever had with either. How could he have been so blind? Rai never put much effort into hiding her emotions, true, always radiating anger and hostility. Which, now that he thought about it, not hiding her strongest, most basic emotions, was actually a pretty efficient way to conceal all the others. Berdnard must have learned that from her.

"Nothing," she admitted rather sheepishly. "He didn't even look at me twice."

"Huh," Lyam said, feeling somewhat insulted on behalf of his kind. The Nephilim might have their gods and monstrous pets, but Prometheans were not powerless and should not be so easily dismissed. "They destroyed our lives, our ship, took our land – well, technically – the least they could have done is acknowledge our existence," he grumbled.

"I, for one, am glad they didn't," Berdnard said dryly. "In my experience, bad things happen to those whose existence is noticed by those who believe they should not exist in the first place."

"All I'm saying is that we put up a fight, so much so, both sides lost," Lyam said in an attempt to stir the subject into less bitter and prejudiced ground. "We hit them as hard as they hit us. Don't sell yourself so short, Berdnard." He cringed at the poor choice of word but, to his credit, did not make matters worse by taking it back or dancing around it. "I bet they are as cautious of us as we are of them."

"They were cautious of something, all right," Berdnard said tautly. His own memory of events was far less heroic than Lyam's. And yet, he never actually felt afraid of the Nephilim. Not – and he would never admit to this, mind – the way he was afraid of Prometheans or even of Narrum. If anything, he had often been tempted to join them.

One self-exalted race is as bad as the other, Berdnard reminded himself, proud that he'd managed to obtain a bit of agency amidst it all. And since he was the only person he trusted anyway, it was enough.

"Did you notice anything strange prior to their disappearance?" Rai asked, diplomatically changing the subject before the emotional states of both men escalated the argument. What had happened during the battle was half assumption, half speculation anyway. The significant records of it had been lost or erased. All they knew had been patched together from the observation of the aftermath and what little remained of the survivors' memories of the event. Many believed, herself included, that if none of them remembered it correctly, perhaps it was for the best.

"No. As I said. Whatever happened to them was swift and sudden. It gave no warning, left no marks, no tracks, nothing."

"How do you know it gave no warning?" Audric asked.

"Oh, look who's paying attention. No warning that I was aware of, satisfied?" the short man replied defensively, close to standing on tiptoes.

Audric lifted his hands in an appeasing gesture. "Just asking."

Audric had a point, though. Lyam inspected the short man askance, not trusting much of what he'd said thus far.

"A rescue ship probably came to pick them up," Rai concluded despondently, convinced this excursion was turning out to be a waste of her time, like everything else they'd done of late. Oh well, at least she got to go on an adventure, rather than pretending to dig around rubble to please a dying woman.

"That's what I thought, at first. But…" Berdnard's shoulders slumped slightly. He hated having to use the F-word, especially around empaths. "It doesn't feel like it." Feelings were luxuries of tall folk and those who'd rather not face facts or think for themselves.

"Come on, hundreds of people don't just vanish," she insisted. "They left."

"They are not people," Lyam stated belligerently.

People had emotions. Narrum had sensations. Nephilim had neither.

They fell silent again.

"Could be related to the moon itself – or the planet," Audric said and was immediately elbowed by Rai. Count on the quiet man to open his mouth at the worse time to say what no one wanted to hear.

"Well, you should ask it, then," said the dwarf.

"Maybe I will," Audric replied in all seriousness.

Rai mouthed what the fuck? at him and got a what? in return.

"Berdnard is aware of our mind tricks, aren't you?" Audric said.

"Not all of them, apparently."

"Audric is just messing with you. We can't talk to the moon," Rai assured him.

"Well, if you ever do, let me know what she says."

"Fuck!" cried Lyam, sprawled on the ground, ash swirling around him like an angry swarm.

Rai crouched at his side, trying to help him up. "What happened?"

"I tripped," he said, glaring resentfully at the protruding rock that'd caused the accident, then at the scrape on his hand, the only injury sustained. "It's all right. I'm all right. Keep going – oh!" He'd started shooing Rai away, then stopped motionless. "Do you hear that?"

"Hear what?" asked Rai.

The rock was screaming at him! – a crushing howl of sadness, anguish and rage. His body filled with adrenaline. He felt the overwhelming urge to run, to fight, to be free. Images flashed before his eyes: Berdnard, naked, strapped to a table, shouting incoherences at him. Glaring lights everywhere. Glass shattering. A serpent trapped in a globe. Eloin suspended in midair, beckoning death. Thoth, looking like a woman writing in his book. Audric right beside him, reading it. A jackal, an ibis, a falcon, an ostrich and a cat, fighting each other under the sun. A tree with mossy eyes played with a girl. And many, many other images that made no sense. Pain followed. First in his stomach, then his head. He cursed, clutching at both. Rai was calling his name, shaking him. But when he looked at her, another Rai looked back. She had tears in her eyes, and there were bars between them. "I hate you!" she screamed in his face.

Then there was nothing.

He came to his senses in the shade of a dilapidated cairn. Rai, Berdnard, and Audric sat a short distance away. Faces ranging from curiosity to concern to boredom.

"What happened?" Lyam's voice sounded as hoarse as his thoughts.

"You fell. And then you fainted."

"How long?"

"Not long. We only just dragged you here." She pointed a short distance away. "From over there."

"The light got to you," said Berdnard.

"Yeah… Can I have some water, please?"

Rai had already put a flagon in his hand.

"Er… thanks."

"Drink as much as you want. I packed plenty."

He glanced at his cut hand, now covered in dirt, and decided not to waste the water cleaning the wound. He was more likely to get dehydrated than septic.

He should be embarrassed, though – and he was. But what he'd experienced went beyond dehydration or heatstroke. Regardless, those were the reasons he gave for his weakness.

"How long until we reach the river?" Rai asked Berdnard.

"At this rate? Days."

"Come on, it's mostly downhill after the ridge, as I recall. Can we make it there before it gets too bright?"

Berdnard balanced his axe on his knee, pondering. "Maybe – if there are no more stops or delays. Other-wise, I'd rather wait the night here."

"We're not waiting," Lyam said resolutely, standing on unstable legs, determined to see this through even if it killed him – a possibility that seemed more likely with each step.

Rai moved to support him, then thought better of it. "Are you sure? There's no shame in –"

"I've never been more sure of anything in my life. I'm fine. We keep going."

CHAPTER 9

The Jackal

*Memories are more than just the sum of a
life's moments.*

– Memory on Record

Walking did become easier once they'd crossed the
ridge.

All gods will help you go downhill. Lyam cursed
himself at the thought. It was another one of those useless mantras that cluttered his mind. It made no sense.
Gravity, not gods, helped you go downhill. And a good
thing it did, for he didn't think he could have climbed
another step.

"How much further?" he asked. Their meagre water
supply was all but gone. Berdnard, of course, wasn't
sharing his.

"Too far – at this pace," the dwarf replied reproachfully.

Everyone but him looked exhausted. Walking was
not something they'd done much of in recent years. The
temple wasn't that big. Despite its seemingly endless
tunnels, they all looped around each other and all led

to the same place. Already they'd walked as much as its entire length tenfold. Not to mention the long climb to the surface even before the journey started in earnest. To make things worse, Lyam felt heavier on the surface. Every step was harder somehow, as if being pushed down as well as pulled.

He chided himself for being so out of shape and packing so much useless crap. His enthusiasm about this venture had dwindled considerably, worn down by the exertion, the unexpected turn of events, the personal disappointments, lies, and the monotonous, nightmarish landscape seemingly conjured by a melancholic Morpheus. There really was nothing to see but grey rock and ash, interrupted by the occasional cairn, which was just more rock and ash assembled into a neat pile. The moon's surface didn't just look desolate, it looked dead. Still, it had a breathable atmosphere and at least one river of liquid water, so it couldn't be dead everywhere. Or not dead for long, at least.

The cairns after the ridge were larger, and the Nephilim had repaired or reassembled almost all of them. The large stones covering their entrances had been either knocked aside or broken, like Berdnard said. The dwarf adamantly opposed any attempt to stop and explore, claiming those were of no importance, just used as private shelters. They had to keep going if they wanted to get to the river before what passed for nightfall. Lyam had had to agree, even if curiosity threatened to kill him like a cat, as Thoth liked to say. Lyam had never quite figured out if the god loved or loathed felines, but he certainly related to them now. It was said cats had many lives. Had Lyam more time and more than the one life, he would gladly give one up to see how the Nephilim lived.

"Berdnard, how can you be sure these won't lead down to the temple?" Lyam asked.

"I'm not. But if they did, we – and by we I mean you folks – would have found the passageways by now. Well, either that, or the Nephilim would have when they restored them."

"Yes, you'd expect so…" Lyam mused.

"Perhaps they didn't dig deep enough," said Audric.

"Because why would they?" Lyam said sarcastically. "Actually, why restore them at all? It's not like they need shelter."

"All creatures need shelter," Berdnard told him flatly.

"Shelter from what? The moon's rain?" Rai quipped. What passed for rain on the moon was a dense cloud of steaming vapour that swept across the surface arbitrarily, turning ash into sooty mud; a fair nuisance to be sure, but nothing that required shelter.

"Why not? Maybe they short circuit when exposed to too much humidity. Maybe they rust. You don't know, lass."

"But you seem to," Audric said, red eyes narrowing.

Berdnard shot him an irritated look. "They like their comforts and privacy to conduct their experiments, or so I've heard. How else would they achieve that, you tell me? Their ship is a wreck. There's nothing but rock on this cursed moon to build with. And we've already agreed that they couldn't be bothered to take your temple."

"Maybe the reason they didn't is because it's not our temple." Lyam had had that thought often enough.

There was something wrong with the place, no matter what Eloin said. The fact that the Nephilim never pursued them there only reinforced his belief. Why wouldn't anyone listen to him?

Audric overcame Berdnard in a few strides and now stood in his way. "How do you know they liked privacy? Or that they were conducting experiments?"

All gazes fell on the short man, momentarily taken aback by the obstinate obstacle in his way.

"Isn't it what they do? Research. Experiment. Study?" Berdnard's tone was uncharacteristically reasonable, almost sheepish.

"You've been in touch with them," Audric said. Not a question.

Everyone came to a halt.

"Please tell me you haven't," Rai said, lips curling.

The short man suddenly seemed smaller, almost childlike, as he looked up at the three taller creatures judging him.

"Just with one," he admitted, pulling at his beard. "His name was Crymure."

"For fuck's sake, Berdnard! How could you?" Rai stomped her foot in outrage.

"How could I not?" he protested. "He got inside the mountain while I slept. Was just sitting there, barely two feet away, playing with my axe while he waited for me to wake up. He had a rictus grin on his face. Nearly gave me a heart attack. You're right. If they wanted to storm the temple and kill us all in our sleep, they would have. I'm certainly no match for a Nephilim. But he only wanted to talk."

"What did you tell him about us?" she asked.

"Nothing!"

"So what did you talk about, then?"

Berdnard fiddled with his moustache, then shrugged. "Everything and nothing. He would bring junk and work on it for hours while we ranted about our misfortunes like two lonely old beings. I learned more from him than he did from me, I can tell you that. He wasn't interested in our troubles, in any case. Nor the temple."

"What was he interested in?" Audric asked.

"The god: Thoth. Fortunately, that was the extent of what I know about that one. So…" Berdnard shrugged.

"All that crap back in your room is his, then?" Lyam asked.

"No. Only the dismantled constructs and a few other bits. Ugly things. Most of the interesting stuff I salvaged myself."

"Why?"

"I'm a collector," he sneered.

"What was the Nephilim working on?" asked Audric.

"Some new type of construct. Apparently, the Narrum managed to destroy all the old ones. Those that were not destroyed in the crash, that is." Berdnard lifted a stubby finger, guessing the next question. "No. He did not succeed. Something about the most important piece being missing. Or not being large enough. I forget which. So no, they've not built a new army out of the dismembered, if that's what you're thinking."

"It wasn't," the man said.

"When was this?" Rai asked.

"He first showed up just days after the crash. And the last time I saw him was three days ago. Right before the Nephilim vanished."

Rai could only gape in outrage. Hard to tell what upset her more, his communication with their enemy or the fact that he'd kept it hidden from her this long. She let her mind shield drop in a moment of pique, allowing Lyam's mind to peek into hers.

'Now you know how it feels,' he told her with everything but words. He tried to remain serious. His lips, however, betrayed a vindicated smirk. She supposed she deserved that.

"How can you be sure they've vanished and are not hiding instead?" asked Audric.

Berdnard puffed his cheeks. "It's not their way. Besides, he – we – agreed to meet the following day. Crymure never missed a meeting. That's when I knew something was wrong. I went looking for him. He, er… sheltered in one of the first cairns we passed."

"The one you didn't want us to look at because it wasn't important." Lyam wanted to kick the man.

Rai actually did, for effect rather than actual injury. "I can't believe you! Sounds like you were friends with this Crymure."

"I guess I was!" the dwarf conceded defiantly.

"Well, if you were such good friends with this Nephilim, why not join them?" she challenged blatantly.

"For the same reason I made no attempts to join you in the temple, lass. I don't go where I'm not welcome."

"You should have told us…" she said, shaking her head.

Her disappointment cut deep. Still, he stood his

ground. "But I didn't. So what will you do about it, lass?"

She turned away from him, angry tears in her eyes. Berdnard's bushy eyebrows drooped and kept drooping as Lyam and Audric turned after her.

∞

They walked in uncomfortable silence for a long while, keeping their distance from each other, as if afraid of learning or sharing their tempestuous thoughts. High above, the planet became larger, angrier, suffocatingly bright. Deep below, the moon cracked under the pressure of his presence. An underground thunder that threatened to split the ground at any moment.

"Berdnard…" Rai sounded like a completely different woman from the one shouting at him earlier, placid and meek.

"Yes, lass?" Berdnard replied solicitously, hoping to make amends.

"Is this part of one of their pets, you think?" On the ground in front of her was a discarded talon larger than a man's foot. Torn flesh still clung where the bone had snapped, still fresh. Instinctively, they all looked about in every direction, searching for the rest of the beast, or the thing that mutilated it.

Berdnard fidgeted with his moustache again. "Strange. Why would they kill each other when they don't need to eat?"

"Something does," Audric said. "Let's hope whatever did this doesn't need to eat anytime soon."

"That's grim," Rai said in distaste, still staring at the talon.

"You'd rather they eat us?" he asked her.

She glared at him.

"Pull yourselves together," said Berdnard before they fell apart again. "And keep your eyes open. We're getting close."

"Stop!" cried out Rai. They all obeyed by reflex.

"What now?" Lyam asked, head and heart pounding as he glanced in every direction.

Audric pulled a large dagger from somewhere.

"What is it?" Berdnard demanded, clearly missing the cause of her alarm as well.

She pointed to a large egg-shaped boulder in the distance.

A four-legged animal stood next to it. It had a rusty-red and black coat, bright eyes fixed on them.

Berdnard exhaled. "It's just a dog! Calm down, lass. It won't attack us if we don't attack it."

"I'm not so sure," Rai protested.

"It's a jackal, not a dog," Audric said. Rai's scowl told him she didn't give a fuck about the difference. Her cheeks and nose had turned slightly pink, and she seemed to have twice as many freckles as usual. They didn't suit her.

Lyam pointed at Audric's blade. "Where did you get that?"

"The holster strapped to my belt," was the answer.

"You need to start being more specific about the origin of your things."

"I was very specific."

"That's not what I meant and you bloody know it!"

Audric closed the distance between them, blade in

hand. "What things were or where they came from is irrelevant compared to where they are now. Or haven't you learnt that already, Promethean?"

Lyam opened his mouth and found he had nothing to say to him in reply. Audric put the dagger away. In the distance, the black jackal sat on his haunches, still studying the group.

"Let's keep moving," Berdnard urged, exasperated. "You two feel free to philosophise as much as you want while we walk. We can all argue to our heart's content once we're in the shade. Agreed?"

"It's following us!" Rai complained several yards afterwards.

"Ignore it!" Lyam snapped. He'd finally come up with a perfect reply to Audric, but the moment had passed, so he took the opportunity to vent his frustration on her.

The psychic lash she gave him in return nearly knocked him sideways. "Ignore that!"

"Hey! You big idiots. We don't have time to chase the beast off or fight amongst ourselves. Let it follow. There is no danger. If it attacks, it's one of it against four of us," Berdnard said.

"Until it's friends arrive," she added waspishly.

"Unlikely. These beasts are mostly solitary. They link to their mates or to their owners. I don't see either," Berdnard said, ignoring her pointed remark.

"I thought the Nephilim's pets were monstrous," Lyam said, remembering the broken talon. This canine didn't seem particularly menacing or friendly to qualify as either monster or pet. Still…

"Nah, it's probably one of ours," Berdnard said.

"There were animals on the Eagle?" Rai asked incredulously, her outrage momentarily forgotten.

"That's what I just said."

"How did it survive this long?" Lyam asked.

"How would I know? Go ask him!"

"If it came with us on the ship, the Nephilim must have taken it in. Fed it, cared for it," Lyam decided. But why would they? "What will happen to it now that their masters are gone?"

"It will either adapt or die. Like all life when circumstances change, including ours. Now quit staring at it, damn it. Move."

"It'll starve," Lyam replied pragmatically.

"Not if he catches one of us first…" Rai grumbled, not taking her eyes off the approaching animal. "Ugly beast."

The canine snarled menacingly.

"It heard me! It understood what I said. I'm telling you guys, that thing's evil."

"No. He just doesn't like you," Audric said.

"He? Are you communicating with that creature?"

Audric didn't answer her. He was already walking towards the animal.

"For fuck's sake! Are you insane? Come back!" she shouted, to no avail.

Berdnard threw his hands in the air in defeat, then sat down and drank some water, wishing it to be ale, cursing each of them lavishly under his breath between each swallow.

They've all gone mad, Lyam decided, not feeling

particularly sane either. He rolled his eyes to the sky and immediately regretted it. *It's this damned light!*

Audric crouched alongside the jackal, one hand stretched out holding a piece of nectar.

"Hey! What are you doing?" Rai bellowed in disbelief.

Two pairs of eyes in three different colours glared back at her. Both mouths showed their teeth: one set in a snarl, the other in a defiant grin. Then man and beast stared at each other as if coming to some sort of understanding.

"Oh, look: the beginning of a beautiful friendship," Berdnard said sardonically, taking another swig and murmuring "Eejits" to himself.

"You're one to talk about friendships," Lyam snapped at him, coveting the bottle. His mouth tasted of ash, literally. The air was thick with the stuff. His lungs too, he reckoned. "When we're back, we're going to have to explain this Crymure to Eloin. At length."

"I look forward to it," the dwarf said, taking another long sip of water to further taunt him.

"You better keep that thing away from me," Rai warned Audric as he returned, the jackal by his side. They took a step in her direction. She stepped back.

Berdnard stood up and dusted himself. "Now, shall we finally continue to the river?"

"Yes, please," Lyam sighed.

Chapter 10

The River

Memories are the only possessions allowed in the Underworld. They are its currency.

– Memory on Record

An obelisk, almost ten feet tall, jutted from the ground. So well designed to blend in with the moon's colourless landscape, they'd only noticed it once close. Narrow steps led from its doorway, down into darkness.

Now that I must investigate, Lyam decided. "What is –"

"A needle," Berdnard replied before Lyam finished the question. "That's what I call them, anyway. The Nephilim built them. There're a few between here and the river. You've seen one, you've seen them all, so keep those long legs moving. We're almost there."

"The Nephilim built them?" Lyam parroted, standing still. Piling up stones to repair an already built Cairn was one thing. The image of the Nephilim, with their long robes and intricate jewellery, actually cutting stone and assembling it into something like this from scratch was just out of his mind's reach. "Why?" For them to have gone to such trouble, their purpose had to be important, surely.

"It's some sort of communication device. They were trying to contact their homeworld. It makes no difference now. They're pretty, but not relevant. Come on," he beckoned urgently to little effect.

Much like the cairns, the obelisk did seem to have been abandoned. Still, that did not make it irrelevant. Especially if they worked.

"You stupid dwarf. On top of everything else, it didn't occur to you to mention these? Eloin should be informed." Lyam addressed both Berdnard and Rai, who clearly had seen these 'needles' before.

"Eloin does," Berdnard replied reluctantly. "And she doesn't care. Now let's go."

Lyam didn't move. "How can she not care? If we –"

"We can't use it to communicate with anyone; we don't remember anyone. And even if we had the coordinates of our home world or allies, then the Nephilim would too," Rai said.

This left Lyam's mouth ajar, the harsh words he was about to say stuck unuttered in his throat. She was right. And that made him even more upset. "Why am I only now learning about this?"

"Because you didn't care to ask before!" Berdnard gave him an exasperated look. "You are a truly insufferable man, you know that? Why, why, why! is all you care about. You need to first learn the what and the how before learning the why. Even I can see why the captain kept all this a secret. As I was saying, these are quite small – irrelevant. There's a proper tower by the river. I reckon if we're going to find any answers about the Nephilim's disappearance, it will be there. Now, for the last time – move!"

Lyam was apoplectic with indignation. His first instinct was to ask why again, of course. He just about managed not to.

"Why?" Audric asked in a fair imitation of Lyam's petulant tone. "What's so special about this tower?" His mocking smirk gave the impression he'd already guessed the answer.

Berdnard shot daggers at him but answered nonetheless. "It's where they keep their gods."

With a strength he didn't know he had, Lyam grabbed the short man by the lapel of his coat and lifted him up to his face. Rai gasped, caught by surprise. So was Berdnard, momentarily too disconcerted to fight back. "You brought us to a trap, dwarf?" He shouted the question – or rather, the accusation – louder than he thought himself capable.

"No! Put me down. What's wrong with you?"

Audric's grip closed firmly on Lyam's forearm. He shook himself, unsure of what just happened, and put Berdnard down gingerly. "I'm sorry. I don't know what came over me," he said truthfully. He was upset, true, but he'd never been violent. Not like this. *Not that I recall,* he added to himself.

"It's the planet." Berdnard sounded a bit shaken. "Perhaps the Promethean is right. We should stop and… investigate the needle until the light subsides."

"No," Audric said. "I want to see this tower." He sneered slightly. "And I won't have you two confined in a small, dark space." The jackal growled agreement before both walked away. The others spared a glance between themselves and followed.

Lyam's mind digressed to Eloin and her deceit. Had it been her deceit, though? he wondered. She doesn't trust me. Doesn't listen to me anymore. She only listens to him, only cares about what he wants.

Rai laughed at his brooding reflections. "Jealous of a god, darling?"

He bristled at her intrusion. Maybe he was not as circumspect about his emotions as he hoped, but she could really use some boundaries. In any case, he was too tired to argue about it now. "I'm not jealous. I'm… wary, that's all."

"That's an understatement," she said, aware of his true feelings. "What is it about Thoth that upsets you so?"

He turned to her then, confused. "Him being a god doesn't bother you? I bet he can kill you with a thought."

Rai half shrugged. "I bet one of the twins can kill me with a punch. I'm still friends with them."

"It's not the same thing." Lyam drew a long breath to smooth the petulant, whiny tone of his exasperation. Up until Audric mimicked him, he hadn't even noticed it. Now he could not ignore it. Curse the man. "Gods are weird. They have powers we don't understand. And the way they pretend not to care about us while at the same time they won't leave us alone bothers me. I'm surprised it doesn't bother you."

"I just never felt that way about them," she said truthfully.

Lyam shook his head. "Humanity spent millennia

killing each other trying to prove their chosen god was the real one and later drove themselves mad, trying to figure out if there was actually a god in the first place. As it turned out, our ancestors had already found the answers to those questions. There are many gods. And they're all cunts. What have gods ever done for us? Nothing. We are nothing but entertainment to them. In their way, the Nephilim achieved what we never have. They learned how to harvest their powers."

"But for their own good, not ours," Audric said.

"When it comes to gods, what's good for the Nephilim is good for us," said the dwarf.

The muscles in Audric's jaw tensed.

"We're better off without gods or Nephilim," said Lyam.

"On that, we can all agree," Rai said, hoping to put an end to the conversation.

It was no secret that the Nephilim enslaved gods. But gods were a tricky subject, always open to debate. The two main contention points concerned the nature and extent of their powers and how far they could be trusted – if they could be trusted at all. Eloin saw them as potential allies. Lyam… not so much. Rai never gave them much thought. And only the gods knew Audric's mind on the matter.

To complicate things further, not all deities were the same. There were gods – virtually immortal beings whose talents allowed them to bend or even break most laws of the Universe – and then there were Gods – entities of such power they were part of the fabric of the Universe itself. Forces rather than beings. Any attempt to understand, let alone empathise with them, would likely turn a mortal insane.

One thing was certain: gods had every reason to hate the Nephilim, but they also had reason to hate the Prometheans for their post-human cousins, the Lokians, who'd created the Nephilim in the first place. If for no other reason than the fact they did not seem able to distinguish between the two top echelons of humanity. Thoth had once said that to gods, all humans looked alike. Sadly, the same could be said about gods to most humans.

Post-humans had long stopped counting on deities, and unlike their ancestors, they'd never worshipped them. Until now, that was. Thoth, and life in the temple, had forced them to regress to a more primitive spiritual stance. The prospect of meeting another god both intrigued and concerned the group, for a god's hate, much like their power, can be a fickle thing, and not always aimed at those who'd caused it.

∞

The moon's shadow moved closer to the centre of the planet. The contrast between light and darkness resembled an event horizon, as it reflected the radiation of the red giant behind them. It would soon become too much for their unshielded eyes to cope with. 'Almost there' resonated from every mind like a mantra with each step.

The Nephilim had vastly reworked the valley's landscape. It almost didn't seem to belong to the same moon. The closer they got to the river, the more it changed, with dozens of new cairn-like shelters, obelisks and even a few watchtowers. The Nephilim not only knew how to build but how to build well. And they'd been busy. They had even paved paths between structures. Lyam felt ashamed on behalf of his complacent peers. The machines hadn't just huddled together like sheep, hiding in one place and making do with their borrowed environment while waiting for a miracle, they'd spread out and adapted the environment to them. They'd tamed it. Shaped it to their needs.

"How did they move all this stone?" Rai mused aloud.

The gods help those who help themselves. Lyam chuckled bitterly to himself at the aphorism. Even if they do it against their will, he added. Nephilim had long ago learned how to force gods to help them. To do what, though? At first, the buildings' locations seemed random, chosen for easy access to materials or by personal whim, but upon closer observation, he discerned a pattern, a purpose. They'd set a perimeter around their crash site, the river and this mysterious tower. Lyam wanted to stop and investigate the structures, a reprieve from the planet's glaring light, if nothing else. But he dared not confront the dwarf, in case what had caused his previous behaviour – whatever it had been – got triggered again.

Berdnard set a relentless pace, made more impressive by the length of his strides. The jackal guarded the rear of the party, all but marching them along. There was no turning around now, so they just marched towards the river in grudging agreement.

When the crash site came into view, Lyam noticed something odd about the ship – or what was left of it: It didn't look like any of their other ships (although Lyam had no idea how he knew that). There didn't seem to be a lot left to salvage or worth protecting. Still, they'd done it anyway. A huge stone wall had been built around it. As much as Lyam wanted to believe the endeavour had been for their sake, he seriously doubted it. Berdnard was right. The Nephilim didn't give a shit about them. And that meant Eloin – devious, scheming Eloin – was also right. There was something else they feared. Something truly worth fearing.

"Stay close. Stay low. We'll be able to see the tower clearly once past that cairn. Which means, if they're there, they'll see us too," Berdnard said, motioning everyone to crouch to his level.

"That doesn't look right." Rai's words expressed what they all thought, lying flat on the ashy ground, overlooking the river basin and the tower erected next to it. The tower itself looked fine. If anything, its revelation was anticlimactic. Square and squat with a flat top, it resembled more the remnants of a mausoleum rather than a stronghold. What made them all share her assertion with open mouths and wide, disbelieving eyes was what they saw beyond it. Or rather, what they didn't see.

"Where's the river?" There was a knot in Lyam's stomach, and his mouth felt dry from more than just thirst.

Berdnard licked his lips, fidgeting with his moustache so frantically he pulled out a few hairs. "I don't see anyone, no movement. You?" he asked them. The planet's glare made it almost too bright to see anything in the distance, and his eyesight had never been that good to begin with, especially over long distances. "I guess they are gone."

"How do we know they're gone and not just hidden?" Rai asked.

"They don't hide. It's against their nature," the dwarf said.

"That's true," said Audric. "Nothing moves. Nothing lives."

"Where is the fucking water?" Lyam practically shouted this time.

No one had an answer.

CHAPTER 11

The Abyss

*The soul is drawn to the things the mind
wishes to forget.*

– Memory on Record

When Audric stared into the abyss, darkness stared back.

"How deep does it go?" Rai asked no one in particular, peering over the abrupt edge.

Audric picked up a rock and dropped it into the chasm. Long moments passed. They exchanged silent glances, breaths consciously held, waiting for a sound. It never came. "Deep," he finally said.

Lyam was less concerned about its depth than he was about its very existence. "Are you sure this used to be a river?" he asked Berdnard.

The short man looked up at him resentfully. "Yes. I am sure. And a shallow one at that."

"But you've only seen it from a distance. You've never actually been here, have you?" Rai pointed out cautiously.

"You think I can't tell the difference between a river an abyss, lass?!"

"Maybe the light played tricks on your eyes, or we took a wrong turn somewhere," she said without much conviction. The chasm not only stretched to the depths of the moon, it seemed to run all around it as well.

Berdnard picked up a handful of pebbles at their feet, remains of what had once been a riverbed. "Look here, lass. I may not be as clever and educated as you post-humans, nor do I have the best eyesight, I admit, but I can still tell when stone has been polished by water. This used to be a river. I'd bet my beard – no, my life – on it."

"He's right," Audric said, turning away from the edge. The darkness was starting to make him hear things. "Your Nephilim friend, did he mention anything about their experiments, anything that might have caused this?"

Berdnard shook his head vehemently. "No. They only wanted to contact their homeworld and..." He frowned, as if trying to remember the words. "And something about recovering missing records. Nothing about the river. Or water, for that matter."

"So what happened to it, then? What – or who – in Olympus could cause something like this?" Lyam asked, panic in his tone. He, too, didn't like the images and sounds his mind picked out of the darkness.

"Could be a sinkhole," Rai suggested feebly. "A very large and deep sinkhole. Maybe the constant seismic activity opened a fissure and the river..." She took in the sceptical expressions of the group and threw up her hands in the air. "I don't know, maybe the moon got thirsty and drank it. Oh, don't look at me like that. Geology is not my forte. Do you have a better idea?"

"They must have done it: the Nephilim. Somehow, they've done it," Lyam said, wanting and simultaneously dreading to be right.

She guffawed mirthlessly. "How? With what? And what for?"

"With their enslaved gods, of course. To lure us here. Or leave us to die without water." Lyam tried not to think of how thirsty he was. Of all the things he'd expected to die of, dehydration had not been one of them.

"We have our own water supply in the temple," she pointed out, then blinked. "They don't know about the well. Do they, Berdnard?"

Berdnard wanted to pull his helmet down to his shoulders. "I may have mentioned it…"

"For fuck's sake!" cried Rai.

Lyam rubbed his forehead. He felt dizzy again. Too tired and too stunned to even think properly. The light and heat and thirst had become unbearable. He glanced at the moon's shadow, now a perfect black circle amidst the maelstrom of clouds on the planet's surface. It seemed to want to suck them in, much like the abyss at their feet. "Forget about the Nephilim. It's the moon. It wants us dead. Has to be."

"Get over yourself, Promethean," Audric said. "The moon doesn't give a fuck about you."

"Oh yeah? Maybe it's you she wants to fuck, then."

"Cut it out, you two!" Berdnard waved his axe between the two men before they came to blows. "We're all on edge. Pull yourselves together. We must find shelter."

"Fuck shelter. Fuck the light. Fuck you three. We need to get to the bottom of this!" Rai said, then cursed to herself. "Metaphorically, I mean…"

"Sure. But not here. I don't want to go blind. Besides" – Berdnard pointed to the horizon beyond the ridge – "a storm's coming."

A cloud of sodden ash rolled down the ridge, powered by wilful winds. Already the hot moisture in the air threatened to smother them like a wet blanket.

"To the tower," Audric said, already dashing towards it, the jackal and Berdnard on his heels.

"Have you completely lost your mind, red eyes?"

"I reckon he has, long ago," Lyam said, walking after them. "But he's also right. The tower is the closest shelter. And the only place we might find some answers. Or do you have a better suggestion?"

Rai stamped her foot in frustration and spared another glance at the world-splitting chasm. The father of all bad feelings crept inside her. She wanted to be anywhere else but there.

'Come closer,' a voice sizzled from the depths. She stepped back. 'No, closer. One more step. That's it. Just one. more. step.' She stood on the edge again without realising. 'Come to me now,' the voice demanded.

Rai ran after the men.

PART II

The primordial gods met for the first time in the Abyss, for it was hidden, impartial and unspoiled by light. But it was the event itself, not the meeting or its location, that mattered. For there had never before been such a thing as a first time. There had been no before either. No after. No cause or consequence. Everything happened simultaneously for no other reason than that it did. For that is the beauty of Chaos.

– Memory on Record

CHAPTER 12

The God & the Machine

Scars are memories recorded in flesh.

– Memory on Record

Namrive didn't recognise herself. It wasn't just the partially melted face, the lack of ornamentation embedded in her skin, or even the ill-fitting dress she'd borrowed from Seshat after her own had been incinerated by the Olympian sun god, Apollo, in his futile attempt to burn the Suzerain to cinders. The Nephilim didn't fret about their looks – not much, anyway – and clothes, well, clothes were a mere formality and easily changed. It was her brain, the very core of her being and personality, that had been altered. Try as she might – and she had tried; by the Mentor, she kept trying – she couldn't fix it. And that troubled her deeply.

Troubled, exactly… The Nephilim didn't have troubles, or anxieties, and certainly not identity crises. They had no mental or emotional problems of any kind, in fact, since they'd been designed purposely to overcome them.

She ran another diagnostic through her matrix, and sure enough the errors were still there. Whatever the Suzerain had done to her, it was permanent. Her body could and would be repaired, but her mind – the very thing that defined her – had been irreversibly damaged. The only way to restore her original personality was to reset her mind, which meant deleting all her memories – not an option. Sure, she could backup her memories and download them again afterwards, but knowledge without context, without the experience, the thought processes that led to them, would be as bad as ignorance, and there was no guarantee her mind wouldn't unravel again once they were reinstalled. She'd have cried; she wanted to. But Nephilim hadn't been designed to cry either…

Contrary to common belief, some Nephilim – herself included – had emotional pathways in their matrix. After all, emotions could be useful shortcuts when processing too many variables. But they never reached levels high enough to cause the shedding of tears, nor any other absurd manifestations. Still, the weakness existed. It was through her emotional pathways that the Suzerain had been able to control her mind. And now her emotional responses were off the charts. Too much emotion was counterproductive and hazardous. It hindered the decision-making process. She'd learned that lesson when she'd linked to a dying man. But even that painful experience paled in comparison with how she felt now: diminished, weak, impaired – broken.

She couldn't return to Pallas like this. Especially not on top of her spectacular failure in Niflheim. What would the Mentor say? What would She do? The idea triggered another jolt of anxiety. Had Namrive a heart, it would be tearing itself apart with the effort of keeping her alive. And, as if facing the Mentor's displeasure wasn't enough, she also had to honour her promise to the Maker. He'd claimed Niflheim for himself and demanded it be erased from every database. Removing Niflheim and all that had happened there from their records would be easy – and all things considered, wise. There was hardly any information about the world to begin with. Its acquisition had been fairly recent, and the Suzerain, the creature they'd clearly underestimated to rule it in their name, had kept reports to a minimum. Besides, the Nephilim cared little about worlds linked to the Underworld. The afterlife was of no use to them. They had no soul or spirit; they weren't alive and therefore would not die. If not for Anubis and what he'd taught her, she wouldn't have cared, either.

But erasing a record is not the same as erasing a memory. The Mentor would remember. She would care. Oh yes, she would care deeply.

It was said one couldn't serve two masters. Well… no shit. Namrive had been designed to obey, true, but also to think for herself: Two directives now at odds with each other. The conflict exacerbated by emotion. No wonder her mind kept glitching. The rational course of action would be to just let the Mentor and the Maker sort out their issues between themselves. Except rational doesn't always mean right, and in her current condition, rational did not come easily either.

And then, on top of everything else, there was magic. She'd always dismissed it as just another word mortals used to describe their ignorance about technology and all other things they did not understand. Something it had never suited the gods nor the Nephilim to correct, for it was preferable to have them believing in magic than learning how to develop their own technology – that never ended well. What humans had done to Midgard was a fine example of that. However… what she'd witnessed in Niflheim had not been technology or the product of a god's talent. Namrive wasn't a mortal, nor was she stupid, and yet there was no logical explanation for what she'd experienced. Before she filed any report or faced the Mentor, she had to figure that one out. Her sanity, if not her very existence, depended on it.

She pressed her temples, glitching again. The Nephilim had conquered space, matter, flesh, mortals, and gods. Namrive refused to accept ignorance had defeated her, let alone magic.

No, she told herself sternly. It wasn't magic the Suzerain had used to break her mind but his own technology. Technology she could learn. Learn how to fix herself. She had to. But how?

"Bugs," she moaned, hands holding her head as if to keep it from falling off.

She was making no sense, jumping from thought to thought, unable to follow a logical thread. It was as if she was accessing someone else's mind. She knew the correct course of action would be to come forward, volunteer to be decommissioned, and have her original consciousness downloaded into a new body. Start over. But then… then she wouldn't be herself. The self she was now, the self she didn't recognise and hated. Still, she was reluctant to follow protocol: a rebellion fuelled by what could only be described as self-preservation.

"There's nothing to preserve, you idiot!" she told herself, then cringed when she realised what she'd just done. "I'm talking to myself, like a mortal." She covered her mouth before more words came out unbidden. No, she shouldn't be preserved, she decided. A mind working in this state was like a virus, it would unravel to incoherence, and worse, it might infect others. She had to follow protocol. There was no other way. Her hand moved from her face to the keyboard, shaking.

"Namrive?" Anubis stood right behind her when he spoke. It took all her self-control not to jump at the sound. She hadn't heard him come in – then again, she rarely did. The cursed god's true form might look like a dog, but he was stealthy as a cat.

"What?" she snapped, changing screens. She didn't want him to see what she'd been about to do. Not that he'd understand what he saw, anyway. The god was too proud to learn their technology – or too dense. She hesitated before turning around to face him, not wanting to see the smugness on his canine features. Surprisingly enough, it wasn't there.

He wore his human aspect, a slim, young male with tanned skin and a strip of black hair standing on end along the top of his head.

"What were you doing?" He sounded genuinely concerned, as if he already knew the answer. Was her emotional state so off the scale that it actually registered to his Reach?

Bugs, now you're being paranoid, she told herself, then paused all her subroutines to collect her thoughts before she dared speaking again. "I'm running repairs, if you must know."

"On the ship?"

"No. On me," she admitted. No reason not to. Even a Narrum child could see she wasn't all right.

He placed a hand on her shoulder. "How bad is it?"

She looked from it to his mismatched eyes: one copper, the other burgundy. She'd never wondered why they were a different colour or why he chose such a homely human face. And why would he do that to his hair? She glitched herself for wondering about it all now.

"Nothing that can't be repaired," she said as dispassionately as her old self would have. "What do you want, Anubis?" For he had to want something. He only wore a mortal guise when he wanted something.

He clasped his hands behind his back and smiled that cunning smile all gods seemed to share. "I'd like to thank you for letting Seshat travel with us."

As if I'd had a choice, Namrive thought bitterly. Amidst the chaos of those last moments in Niflheim, it was either bring the goddess of writing along or not leave at all. Still, she appreciated the formality of his gesture, for she sure could use the illusion of still being in control. She wasn't, though.

"I agreed to bring her on board. Whatever happens next is not my responsibility. Seshat has a talent that, frankly, is of little use to us, but she's still a goddess. Some might find her useful in other ways. I cannot – no, I will not – protect her."

"I understand," Anubis said dutifully, pleased to learn Namrive only knew about Seshat's talent for writing, not her ability to take the aspect of any character in her stories. Then again, for the Nephilim, changing bodies was as common as changing clothes. Regardless, Namrive had a point. They always found a use for gods, even for those whose talents they had no use. He knew it well, for he'd been one of them.

There was something different about Namrive, he reflected upon close observation. When he'd entered the room, he could swear he'd sensed her mind, which made no sense. Reach only worked on the living. Unless her mind had been altered, gifted by a god, for example. Cats knew he'd wanted to do it often enough, if only to understand how that artificial matrix they called a brain worked. But then again, it was likely to be as convoluted as their reasoning. He was better off without that particular insight.

He turned to leave, then hesitated. There was definitely something in his Reach. It sounded like a high-pitched howl muffled by static.

"Namrive… what really happened to you back in Niflheim?"

Anubis had left Namrive alone for one day and missed an entire chapter of her life, apparently. She told him she'd been caught in the crossfire between Apollo and the Suzerain – an immortal tyrant who had no love for either gods or Nephilim – and that a sorceress nymph had somehow taken both of them down with her through a portal, only cats knew where to. Seshat was dying to learn the whole story. In truth, so was he.

Namrive cracked her neck, the loud metallic snap at odds with the delicate feminine figure she possessed. "I do not wish to talk about it," she said tartly.

"Talking has its uses. It helps organise the mind. Puts things in perspective. When you talk, you sometimes notice details you missed or forgot," he insisted.

"I wish I could forget…" Namrive practically sighed as she spoke, the words an anathema coming from her. "Our minds are not like yours. We don't forget or miss anything, and we can't remember what we don't…" She had to stop before she embarrassed herself further. Bugs, she sounded so weak. "It's the Mentor I'm concerned about. And talking will not change that." Which was true enough. "I can't be worried about you and Seshat while dealing with her, that's all," she added, despite herself.

"You worry about me?" he asked, feigning astonishment.

She grimaced, but she couldn't take it back now. It's the thing about words. Once out of your mouth, it's like they sealed the thought. "I worry about a lot of things now. That is the problem. I'm not myself, Anubis. I'm glitching. I need to be repaired," she confessed.

She dipped her head as if ashamed. The motion looked unnatural, downright artificial, and yet it made her somehow seem more earnest and genuine than ever. She sounded ill rather than glitched and Anubis had no talent to deal with illnesses of the mind.

"Well, I'll leave you to it, then. If you need anything, you know where to find me," he said.

She almost laughed. "I must look pretty damaged indeed for you to pretend to be my friend."

That quip affected him more than he cared to admit.

"No. I'd not insult you with my friendship, Namrive. But I do owe you a favour. I am an honourable god, despite what my pantheon might say. I pay my debts, even to – especially to – my enemies."

Favours were a god's currency. Either through promises – which most were bound to keep – or pride, they always returned them. For such corrupted entities, they sure valued their integrity. Namrive couldn't decide if that was their greatest weakness or their greatest strength. Then again, making decisions was not her forte these days.

"Anubis," Namrive called when he was about to leave the room. He turned slowly, hands clasped behind his back, patiently expectant.

"What do you know about magic?"

"Which kind?"

"There's more than one?" A grim prospect.

"Er…" So many he didn't even know where to begin.

"Ignore that," she said, fearing the output of too much information. "The god-slaying kind."

"Aaah. Well, technically, there's no such thing. Life and death don't mean the same to gods as they do to mortals, as you know. To us, life is a spectrum and death is just another realm."

"We've killed many gods," she said.

"Yes." As if he needed the reminder of how the Nephilim had been decimating pantheons across the Universe. "By siphoning a god's will to exist, true. But, as I said, death is not necessarily the end for a god. Not while their soul is out there. Nor is it the worst fate we can suffer, either."

"What is?"

"Oblivion."

Anubis left without another word.

"You didn't answer my question." Namrive spoke to an empty room, cursing all gods and their cryptic speeches. Still, he was right. Memory outlived death. And even bad memories were better than none. As damaged as she was now, she was still herself because she remembered who she'd been. If she reset her mind, all that she was would cease to exist. All she'd experienced would count for nothing, for memory without context is just data open to manipulation and, worst of all, misinterpretation.

She cancelled the protocol.

∞

Anubis wondered if he'd made a mistake. He'd wanted to get rid of Namrive for so long. Now the opportunity had finally presented itself. He had her in his paws, and instead of claiming his victory, he'd given her hope. Had he gone soft? No, of course not. He was more ruthless than ever. He told himself it wouldn't be much of a victory now, in her state. The truth was, he no longer felt threatened by the Nephilim, and over time his relationship with Namrive, however grudging, obligatory and unsatisfying for both parties, had been the best he'd had in ages. He would beat her – in time and fairly.

'It's a god's curse that whenever they force fate to suit their needs, they pay a personal price,' Ra had once told him.

He pushed the memory away. Ra was gone. He'd chosen to die in order to be remembered rather than live and risk being forgotten. He'd abandoned his pantheon and all his scions, the coward. Anubis wouldn't give up that easily. He'd already spent too much of his existence in the Underworld. And memories are only as good as those who remain alive to remember them. Which brought him to his real problem. He'd promised Seshat to take her to Mnemosyne, the goddess of memory. It was how he'd convinced her to leave Niflheim. It had been primarily an act of kindness, for he believed peace in the Underworlds wouldn't last, but also an act of selfishness. He needed her. If anyone could get to Mnemosyne, it would be Seshat. He knew he should tell her the truth about what had happened to the Titaness and where he was taking her, but he'd also made a promise to her father, Thoth, who was waiting for her.

I hate promises... he thought ruefully. Well, let Thoth explain to his daughter what really happened to Mnemosyne. He had Namrive to worry about. The Suzerain had clearly done something to unravel her. Any creature would adapt when confronted with their own mortality. The Nephilim weren't creatures, though. They didn't die and certainly didn't change. Except this one had, apparently.

He considered going back and pressing her for more information, then decided against it. Better to figure it out for himself, whatever it was. The fewer questions he asked, the fewer he had to answer. There was still a long journey ahead, and he was running out of good answers.

Chapter 13

The Wandering Goddess

Time and memory move in opposite directions.
May we never meet.

– Memory on Record

Seshat loved to read. As a child – or as close to it as a young goddess got – she used to sneak into her father's realm to read his accounts. Thoth, the god of writing, learning and reckoning, was the wisest in their pantheon, a master of observation and deduction. Nothing escaped his notice. Or judgement. No detail too trivial to be left unaccounted in the narratives of those he deemed worthy of his talent. To be featured in his work as more than a footnote. It was a privilege few gods and even fewer mortals ever achieved. Those who did became legends. For, after all, immortality is meaningless if no one knows you existed in the first place.

She'd always wanted to be like him, but, alas, her talents differed slightly from her father's. She had the power to turn history into story and vice versa. Her writing was entertaining rather than strictly biographical or educational. It lacked gravitas and therefore wasn't taken as seriously. She herself was also far less popular than her father, which was just as well. She didn't write for fame. First and foremost, she wrote for herself, and although a little appreciation for her work now and again wouldn't have hurt, remaining obscure had its advantages. For example, she could write whatever she wanted.

The only thing better than writing her stories was reading them, remembering the thoughts associated with each word and the events they described as if they were happening again in that moment.

"To remember is to live," Mnemosyne used to say. The goddess of memory used to say many things… until she went silent, muted by the Nephilim.

I will find you, Seshat vowed again, then sighed and returned to her task. Namrive had given her access to the ship's computer, and she'd been staring at screens ever since. The Nephilim's records differed greatly from hers or Thoth's. They were joyless, lifeless, practically pointless. And yet far more extensive as well. There were no stories, no fiction or creativity of any kind that she could tell. This wasn't surprising. Their minds were artificial thought processors with no room for imagination. What passed for history in their books was an objective record of events – all events, big and small – exactly as they played out, with plenty of repetition, no editing, no skipping over the boring parts and certainly no concern for word count or reader fatigue.

At first she'd been almost ecstatic with the prospect of so much information gathered in one place, but now, after what felt like an eternity looking at words with little meaning attached to them, she'd all but lost the will to read.

"Cats," she cursed as she finished yet another entry on the ideal hierarchy of concepts for decision-making within a well-organised mindset.

"Problem?" Anubis asked as he entered the room. Of course there was a problem. More than one, in fact. He kept finding excuses not to look through the records with her, and when he did, he paid a lot more attention to her thoughts than to them. Anubis had always been strange. Most gods linked to the Underworld were, to be fair. It was part of their charm. But something had happened to him in the years they'd been apart. Whatever he'd done in the Nephilim's service had changed him. Left him somewhat more… eccentric. And without knowing what had really happened, she hadn't yet decided if she could count on him as an ally, let alone a friend.

"You said I'd find information about Mnemosyne here," she told him, making no effort to hide the accusation in her tone.

"You did," said he.

It was true. She'd found the name, all right. There were millions of entries regarding the goddess of memory: where they found her, how she'd let herself be captured and enslaved in exchange for releasing the five muses they'd held captive, and how crucial her talent had been in refining the Nephilim's minds as well as their record system. What had happened to her afterwards, however, or her present whereabouts was yet to be found.

"You know perfectly well what I mean," she said, on the brink of rudeness. "I never thought there could be such a thing as too much information, and yet that's the only real thing I've learned since boarding this cursed ship." She pressed her temples in an unconscious effort to ease the constant headache caused by the Nephilim's vessel and its wards, designed to suppress a god's powers. "Going like this, it's going to take forever to find anything."

"Good thing you're a goddess. You have forever," he teased.

"Time is not the same as patience!" she snapped, clearly running out of it. She felt irascible as a wet cat. The uncharacteristic mood annoyed her almost as much as its causes. "Is there a way to, I don't know… narrow down the search?" she asked hopefully.

Their system was flawed. The files were organised by type and in some chronological order Seshat could not fathom. The Nephilim, like their creators and their creator's ancestors, had developed a system to measure time, as if the entire Universe worked around their clock. Talk about hubris. And their search function was an insult. It never actually searched for the thing she asked it for but everything related to it instead. She'd kiss a cat for the ability to Reach into the computer's virtual realm and select the right file.

"You can ask Namrive to find it for you," Anubis suggested. Again.

Seshat hissed at him in reply.

Working with Namrive was not an option Seshat's godly pride would ever allow her to entertain. That she'd agreed to be on the same ship as the android in the first place was already stressing her integrity to the limit. The Nephilim deprived gods of their will, their freedom. They'd caused Ra to return to the fabric of the universe, leaving a bereaved pantheon vulnerable to all sorts of power disputes. To be confined with a Nephilim was bad enough. To work with it...

"No," she said stubbornly, and opened the next file. It wasn't the right one, but she would read it nonetheless, and who knows, maybe she'd learn something, damn it.

Namrive entered the room. Both gods watched her like cats, ready to pounce on their prey. She walked slowly to the main workstation, seemingly unperturbed by their attention, though making an effort not to limp. There she began typing with her left hand, the right lacking dexterity and the fingertips required to perform the task efficiently.

The right side of Namrive's body was a ruin, having been caught in the crossfire between Apollo and the Suzerain. Seshat almost felt sorry for her. A mortal would have died; a god would have healed. A Nephilim, it seemed, could do neither and so just went on damaged until it downloaded into a new body. Their imitation of immortality was as flawed and insulting as their search function.

Seshat had met other Nephilim, back when she was the Suzerain's chronicler, and she had no love for these sentient machines designed to steal the willpower of gods. Their creators had been descendants of humans, hand-picked by Loki at Prometheus' request in an effort to save humanity from the gods. Both Loki and Prometheus were tricksters. Suffice it to say, things had got out of hand, and now there were hardly any actual humans left and not many free gods either.

A familiar wave of irritation ran through her soul whenever she thought of Loki and the chaos he'd brought to her life. He and Psyche, the ornery goddess of the soul, would have to deal with the Suzerain without her, for no god, mortal or Nephilim would ever be safe while he existed. But that story she'd have to miss, unfortunately. All she really cared about now was finding Mnemosyne, for without memory, all stories were meaningless.

Namrive finished whatever it was she was doing and turned to face them. No one spoke for a long moment, not even telepathically. They just stood there, doing nothing yet ready for anything.

"We'll be arriving at our destination shortly," she announced.

"Already?" Anubis asked, confused.

Finally, Seshat thought. The Nephilim's stellar chariot – or spaceship, as they called it – was imbued with the same material as the interior of the Stump in Niflheim, designed to damper a god's will and render them almost powerless. Seshat couldn't wait to be free of it. Her search would go much faster, if nothing else.

Namrive's eyes focused on her as if she'd heard her thoughts. She hadn't, of course. The Nephilim didn't have Reach, but their deduction and observation skills were uncanny. She'd been against taking Seshat with them, and had Anubis asked for her permission, he would have been denied. But everything had happened too fast for her to protest. Seshat herself had been too caught up to object and, all things considered, she had to admire Namrive's pragmatic restraint. She was yet to show even the slightest hint of resentment towards Anubis for bringing Seshat aboard, and if her presence disgruntled her, she was much better at dealing with it than Seshat. Then again, that might be due to her artificial physiology and mindset rather than good nature.

"And what is our destination?" Seshat asked politely. It only then occurred to her that she didn't know. All she'd cared about was getting access to the Nephilim's database. Then again, to a god, one world was as good as another in the great expanse of the Universe.

"Pallas. The Nephilim homeworld," said Anubis.

Except that one! Seshat almost blurted.

"Not exactly. I am going to Pallas – alone; you two are going to Sombra," Namrive said matter-of-factly,

"What?" The god of the dead practically barked the question. His jackal aspect showed through his human features, as it often did when he lost his grip on his emotions.

"We've just received a distress call from Sombra," Namrive said. "The issue is more suited for your skill set than mine, Anubis. Taking into account the catastrophic turn of events in Niflheim and the passenger on this ship, I decided it was more prudent to stop there first."

"You decided?" Anubis growled, eyes glowing with outrage.

Namrive kept her poise. "Yes, Anubis. It's my ship, therefore it's my decision. When you have your own ship, feel free to choose its destinations. Right now, be grateful that you and your guest are allowed to travel on this one. Or perhaps you'd like to try your deep-space translocating abilities again?"

His ears pressed flat against his head. He groaned. Translocation was an ability common to most gods, but only a few were able to do it across vast distances with any sort of accuracy. Scions of Ra were particularly challenged in that department, their affinity with stars meant that they often ended up inside one – a less than desirable destination. Still, Sombra was worse. He'd rather be sent to Bastet's world to face her and all her cats than return to that cursed moon. Especially now.

He tried to inhale and choked on his own breath. The thing about breathing was that you had to do it often, otherwise you'd forget how to do it properly.

"Problem?" Seshat asked pointedly.

"Yes. A big problem. I can't go back there, Namrive. I don't want to go back there!" His blatant honesty shocked even him.

Namrive tilted her head like a curious kitten who'd just spotted an injured bird. "I figured you'd like it. After all, you are worshipped as a proper god there."

Seshat raised both eyebrows at that.

"As a Nephilim god…" he grumbled exasperatedly.

Seshat's eyebrows drew close together.

"I… er… oh, for cat's sake. You'll see," he replied to her telepathic questioning, rubbing his neck as if it pained him.

"I cannot wait," Seshat said dryly.

"Good," said Namrive. "Glad that's settled. I've already sent a message to Thoth, letting him know you're coming back." She turned to Seshat. "He cannot wait to see you, by the way."

Seshat's tight control on her emotions unravelled.

"Wait, who?" She turned to Anubis, eyes burning in a half-pleading, half-accusatory glare.

Namrive remained impassive as a statue, trying not to smirk.

Anubis could have mewed. "Ah, yes. Didn't I tell you, Seshat? I've been working with your father for a while. I'm sure I meant to tell you before, but you were too busy accusing me of treason. Must have slipped my mind." He smiled forcefully.

Seshat's mouth opened; words came out a few seconds later. "You and Thoth... Since when?"

He grimaced. Lying would be pointless now. "Since you left for Niflheim."

'That was decades ago!' she shouted telepathically.

'According to some calendars...'

'Huh?'

'Time is relative, you see. Chronos, He –'

Understanding dawned on Seshat. No wonder she was having so much trouble finding her way through the records. She'd completely misinterpreted the Nephilim's chronological scale, assuming it had been based on a mortal's perspective of time. The gods glared at each other, bristling.

"Well then. Glad that's settled," Namrive said matter-of-factly, actually surprised at how little she cared about being excluded from their telepathic argument. Gods might be able to hide their thoughts from her, but their body language spoke volumes. It was something they only did when they were together, she noticed. On their own, a god was an enigma, practically inscrutable. But put two or more together and it was like watching mimes.

She smiled at her insight. "Meet me in the teleportation room in forty-six hours." And she left feeling a bit better about herself while Seshat and Anubis clawed their minds to shreds.

Chapter 14

The Truth in the Lies

A good liar must have a flawless memory.

– Memory on Record

"You lied to me!" Seshat shouted in Anubis' face.

Anger suited her, he realised. The way her eyes burned within their thick outlines of kohl and how her straight black hair brushed against her bare shoulders had always fascinated him. Unfortunately, she could be as dangerous as she was gorgeous in a fit of pique.

He lifted a finger between them. "No. I haven't told you the whole truth. There's a difference."

"Tzzzz!" She scratched his face from hairline to chin.

"Ouch! Now, now. Manners, Seshat. Keep your claws to yourself or you'll never learn the entire story." Anubis massaged his already-healed cheek as he spoke.

Seshat prepared to summon Quetish. The sphinx would teach Anubis not to bend the narrative to suit his personal needs, for sphinxes cherished wisdom and truth above all things. They were immortal beings but not quite like gods. Able to slip between realms at ease, they were often bound to reality by linking to a specific person or place, cursed to guard it, or simply decorate it. Seshat had broken Quetish's curse to Thebes and offered her all the knowledge she could learn inside her private realm in exchange for a more convenient and formidable method of transportation in the physical worlds rather than her unreliable translocation. Quetish owed her allegiance. She would fight for her. But she decided against it. The sphinx would not appreciate being dragged into this mess, to be confined in the ship. She was still sulking about having to leave Aedan in Niflheim. One more offence and Quetish might become the Dharkan's mount instead – in more ways than one. Seshat rolled her eyes, focusing back on Anubis. Her mind always wandered when she wanted to flee. There was no escape, though. She had to fight this one out – alone.

"You've been working with my father. How could you!"

Anubis mimicked her inflated shock. "You say that as if it's a violation of the laws of the Universe. We've always worked together! I weigh the souls; he records their deeds."

"I thought you stopped that nonsense when Horus defeated Seth!"

"We did! But then the Nephilim came along and… Oh, cats… there's so much you don't know." He sounded tired now, rubbing his forehead.

"Well, we have hours to spare, apparently. Entertain me with your story." Seshat still wasn't sure what an hour was in Nephilim terms. But any amount of time spent on the ship was too long, in any case.

Anubis complied with a long-suffering sigh. "I told you the Nephilim have conquered death and therefore know little about it. They use me to advise them on matters of the afterlife and the Underworld. That is the truth. I also told you I wasn't the only one working with them and that they were not interested in your talents because their record-keeping was better than yours. Had you not been so offended by the idea, you might have Reached the true meaning of my words. After all, there's only one god more obsessed with knowledge and more meticulous in his accounts than you."

"You dare to suggest it's my fault I misread you?" She was incandescent in her fury. Had she been in full control of her powers, she'd have vaporised the ship.

"I'm saying you've been a bit dim for the past millennia, Seshat. Distracted by the wrong characters: Eros, Loki, Chronos, Mnemosyne, the Suzerain. Meanwhile, new stories are unfolding. Or, in this case, an old one carries on. Stories don't end just because you're no longer interested in them."

"And who gives you the right to dictate what I should be interested in? I was doing quite well before you decided to rescue me."

"Oh please, you were losing yourself in Niflheim, only a few chapters away from self-destruction. Playing your own characters, embellishing stories, sending messages across time – don't even try to deny it!" He wagged a finger at her. "You were miserably bored and unhappy. An unhappy god makes mistakes, and those mistakes affect other gods."

"You selfish, hypocrite, cat!" she scorned. "No god was more unhappy than you when you were weighing souls. And now you're doing it again! For what reason?"

His impeccable posture slacked as he contemplated

that fact. "A similar one, actually," he admitted sheepishly.

"It can't be to punish Seth or to rid the Underworld of those touched by his influence. He's gone now. The Nephilim caught him – or Horus gave him to them – either way, they got him."

"Yes… they got him all right. Despite all their short-sightedness and arrogance, the Nephilim actually developed cages that work. You experienced one first-hand back in Niflheim. But there's a flaw in their design, you see. The Nephilim can't use Seth's soul to power it. Old souls, especially those of our pantheon, have a way of disrupting the er…" – Anubis struggled to remember the word – "circuitry of the thing. Something like that."

Seshat blinked. "You mean… the Stumps are powered by the souls of their prisoners?"

"Why… yes."

"That's cruel!"

"The Nephilim call it practical."

She paused, realisation dawning on her. "Oh, cats! They can't control him, can they?"

Anubis nodded gravely. "That was what Horus intended. After all, how best to defeat an organised enemy than to have them deal with a god of chaos? Unfortunately, it didn't take the Nephilim long to realise Ra was the only one able to control Seth. But Ra, of course, was still angry with Horus and refused to play a role in his plan. When the Nephilim came for him, he removed himself from the situation by turning himself into a star." Anubis shook his head at the memory. To watch a god return to the fabric of the Universe was a terrible thing, a reminder of both their potential and their fate.

Gods can't worship other gods, but Ra was closer to Chronos and Gaea than most deities, and the relationship between him and his scions involved a level of respect and admiration not seen in any other pantheon. He took a deep breath. "Anyway, that's where Thoth and I came in."

"I don't get it. What passes for humanity these days have all but lost the ability to think for themselves. They may still have the free will that comes with their souls, but they rarely use it. What are you weighing, Anubis?"

"It doesn't matter what they think. In fact, it's better if they don't. Only their actions and, of course, their souls matter."

"Is the goddess of the soul aware of this?"

"Cats, no! I've tried very hard to keep it out of her Reach. Besides, Psyche has her hands full with the Nyx situation. It's going to be a while before she notices what we've been doing." Or so he hoped.

"And what have you two been doing, exactly?" Seshat asked again, straining for patience.

"Feeding the beast," he said sheepishly. "Strengthening it, to be more precise. While pretending to do otherwise, of course."

"By all the cats in the universe – why?" she almost cried.

He grimaced. His next words would cost him dearly. The truth always had a high cost. "To help Nephilim like Namrive eliminate their most thorny antagonists."

"Other gods," Seshat guessed. "So I was right. You are a traitor." The words were uttered with loathing.

He smirked at her. "No, Sunshine. We are only a nuisance to them, a source of exotic power at best, nothing more. Their real threat is their creators and, of course, themselves."

She frowned. "The Nephilim are at odds with each other?" She found that highly unlikely. They practically shared the same mind, the same design, at least.

"Any being who can think for himself will eventually disagree with the status quo."

"Free will is a bitch," Loki had always said.

She focused back on Anubis. Something about what he'd said didn't sound right. "I thought the Nephilim's creators had died out like the rest of their kind." Humans, as Prometheus had created them, no longer existed. Most of humankind had evolved into beasts, daemons, and even stranger things.

Anubis tilted his head from side to side as if weighing his reply. "Sort of. The original humans selected by Loki are gone, yes, but some of their descendants still call themselves human. Or post-human, to be precise." Seshat curled her lip slightly. Anubis waved his hand dismissively. "You'll understand when you meet them."

"I'd rather understand now. So I'm not distracted when I meet them."

"Very well. In a nutshell, post-humans, like all gods' creations, wished to achieve godhood, but they disagreed on how to achieve it. Wars broke out, as they always do, and to abbreviate a long story, eventually they divided themselves into two groups, each with their own philosophy on the matter: Prometheans and Lokians. Prometheans believed they'd been designed to evolve into deities and so the fastest way to become a god was through gene editing and selective breeding of desired traits. Only the most intelligent, beautiful and healthy were allowed to reproduce. That proved to be insufficient, of course, but they keep trying, travelling from world to world looking for that illusive element required for apotheosis, leaving only genocide and mutilation in their wake." He shrugged. "They're of little importance, really, practically extinct now."

"And the other faction?" she prompted. "The one you called Lokians." An ominous designation if ever there was one.

Anubis licked his lips as if he'd tasted something foul. He despised the god who inspired the eponymous appellation of this faction, if not the faction itself. "Lokians, on the other hand, figured out the best way to become a god was to imitate one. They mastered the intricacies of matter and life itself, rejuvenating and replacing their old flesh with younger, over and over again until they became practically immortal themselves. But when even that turned out to be insufficient, they developed a way of animating matter from scratch to host not only their minds but their souls as well, turning their backs on life as we know it.

Seshat nodded absently. So that's how the Nephilim came to be. Their records merely said they were the product of an agreement between the Mentor and the Master – whoever they were – united against the Monster and the Martyr.

"Ironically," Anubis continued, "the closest they came to godhood was in their disappointment with their creations and – ah, yes, this reminds me – be aware when you encounter them, both factions have Reach."

Seshat raised an eyebrow.

"Yes, I suspect a god was involved." Reaching her thoughts, he added, "Not Loki, for he was still imprisoned in the Underworld when all this happened. But some other trickster, I'm sure."

"How come I haven't heard of this until now?"

"You've been in Niflheim for too long, Seshat," said Anubis. "An age passed while Chronos held that world hostage. We might have the luxury of time, as the mortals say, but He is luxury itself." Anubis glanced down at the gemstones set in golden rings on his fingers. "We just wear it."

"Cats…" She knew humans had been scattered from Midgard across the Universe long before they'd evolved enough to venture into space. Odin and Thor in particular had taken a fair share of subjects from right under Zeus' beard shortly after their creation. She'd even tracked and recorded the rise and fall of some of these new civilisations for a while, but their stories were always the same, regardless of the world they were set in. Always short and violent, or worse, boring. Had she been asked to guess which, of all the species in the Universe, mortal and immortal, would become a threat to gods, humans, so fragile, short-lived and in a constant quarrel with each other, would have been at the bottom of her list. She would not underestimate them again, that was for sure.

"Right," she said, taking it all in. "Still, none of it explains Seth or your dealings with Thoth."

"I'm getting there. Not everyone is as good at telling stories as you, Sunshine. Be patient."

He's enjoying this, she realised. And purposely using

speech to tell this account so she could not pin down his true feelings on the subject, the cat. She pressed her lips into a taut smile and encouraged him to continue with a gracious gesture.

"Remember when Horus, in his attempt to show how magnanimous he was, spared Seth's life after he'd defeated him, claiming that there would be no order without the constant threat of chaos?"

Magnanimously vain, she thought. The whole affair had been a plot to humiliate and incarcerate Seth, a god whose greatest crime was not being like the other gods. She'd refused to take any part in it.

"You always had a soft spot for gods of chaos," Anubis teased, reaching her mind.

"Again, what does that have to do with anything?"

"Well, let's just say Horus made a mistake."

"You already said that."

"I did, didn't I? I never tire of saying it." He grinned. There was no love lost between Anubis and his half-brother Horus.

"Where is Horus now?" she asked, although she could guess.

"In the Nephilim's custody." Anubis shone with glee as he spoke.

She exhaled loudly. Gods could be such petty creatures sometimes. "Let's return to the Lokians." That wiped the joy from his features. "So they created the Nephilim as vessels for themselves."

"Correct."

"That's quite ingenious – too ingenious. They must have had help – from a crafter, not a trickster," she clarified before he had a chance to tell her she was wrong.

Anubis' mirth returned, tainted with excitement. "Oh yes. Care to guess from whom?"

"Hephaestus."

Anubis sneered derisively. "No, Seshat. The Olympian cripple only came into this story much later, after the Nephilim rebelled. He refined the Nephilim's technology so it would be shielded from us as well as work against us, but he was not the one who inspired them to pursue that path. You're close, though."

Seshat hated being tested, but she also loved figuring out a plot. There were only three gods Hephaestus would want to please: his father, Zeus, who had grossly underestimated the Nephilim and paid the price; his wife, Aphrodite, who, if rumours were true, had suffered a similar fate to Zeus; and Athena, Zeus' daughter and Hephaestus' first and long-lasting infatuation, a goddess who valued cold reasoning above all else, a weaver who championed craftsmanship and scorned emotion as a weakness. A goddess of war who came into existence fully grown and ready for battle. The very manifestation of Zeus' enmity towards their kind.

"Oh, cats…" Seshat breathed. It was quite the story to unravel, and yet she wanted nothing to do with it. Only one thing really mattered to her. "What about Mnemosyne? Where does she fit into all this?" The goddess of memory was a Titaness. Titans – at least those who had avoided eternal incarceration in Tartarus after the Titanomachy – were reclusive deities who'd learnt how not to get caught up in Olympian schemes.

Anubis winced, looking for words that would soften the truth. It had been too much to hope for that the tale of Seth and the Nephilim would distract her from her obsession. He sighed. "I told you she was linked and that something terrible had happened. All records have been lost, destroyed or… forgotten. That is also true. Except she was not linked to a Nephilim or held prisoner on a Stump. Not exactly. You see, er… she was on a ship."

Seshat frowned, not quite following.

"She's too precious to keep in one world, and not even a Nephilim's mind was able to cope with that much information. So they built something that could. And they used her to compile their knowledge across worlds."

"That's why I can't find a record of her anywhere. Because she's everywhere," Seshat realised. "She is the records!"

"Precisely. Wait!" he urged before she turned supernova on him. "I told you something terrible had happened to her world. That wasn't a lie either. Again, not exactly! The ship's gone. They can't find it. But I figured you probably could. You see, she's not dead; otherwise we wouldn't be having this conversation. We wouldn't even remember the words to! My guess is that she's incorporeal. If anyone can bring her out of hiding, make her manifest herself in this realm, it's you, Seshat."

"You want me to find her for them so they can bind her again? You want me to betray her?!" She wanted to claw his eyes out.

"No. I want you to find her and keep her safe, for all our sakes." He had enough sense to stay out of arm's reach as he spoke.

"You –" She had to take a deep breath. "You don't want me to find her. You want me to bait her! Oh, Anubis, I wonder how much your soul weighs now," she said bitterly.

That stung. "It was not my intention, not my choice. But… yes. Now it seems we need to finish what I started before it's too late, so…" He spread out his hands. "Apologies, Seshat. Believe me, I did not want you involved in this. I'd rather return to Niflheim than to that place. But alas… priorities! Seth needs to be dealt with first. The search for Mnemosyne will have to wait."

Everything about his demeanour told her that the last bit, at least, was sincere. But it wasn't enough.

"How can I trust you, after everything you've just told me? Everything you've done?"

He changed to his true aspect, took a step forward and looked her straight in the eyes. "Frankly, Sunshine, your trust is irrelevant. You'll do what you have to – as I have. And that's that." He turned to leave, then looked over his shoulder, dejected. "It's all we gods ever really do."

∞

Seshat's gaze lingered murderously after Anubis, long after he left the room. He was right, though. She'd been overconfident and blinded by her need to close the book on Mnemosyne. So much so, she didn't realise she'd inadvertently walked herself into a different story. Anubis had written her into a corner, and now she had to play her part if she ever wanted to write anything else.

"Very well," she said to herself. First, she had to learn more about the Nephilim. She'd learned a lot already, true, but not enough. These recent revelations taught her she had to learn it all. The entire story from long before they were created. Ideally, all the way back to their creators themselves. To their creators' creators. To why Prometheus and Zeus created humans in the first place. If only she could meet one of the original Titans, or the Ogdoad, even. Perhaps then the universe would finally make sense. Failing that…

"A goddess should always be prepared," Hathor used to say.

Seshat turned to the computer again. "I wish to learn everything there is to know about Lokians, Prometheans, the Nephilim, Athena and Pallas. Go."

CHAPTER 15

The Turn of Events

Narratives are the product of memory,
not truth.

– Memory on Record

Anubis stormed into Namrive's quarters. He tried to rein in his temper, but he was tired of pretending to be a temperate deity, let alone patient. "Did you get all that?"

She'd witnessed his argument with Seshat, of course. There was no privacy on the ship, riddled with artificial senses as it was, some almost as precise as a god's Reach.

"I did indeed." Namrive's mouth spasmed as she attempted a smug smile. Better to remain serious, she decided upon seeing his reciprocating snarl. He wore the jackal – his real aspect and a far more impressive facade than a human's. "Don't waste your breath," she said pre-emptively to his intake of air, focusing back on the screen to further aggravate him. Gods like him hated being ignored.

"Breath comes and goes," he said. "It's my words and sympathy I've wasted, apparently. I offered you an olive branch earlier, and in return, you condemn me back to Sombra. Is that your idea of punishment for bringing Seshat with us?"

"I'm not a god," said Namrive. "I don't deal in punishments. You're going to Sombra because there is where you're needed."

"No. That's where you assigned me."

"Same thing." She feigned confusion. "Why are we having this discussion, Anubis?"

He released his breath. "What is Thoth's still doing there? We were done."

"No. You were almost done. We should have stayed until the end. By leaving, we invited fate to intervene and make a mess of things. I swear, you gods are your own worst enemies." She tried to shake her head, but it would only turn to the left, making her look as glitched as she felt. Fortunately, Anubis was too angry to notice.

"Apparently!" he growled. "Do you have any idea what this little detour will cost me?"

"Clearly not," she replied, eyes wide, trying to deduce the real reason behind his tantrum. Anubis was many things; prone to emotional outbursts was not one of them. She had to understand what had triggered this state. "So your girlfriend is Thoth's daughter? Funny, he never mentioned offspring."

"She's not my girlfriend." Not anymore, if indeed she ever had been, he added to himself grudgingly. "And you know very well we only mention what we must."

Namrive wanted to scowl, but given the state of her facial expressions, she didn't dare try. "Yes, I am aware of how much your kind values cryptic mystery. The Mentor forbid mortals ever learn how banal you really are."

Anubis' deep-seated growl would have raised the hairs on her nape – had she any.

"You speak of the Mentor as if she's not one of us," said he.

"She's not banal."

"No, she's the very epitome of a mind without a conscience."

Not long ago, such a statement would have been the end of Anubis, despite the fact Namrive could not fault his observation. He grew bolder as she got weaker. But she would use that weakness.

Unable to stand as straight as she'd wished, Namrive turned around and leaned on the console to keep her balance, doing her best to appear nonchalant.

"You claim to have a conscience, but still you… hmmm" – she paused, looking for the word – "how do you phrase it, ah yes, bent the truth regarding the nature of your work with Thoth to Seshat. Is that how you treat your friends or just your kin?"

"To us gods, too much honesty always leads to trouble. It has nothing to do with conscience, affiliation or loyalty. Only survival," he told her.

For immortal beings, gods sure worry a lot about survival, Namrive reflected. Anubis might claim death was just another realm, but it had to be a pretty unpleasant one if even he, a god of the dead, was so averse to it.

"You'd rather lie than face the consequences of your actions in reality," she scorned.

Anubis stepped into her personal space, forcing her to stand upright in order to not suffer the humiliation of being nose to snout with him. She'd never been uncomfortable in the presence of a god – certainly not in his presence – but there was something to be said about gods and their anger. Wrath made them formidable. His gaze burned her with a fire that did not belong there, and suddenly, she felt very uncomfortable.

"Are you screwing with me, Namrive?" he rasped erringly.

She had to think for a moment. "I'm not sure I understand the question."

He narrowed his eyes to slits. "It's easy for you to judge, Nephilim. You have your reality – your only reality – so neatly defined. You think that by measuring it down to the atom you can control it, even predict it. Here's the truth: you control nothing. At any moment, gods like Chronos can unravel it all just like this." He snapped his fingers for effect. "Come back to lecture me on reality and consequence after you've travelled across endless realms through the eons, with nothing to guide you but memory. Because you see, truth can be as relative as time. And just as destructive."

Her mind was clearly not functioning well, for she could not think of an appropriate reply to this. So she did the next best thing: she deflected.

"Speaking of memory, what is Seshat's obsession with Mnemosyne?"

Anubis hung his head, despondent. It was hopeless to try to explain a god's experience to a Nephilim. They would never be able to communicate, let alone understand each other in that regard. So he answered her question. "They were lovers."

Namrive laughed then; the staccato cackle seemed to mock joy to Anubis' ears. "Liar."

"It's the truth," he said despairingly.

"Perhaps. But it's also the answer you expect me to be satisfied with because you're aware of my proclivities. However, it's not love that drives Seshat, nor even lust. It's fear. And I want to understand why. Is there something the goddess of memory knows that we don't?"

He almost gaped. "Wow! Let me think… How about – everything?"

Namrive cursed her bugged brain again for the poorly articulated question, then tried a different approach. "You, too, fear Mnemosyne, and it's not because of her knowledge. What aren't you telling me?"

"Cats, Namrive. Your circuitry must be truly burned out. It's not what she knows, but what she is." He took a breath, not wanting to delve any deeper into that explanation. "Never mind. You're right. My anxiety is of a different nature. I promised Mnemosyne to Seshat, you see. I am a god; it's important that I keep my promises," he said grimly.

"Then you have nothing to worry about."

Anubis stood very still, holding breath and blink alike. "Namrive – what do you mean by that?"

Namrive relished her next words. "You see," she said, mimicking his tone. "Before, I too spoke only a partial truth. The distress call came from Mnemosyne's ship. Or what was left of it to be more precise."

"What?" The word sounded like the low bark of a startled canine.

"Prometheans found it orbiting Sombra. I'm not filled in on the details of what happened. It seems that they've collided or something, which is highly unlikely, of course, but there you go. Whatever happened, it did not end well for either party."

He almost howled. "What in Ra's name was the ship doing in Sombra's orbit?"

"Thoth summoned it in. Said he needed Mnemosyne to edit Seth's memories before the big event."

That made no sense to Anubis. If he didn't know any better, he'd say the god of reckoning was mad, but a mind like Thoth's would never unravel into madness. Besides, he hated Mnemosyne. How she just absorbed knowledge by simply existing, while he had to painstakingly write it down. He must have been desperate to even consider asking her for anything. "What's wrong with Seth's memories?"

"How would I know?" Namrive tried to click her tongue; it sounded like a hiccup. "We really shouldn't have left for Niflheim until we were certain of the outcome of that venture."

"You wanted to go!"

Now that Anubis thought about it, it had been uncharacteristically impulsive of Namrive to drop everything to go check on what had at first seemed a malfunctioning portal on a trivial world. Sure, they couldn't risk another Nephilim being sent in their place and finding out the Suzerain had been supplying them with Narrum souls (souls that technically no one would miss) but it had been quite the cosmic dash through three wormholes from Sombra to Niflheim over an assignment that, under normal circumstances, she would have deemed beneath her. Not only that, they were now returning via the longest route, avoiding monitored systems and wormholes alike.

"Yes... It was my call. My responsibility." She sounded contrite. But of course, he must have misheard. Nephilim were not capable of such a thing.

"What about the post-humans? What were they doing there?" Anubis prompted while his mind and Reach desperately searched for anything to account for her behaviour. Ironically, her disfigurement made it harder for him to read her. Her mind, though... he could definitely sense it, he just didn't quite understand what he was sensing.

"Not a glitching clue," she replied with a sigh. "Either they'd figured out what we were doing – although why they would care is beyond my speculative abilities – or they got extremely unlucky in their flight path." She considered this. "Luck likes to mock us, doesn't she?"

"Tyche has one of the most twisted senses of humour you'll ever find in a deity," he admitted, then added, "Regardless, the post-humans are the least of our problems. They wouldn't know where they'd landed, even if it swallowed them. And I doubt they'll survive long." He perked up at the prospect of a well-populated underworld to play with.

"Actually, they've been living in the temple for years now. It's all Thoth can do to... distract them, so to speak."

"Years? As in, Midgard years?" Anubis cursed Chronos for his capriciousness and abuse of power. From his perspective, he'd only been away a few days, for cat's sake. "How would they even find the entrance to the temple?"

"Ask Thoth. He too has a sense of humour, it seems," she replied, clearly unimpressed by the deity's initiative.

Anubis wrought his hands behind his back, thinking

furiously. Thoth had no sense of humour at all. Nor was he prone to acts of kindness, let alone recklessness. "He must have needed their souls to control the situation, forestall Seth, or something. Create a balance…" he speculated. That was bad. Really bad. Cats only knew what sort of souls Thoth sent down that well without him there to weigh them.

"Is there any way we can contact him directly?" Anubis asked, hoping against hope to find something to help him get a better insight into the situation. Reach was out of the question. Sombra's underground was as shielded as the Nephilim's ships.

Namrive half shook her head again. "Crymure wouldn't risk contact around so many empaths."

"For cat's sake! We need more information. I can't just drop in there blind."

"You're resourceful," she said meaningfully and unsympathetically. "I'm sure you'll find a way to make contact with one of your own priests. I can lower the ship's shield if it helps." She didn't wait for his acknowledgement to input the command.

"Thanks." It did help in more ways than she'd intended. Already he felt so much better despite the annoying realisation that, one, the psychic shield could be lowered, and two, that she knew more about his talents than he thought – bitch.

"The situation appears to be pretty bad there, so whatever you do, don't make it worse. For my sake, as well as your godly hide," she warned. "I really can't afford to present another failure to the Mentor. Neither can you."

He wanted to strangle her. "I had nothing to do with your screw-up. How dare you bring this down on both of us!"

"At least I didn't bring anything with us," she pointed out blatantly, still not convinced about Seshat's innocence or his own self-proclaimed lack of involvement in the devastating events that had taken place on Niflheim.

Anubis seemingly deflated. "Cats, Namrive. Do you have any idea of how dangerous it is to go back there now, so close to impact?"

"Would you rather switch places? I'll go to Sombra, and you can explain yourself to the Mentor."

No, he really didn't like that option.

"I thought so."

His jackal ears pressed flat against his head. It made him look almost puppyish. "What if it's too late? If I fail… If he gets out before we… or if we get caught or sucked into it…" He trailed off, genuinely perturbed by the idea.

She wanted to touch him, comfort him. And could have kicked herself just for thinking it.

"You're too proud to fail," she said, to no effect. "Look, I'll make you a deal. Your kind loves deals, right? So here's mine: finish what you started with Thoth –"

"Then what?" he interrupted, ears flipping forward, intrigued despite himself.

"Then you're free – from me anyway – I promise, for all that might be worth to you." She meant it, though. "I'll tell the Mentor that Hel and Hades took offence to your presence on their world and captured you. If there's something I've learned in the last few days – besides to not dismiss magic, that is – it's to not get involved in a god's schemes, especially those who dwell in the Underworlds."

This seemed to animate him a little. "Brain damage has made you wise, Namrive."

She let the insult slide, for it was too close to fact. "I just have different priorities now."

"Such as?" He didn't wait for her answer. "Ah, yes: the Suzerain. Good luck with that."

"I'd rather have magic," she said without thinking. Still, Anubis Reached the truth of her words well enough.

He stared at her with a newfound appreciation for how she'd changed and lamented the fact that she was a Nephilim, for she might have made a pretty damn good goddess. Did the Suzerain know what he was doing to her when he hacked her brain? Could he have been that cruel? Yes, Anubis decided. Yes, he was.

He changed to his human aspect and touched her ruined cheek. "Luck is better than magic, Namrive. But you can't rely on either. Remember that."

She nodded, lost for words, feeling a bit dizzy.

"Goodbye, Namrive." He smiled, kissed her forehead, and headed for the door.

'Until we meet again, Anubis,' she said to herself as he left.

And although he did not turn around, he smiled because this time, he'd definitely heard her.

CHAPTER 16

The Mentor

Zeus was a necessary affair.
The Nephilim a calculated risk.

– Memory on Record

Namrive strode along the colossal diamond-shaped hall, her head held high, her step steady and assured, her mind set. She'd dropped Anubis and Seshat off in a shuttle within flight range of Sombra. All he had to do was sit back and let the ship's computer follow the trajectory she'd personally calculated, and they'd land on Sombra, right next to its Stump, without incident. Of course, that wouldn't happen. Anubis would try to pilot the ship himself and likely crash the thing. Maybe even end up on the bright side of the moon. Oh, what do you care? she asked herself. In fact, she didn't. She just couldn't get him out of her head since their last conversation for some reason. Not now. Focus.

Athena, goddess of war and wisdom – two talents that had always seemed incompatible to Namrive – sat on her golden throne, flanked by massive pillars of pristine marble and the twins Belus and Agenor, awesomely radiant in gilded armour to rival Apollo's own. An owl perched on a pedestal beside her, huge eyes fixed on the approaching supplicant like a predator's on its prey.

"Mentor." Namrive spoke reverently, bending her knee in a curt and precise curtsy.

"Ah, Namrive. You have returned." The goddess's tone implied a certain dissatisfaction. Then again, Athena always sounded dissatisfied. She leaned forward and bored her gaze into Namrive with the kind of scrutiny only gods were capable of. "I see you've been repaired but not upgraded. Don't you approve of the new model?"

Namrive inclined her head. "I do, Mentor. A model capable of hosting souls locally certainly has its merits and advantages, but I've grown attached to this body." And its personality, she might have added, but too much truth can get you in trouble, as Anubis would say.

Athena curled her lip slightly. "Some claim that being too attached to one image is a weakness." Long moments passed. She leaned back again. "I believe one should remain true to one's identity. Gods shouldn't hide behind glamours, wear masks or change bodies like children in costumes pretending to be their foes. Neither should Nephilim. I'm glad you're able to be repaired. It would have been a waste and shame otherwise. After all, I patterned your design." A fact Athena never ceased to remind her of.

"Yes, Mentor." Namrive inclined her head further as she spoke. What had once been a source of pride and drive now became an irritation. It put her in mind of a parent always reminding their children that they were alive because of them, as if they'd chosen to be alive, let alone born to their family.

"So tell me, did you meet my father during your time in Niflheim?" Athena asked with the subtlety of a gong.

Namrive blinked. So much for secrecy, it seemed. Her left side still glitched now and again, and her brain remained affected by whatever the Suzerain had done to it. But her mind was clear. Clearer than ever, actually. She doesn't know. Can't know! Namrive thought, hopefully – desperately. And she sure would not be the one telling her what had happened to Zeus. "No, Mentor. I never left the Stump." It was the truth.

The goddess licked her teeth. "Mmm. Why go all the way there, then?"

"Anubis said he was curious about the Merge." Another truth, just not at all related to the question.

The owl's eyes narrowed to slits. "Since when do you do what Anubis wants?" Athena asked.

Namrive risked a smile. "Since what he wants sometimes is what we need. It's one of the reasons you, in your wisdom, assigned him to me."

The owl bobbed her head. Athena remained still. "And where is Anubis now?"

This is it, Namrive thought. The moment of truth – or deception, to be precise. Nephilim can't lie. Not to the Mentor. And yet she would have to, somehow. A lot depended on it. She'd rehearsed this answer dozens of times. *Breathe,* she told herself, even though the very notion was alien to her.

"Hades and Hel were reluctant to let him go." They couldn't have been more eager to send him away, in fact. The statement did pass for truth, though, since before they'd decided to kick him out of their world they had argued at length about where and how they would curse him for Eternity. In the end, they'd agreed the last thing they needed was another psychopomp in their Underworld.

"Were they now?" Athena glared through cold, hard-set eyes.

Namrive felt her skin prickle, her synapses glitching, her very self holding a metaphorical breath before what could well be her end.

"Interesting…" The goddess drummed her finger on the throne.

It was Namrive's turn to remain silent, frozen in place. She doubted she could have moved even had she wanted to.

The drumming dragged on, the only sound in that colossal hall, for what felt like a lifetime, until Athena suddenly flicked her fingers in the air. "Ah well, he's my father's problem now. Tell me more about this Suzerain character."

Namrive's legs nearly gave out. The relief was too quickly followed by more terror. Then anger took over, and she held on to it like a clamp.

"It appears he found a way to enhance our technology with magic," Namrive said. No point lying about that.

The corners of Athena's mouth turned downwards. "That is impossible. The two are incompatible by design."

Go to Niflheim and you'll have to redefine impossible, Namrive wanted to say, but instead she said, "I would agree but…" Namrive paused. She did not wish to lie about this part of the story. Not because she shouldn't, and many would suggest she should, considering how it made her look. But for once, subterfuge would not get her closer to answers or revenge, and she badly wanted both. She took a step forward, summoning earnestness. "Mentor, he bested me." He bested your father too, she wanted to say, but that would only stir the goddess in the wrong direction. "He learned how to adapt our technology to make him invulnerable to gods' talents as well as giving him an advantage over our own. I cannot explain how or why. I just know what I saw, what he did to me. Something made it possible."

Athena chewed on this information for a short while, straining for composure. "And he seemed so reliable. So humble, so dedicated, so…" She gritted her teeth, stood up and stomped her foot. "I hate dryads! They have no soul. It only takes a breeze to blow their wills in different directions, like leaves in the fall. They are Chronos' creatures; cursed like trees who bear his marks. Every single one of them. Worse than humans. Bah! Father should have eliminated them eons ago. Curse him and his damned lust! I swear, ninety per cent of the pantheon's problems are caused by his inability to remain chaste." Namrive had no argument there. Although she did sometimes wonder if the other ten per cent might be caused by Athena's impenetrable chastity and Hera's jealousy.

The goddess summoned her lance and shield, ready for battle, and marched back and forth across the room.

"The fates have played their hand," she proclaimed. "A better hand than I expected, I have to admit. However, now we know where we stand. What to expect. How to fight back. And we shall." She radiated intent as she spoke, as if addressing a vast audience or an army only she could see.

"Do we?" Namrive spoke without thinking. A few tweaks still needed to correct these unfortunate glitches between her brain and mouth. "Know where we stand, I mean," she amended quickly.

"I do. You will stand where I tell you."

"Of course." She practically bowed this time. "I am at your disposal, Mentor."

Athena glided from the dais to stand looming above her – ten feet of glorious animosity matched only by her ruthless vitriol. "Prove it," she demanded.

Namrive did not glitch. The goddess's callousness had always unsettled her, but it no longer frightened her. Not really. She only feared what Athena could do to her and only so far as it might prevent her from doing what she wanted to do. "How may I?" she asked almost piously.

The goddess, moving too fast for her to see, clasped Namrive's jaw in one hand. Her grey eyes turned red. And somehow she heard the answer before Athena spoke. "Bring me the Suzerain's heart."

Namrive would gladly tear his heart out. But she wasn't even sure he had one, let alone where to find him.

"Asgard," Athena practically snarled the word in reply to her unspoken question.

She can hear me think, Namrive realised. Anubis, what have you done!

Owl and goddess stared at her intently. Namrive bowed this time, deep. "It shall be done." What else could she say?

Athena appeared placated. She gestured towards the exit, and Namrive turned to leave. She did not dare to ask how the Mentor came about this piece of intelligence, but she was glad she had it. As to the rest, well…

"One more thing." The haunting voice echoed at Namrive's back midway through the hall.

"Yes, Mentor?"

"Next time you make a deal with a deity behind my back, make sure you know who you are dealing with."

Namrive froze. Her knees began to shake. Her mind reeled, unable to decipher which deity the goddess referred to. She had made quite a few deals lately, after all. The Maker had been just one of them. An answer eluded her. Caution urged her not to answer at all. Thankfully, she didn't have to.

"Do not disappoint me again, Namrive." Athena spoke without even turning, and still Namrive was sure she could have smote her where she stood had she wanted to. Why didn't she?

"Mentor…" was all Namrive managed to articulate over her shoulder before she left. It seemed war and reason were not dissimilar, after all. Athena's cold rationality and uncanny deduction had nearly unmade her and all her plans. Asgard, she mused. The last true bastion of the gods. She had no wish to travel there. No wish to set foot on any of the Aesir's nine worlds, in fact. Although it made sense the Suzerain would hide there – amongst his greatest enemies. Right under their noses, biding his time until he caught them unawares. Just like he did to me. Namrive headed straight to her ship, where she locked herself in her quarters, held a pillow to her face, and screamed. Whether in horror or excitement, she wasn't sure. But she felt much better afterwards.

PART III

Chronos arrived with a bang – the echoes can still be heard across the Cosmos to this day – and immediately began to separate events into cause and consequence. The concepts of past, present and future followed. Thus, I came to be what I am now, an entity forged out of the desperate need of a wounded Universe to make sense of this intruder's narrative.

– Memory on Record

CHAPTER 17

The Tower

*I remember him, as he remembers himself, as
he remembers me. I remember his life and his
death. I remember my life after he died.*

– Memory on Record

"Huh," was Lyam's first assessment of the tower perceived under the illumination of Audric's lantern. The walls had to be at least ten feet thick, making the interior much smaller, and yet somewhat more impressive than the exterior suggested. There was no writing, markings, or decorations of any kind, only what looked like a couple of suspension chambers set vertically atop some sort of force field generators, their power sources depleted. But clearly the lack of decor didn't mean it'd had no purpose or that it had been constructed in a hurry or on a whim. Every stone had been precisely cut and set. Every angle accurate and flush. Not that he'd expected anything less than perfection from the Nephilim, mind. What he hadn't expected was how erringly similar it looked to the pyramid buried beneath the mountain.

"It's empty." Rai sounded both relieved and disappointed. "Now what?"

"Now we wait," Berdnard said, sitting down on the ground, axe laid across his lap, despondently resigned. A storm unlike any other raged outside, the air almost too dense with soot and moisture to breathe without a mask. But inside, despite the drifts of ash covering the ground, it was surprisingly fine.

Rai cursed to herself, leaning against a wall, then took a nectar bar from her pack and started chewing. Lyam couldn't tell if she ate to cope with anxiety or if being anxious made her hungry. He just hoped they didn't have to wait long, for there wasn't a lot of food or time left.

The place was empty, all right – too empty for comfort. "Rai, can you feel this?" he asked.

She just stared at him in annoyance for a moment before sputtering a muffled. "What?"

"Nothing." He'd sent her a burst of emotion strong enough to make a Narrum cry. As he suspected, Reach didn't work inside this tower. It was like the rest of the moon, the very Universe, had ceased to exist beyond his perception. All that was left was this residual hmm, like the sound of silence itself. He glanced wistfully towards the exit. Audric stood there, as if guarding it. The jackal sat at his side, both staring up at the suspension chambers, their heads slightly tilted to one side.

Lyam shook his own head and sat down, exhausted and dispirited.

"So tell me more about your friend, this Crymure," Rai prompted the dwarf while she chewed, clearly still cross with him. "Who was he amongst their kind? Did he have a rank or a title? Was he linked to a god? What made him such a good friend?"

Berdnard smoothed his moustache, pondering the barrage of questions with a heavy heart. He would never live down his liaison with the Nephilim, it seemed. He really didn't wish to talk about it, but considering their current location and Rai's aggressive curiosity, he might as well wish to be taller.

"I'm not sure." The answer applied to all her questions. But of course, it would not suffice. "He seemed common enough," he elaborated. "Could almost pass as one of you folk, if not for the eyes, constantly flicking, and that terrible sense of humour." Berdnard shook his head in remembrance. "He claimed to be an inventor who'd got himself into trouble with his kind for meddling with magic and the Underworld. Magic, humph." The vehemence of the interjection expressed what he thought of that particular pursuit. "I guess even the Nephilim have their eccentrics… What else can I say? He was an outcast, like me. Two outcasts don't make a rebellion, lass."

"I thought they'd culled all magic users from their ranks," said Lyam. "They won't even link to gods who practise spell craft."

"As did your kind," the short man pointed out sardonically.

Lyam sucked his teeth. "Reach is not magic."
"Oh no?"
"No. Telepathy only seems magical to your kind because you can't grasp it. Evolution is not magic; neither is technology."

"Evolution, bah. You truly believe you're so much

better than the rest of mankind. And who taught you that technology? For you did not come up with it yourselves. Gods did. Gods are scientists!" He burst out laughing at the notion.

"More like scientists can look like gods to simple-minded mortals like yourself," Lyam said spitefully.

That stopped Berdnard's laughter. He snorted instead. "Your memory might be gone, but the personality remains the same."

"What do you mean by that?"

"Nothing. Don't like being called stupid, is all. At least Crymure pretended to be my friend," he grumbled.

"And what am I?" asked Rai.

Berdnard shook his head ruefully before answering. "He was better."

"Unbelievable!" She took another angry bite of nectar.

Lyam would feel sympathy for her had he not felt somewhat vindicated by the dwarf's attitude. Taking advantage of his candid mood, he asked, "Did Crymure ever tried to contact Eloin or Thoth? You said he was interested in the god."

"Of course he did. He even tried to offer us a trade. Nothing came of it, of course. Thoth was not interested in him. He wanted nothing they offered, and what they wanted we couldn't offer. I was a poor mediator, in any case."

"What did they want?" Audric asked.

Berdnard frowned at him sideways across the room. "Us. Working together."

"Doing what?" asked Lyam, not wanting to be out-questioned by the other man.

"I never found out. The elders put an end to the negotiation before it even started."

"When was this?" Rai asked suspiciously.

"Right before the mutiny. Then Eloin took over, and she was even less interested in the deal. She had the nerve to forbid me to talk to Crymure again. Another one who thinks she still owns me," Berdnard huffed.

More than once, Lyam had wondered about the extent of Eloin's part in the massacre of their elders. Only he was aware that she'd deliberately let the tensions between both factions escalate in hopes to cull the Narrum numbers. The aftermath had established her as ruler.

Still, she'd always been opposed to an alliance with the Nephilim. Why? he now wondered. Clearly she wasn't too worried about them and, all things considered, an alliance might have suited both factions. Or it might have interfered with other alliances, a nagging voice said.

"And you've been socialising with a machine ever since…" Rai sounded miserable. "How long will this cursed storm last?" She glanced wistfully towards the exit.

"Fuck knows," Berdnard replied.

"I thought these storms didn't last long," she said. Her eyes met the jackal and narrowed in annoyance.

Berdnard began to idly draw lines on the ash with the tip of his axe. "This one's special."

"Of course it is…" Lyam's spirits had reached a new low. Nothing had happened the way he'd expected. He wasn't sure what he'd expected, true, but of all the things he'd imagined finding about the Nephilim and their disappearance, this had certainly not been it.

Between the deceptions, the oppressive light, the tower blocking his Reach and the fucking abyss, he was starting to lose his grip on sanity.

"Let's take the opportunity to analyse all this. This tower, for starters. What do you make of it?" He sounded like a weary old scholar, prompting reluctant pupils. But he had to keep his mind engaged, tethered to his senses, or it would unravel.

"Who the fuck cares about an empty building when there's an abyss right next to it?" Rai said, chewing vigorously. It was for the best they couldn't Reach each other's minds. Hers seemed to be unravelling faster than his.

"Just indulge me," he said patiently, determined to marshal his thoughts in order with a few answers. "How did they build it?"

Cairns and obelisks were quite small and relatively simple, but the tower was on a whole other scale.

Rai puffed her cheeks. "With their bare hands. Why not? They are strong and sturdy. They don't tire and they rarely break. I bet they could have built anything they wanted."

Could they have built a ship from rock? Lyam quickly dismissed the stupid idea. "Sure, then why a tower and why here? Up the hill would have made more sense for a lookout, no?"

"Because it was close to the river."

"They don't need water."

"But gods do," Berdnard said, his smooth moustache now curled as a corkscrew. "At least I think they do…"

"Some… perhaps." Lyam realised he wasn't actually sure himself. He sighed before approaching the subject from a different angle. "All right. It looks like they kept their gods prisoner inside those chambers. They're empty now, so we can assume they took them along when they left." He frowned, disliking the notion. The frown deepened as he took in the whole structure again. "Why build it so large, though?" If all they needed was a place to put the soul cages, pretty much any cairn would do.

"Maybe they liked to look at the gods when they're powerless," Berdnard suggested. "Or they needed a place to congregate and have pointless, boring discussions like this one."

"No. They don't need to congregate. They can communicate across vast distances. Their Reach is better than ours. Their minds constantly in sync," Rai said.

Lyam blinked at her. "How – do you know that?"

"I just do," she sneered back at him. "The same way you know all your maxims and platitudes."

Audric, seemingly indifferent to the discussion for the most part, raised an eyebrow. "Care to elaborate on that, redhead?" He managed to sound both intrigued and hostile. The flame in the lantern flickered to match his mood. That's when Lyam realised he'd never actually seen the man light the damn thing. A magic lantern. He cursed Thoth under his breath.

Rai puffed her cheeks, then took in a deep breath. "The Nephilim excluded social demands from their programming, along with extreme emotion. Each interaction between members of their kind is based on trade, much like it is between gods. To them, the descendants of humankind are slaves to their social and emotional needs, making them no better than sheep. We share the same philosophy, to some extent, that's why we were able to achieve so much more than the Narrum and the other minor races – no offence," she added half-heartedly to Berdnard.

The dwarf showed her his stubby middle finger.

"Who told you that?" Lyam asked. Those had not been Rai's words, he was sure.

She took another bite of nectar. "I read it somewhere: a textbook or something. It stuck with me for some reason. Want to hear the rest?"

"No," Berdnard said almost simultaneously to Lyam's and Audric's "Yes."

"The majority wins." She pressed her lips in annoyance and closed her eyes before continuing. "Very well, here goes. Our ancestors understood the downside of emotion, especially when paired with low intellect, so they programmed the Nephilim to value individuality and critical thinking the same way they did. What the original humans called herd mentality has been eliminated from our kind, replaced by a limited form of telepathy – Reach." Her eyes remained closed as she grew more confident reciting the text from memory. "But while the ability to Reach into another's mind unified the Nephilim to a common goal, post-humans became less trusting of one another. If anything, our ability to share emotions and ideas directly to each other's minds made us less able to trust and cooperate. We became cautious, more aware of judgement, and subsequently guarded to the point of coldness. True emotion is a gift we only share with those we love" – she spared a sheepish glance to Lyam – "For too much emotion and feeling strongly about emotions – especially other people's emotions – is what turned humanity against each other in the first place. It precipitated prejudice, hate, war; it led to the division between us and the Narrum – who chose to remain as the gods made them. The animosity grew to the point where we couldn't even share the same planet. And despite thousands of years of selective breeding across different worlds, this urge to antagonise those who do not feel and think like us is still there, embedded in the fabric of our being by the Maker." She paused as if suddenly understanding the words. "The Nephilim's artificial mind is free of that curse. That is why the Mentor chose to enlighten them instead of us. She turned her back on humanity, for we were, and still are, unworthy of Her gift."

"Sounds like a load of bullshit, lass," Berdnard said in distaste.

"Don't you mean the Matron?" Lyam asked, referring to Hera, who had briefly aided the Prometheans when they first ventured into the stars.

"No, I'm sure it said the Mentor, why?"

"Nothing. It's… er… interesting," Lyam said diplomatically, secretly gobsmacked that she'd kept all this to herself as well.

She shrugged, nibbling nectar, clearly not hungry anymore. "It must have been important enough for me to memorise it. To stick despite… well, pretty much everything else being gone. The bottom line is, the Nephilim are not social beings," she said sharply to Berdnard. "They tend to keep to themselves and they love to disagree." She cast about her. "Something on this scale required agreement and cooperation."

"Even gods cooperate when they have to," Audric pointed out.

"Exactly!" Lyam said after filing this latest grievance along with the others to deal with later. "So what made them do it? And to build this? Why not fix their ship or storm our temple? Why remain here, when they could have gone anywhere on this moon? Explored. Learned. That's the sort of thing they like to do, right? I doubt the planet's light affects them. They're designed to withstand high levels of radiation, even the vacuum of space. Not build monuments."

"This is not a monument. This is – or was – their power source. There's nowhere to go. Nothing to learn. All they wanted was to leave this moon," Berdnard said, standing up. There was disgruntlement to his tone, irritation in his stance.

"You claimed you didn't believe your friend would leave without a word," said Lyam.

"Clearly, I was wrong, and he was not my friend, just another clever machine probing a dull specimen for information about his more interesting cousins." He paced the room, furious with himself for believing Crymure had actually enjoyed his company. To him, post-human and Nephilim were just two sides of the same coin. "If that chasm outside is any sign, the moon's breaking apart. Unsurprising, it being caught between star and planet. I reckon they left the first chance they got. No time for goodbyes."

"Too simple, no?" said Lyam.

"What is it you people say: the simplest explanation

is usually the right one?" Berdnard kicked at the ash. "The moon's orbit is decaying. It's being pulled by the planet's gravity. I bet that's what's causing all these tremors."

"How do you –" Lyam began.

"I'm short, not stupid! Just because I don't have your Reach doesn't mean I can't think. The human brain was good enough before you started messing with it. Have you ever considered that Reach actually hinders your mind?"

"No," Lyam and Audric replied simultaneously, eyeing each other in surprise.

Berdnard sniffed. "So you can agree on something after all. Humph. The enemy of my enemy is still my enemy, I guess." He scowled at both men in turn, then kicked the ash again.

His boot hit something.

"What was that?" Rai sprang from the wall in alarm.

"There's something on the ground," Berdnard said, bending over to clear it. "Hey, gloomy one, bring the light closer, would you?"

Lyam's stomach sank. Somehow he knew exactly what they would find, without having to look at what the Narrum's boot had revealed under the ash: a snake eating its own tail, and in the middle of it, a hatch. Except this one was much smaller than the one at the pyramid. And it had a handle.

"Don't touch it!" he urged, but Berdnard was not only touching it, he was already pulling at it.

"It's unlocked." He tugged the hatch open to reveal a ladder leading down into darkness.

Everyone froze, torn between dread and curiosity.

"What do we do?" Rai asked.

Audric answered by stepping onto the ladder.

Lyam grabbed his arm. "Don't."

Audric's eyes seemed to flash redder as he pushed the hand away. "Hold this." He gave Lyam the lantern and continued his descent.

Lyam moved to follow, and the jackal growled ferociously. He held up the light. The rungs ended only a few feet down the hole at the aperture of a small tunnel. Audric had to crawl his way in. Everyone was too stunned to object. They just watched as he vanished into the gloom. There was silence. The jackal whined softly, impatient. Moments later, Audric's head reappeared from the shadow.

He wasn't alone.

Chapter 18

The Well

*Memories are like souls, shaped by the minds of
those who possess them.*

— Memory on Record

The woman was tall and slender with an oval face,
high cheekbones, long nose and full lips. Her eyes were
enormous and completely black, like her long hair. She
wore a silver bodysuit, matching her skin tone almost
flawlessly, in a swirling pattern that seemed to ripple
in the lamplight as she climbed up the ladder with an
unnatural, fluid grace, as if gravity didn't quite apply
to her.

"She's one of them!" cried Rai.

The woman stopped her ascent to assess each of the
members of the group in turn, expressionless. Her gaze
lingered on Lyam. She blinked once and retreated into
the shadow. The action suggested disinterest rather
than fear.

"What do we do?" Berdnard asked, curling his
moustache compulsively.

"We don't engage," Lyam said, remembering Eloin's words. But there was something else he remembered: the likeness of the woman in Audric's room. This was her; he would swear on it. And yet Audric acted as if he'd never seen her before.

"We can't just leave her there," Berdnard insisted.

"Oh, yes we can," Rai said.

"No, we cannot. Come." Audric extended his hand in a sharp beckoning gesture, more command than invitation. The woman retreated further into the shadows. Lyam couldn't tell if in defiance or weariness. He relied too much on his empathy. Without Reach, every behaviour seemed ambiguous.

"Try a piece of nectar; it worked with the dog," Rai suggested spitefully.

Audric glared at her. The jackal growled, and Rai backed away, cursing man and beast alike.

It took some convincing and a bit of cajoling on Lyam's and Bernard's part, but eventually the woman climbed up out of the ground. Then she just stood there, aloof, almost dazed, as they all frowned at her in silence.

She was unlike any Nephilim they'd ever seen, with an aura of immortality about her to put most goddesses to shame, but there was no denying her artificiality. Her black eyes flickered now and again, and vein-like circuitry glinted from under her skin all along her neck. A piece of imbued hardware bulged at her temple.

"Is she a goddess?" Berdnard whispered the question.

Amusement crossed her handsome face, more a ripple of luminescence than an actual expression. She touched Berdnard fondly on the forehead, producing a gasp from the startled half man.

"She certainly acts like one," Rai snorted. Keeping her distance. "Well, are you?"

"No," the woman replied without even looking at her, a hint of disdain in her tone.

Rai hadn't expected an answer. Especially not that answer. She crossed her arms and cleared her throat belligerently. "Well, then."

"Who are you?" Lyam asked.

The woman looked at him as if confused by the question. Her eyes remained as dark and mysterious as the abyss outside, showing nothing, not even the flame's reflection.

"I am myself." Her voice had an ethereal feminine timbre that seemed to echo across the large empty room.

"Do you have a name?" Rai demanded.

"Many." The woman smiled the answer at Audric, her face animated by silvery radiance, paying no more attention to Rai than one would to a pebble.

The redhead straightened herself, hands on her hips. "She's a tease! She'll have you three wrapped around her little finger by the time the storm ends." She glanced hopefully towards the exit. "Gods, it had better end soon…"

Lyam shifted his attention back to Audric, hoping for some input. The man looked more stoic than ever. He exhaled, then smiled back at the strange woman and resumed his questioning as politely as he could. "One name will do, if you please."

"Pick one," she teased.

"Oh, for heaven's sake." Rai threw her hands in the air and moved away cursing man's stupidity.

Lyam clicked his tongue, unsure of how to deal with either woman. "What about… Pandora?"

"Seriously?!" Rai sputtered from across the room.

"Pandora…" The woman repeated the word, savouring it.

"It's the name of the first woman, according to legend," Lyam explained.

"I know," she said, smiling broader. "I like it."

"Good! So… Pandora: Do you live here?" he asked.

"I am here."

"Yes, but is this where you live?" he insisted, secretively thinking this Pandora might not have all the gifts.

She tilted her head coquettishly. "I'm not sure I understand the question. I live no matter where I am." She paused, smiling. "But yes, I suppose here is where my consciousness is now. In this body."

"And your soul?" Audric asked gravely.

She turned sharply in his direction, eyes boring deep into his, a slight frown on her brow. "You know about souls."

"Everyone knows about souls," Rai said petulantly. "Forget it. She's not a goddess. She's one of them. And she's broken, by the sound of things. I bet that's why they left her behind. She's of no use to us."

If Rai's assessments offended the strange woman, she didn't show it.

Lyam rubbed his forehead, straining for patience. "Are you alone here?" he asked, for lack of a better question. Clearly, he'd not been prepared for this turn of events either.

Pandora only nodded; her gaze remained fixed on Audric as if entranced.

"Where did the Nephilim go?" Audric's tone and stance remained seemingly impassive to her scrutiny or silvery radiance, but his hands, closed into bloodless fists at his side, betrayed him.

"To the river," she whispered charmingly.

Rai and Lyam exchanged worried glances. "And… where did the river go?" he asked.

"Down the well."

A terrible idea began to take form in Lyam's mind. "Audric, how far down does that tunnel go?"

"Not far. It's blocked."

"You mean blocked as in buried like the pyramid at the temple?"

"No. It's properly walled up like a cell."

Lyam turned to Pandora again. "Why were you down there, alone?"

"It's quieter."

He frowned. The whole place was as quiet as a tomb. Except for that increasingly persistent hmm in the back of his mind. "What do you mean? What can you hear?"

"The souls."

"What souls?" Rai asked.

Pandora gave her a levelled look. "The souls of those who haven't measured up. They talk and complain and they scream. They want to be remembered." The strange woman's eyes grew darker. "They won't. They're weak. And so they're doomed." She said those last words with such loathing, chills ran up their backs.

"Aren't you cheerful," Rai said dryly, taking a drink.

"Can I have some?" Lyam asked hopefully.

She reluctantly offered the bottle to him.

"Thank you." He drank greedily, having momentarily forgotten how thirsty he'd been for most of the journey. Then he stared at the bottle, a dreadful realisation in mind. "We have to return to the temple," he said.

"I agree," Berdnard said. "But unless you want your lungs filled with ash, we'll have to wait until the storm subsides."

"There's no time. We have to move now! We have to warn them."

"Of what?" Rai took the empty bottle back with a resentful glare.

"The Nephilim. They're coming from below! Through the well. The river and it must be connected. They'll drown us."

CHAPTER 19

The Woman

Memories were meant to fade.

– Memory on Record

"Hold on. Calm down, lad." Berdnard struck a pose, axe in hand, looking more threatening than appeasing. "I'm all for going back, but what you're suggesting makes no sense."

Lyam motioned in frustration. "The Nephilim don't think like we do. What to us is insanity to them might be a perfectly logical plan to regain control of their temple."

"I agree with Berdnard," Rai said dubiously. "It doesn't make sense. Besides, the river isn't just dry or drained; it's gone. The very ground gone along with it. If that's some fucked up consequence of using captive gods to break a few laws of physics to somehow divert the water to overflow our well, why leave her behind to tell us about it?" She shot a suspicious glare at Pandora.

"She only said they went to the river," Berdnard clarified.

"And that the river went to the well!" Lyam's head throbbed with exasperation. A constant hum chimed in his ears, as if he was on the verge of fainting, driving him mad.

"So the Nephilim simply dived down to the depths of this moon and then swam up under the mountain?" Berdnard sneered.

"They don't need to breathe," Lyam said through clenched teeth.

Berdnard blew out his moustache. "If that's what happened, well… then it's already too late to warn anyone."

That's precisely what Lyam was afraid of. "We still have to try. We can't just stay here!"

"For now, we do," the short man said, waving a hand in a futile attempt to clear the air around him.

Lyam groaned in frustration. The storm showed no signs of abating. If anything, it was getting worse. A cloud of ash and stone dust now filled the room. He could feel it inside his nostrils, deep in his throat, see it caking his clothes. He could only imagine how bad it must be outside. Even if they somehow managed to breathe in it, they'd certainly not be able to find their way back through it. He was stuck. Again.

"Why do you insist it's their temple?" Audric asked. He stood slightly behind the strange woman as if guarding her. The juxtaposition highlighted the similarities between them – the extremely pale skin, black hair and symmetrical features on the verge of aesthetic perfection – but also the differences. Pandora's cold radiance clashed with Audric's smouldering coldness, his stance reflecting a storm raging in his mind greater than the one rolling outside.

Lyam cast about the room, arms spread out in demonstration. "Similar materials; similar style."

"Different shape; different technique," Audric counterpointed.

"Likely a different purpose, too," Lyam conceded. "But I'm telling you, it's their temple. I bet this whole moon is theirs, too."

Pandora chuckled.

"What's so funny?" Lyam snapped.

"The mortal ego. You fear death so much, you believe it to be the goal behind every action taken by those who oppose you." Spiteful mockery in her tone. "You know so little. Matter even less." She laughed then: a sad laugh, free of derision or malice, and murmured, "Only a planet can own a moon…"

Berdnard's frown deepened. "Crymure would have given me a heads-up. Sure, he cannot be trusted. No one can. But if his indifference to the temple wasn't real, his uneasiness about the moon and the accursed planet it orbits around certainly was. The Nephilim hated being here. They wanted to leave this rock, not dig themselves deeper into it. And if they coveted the temple, I already told you, they would have taken it. I'm certainly no gatekeeper. And not even the big twins can match their mechanical strength."

Lyam considered this. "But we outnumber them ten to one, and the Narrum can be quite savage – oh, don't pretend to be offended, Berdnard. You'd relish a chance to hack into one of them with your axe."

"Not just one; not just them either," the short man grumbled, balancing the haft of the aforementioned weapon in Lyam's direction.

Lyam chose to overlook this. "The point is, they would not take the temple without having to engage us in close combat and risk considerable damage. Their ship's destroyed. Likely, so too are the means of repairing themselves. That has to be an inconvenience." He paused, considering an alternative hypothesis. "Then again, they might have had nothing to do with whatever happened to the river. It just gave them an opportunity."

Rai kept shaking her head as Lyam spoke. "But there's nothing in the temple worth the trouble. Except maybe the nectar, but they don't need to eat. Besides, they seemed pretty settled here. And they were clearly working on making contact with their kind. To simply abandon it all for no good reason…"

"There must be a good reason; we just haven't found it yet," he said. "Eloin believes there are more tunnels, that the real temple is buried beneath that hatch. If she's right, if that hatch does lead to something larger or powerful, something of value, maybe that's what they're going for."

She puffed her cheeks. "Unless it leads to a wormhole, it really doesn't help much with the whole 'getting off this rock' goal, does it?"

"Rai… you don't know –"

"No, Lyam. I do know. I too can sense something from whatever is buried under that hatch, and trust me, it's not a way out. Not a good one, at least."

"No…" Lyam agreed. "It's the fire beneath the frying pan."

"Maybe that's what the water is for." Audric chuckled to himself at some private jest only he understood.

"Those little cryptic quips of yours really aren't helping, red-eyes."

"I'm just saying what you're all too afraid to think, redhead."

Pandora turned to look at Audric quizzically.

He shifted his attention to Lyam. "You are wrong, Promethean. The two structures look similar, but they are very different. One is built from stone, the other carved from it. This tower is stark and functional, a conduit, designed to drain gods like batteries. The temple is lavishly decorated, dynamic" – he paused, his broodiness lifting momentarily in contemplation – "almost as if it's alive."

"Nonsense," Lyam insisted, taking offence.

"Is it, though? The Nephilim's style is practical and precise, and they'd rather have gods working for them than having to do the work themselves. As impressive an accomplishment as this tower is with the material and tools at their disposal, surely they could have done better. They didn't because they built it to perform a function, not host a ritual." He eyed his audience mischievously. "Now who do we know that likes to host rituals?"

"You're saying gods built the temple?" Rai asked in reply.

"No, redhead… I'm saying mortals built it for them." He enunciated each word slowly, as if addressing a child, his gaze fixed on the hint of a smile on Pandora's lips.

"What for?" Rai contended in a similar tone.

"That's what we need to figure out, isn't it?"

"Sounds like you already have," Pandora teased.

"My deduction skills only go so far. So does my restraint," Audric warned.

The woman they called Pandora beamed at him. "Humility doesn't suit you – red eyes." She uttered the nickname with eerie familiarity.

Lyam decided he'd had enough of their wordplay. "Who is she?" he demanded.

"I don't know," Audric said.

He sounded sincere, but Lyam would not be played for a fool again. He reached for his pack, took out the likeness of the woman he found in Audric's room, and held it to his face. "I think you do."

Audric's eyes burned like the coals in a smouldering fire, just waiting for a bit of fuel to turn into a furnace. "You had no right."

Lyam grimaced. The hum in his ears had become louder, almost unbearable. "Perhaps not. To be honest, I don't know why I took it. I just had this impulse and, well, that hardly matters now, for I'm glad I did. I'm sick of being lied to. So, tell us the truth. Who is she?"

Rai took the tablet from him, eyes darting between it and Pandora. "What's the meaning of this?" She passed the image along to Berdnard, who raised his bushy eyebrows in startled consideration.

"Who the fuck is she?" Lyam demanded again, more forcefully.

"The woman in the picture is my wife." Audric snatched back the image and put it somewhere inside his cloak, then closed his eyes and paused for a short exhale. "Was my wife." Burning red eyes locked onto Pandora's cold dark ones. "I have no idea who or what she is, for she's certainly not Dayna."

"Could have fooled me," Berdnard said sceptically.

"Have you ever had a wife?" Audric snapped back at the short man.

"No."

"That's why you'd be fooled."

"The similarities are uncanny," Rai said, still in awe.

"You think I haven't noticed that?" Audric replied rhetorically.

"So, what happened to your wife?" Lyam asked, straining to understand this.

"She died."

"When?"

"In the crash."

"He lies. She wasn't on the Eagle," Berdnard said.

"And how would you know that, little man?" Audric asked sharply.

Lyam had no memory of her on the ship, either, which was hardly a surprise. No one remembered much from before the crash. Then again, maybe he did remember. Maybe that's why he'd taken the image, because on some deep level he remembered her.

She saw her then, wearing a cloak identical to Audric's. He'd bumped into her amidst the confusion after the crash. She pressed a finger to her lips – then ran it across her neck before she – He shook his head to clear it, and the memory was gone.

Berdnard walked up to Audric, axe in hand. "Come to think of it, neither were you. I did not see you until after we crashed."

"Is that a fact." To everyone's further stupefaction, Audric smiled – the sort of smile that would make others cry.

Berdnard uttered a curse the moment he realised his mistake.

"Berdnard… are you saying your memory is intact?" Lyam asked, slowly, almost cautiously, his mind in a daze, not quite believing what he'd just asked.

The silence that followed lasted only a few seconds but felt like Nephilim's years.

"Yes!" Berdnard admitted defiantly.

Audric crossed his arms, pleased with himself.

Rai stared at both men. "You weren't aboard? And you… you remember? How?" she shook her head. "I always wondered…" She trailed off as if realising something.

"What were you doing on our ship to begin with? I found it odd that you were part of our crew, but still…" Lyam trailed off. Not all Narrum had subpar intelligence, and Berdnard clearly had showed enough of it to classify as a lower-ranking member. His his physiology made it highly improbable, though.

"You really don't remember me, do you?" Berdnard's expression was one of genuine surprise, mixed with frustration, resentment and disappointment.

Lyam's exasperation returned tenfold. "No. And let me tell you, I would!"

Berdnard laughed mirthlessly. "No, clearly you wouldn't. I was part of the science team dedicated to anthropogenesis."

Lyam blinked. "Were you? Really? I think I was part of that team, too."

"Aye, you were."

"Did we work together?"

The dwarf snorted. "You can say that."

"What was your specialty?"

"I was the test subject, you piece of shit."

The hostile animosity drained along with the blood from Lyam's face. There was a moment's silence. Audric's smile turned into a smirk. Rai began chewing another nectar bar vigorously. Lyam forced himself to close his mouth.

"So you remember it all? The battle, the crash. What life was before?" he asked.

"Not all. Like all nonessential crew, I was in stasis during the flight. But my memories weren't considered worthy of backup. No one cared if some were lost. And many were over the years, let me tell you. I remember little from my life before being taken aboard the Eagle, but I remember those on it very well and those who performed the experiments on me even better," he added grievously. "After the crash, I woke up alone. Apparently, I wasn't worth rescuing either. I followed the screams. When I realised no one remembered anything, I figured I would just blend in, pretend to be Narrum. One of the elders put an end to that notion. Actually, he saved me from being ripped apart by them. As it turns out, some things go beyond memory: prejudice, aversion towards the other. There's no place for creatures like me, not even amongst the Narrum – which are not my kin, by the way. You people can't even tell the difference." He puffed his moustache. "The irony is, I probably know more about digging through rock than any of you, Prometheans." His gaze lingered on Audric. "I could have had that temple cleared long ago."

"How so?" Lyam asked, still stunned by the revelations.

"I used to live in a mine – before being taken onto the ship. There are others like me still stuck there. Slaves. You call yourselves higher, evolved. Post-humans. Humph – more like post-humanity to me."

"This is madness. You're lying!" Lyam shouted. "I would never harm another human being. I'm an empath. I can feel their pain!" And hear things too, apparently, he added to himself. That awful noise just would not stop. Yet no one else seemed bothered by it.

"That was part of the point of the experiments," Berdnard told him. "Your kind can feel everything, yes. So much so that emotions are no more than colours to you. Some more pleasing than others, but still, just something in the background – behavioural ornaments. You've grown desensitised to them: callous, unfeeling. The memory loss changed your personalities. Made you more human again." He sniffed disdainfully. "I've wondered how long that would last…"

Lyam walked backwards, away from the group. "No. No, even if that was true, you can't possibly hold us responsible for something we don't remember."

"Oh, yes I can."

His head was splitting. He pointed at Berdnard. "I don't believe you." Pointed at Audric. "I don't trust you." At Rai. "I barely recognise you." And finally, at Pandora. "And exactly what the fuck are you?"

Pandora gave him her full attention. "I was once post-human. Transformed to host a soul – a very special soul. But the soul got away. It was too strong. This design too flawed," she said matter-of-factly.

"Told you. She's just a broken doll left behind by her makers," Rai said through a mouthful.

Lyam buried his face in his hand. "How come you're so calm about all this?"

"Calm? I'm not calm. I'm sick of it all!" Rai spat the piece of nectar she'd been chewing, unable to swallow it. "You want to know what else I remember besides boring texts? I remember wearing dresses and swimming in a sea." Tears gathered in her eyes as she spoke. "Now I hate dresses. And I not sure if I can swim, even if I wanted to – which I don't. Nevertheless, I seemed to have done both and enjoyed both in the past. Most of my memories are like that. They might as well be someone else's memories for all that I can relate to them. Memories from another life in another world we no longer belong to. This is the only life I know. The one I am living right now and therefore must care about above the one I lived before. Otherwise… I might go insane. This is who I am now. This is what I like to wear." She pointed to her rough trousers, sweat-stained shirt and ripped jacket. "It's bad enough to keep track of the things we do remember, of the mistakes we make in the present. Leave the past alone, I say. At least until we are far away from this place." She covered her ears and shut her eyes. "Argh, Fuck! Am I the only one who can hear the abyss screaming?"

Ah, that's what the hmm is… Lyam realised. His eyes glanced around the room, resting on Audric, who did not seem bothered by any noise, standing impassive, almost bored with their emotional turmoil. He was the one who'd set this argument in motion. The one who allegedly hadn't been on the Eagle. He'd always rubbed everyone the wrong way. Now Lyam had to figure out why.

"We're not going anywhere until he explains him-self."

Audric's gaze narrowed slightly. "I will not explain what I don't understand. But –" he added, before Lyam could interject, "I will tell you what I am on the way back." He pointed to the exit. "The storm's passed."

CHAPTER 20

The Chaos

If you forget, you never learn.

– Memory on Record

"I'm all ears," Lyam said the moment they stepped out of the tower, still struggling to breathe in the dense, damp air.

Audric spared him the type of glance often given by those suffering fools. "I'm Lokian."

Berdnard whistled. Rai guffawed. Lyam's nostrils flared and he punched him in the face. "I knew it!"

"No, you didn't," Audric sneered, hiding the blood from his split lip.

Lyam pulled back for another punch. Audric, moving inhumanly fast, grabbed his hand and twisted his arm behind his back, making it perfectly clear that he would not tolerate another hit.

Lyam's face distorted in loathing. "That's why no one likes you. We all knew, instinctively. We did!"

Audric shoved him loose. "Stars, you're dim. And arrogant. The two really don't complement each other.

You all don't like me because I never cared to be liked or pretended to like anyone in return. My indifference shaped your opinion of me, not stirred some deep, hidden wisdom."

"What sort of Lokian?" Rai asked, still more averse to the jackal than him.

"A criminal. Likely a murderer in custody on our ship. That's why the dwarf didn't remember you," Lyam replied.

The Lokian curled his lip in contempt for Lyam's assumption. "I've been right here. I've been here since before you arrived. Likely, since before you were born."

"Doing what?" Rai practically squealed the question.

Audric's gaze took in both Lyam and Pandora, then the jackal, before finally resting on the turbulent planet in the sky above. He'd hoped to have this conversation in the shade, preferably once back inside the temple.

Hopes and dreams; almost as useless as plans.

"Weren't you in a hurry to return to the temple and save the people?" he said to the Promethean.

Lyam swallowed. He'd forgotten all about that. How could he have forgotten that? "Yes, er… of course I am. We must return now. But you can still talk and walk, can't you?" He gestured for Berdnard and Audric to lead the way along the edge of the abyss, so he could keep them in sight – for he certainly didn't trust them behind him.

Audric fought the urge to plunge the man into the chasm. Would he qualify? he wondered. But honestly, he didn't really care right then. He just took Pandora by the arm and began a brief – very brief – summary of the most recent years of his life as he ploughed on through the ash.

The years he'd spent in the service of Anubis.

∞

Audric would always remember his first Purge. The man had been despicable, his guilt proven beyond a doubt. He'd raped, then killed, a beautiful woman who he'd claimed to love because she'd refused him. In his world, he'd been perceived as the victim, even praised for his actions, and the woman blamed for her ingratitude and defiance. But jealousy, self-righteousness or notions of virtue and honour twisted to fit the villainy of the likes of him no longer had a place in the Lokian society. The Universe had been enriched by the removal of his rotten soul. Others had followed: a vain, ugly girl who'd disfigured her beautiful sister. A mediocre performer who'd poisoned a much more talented rival so he could take his place. A mother who'd convinced a physician to castrate her son because she'd wanted a daughter. And others, many others, brought from many different worlds, different realms and even different times, all just as guilty, all just as rotten. On some of those worlds, many of these actions were not even considered crimes, the laws having been written by those as evil as their perpetrators.

But gods cared nothing for the laws of men. They cared only for their deeds and, of course, their souls.

Audric had once worried they would run out of souls to Purge into the Well. Now he knew better. As his wife Dayna used to say, ever since Pandora – the real one, not the woman next to him – had opened that box, there'd been no shortage of despicable evils in the Universe. They'd vowed to purge humanity from all who embodied them. Only then would they finally be worthy of becoming gods.

"You're a priest?" Lyam asked in disbelief after he fell silent. To Prometheans, priests were no better than the pets of gods.

Audric detested the word, for it drastically reduced the extent and importance of his duties at the temple. "I'm a liaison between gods and mortals. I mediate rituals and guide souls on their journey to apotheosis or the Underworld. A psychopomp, if you will."

"A priest," Rai reiterated curtly, voice muffled beneath a scarf covering most of her face. "Only gods and angels can be psychopomps."

He glared at her but chose not to argue. It was, after all, just a word. Dayna had always taken pride in calling herself a priestess. Why shouldn't he?

"Where's this apotheosis?" Berdnard asked, wading through ash up to the dangling tips of his moustache.

They'd left the tower's shade and were slowly making their way back along the chasm towards the obelisk. The storm had been unlike any other. It'd left the moonscape unrecognisable, thick in wet ash and stone dust with only the tops of a few buried landmarks as guides in the planet's glaring light.

"Apotheosis is not a place. It's an old pipe dream of our ancestors – it means to become a god," Rai explained.

He snorted. "No wonder you tall folk are always so aggrieved. Might as well wish to become a star."

"Some gods are stars," Pandora said.

"Perhaps," Rai continued testily. She'd been against bringing the Nephilim. One vote against three. Sometimes she hated democracy, for the majority was not always right. "But humans can't become gods, no more than Narrum can become Promethean. If there's one thing I remember clearly, it's that only the scions of a god can become gods."

The dwarf shook his head. "How did you people develop this shared obsession? And you do realise the reason you can't tell each other apart is because you – Prometheans and Lokians – are both the same. Right?" he added, as one might add fuel to a flame.

"Wrong." The three spoke in unison.

"I stand corrected." Berdnard's words were laden with sarcasm.

Rai sighed as if pained, glancing at the abyss before she recited from memory. "A long time ago our ancestors left their home planet to pursue this dream, away from the Narrum, who were beyond improvement, never mind divinity. Except they couldn't agree on how to make the dream come true. There were those who believed it was a matter of finding this mythical substance, Ambrosia, the resin of a tree that only grows in the Underworld –"

"Hold on a moment, lass. Does that mean that in order to acquire this resin, you'd have to die first?" Berdnard's laugh roared across the abyss and back. "The gods are clever; you people, not so much."

Rai wanted to kick him.

"That was the belief of the weak majority," Audric elaborated tautly. "Others, more sensible and disciplined than the average human, believed that it was possible to transmute their souls through reason and willpower."

"Ah, yes," Rai said airily. "But they soon found out that no amount of willpower would ever overcome mortality, not in the short lifespan allotted to mankind. And so they developed ways to replace their flesh with more durable material, often stolen from other species, easier to rejuvenate with their technology."

"How would that work?" asked Lyam, to whom the human genome was sacred.

"They tried to cheat death by not really being alive or human," she said, still reciting the information from a place in her memory she could not quite identify. "But even that only bought them a bit more time. And time itself is never enough. True immortality was their goal, so they emulated the gods by designing their own creations. They made them stronger and sturdier than any mortal, their minds faster, brighter. The idea was to use these artificial bodies as immortal vessels for their memories and souls. But in their hubris, they also gave their creations free will. And as soon as they learned how to think for themselves, the Nephilim realised a god's soul was much more powerful than a human's."

That's fairly accurate, Audric thought, impressed and slightly annoyed that she remembered so much and yet so little.

"A Nephilim priest…" Lyam mused aloud, still having trouble with the concept, it seemed. He liked to reiterate things, then twist them around in his mind like a particularly curious but not very bright child. Audric wondered if that was related to his memory loss or his training as a Promethean scientist. Then wondered on which side of the scale would his soul fall. Can a man be judged without the memories of his crimes? Should he? Would the soul remember?

Audric sighed, unable to come to a conclusion. "I am not a Nephilim," he clarified patiently.

"No. You're a Lokian," Rai said in disgust.

He turned on her then, exhausted by her misguided hostility. "And so are you, redhead. You're just one of their lab rats, like the dwarf. A Lokian lab rat."

In one swift motion, Rai reached inside his coat, took the dagger from his belt, and laid it against his throat. "You lying piece of shit!"

Audric smiled ruefully, not one bit worried about the blade pressed against his skin nor their precarious proximity to the edge of the world. "You were captured by these so-called scientists who, in truth, are no better than torturers, to be studied and experimented on. They've never had the balls to experiment on themselves, but they still want to understand how we work. They are jealous of our longevity. Their goal is to steal our technology, reverse-engineer our evolution to speed up theirs. Your memory might be damaged, but nothing can erase the spirit, much less the soul. You'll never forget what you are. That's why you remember every word of those texts so well. They are the record of our history, the core of our identity. The knowledge has been written in our souls. Not even Mnemosyne can erase it."

Pandora's chuckle gave them all pause. They'd almost forgotten she was still there. "It isn't wise to challenge the goddess of memory. She might take offence and make you forget everything, including how to breathe."

Lyam ignored her as he stepped closer to Rai with the caution one employs when dealing with a dangerous explosive. "It's all right. I know it's not true."

"Only the truth can trigger such rage," Audric said, still calm and smug, but his eyes had turned such a dark shade of red, under the planet's light, they looked almost black. "You're a rebel, Rai – a misfit. You always knew you were not like the rest of them, and you're friends with the dwarf because you related to his circumstances. You're one of us. And you know it. Deep down, you've always known."

Rai's hand shook. Her jaw tightened until her teeth hurt, but she did not move. No one did for what felt like a very long time. Finally she dropped to her knees and screamed herself hoarse into the abyss.

"Shut up, shut up, shut up!" She held her head in both hands, crying out in pain. "Everyone, shut up, please. It's too much! Too loud."

Lyam placed his hand gently on her shoulder, glaring at Audric. "If she's not a Promethean, how come she can hear the screams?"

"We all can. She's just lost the ability to cope with the noise." Audric snatched up his dagger from where she'd dropped it, touched his neck and thanked the stars the blade was blunt.

"I can't hear anything," Berdnard said, utterly confused, and no longer amused by their philosophical quarrel.

"Your kind has long lost the ability to listen to the things they don't want to hear," Audric said reprovingly.

"Well, that sounds like a good thing to me, right now, if this is what it does to you!" the short man replied without skipping a beat.

Rai was in tears, rocking back and forth and murmuring "Make it stop. Stop, stop," over and over again.

"Come, let's move away from the noise. I can't stand it either." Lyam helped her up and all but carried her away from the edge. "We can continue this discussion when we're far from this…" He pinned Pandora with his glare. "Just what the fuck is down there?"

"Souls," Pandora said matter-of-factly as she all but glided through the ash as though every particle parted before her. There was hardly a speck in her hair or on her bodysuit. More alarmingly, she appeared to have a destination in mind.

"The souls you were designed to host?" Audric asked, trailing after her. The jackal was behind them, leaving a trail of displaced ash behind him.

"I was designed to host one soul only," she said without turning.

"What happened to it?"

"I told you. It fled."

"Where?"

She stopped and smirked at him over her shoulder. "That's what everyone wants to find out."

"Are you hosting a soul now?" he asked.

Her head tilted from side to side as if considering the question. "I'm not sure if soul is the right word."

The look she gave him made his heart ache.

She's not Dayna, he reminded himself for the hundredth time. "What is your real name, Pandora?"

"Whatever name you choose to call me is real. I've never had to name myself. No one ever called me until…" Her step faltered as she eyed what was left of the Nephilim's ship contemplatively.

It is a strange ship, Audric realised now that he looked at it. Larger and longer than most, it looked as if it hadn't been designed to either land or fight. Which would help explain its current state.

"Hey! Wait for us," Lyam demanded. He'd fallen behind along with Berdnard, both struggling with Rai, who had fallen into a dull torpor, reluctant to move.

"Get over it, girl, you're stronger than this," Berdnard was chiding her as a means of encouragement.

Audric caught up with Pandora and grasped her firmly by the arm. By rights she should have yelped or protested, but she made no sound. Her eyes never left the wreckage.

He followed her gaze. "What did the Nephilim call you?"

"Sombra," she whispered.

He blinked, bemused. "Why?"

"Because I cast a shadow."

Her eyes met his, and for a moment he thought he caught a glimpse his wife looking back, then he saw the truth and let go of her arm, bewildered for the first time in centuries.

They stared at each other for a long moment, so many words unsaid, until a loud slap brought them out of their reverie.

"Snap out of it, girl!" Berdnard shouted, shaking Rai for all he was worth, trying to drag her limp body upright.

She blinked a few times, then looked about as if she didn't quite understand where she was or who she was with. Then she stood, dusted her clothes off, adjusted her backpack and nodded to herself. "Yes, I understand," she said introspectively.

"Understand what? Rai, who are you talking to?" Lyam asked.

She beamed at him. "I remember, Lyam. I remember it all." She spoke exultantly. "I had a wonderful life. Up until…"

"Girl, you're really freaking me out," Berdnard said.

She patted him fondly on the cheek. "I'm sorry." Then turned to Lyam. "We had fun, didn't we?" She kissed him on the lips. "Ignorance is indeed bliss."

Before he could say anything in reply to that, she punched him hard in the face, turned and ran to the stygian abyss, leaping head first, arms spread wide, giving herself to it freely.

A choked sound came from Lyam's open mouth, a gurgle from his bleeding nose. Berdnard dropped his jaw, then his axe. Both men stood there, still and silent, two forlorn statues covered in grey ash.

Audric's heart raced inside his chest, for he too had heard what the god of chaos had said to Rai. 'Join me and we can both be free.'

Pandora released a breath he hadn't realised she was capable of holding and said, "Your friend just declared war on Fate."

Interlude Part I

The Empty Bucket

*Time is my adversary. And I am his. But we
not enemies, for neither of us would matter
without each other.*

– Memory on Record

Jolyan hoisted the container out of the well, cursing gravity and the gods' cruelty alike. It wasn't enough that they'd denied humans immortality, they'd cheated them out of youth for most of their short lives as well. What was the point of longevity if youth lasted only a few decades? You then spent the rest of your life tired and wrinkled and weak, despairing as your mind and body deteriorated before your eyes until you finally died. Some would say ageing was a privilege, others a kindness to induce a weariness with life and therefore ease the transition into death. Fuck that, she decided, as she poured the water into a canteen with unsteady, arthritic hands, spilling most of it in the process, meaning she'd have to drop the damned thing back into the well to fetch more.

She shouldn't be doing this task. She was too old for manual labour, too old for most things, in all fairness. But she was too proud to ask for help and too stubborn to die as well. She'd dedicated her life to fighting death, especially her own. She'd learned to fix all sorts of insidious ailments the sadistic gods had conjured to afflict the lives of mortals: she'd cured infections and diseases, sutured wounds, set bones… Keeping people alive was a never-ending struggle and one she was fated to lose for she would never be able to fix death itself. Sometimes she wondered if that was why Death had left her alone this long, so she would suffer until she begged for an end. Then she would chastise herself for her hubris and self-pity afterwards.

Death isn't even aware you exist, you fool, no more than Life is, she reminded herself. Whatever the gods had set in motion when they'd created mortals had long since gotten beyond their control. They were on their own. Except when they weren't…

There was a god – an actual deity, for crying out loud! – living in the temple with them. A wolf amongst sheep; anyone could see that, and yet none dared to act against him or even comment on the situation because sheep only turn on other sheep.

Like most gods, Thoth did little but observe and insinuate ideas into susceptible minds like Eloin's. Jolyan cursed him as she wiped the sweat from her brow and braced herself to hoist the container once more. Whoever had built this well clearly had not needed to fetch water or had other means by which to do it. Maybe it wasn't a well at all, just a hole in the rock that happened to lead to an underground river. Either way, that was beside the point. They needed water, and this was the only means she had to get it. Speculating about its origin or purpose was as futile as speculating on Death's motives for keeping an old woman alive while young Eloin would not live long enough to see her first grey hair. It wasn't like Jolyan cared that much for Eloin, mind. Death could take all Prometheans as far as she was concerned. Just not while they were under her care. That she took as a personal affront.

Again Jolyan reminded herself Death didn't care; again a voice in her head told her she did.

"Jolyan!" a high-pitched voice screeched.

She recognised it immediately. "Fuck my life," Jolyan whispered and for a moment considered following the bucket into the hole.

Merian, a pear-shaped woman prone to eating and childbearing, galumphed down the tunnel towards her. "I'm so sick," she wailed, clutching her enlarged stomach.

Jolyan took a fortifying breath. "Something you ate?" The question was almost rhetorical. Merian's ailments were always related to her stomach.

"I ate nothing but that awful nectar." Merian spat to illustrate her disgust. "I can't eat that shit anymore, Jolyan. The baby needs meat."

Jolyan frowned in disapproval. Of course, Merian was pregnant again. Women like her always used pregnancy as an excuse to get more: more food, more space, more stuff. The fact that more children meant there was less of anything available for everyone, including themselves, did not factor into their greed. And if there was one thing Narrum did well, it was breed. Not Jolyan, though. Death had claimed her only daughter while still in her womb, then Life denied her another one. And so her battle with both deities began. She'd brought countless souls into life and delayed the death of many others. It had to count for something, even if quantity didn't always mean quality.

Merian leaned closer. "Say, is anyone about to die soon?"

Jolyan couldn't tell if it was the woman's sour breath, the wart on her nose or the question itself that made the bile rise in her throat, and not for the first time she wondered if Merian, and others like her, were one of those afflictions conjured by the gods rather than their victims.

"No," she replied curtly.

Merian leaned closer still. "I heard the captain ain't looking good. Mayhap you could give her a push, eh? Promethean meat is still meat." She grinned, her mouth half-filled with rotten teeth. "You set us free and feed us in one go. Clever, eh?"

Sometimes Jolyan hated being Narrum. It was no wonder Prometheans despised her kind. She'd bet most looked, sounded and thought like Merian to them. Fuck, most of them did… Prometheans saw themselves as better than Narrum because of their enhanced abilities, which they claimed made them closer to gods. Perhaps that was true. After all, they were lazy and introspective like gods, only much less powerful, thank fuck. Otherwise, they'd likely have got rid of the Narrum long ago.

"You heard wrong," Jolyan lied. "The captain is just tired. And without Eloin, we'd all be eating ash and rock on the surface instead of nectar. If I were you, I'd pray she has a long, healthy life."

"I only pray for meat," the woman said spitefully.

Jolyan refrained from pointing out how the gods had answered their previous prayers.

The first thing the Narrum had tried to eat, trapped underground with nothing but the clothes on their backs, were the ants, then the moss. As it turned out, both were toxic. Half the Narrum who'd survived the crash died in those first few days. Those then fed the remaining half for a few weeks. During that time, Prometheans – who wouldn't demean themselves by eating insects, moss or flesh – found the stored nectar. But as nutritious as nectar was – and Jolyan would even praise its taste – it didn't satisfy the appetites of Narrum like Merian. They'd rebelled, killing the Promethean elders and as many of the others they'd envied or feared in the process. That left enough corpses to last the Narrum another couple of months. In the meantime, Eloin assumed command. The great pyramid was discovered, and their numbers remained fairly stable ever since, although with a lot more infants than adults despite the high mortality rate in newborns.

Eloin, unlike her elders, had been wise enough to turn a blind eye to what the Narrum did after someone died. As long as the death had been natural or accidental, no questions were asked, no judgements made. There were a few nonaccidental accidents early in the excavations, but they'd ceased once Eloin declared that those responsible would suffer an accident of their own. Everyone became extremely cautious after that. Most refused to work, in fact – to avoid accidents, they'd said.

Prometheans, of course, were entirely off the menu. And so they'd ended up having to do most of the work. Jolyan could have warned Eloin of this outcome, but she hadn't been her physician back then, and all things considered, it'd helped to keep things peaceable between the two disparate peoples, for only two things pacified a Narrum: leisure and food. It was a thin compromise and one Eloin was too feeble to improve upon, no matter how much the slow progress frustrated her. Besides, making the Narrum docile in her presence already took most of her energy.

Jolyan wondered what Narrum like Merian would do if they realised all Prometheans had abilities, not just Lyam? Then she frowned. Had she been under their spell as well? Eloin had promised never to use the ability on her in exchange for fair treatment. 'Trust must go both ways,' she'd said. But then again, how could Jolyan tell if she'd lied?

"Why are you frowning again?" Merian demanded, scowling open-mouthed at her.

"Nothing. My back hurts, is all."

"They are working us to death," said Merian, who Jolyan had never seen pick up as much as a pebble. "They are like the machines, using us to make babies because they can't."

Jolyan grunted in derision. There were no Promethean children, true. Not even on the Eagle. Or if there had been, no one remembered them. No one seemed to miss them either. And she very much doubted they'd want Narrum children. As to why the Nephilim wanted them, though… well, some things even Jolyan would rather not know.

"We have to do something," Merian affected an air of importance as she spoke, clearly quoting someone else.

Jolyan sighed. With that, she could agree. Having the Narrum do something useful and productive for a change would go a long way towards improving their quality of life and their relationship with Eloin and her kind. Of course, that was not what the hideous woman meant.

"We have to bring the god to our side!" Merian shrieked, frustrated by Jolian's indifference. Her voice was as brittle as her mind; it didn't take much to break.

"Thoth's on no one's side," Jolyan told her sternly, hoping it would sink in this time. Nothing good ever came to those who relied on gods to solve their problems.

"He says the value of each person is in their soul, not brain. The anima, says he. We all have it but only a few use it." Merian pointed at herself as she spoke. "Let me talk to the god. Show him my belly. My soul. He would not say no to a pregnant woman. And I wouldn't say no to him."

It was all Jolyan could do to remain civil.

She pulled on the cable. It was light – the container empty. She cursed, dipping it back down. Again, it came up empty. Her frown deepened. She scraped a handful of glowing moss from the wall, placed it in the empty bucket and lowered it gently. What she saw – or rather what she did not see – told her Death had just made her life a lot harder.

Interlude Part II

The Mob

Jolyan walked as fast as her old legs would allow her. By now, the news of the empty well would have reached the ears of the most troublesome of her kind, Merian's legs being shorter but also much younger than hers. She had to get to the pyramid before the mob did. They wouldn't catch Eloin, or any other Promethean, off guard, of course; they'd be able to hear them miles away with their accursed telepathy, but they would still catch them, nonetheless. And if they caught them alone…

That's what Prometheans lack, she reflected. Sure, they were able to connect their minds to each other, but not act as one mind, much less a mindless crowd. And a mindless crowd was a great deal more dangerous than a heartless individual.

It was hard to imagine Narrum and Prometheans shared the same ancestors and had once been the same people living in harmony. According to myth, humanity had been created by the Titan Prometheus, then raised by the mischievous Loki. Both gods of fire, both tricksters whose passion was to annoy other gods. However, Loki was also a god of chaos and strife.

The conflicts always began small, stemming from different opinions, tastes, or lifestyles. Their disagreements amused the trickster god, who encouraged debate, claiming disputes were crucial for a well-developed intellect. He tried to teach people how to think, instead of what to think, and how to agree to disagree. But people are not gods, and even gods struggle with that particular lesson often enough.

As the species' population grew, so did their differences. And when Loki was no longer present to moderate their grievances, many forgot his teachings. Lines were drawn. First, they split into groups. Groups turned into tribes. Tribes became nations, each with their own set of morals, laws and values. Humanity continued to grow in both number and intolerance. Resources became scarce, land did too, and many were forced to move to different lands, different environments, some more suited to their needs than others. Islands became particularly coveted during this period. One faction, who kept to their god's teaching, learned how to build ships and extricated itself from the conflict. Others became superb swimmers, took to the water and were never seen again. Some say they found a way to live in peace under the ocean and were said to sometimes be seen judging humanity from afar.

To most humans, however, life became about either win or die. There was little incentive to think, plant, or produce, only to fight and brag about the spoils. Meat became the prime form of sustenance and the only currency. It didn't take long for animals to go extinct, but humans never seemed to. And so eating your enemies became both the ultimate victory and reward amongst the Narrum.

Any attempt at truce always ended in assimilation, subjugation or genocide, until finally there were only two factions: Lokians and Narrum. Lokians – the descendants of those who'd chosen not to fight and had instead claimed the largest landmass across the widest ocean, where they'd spent most of the warring years developing their technology while never taking more than they'd needed from their environment – decided to leave in case the Narrum ever overcame their natural aversion to water or learned how to build proper ships.

First, they fled the planet, then the solar system, and eventually the galaxy altogether. When they'd returned, many centuries later, they claimed to have achieved a post-human status – which sounded like a fancy way of saying they were better than the humans they'd left behind. And to be fair, by then neither faction resembled their ancestors anymore. Lokians had become lithe and as tall as their egos in the artificial gravity of their ships, standing heads taller than an average Narrum, who had grown squat and grounded by their diet and the world's strong gravity. But the greatest difference between them was their intellect. Of course, just because the Narrum weren't able to split the atom – or even locate one, mind – didn't mean they were stupid. They just had very different priorities in life, such as consuming and breeding, as well as different ways of dealing with things, cruelty being paramount in every dispute.

The elders of both factions tried to negotiate a truce, but it soon became clear that there would never be a reconciliation between the two peoples, no more than a snake could be reconciled with a mongoose. And so the Lokians left again, leaving the Narrum to strip their planet of all its valuable resources, including themselves.

That was when the gods came – the wicked ones – drawn by their desperate prayers. Even they were appalled by what they found and, thinking humanity no better than vicious beasts, killed the worst of them, then enslaved the rest, taking thousands to other worlds. Entire tribes vanished overnight. Those that remained took it as a sign of their righteous superiority and new conflicts ensued to claim the ruins.

Then the Nephilim came with their Faithful machines and took their children. People took it as a sign to have more children. Finally Jolyan's great-great-great-grandmother, an elder and healer such as herself, used an old communication device left behind by the Lokians in good faith in case they needed aid. This act of defiance cost her her life, but halfway across the universe, they'd received her call for aid, and three generations later they arrived. By then, whatever society the Narrum once had, had completely decayed. They'd become a people unable to sustain themselves or evolve, constantly running and hiding from the Nephilim and their culls. The Lokians themselves had become colder than the machines and more ruthless than the gods. They called themselves Prometheans now, after the creator, and instead of aid, they'd rounded up most remaining

Narrum onto their ships so they could study them in order to understand how humanity had deteriorated to such a state.

The answer seemed pretty obvious to Jolyan. But then again, she was no scientist.

And now just because some twist of fate and bad luck had put these two descendants of humanity together again in the same hole, they were supposed to get along? Everyone knew it was just a matter of time before the next crisis unravelled.

Lack of water was a pretty big crisis.

Lost in her thoughts as she was, Jolyan failed to spot Ninguém crossing her path, and she crashed into him. It was like hitting a padded wall – she bounced right off.

"Aren't you too old to run, woman?" he asked amiably. His hands had fastened around her arms and torso like clamps, rattling her bones when he lifted her from the ground to steady her, and she bit her tongue when he placed her back down on her feet again.

"The well… The water… is gone." Much like her breath and dignity, she noted.

"Come again?" He and his twin brother, Nenhum, were always polite to her, at odds with how they would usually address anyone else. She wasn't sure if that was because she was a woman, old, or Eloin's healer. Likely all three. And that was fine by her.

"The well is dry. The water is all gone," she repeated, craning her neck to look at him.

"Are you sure?"

"Yes, I am sure. I'm old, not blind! Merian saw it too. I need to warn Eloin before –"

He must have Reached into her mind and confirmed

what she'd seen, for he picked her up again and started running before she finished the sentence. "It's faster this way," he explained before she could protest. "Nenhum is already on his way to the pyramid. No harm will come to Eloin. You have our word."

Jolyan didn't give a shit about their word, only their actions. Prometheans claimed telepathy was the gift that brought them closer to gods. Her cynical self believed it just made them too wary of each other, always concerned with what others might think, and too lazy to actually talk about their issues. Still, clearly it had its uses.

When they arrived at the pyramid, a group of Prometheans had already arranged themselves in a perimeter around the hatch, holding improvised tools as weapons. Eloin stood at its centre, next to Thoth, who seemed to glow brighter than ever. A few Narrum desperate to gain the god's favour were also present. They looked scared, conflicted about what to do or where to stand. Jolyan could relate, if there was ever a time to pick a side, it would be now.

Ninguém carried her past the Prometheans and set her down gently next to Eloin.

"It's all right," Eloin said, taking her hand and giving it a reassuring squeeze when she smiled.

She's burning up, Jolyan realised. She wanted to chastise her for not being in her room, resting as she should. For making things so much harder for both of them. But the words just died in her throat. Eloin, much like death, brooked no argument.

"Thoth warned me about the well."

"Did he now?" As usual, Jolyan felt a chill running

up her spine in Thoth's presence. Light should be warm; his was not. She held his flinty gaze. An easier feat than to look into Eloin's feverish one. "Did he warn you about another riot as well?"

Eloin pressed her lips, avoiding the god's glare. "We are prepared for another insurrection, yes. And the hatch is finally uncovered. We're opening it now."

"Aren't you going to wait for Lyam's return?"

Eloin smiled sorrowfully. "Lyam's return is uncertain, and my time is limited…" She glanced up at Thoth then. There was so much in that look: trust, fear, faith, hope, doubt. "We are ready."

The ground began to shake. For a moment Jolyan thought it was one of the moon's fits, but they were never this rhythmic. Or this loud.

They're coming.

Dozens of Narrum descended from the tunnels, shouting hateful incoherencies. The entire population, it seemed, children and all – those able to walk at least. They were all armed with stones, and there was no way this handful of Prometheans with their pointy sticks would fend them off. Jolyan let go of Eloin's hand and began walking backwards. To where, she did not know. There was nowhere to go.

"We can't let them ruin this," said Eloin.

"I agree. We shall kill them all." Thoth's godly decree.

"That's not what I said!" she protested.

"It's what you were thinking," he said matter-of-factly.

"I haven't finished the thought yet!"

He waited.

"I can't think of anything else…" she admitted, biting her lip. They only needed a few more souls. There was no need to kill anyone. Then again, there was no need to keep them alive, either. And you can't reason with a mob.

"Why not let fate decide?" Thoth suggested with a glint in his eyes.

Better fate than me, thought Eloin, tired of making decisions.

Thoth rose into the air. Blinding light filled the room.

The mob screamed.

PART IV

The First Memory

"We have seen our end," the Morai wailed as one.

"I can't see at all," said Kauket, to whom darkness meant sight.

"And I," said a bewildered Hyperion, "am alight." He tossed his flames into space, inadvertently creating the very first star.

"We must banish the intruder," Phanes declared as he began to change under the star's light.

"It's too late for that." Ymir pondered the new word gravely.

"I can kill him. Erase his existence," Nyx suggested, intrigued by the concept of death.

"Bad idea," one of the Morai cried, pulling at her hair.

"Can't be done," another added, nails digging into her cheeks.

"Death will become you…" the third one whimpered.

"Anyone have a better suggestion?" Nyx challenged the many who remained silent, defiant or perhaps indifferent to her proclaimed fate.

"I do," a wicked voice whispered from the primordial shadows cast by the newborn sun. "Seduce him."

– Memory on Record

CHAPTER 21

The Dream

Do not mistake ignorance for innocence.

– Memory on Record

Lyam stretched opposite Rai on the narrow cot, massaging her feet. Ants crawled along the walls and ceiling of the cell, their luminescence giving a scintillating sheen to the dew clinging to her bare skin with each deep breath.

"Well, you definitely remember a few things," she teased.

"Just like riding a bike," he replied, not quite sure what a bike was but too lazy to care. He'd been trying to seduce the fiery redhead since the crash and still couldn't believe he'd succeeded. Even if her reasons had more to do with spite for Eloin than lust for him, he didn't mind. He just hoped the memory wouldn't fade, like all the others had.

"Why only our long-term memory, though?" she asked, Reaching his thoughts. "Why not melt our brains entirely?"

He cursed himself for always letting his mind wander unshielded after sex. Hers, as usual, remained well out of his Reach, so he had to ask, "What do you mean?"

"It's a very selective amnesia. It only affects our explicit memory and in a very specific way. It can't have been an accident."

He sensed suspicion rather than idle curiosity, glad that his empathy still worked better than most. "Are you suggesting the memories were erased on purpose?"

"Yes. Think about it. If the memory storage system had collapsed during the crash, we shouldn't be able to remember anything. More suspiciously, not everyone was plugged in. And then there's the Narrum. Their brains differ from ours, and yet they were affected in exactly the same way. Don't you find that strange?"

He did. But stranger things had happened since. The pyramid, for example. The moon itself. The damned thing had been on his mind ever since they'd taken shelter here, and he was far more concerned with their present and future than with whatever might have happened in the past. Nevertheless, he pushed the thought away to indulge her. "Who would do that? How? And why? Ignorance is never a good thing."

"Ignorance is bliss," she quoted.

Lyam shook his head, amused, for he too remembered the oxymoronic maxim as soon as he'd uttered the word ignorance.

"See, that's precisely my point. Why do we remember these sayings or the lyrics to songs we can't sing or quotations from books we don't remember the titles of, but most of our own personal experiences, including anything that happened during the voyage, especially the battle, are gone?"

"Some remember the battle. The elders did." They having been amongst the first ones awake after the attack.

"So they claimed."

"You think they lied about it?"

"Sure. I would have lied if it helped keep people calm under the circumstances."

"Clearly, it didn't," he said dryly, remembering the riots. Now that was something he'd willingly forget. If it was up to Lyam, no Narrum would be allowed in the tunnels. They were vile, dirty and dangerous creatures, incapable of reason or empathy. Every Promethean knew that – they could read their minds, for heaven's sake! Why pretend otherwise? Sure, they were stupid, but not that stupid. Eloin would regret keeping them around. They were a liability, and useless to boot, no matter what Thoth said.

"And they only said the Nephilim attacked first. That by the time we reacted, tried to fight back, it was too late. They chose to crash here rather than being pulled into the planet. But the fact is, the Nephilim crashed, too. I believe the elders had no idea what happened. They built a narrative around the bits and pieces of evidence available. Whatever was done to us happened during sleep, and the Nephilim are just a coincidence."

The conversation prickled his mood. "So you're suggesting that someone – one of us – sabotaged our memories during the flight?"

"Why not?"

"They would have been caught, for one." The first thing the elders did once everyone settled was interrogate every survivor. The elders hadn't achieved their status because of their age, but their skill. Not even Audric would be able to hide something like that from them.

She slapped him playfully in the head with her foot. "They erased their own memories as well, of course. The best way to get away with a crime is to erase all evidence of it, including, and especially, the memory of doing it." She paused introspectively. "I remember that from some manual."

"Maybe you did it, then."

Rai shrugged. "I'm not excluding myself from the list of suspects. I have the right temperament and a fair knowledge of memory systems, for some reason," she added as an introspective afterthought. "I suppose I'm wicked enough for the part. I don't feel guilty, though. Then again, can you feel guilty for something you don't remember?"

"How would I know?" he teased.

"But that's not what keeps me wondering," she continued absentmindedly, ignoring his reply. "Prometheans only sleep during long voyages. And only embark on such voyages when there's a destination – a pressing one – which suggests we came here on purpose."

Lyam exaggerated an exhale. "Or were set off course by chance."

"Chance is never random. Not even casual or distracted. She always knows exactly what she's doing," Rai quoted.

He yawned. The idea was ridiculous. Who would benefit from such a thing? Besides, what did it matter now? There were better things to do than speculate on guilt, what was or could have been. He sat up and pushed Rai's legs apart and began kissing along the inside of her thighs. "Wicked, you say?"

'You have no idea,' she sent telepathically between moans.

The floor dropped from under him. Rai got pulled through the blanket into darkness. Cracks spread along the walls. Ants crawled over his bare skin. He tried to shake them off, to squash and smash them desperately, viciously. But there were just too many of them, biting, crawling around him, over him. They got beneath his skin. Their glowing bodies growing brighter and hotter. They filled his eyes, his throat. He couldn't scream. Couldn't see. They were so bright! Just like the planet's light, he realised.

Darkness. Silence.

The ceiling collapsed upon itself, and he fell upwards into a maelstrom of oblivion.

'Bring her to me,' the darkness thundered.

∞

"Wake up!" another voice shouted, far less menacing, but also a lot closer. Lyam opened his eyes to see the flame of Audric's lantern reflected on the blade of Berdnard's axe. He was soaking wet, covered in sweat and soot, curled up on a stone floor in a confined space. His whole body trembled from both cold and dread. His head hurt horrors, his skull even more so, and he'd bitten his tongue.

I was dreaming. The relief brought by the realisation lasted until his full memory returned.

Rai's dead.

That was only one bad memory. He remembered them all now – everything. His entire life. And what a wretched life it'd been.

"Oh, gods." He managed to sit up before he threw up. His mind tried desperately to cling to a vestige of hope that it all might have been part of the dream. It wasn't. He buried his face in his hands, still gagging, glad that he hadn't eaten in days and so there was little in his stomach worth retching.

"Where are we?" he uttered in a muffled rasp.

"Inside Crymure's cairn," Berdnard replied.

We've made it, then. Lyam almost wished they hadn't, though.

They'd been marching non-stop in stunned silence since leaving the chasm. Sodden ash clung to them, the ground and everywhere, layer on top of layer, making each trudging step heavier, harder, slower. Their spirits as laden as their clothes.

And then it had come.

The last thing he remembered was a shimmering black wall thirty feet high racing towards them, sweeping everything in its path. And the wind… such strong wind filled with moisture and the stench of brimstone. Its roar unlike anything he'd heard before. The roar of a living entity rather a force of nature.

"What. The fuck… Is that thing?" he'd stammered.

"The river," Audric told him.

Lyam hadn't believed the man to be actually capable of emotion until he hit him with all of them at once. They ran. Ran and kept running until…

"I stumbled." He touched his head and winced.

There was a significant cut on his forehead; dried blood covered half his face. Bloody mud clung to the rest of him.

"Yeah, you did," Berdnard said. He too was caked in mud from helmet to boots and sounded mightily affronted. "And you fell right on top of me. Hit your head on my axe and fainted. Humph. Do you have any idea of how much you weigh?"

"Er…"

"A lot! You broke me ribs. I couldn't breathe. Couldn't get up. If not for the Nephilim, we'd be dead. She carried us both. Ain't that priceless."

Lyam blinked at Pandora, who sat primly across the room next to Audric, impeccable and serene as usual, without even a stain on her. The jackal was nowhere to be seen, which was just as well. "You carried us?" Somehow, of all the things he'd been through lately, that seemed the most incredible.

"One under each arm. And me kicking in protest the entire way." He winced as he clutched his right side, clearly in pain. "I'd cut off my beard in shame, but even the Lokian here struggled to keep his feet on the ground. It was that fierce…" He sounded livid, but there were tear marks streaking the dwarf's cheeks.

Lyam's gazed narrowed at Audric. A Lokian… right. He'd almost forgotten that unpleasant revelation amidst all the even more unpleasant ones. He should have seen it. In hindsight, it all made sense: his looks, demeanour, attitude. How Lyam hated hindsight. All Prometheans did.

"Thank you, I suppose," Lyam said to Pandora. The insincerity cost him little at this point.

Her smile told him she was aware of his true feelings, perhaps even his memories, and he wondered if the valiant act had been a kindness or a punishment.

"Sounded like a pleasant dream," Audric said as he wiped dirt from his face with a piece of cloth. Not that he needed to. The matted hair and added filth made him look even more roguish somehow. Lyam repressed a pang of jealousy at the realisation.

"I do not wish to share my dreams with you," he said, looking for his bag. He wanted to change his shirt at least, but alas, it seemed Pandora had only carried his body, not his pack. Shit. He looked around, hoping to find something that would make himself more presentable.

"So… this is where Crymure lived?" It was a dismal place, empty apart from a few boxes filled with bits and bobs with no apparent use and a gilded robe – that Lyam wouldn't demean himself further by wearing under any circumstances.

No wonder he sought Berdnard's company, he reflected gloomily.

"Even gods seek company on occasion," Pandora said, confirming his previous suspicion. He wished he hadn't chosen that name for the woman. It fit almost too well.

A punishment, then, he decided. "You know a lot about gods," he said to her. Sadly, his own knowledge on the subject had not increased overly much. 'Gods cannot be trusted' remained the gist of it.

"Memory is knowledge. And knowledge is key." She caressed a golden bracelet studded with three gems – two of them broken – on her forearm. Lyam recognised it as the one Audric had taken from Berdnard's stash. A gift, bribe or reward for carrying them, perhaps?

"Key to what?" he asked warily.

"Salvation."

"I doubt anything short of divine intervention will save us," Berdnard grumbled.

"It's divine intervention that brought us here," she told him.

"I thought you had," said Lyam.

Pandora smiled and winked at him.

Nephilim can't be trusted, either. Nor Lokians. And Berdnard, whatever he was, had already proved himself untrustworthy.

The room felt smaller by the breath.

Lyam glanced at the large flat stone wedged tight against the entrance. "Is it still, er… wet outside?" The concept of rain did not quite apply to what they'd encountered earlier.

"We are to wait here a while," said Audric, his expression and mind unreadable.

"I'd rather leave now. I don't hear anything. It's probably over. We should check. We're so close to the temple. If we –"

"We wait," Audric reiterated.

"For what?!"

"We'll know for sure when it arrives," Pandora said.

Lyam didn't need empathy to sense something was afoot. He threw himself against the capstone, pushing and cursing at it for all he was worth. It made no difference. This stone was no different from the one he'd encountered earlier. A wise man once said the definition of madness was trying to do the same thing in the same way while expecting different results. "Fuck!"

"If we're not sharing dreams, what about memories?" Audric suggested. His mind poking for answers as insistently as his words.

"I'm not sharing anything with anyone!" Lyam protested.

"Might as well share something. It'll help pass the time."

"Waste time, you mean. We need to return to the temple, not sit here reminiscing." His head throbbed with the effort of both the physical and mental strain to move the stone and keep his mind shielded from Audric. His head wound had reopened, fresh blood now mixing with the sweat on his brow. It was futile to try to move the stone alone, just as it was futile to avoid Audric's questions. He'd been thoroughly ensnared, it seemed.

"Fine." Lyam slid his back down against his immovable adversary, defeated by the stone but determined to stand his ground against the Lokian. "Let's share. You go first."

Audric smiled. "What do you want to know?"

So many things, he thought, and yet right then only one came to mind. "Why did she jump?" Lyam practically whined the question.

"She was weak," Pandora said. "Too much energy spent fighting an inner rebellion. Not enough left to fight off the enemy."

The answer filled him with rage. He directed it at Audric, who had forced him to confront that memory.

"We should have left the Nephilim in that tower. I don't give a shit that she looks like your wife. She gives me the creeps. And she knows what's down in that abyss. She probably made Rai jump, too. She –"

"She had nothing to do with Rai's decision," Berdnard said. "Her mind had begun to unravel long before we found this one. And not just Rai's mind, either. You two are not the same men who left my shelter yesterday. Whatever's in that abyss, you're both susceptible to it. It has a hold on you. It twists you, somehow." He shook his head. "I saw it take her over. Didn't understand what I was seeing and then…"

"Then maybe you shouldn't have hit her." It was a low accusation. Unfair and untrue, but Lyam just wanted someone to blame. Wanted something to make sense.

Berdnard turned apoplectic. "Don't you dare blame me, Promethean! Rai could take a punch. Metaphorically and physically. Do not diminish her memory by suggesting that's what broke her mind."

"Not broken. Awakened," Pandora said.

"Huh?" Both men grunted in unison.

"The moon calls on every soul. But only the worthy dare to listen."

"Listen to what?" Lyam demanded, remembering that eldritch voice all too well.

Pandora spoke as if they were not even there. "A soul by itself has no purpose. It needs a mind to animate its will. The greater the mind, the more complex the soul becomes. And complex souls can learn how to wield the power of a god."

"Are you saying my soul is not complex enough, is that it?" Lyam said.

Pandora smiled that knowing smile of hers. "Not at all. I'm saying you lack the hunger to live as gods do."

"And what do you lack, huh? Why are you not a goddess?"

She gave him a quizzical look. "Because I am what I am."

"For fuck's sake…" He refused to deal with this shit right now.

Audric cleared his throat, seemingly annoyed by her interruption. "Listen to who. Not what."

'So you know,' Lyam sent to him.

'I do. But is what I know the same thing you think you do?'

Lyam cursed the man. Lokians loved playing games, he remembered. He remembered pretty much everything about them, in fact. The knowledge made him look at Audric in a completely different light.

"I take it you're a higher," he said peevishly.

Lokians were elitists. They had chosen the egalitarian way to civilisation. Not by pulling everyone down to the lowest possible denominator like the Narrum but by trying to elevate each individual to the highest standards. Unfortunately, that too had proved to be a mistake. Not everyone was created equal or had the same ambition and so not everyone was able to achieve the highest echelons. After all, there could be no perfection without flaws. No hills without valleys.

"No. I'm somewhere in the middle." Audric actually managed to sound proud in his humility.

"How so?"

"Choices," he said plainly. "To be a higher, you need to dedicate yourself wholeheartedly to the endeavour.

Let go of all that binds you to reality and flesh. It takes centuries of discipline and meditation. I was not ready for that yet." His eyes betrayed a glance at Pandora, listening intently to his every word. "I chose to spend those centuries with the one I loved. Apotheosis could wait."

It was hard to imagine anyone more disciplined and cold than Audric. And to hear him talking about love grated Lyam in every way. Then something else triggered his attention.

"Centuries?! How old are you?"

"Three hundred and fifty-one standard Midgard years."

Lyam gaped. No true human achieved such longevity.

"I was born, not engineered in a lab," Audric sneered, reading his thoughts.

"Then you're part machine – like her!"

The way Audric glanced at Pandora could define grief. "No. Not the same. I've rejuvenated many times, yes, but I'm entirely biological. And I still have my soul."

For the first time, Lyam sensed a crack in the other man's emotional shield. His first instinct was to exploit it.

"And still, you were not good enough to become a god. Is that why you became a priest?"

Audric's red eyes narrowed to slits. "Being a god is not about being good. There's no good or bad on the way to apotheosis. There's not even right or wrong when it comes to how you choose to travel your path. There's just one goal: know yourself. And a simple rule written in many different ways, across many worlds." He paused for emphasis. "Live and let live."

Lyam snorted. "Says the man who killed over a dozen Narrum during the riots with his bare hands."

"They broke the rule. Tried to kill me first. Granted, they thought I was one of you, but ignorance does not excuse hostility. Just because we don't kill for sport, spite or science doesn't mean we take threats to our lives lightly."

Lokians had very different interpretations of science and how far it should go in its quest for understanding.

"If you despise us so much, why the fuck did you help us after the crash?"

Audric tensed his jaw. "I was against it. Told Thoth as much. But the gods know more than we do. And they make their own decisions." His eyes turned almost black as he looked back on that day. "There were only a handful of us left in the temple when you crashed. We weren't even supposed to still be here but... something bad happened. We came to the surface at Thoth's command. He wanted to free the gods held in the Nephilim's ship, but because of you, the machines deployed all their Faithful and we couldn't get to them." He shrugged. "So we fought. What else was there to do? We were already fucked. Things started to go wrong right before you crashed. I reckon that is part of the reason you did. The moon became unstable. Our work unravelled. We needed more souls, so we had to bring you in. Thoth cast a glamour so you would accept us as part of the crew, but your elders... they knew. They recognised us for what we were – their long-lost antagonists. They believed we caused the crash. And why not? We'd created the Nephilim. We had to be on their side, right?" He tsked. "You people were never capable of thinking past the obvious, always deaf to explanation. Always ungrateful." He spared a darting glance at Pandora, who was listening intently. "I saw her fall amidst the fight. Knocked to the ground by one of you. The Nephilim took her body before I could get to her." His hands closed into fists.

Lyam swallowed. "Why would they take her?"

"Dayna was a priestess of Hathor, older and closer to apotheosis than I am. They must have considered her an ideal host for a powerful soul." He looked at Pandora again, eyes burning with sorrow.

His mind shield faltered long enough for Lyam to glimpse a memory.

"Thoth caused the Narrum to riot so they would murder the elders."

Audric nodded. "The elders agreed to silence in exchange for safety, but once safe they soon reverted to their arrogant selves and demanded that Thoth choose: us or them. He obliged the way gods often do. He made us fight. The elders perished but so did most Lokians. The survivors had enough and left. I doubt they made it very far."

"Why didn't you leave?"

Audric licked his lips before answering. "My allegiance is not with Thoth. He can't help Dayna. I'm waiting for the one who can."

"Does that mean someone is coming to rescue us?"

"Someone is coming, yes."

That sounded more ominous than reassuring, Lyam reflected. "You mentioned a glamour. I guess that explains why everyone acts wary around you. But Eloin is not glamoured, is she?"

There was something about the way Audric shook his head that confirmed Lyam's suspicion about his dear sister. "She knows everything. Always has. From the very start. She was the one who suggested we used the Narrum to get rid of the elders. She's willing to do whatever it takes to learn the secrets of the pyramid.

"That bitch."

"It's not her fault. She's dying. The dying are less susceptible to illusions, but more vulnerable to hope." Audric gave him a meaningful rueful smile. "Gods love hope."

"No shit." Thoth's using her. That much was plain. Why, though? What can she do for him he cannot do for himself? "Tell me, what's under that hatch? The truth, if you please."

"The reason we're on this moon – a gateway to another realm."

Lyam blinked a few times. Truth often had the power of knocking you sideways. "A nice one?" he ventured.

Audric almost laughed. "No."

Silence followed by a muffled curse from the dwarf. Suddenly Pandora's bracelet began to glow. She stood up.

"They're here." She spoke as if everyone should know who they were. Berdnard clearly didn't, and Lyam fell backwards before he could ask as she shoved the huge stone aside like it was made of cardboard.

Outside, the sky glared brighter than ever. The awful planet filling most of it. Lyam cursed, shielding his eyes. What sounded like a dying engine puttered in the distance, getting closer.

A Nephilim shuttle zoomed overhead, leaving a trail of smoke in its wake as it lost altitude. The thunderous crash left a ringing in Lyam's ears. But what really messed with his perception, when he dared to look, was what it had crashed into.

"Is that a tree?"

"Something like it, yes. A primordial ancestor of what we now call World Trees. They are to World Trees what Titans are to gods." Audric actually sounded excited saying this.

A tree the size of a mountain. Lyam tried to get his head around it. "How…?"

"The rainstorm washed away the ash of ages."

That had not been what Lyam had asked, but the question became unimportant when something much smaller and closer caught his attention: a beautiful woman stood naked only a few strides away, hissing at the muck in her hair. Her skin glowed like golden starlight. And her eyes, lined with kohl, glared like the Midgard sun when she saw them.

"Cats!" she said.

CHAPTER 22

The Gods and Their Monsters

Those you forget may have not forgotten you.

– Memory on Record

"Are you sure you know what you're doing?" asked Seshat, pressed flat against the co-pilot seat. She didn't think it possible to feel more uncomfortable than she'd felt inside Namrive's ship. As it turned out, the smaller the ship, the more uncomfortable it got. The shuttle was a glorified sarcophagus, with its failing engine torn between the gravitational pull of two celestial bodies at odds with each other. Red lights flashed brighter than lightning bolts, alarms blared, metal creaked and somewhere, something was definitely burning.

Tartarus, she reflected, was a spaceship.

"Yes!" Anubis shouted. "I've done this before." Under very different circumstances, true, but he had no inclination to elaborate on that.

"According to the navigator, we should have landed already. Maybe Namrive sabotaged the shuttle?" Seshat suggested.

"She wouldn't do that. It's beneath her," Anubis said through clenched teeth. He doubted it would even occur to Namrive to miscalculate a trajectory.

"Her kind is set on eliminating and enslaving every god in the universe. They steal, ambush, murder. They feel no guilt, have little respect for life and treat us like power generators. But sabotaging this vessel is beneath her?"

"The Nephilim are bound to their rationality and perfectionism, as we are to our promises. She would never deliberately make a mistake. If she wanted to harm us, she'd set the ship to auto destruct or to crash into a star."

"That wouldn't kill us," she said.

"Precisely. So why bother? It's the ship. It's not working properly."

It looked to Seshat like Anubis was the one not working it properly by the frantic way he pressed random buttons and pulled at things. Still, they had finally managed to breach what passed for an atmosphere on the accursed moon. "Wow… this is bleak," Seshat said and meant it. Rarely had she been on such a godforsaken realm.

"You can understand why I was not in a hurry to return," Anubis said.

"Sure. And I look forward to understanding why you came to be here in the first place."

Anubis pretended not to have heard her pointed remark and pointed at the screen. "Look, there's the moon's Stump. If I can only steer in its direction…"

Through the haze of ash and smoke that made up

the moon's upper atmosphere, Seshat could indeed see the outline of a Stump. Much larger than the one on Niflheim, or any other world she'd been to, this mutilated World Tree appeared to be petrified – a part of the moon itself, not just growing on it. And their current trajectory indicated they had a better chance of crashing into it than landing on it.

"I can do this," Anubis said to himself as much as her. He held on to the controls as if his life depended on it. It didn't. Only his pride did, and she sure wasn't getting herself injured for that.

"No, you can't," Seshat said candidly. She saw the surface clearly now, and having had enough of this mad ride, translocated to it.

For once she'd calculated the distance to her destination perfectly, but failed to take into account the terrain at the destination itself. What had looked like a smooth clearing amidst the rocky moonscape was, in fact, a mud pool of soot. She sank right through it.

The goddess of writing took pride in knowing every word in every language and never before had such an eclectic profusion of expletives been uttered in the Universe.

Furious and humiliated beyond measure, Seshat took comfort in seeing the shuttle crash just short of the Stump, Anubis still inside, tenacious until the end.

"That will teach you not to play with Nephilim toys, you bloody cat," she said, still willing away the muck from her hair.

A pitiful moan reached her senses. She directed her Reach back to the wreck and Anubis. His body was in pretty bad shape and would take some time to heal but, pride and pain aside, he was none the worse for it.

'What doesn't kill you makes you stronger,' she told him in mock sympathy.

He mewed. 'Catshit. Sometimes what doesn't kill you just makes you wish it had!'

'Next time act like a god instead of a hero.'

'I bet you can't wait to write this down.'

'Quite.'

The smug smile tugging at her lips was short-lived. Absorbed as she was in their banter, only then did she realise she wasn't alone.

Three grey shapes and one luminous silver stood behind her, materialised from one of the ancient structures dotting the landscape. Their expressions ranged from amusement to confusion to sheer panic as their eyes darted from her to the ruined shuttle. But what really surprised her was how odd an assortment of creatures they were: a post-human – judging by his similarity to the regular humans from long ago – a dwarf, a Nephilim, and something she couldn't quite identify somewhere between a post-human and a Dharkan, the immortal creations of Hel.

'Anubis, we have company.'

'No, you have company. I have a metal rod sticking out of my chest, both my legs are shattered and burns all over my body.'

'I don't care. Get over here. Now.'

'I can't. Not yet. You're a goddess, for cat's sake. Deal with them.'

Very well. She flared incandescent. "Do not come

any closer; I'll burn you to cinders!" she shouted in her most vehement tone.

No one moved. The human and the dwarf shielded their eyes but continued to stare at her, open-mouthed. No wonder; she had willed away her dress along with the mud. She cursed and conjured a cloak, regretting the fact it was too late to assume a more imposing aspect altogether.

"Who are you?" she demanded, trying to sound as regal as she thought a goddess ought to be. Three different telepathies assaulted her mind by the time the dwarf finished introducing himself out loud.

Seshat made an effort to remain calm. Anubis had warned her that post-humans had telepathy, but she had not expected such a strong mental intrusion from the Nephilim with the ominous appellation of Pandora. She assumed it had to be a more recent – certainly more organic – model than Namrive to be able to Reach her – a disturbing prospect.

"I am Seshat, goddess of writing." Spoken aloud, the title sounded far less awe-inspiring than, for instance, 'the goddess of fire' or 'the goddess of war' would have, which probably explained the immediate apathy of her new acquaintances. Seshat used to relish being underestimated, for it gave her plenty of opportunity to observe and outsmart her opponents, but ever since she'd impersonated the Suzerain and had a taste of how it felt to be both worshipped and feared, she now craved more than a mere acknowledgement of her being. "I am a scion on Ra," her pride demanded she add.

The Promethean and the dwarf stared at her with blank expressions, the Nephilim smiled enigmatically, and the one who described himself as a Lokian – which pretty much told her everything she needed to know about him – said, "A pleasure to finally meet you, Seshat. Thoth has spoken highly of you."

"Has he?" She wanted to sound cross, but the words came out too euphoric for the effect. Thoth rarely spoke of anyone, let alone highly.

"Yes, he's been waiting for you."

"Has he now." This time, the deadpan tone took no effort. *He expects something from me. He always did. It was his high expectations that drove her to play other characters, to remain unknown, unnoticed – unappreciated. To be anywhere in the Universe where he wasn't.*

She took a calming breath, which resulted in a fit of coughing.

Why is there so much ash in the air? Seshat wondered, exasperated with it. The whole moon resembled a neglected hearth, scorched and covered in the stuff, as was her newly conjured cloak already. Only the Nephilim remained pristine. Seshat yearned to figure out what her bodysuit was made of in order to will one for herself, but she'd rather let a cat bite her face than admit any sort of ignorance to one of her kind.

'Half this moon is constantly burning with the sun so close behind it,' Anubis explained, sounding strained.

How can mortals live here, then? How can they breathe? She coughed again. Breathing wasn't her forte, even in the purest of atmospheres. *You'd have to have lived as a mortal, like Psyche, or a Wyrd like Odin, to know how to do it properly,* she reckoned.

"The same way they can live everywhere else. Because of us," said Anubis as he materialised next to her. He stood stiffly, leg bones not yet fully healed, his skin still raw and the strip of hair on his head not yet regrown to its usual length, but still he shone in his most ostentatious regalia. He always knew how to make an entrance.

"My lord," said the Lokian.

Anubis seemed to grow a few inches taller with the deference, shining brighter.

"Lord?" Seshat echoed.

"Yes, Seshat. Why the surprise? After all, and as you so often like to remind me: I am a god."

She rolled her eyes. Hades had a similar affliction. It had to be related to being a god of the Underworld, she decided.

"It's good to have you back," the Lokian continued. "What took you so long?"

She couldn't tell if the Lokian's tone was deferential or deprecatory, only that neither option fit his character's demeanour. And the way he glanced at the Nephilim, the tension and familiarity between the two told her he cared for her a great deal more than he did his lord.

Seshat pulled Anubis roughly aside. "These mortals don't make sense. You told me post-humans were enemies of the Nephilim. Now, I'd bet my best quill this Nephilim and your pet here are lovers!" she hissed in his ear, for she did not trust Reach around so many telepaths.

"Priest," he corrected her, then frowned at the odd group over his shoulder. "Yeah, I'm not sure what's happened to Dayna; her soul is missing. And the stars know how a dwarf and a Promethean came to be in each other's presence. As for Audric, well, he's always been haughty – as all Lokians are – but he's loyal enough. And most importantly, he's competent."

"Competent at doing what? What in Ra's name have you been doing that requires priests, Anubis? Those days are aeons behind us."

Anubis licked his lips. "Well, funny you mentioned Ra. It is sort of in his name that I'm doing this. You see, while organising a proper effort to keep Seth contained, I, er…" – he forced a chuckle – "I mean, in truth, I had little to do with it. It was really Thoth and Hathor's idea. You remember how much they enjoy their rituals, right?" Seshat's eyelids had been narrowing by the word and were little more than horizontal slits of radiant outrage at this point. He grinned for mutual reassurance. "Right! Well, the bottom line is, we sort of turned it all into a ritual – for efficiency's sake – and we both know how mortals love a good show."

"What sort of show?"

"Ah, well, as an incentive for supporters, you see, we sort of inspired the higher humans to work with us in order to pursue a spiritual path to apotheosis. That's all."

"You made up your own religion?!" she nearly screeched.

He wagged a finger. "No. Not made up. I already had one, in case you've forgotten. I merely updated it and adapted it to fit these new worshippers and circumstances."

She wanted to scratch his face down to the skull. "The last time you led a religion, the dead nearly escaped from the Underworld. Osiris ended up having to take over control of it from you – which was what you'd intended, of course. What do you and Thoth intend to accomplish this time?"

"I already told you. We're keeping Seth contained."

"On a moon?"

Anubis looked up involuntarily. "Not exactly."

She followed his gaze with her Reach. "Anubis! What have you done?!"

"Only Ra can control Seth; and Ra retired into a star, so…"

"You turned Seth into a planet?!" This time she did screech.

"Not exactly. Come on, you know I can't do that. He's, er… linked to it, that's all."

"You mean cursed!"

"No. The Nephilim don't use curses. Not… exactly. Namrive explained the process to me once. I didn't pay much attention, apologies. It sounded so boring. I swear their explanations can be as dull and convoluted as their technology. In any case, it doesn't matter, for obviously it hasn't worked very well. Seth managed to pull this moon into his orbit. Again, don't ask me how. He shouldn't be able to. It's not his talent, but by doing that he managed to shield himself from Ra's influence. Only a little shade, but enough to allow him to eventually work himself free from Ra's grip. Thoth's working to forestall that outcome, but no matter what we do, it's going to happen, and soon, as you can see. Our goal now is to minimise the damage by, hopefully, appeasing the beast before he gets free."

"Is everything all right?" Audric asked diplomatically.

Not even slightly! Seshat wanted to snap, but Anubis spoke first.

"Where's my jackal?" the god asked. Then he grinned. "Ah, there you are!"

Indeed a jackal scampered through the bleary landscape. Not a real animal, Seshat realised, only an aspect of Anubis. Still, he would look, sound and feel real to anyone who was not a god. The jackal sat in front of Anubis, who reached down to pet him. "Good boy." The moment they touched, the canine vanished into thin air. Several 'oohs' of astonishment from the mortals followed.

"Nice trick," Seshat said grudgingly. "Astral projection?"

"Not quite," he said. "But useful nonetheless."

Anubis had always been an odd one – most Underworld deities were, to be fair – his power based on an assorted mix of talents more suitable to a sorcerer than a god. She would do well to keep that in mind. "You've been hiding talents from me, god of the dead."

"You have your Quetish and your characters, Seshat. I have my jackal and the ability to cross into the Underworld at will. It all balances out," he said, as if reading her musings.

She was about to give him a piece of her mind about balance when something beyond him caught her attention.

Her eyes widened. His words forgotten as soon as the creature registered in her perception. A real creature, not a figment of a god. "Oh, cats..."

People, mortals especially, often use the word monster to describe anything they fear or that's larger than them. From a god's preceptive, there are actually very few creatures that would qualify as monsters in the universe. The Manticore, a giant winged feline with the tail of a scorpion, was one of them. And one now stood atop a pile of stone, silhouetted against the angry sky.

The mortals shared an intake of breath when they too saw the creature.

"Please tell me that's one of yours," she said to Anubis, knowing fully well that his talents only applied to canines.

Anubis did not need to look; the image appeared in his mind as clear as her startled face, but he turned his gaze nonetheless. "No. Must be one of the Nephilim's pets. They've been experimenting with" – the Manticore lunched itself into the air towards them – "run!"

As the rest of the group dashed towards the charred Stump – not an easy task when most of the ground had turned to slush – Seshat stood her ground and summoned Quetish, for she would not demean herself by running like a mortal. Besides, she'd just gotten rid of all the muck.

The sphinx – a winged monster featuring the head and upper torso of a beautiful woman, the body of a lion and a propensity for killing anyone unable to answer her riddles – materialised at Seshat's side with a put-upon attitude. "I guess we're not in Niflheim anymore," Quetish purred, stretching her wings. Then froze abruptly mid-stretch as she sniffed the air, lips puckered in distaste. "For Oedipus' sake, Seshat, where have you dragged me to this time?"

"I'll explain later!" Seshat said as she climbed atop the sphinx. "Go, go, go!"

Quetish's claws dug into the ground at the sight of the Manticore. "What's he doing here?"

"I don't know! To the World Tree – Please." No god liked to plead, but one could never be too polite to sphinxes.

Quetish had half a mind to break their bond, but did as she was told. "You could have translocated there and spared me this humiliation. I'm not a horse, you know. Look at the state of my feathers! Do you have any idea of how hard it is to clean ash from fur?" Seshat didn't, but the momentary pangs of guilt and embarrassment were not enough to dissuade her.

"I need to impress these mortals," she offered as a lame explanation for her ungodly behaviour.

"There's another one!" Berdnard practically shrieked as they flew overhead.

"Yes, they sure need more impressing," said Quetish, her characteristic sultry tone charged with judgement and annoyance.

"They're not going to make it," Seshat realised. Of course they wouldn't. The Tree was still a couple miles off. The Manticore only a few hundred yards back.

"Is it important that they do?" Quetish asked.

Seshat had to take a moment to consider this. Normally, no. Mortals were not particularly important. But this was such a peculiar group. A part of her wanted to learn their story, while at the same time, another wanted to close this book altogether and start over somewhere normal in a distant star system. "I'm not sure. But if there's one thing I learnt in Niflheim, it's not to under-estimate mortals, especially humans."

"Then perhaps the best way to impress them is to save them," the sphinx suggested.

"That's not what gods do," Seshat said. Quetish's eyes rolled towards the sky in reproachful exasperation. She alighted. "Get off, Seshat. I'll deal with this. The Manticore's after me, not your mortals."

"You?! Why?"

"It's a long story."

"One you never told me!" Seshat protested.

"Every sphinx has secrets." Quetish winked and took flight again in the Manticore's direction.

CHAPTER 23

The Mortals and Their Gods

Time's not invulnerable. Its greatest strength,
the thing that confounds and frustrates us all,
is also his greatest weakness.

– Memory on Record

Seshat watched Quetish and the Manticore vanish behind a cairn in a swirly blur. Wings, claws, teeth and tails lashed frenziedly at each other. She couldn't tell if they were fighting or mating. Then again, with Quetish, one invariably led to the other. She'll be all right, Seshat assured herself.

The personalities of sapient creatures of myth were strange. Their motivations as inscrutable as those of celestial bodies. Altruism or self-sacrifice were not traits Quetish possessed, though. The sphinx never acted out of anything but self-interest or lust. Which meant that whatever Seshat was about to face was probably more dangerous than a Manticore, that despite its cantankerous ferocity and capacity to cause an excruciating amount of pain, it would be no more than a few unpleasant sentences in the long volume that comprised a deity's life. Still, she would gladly not have to write them.

Seshat spared a glance at the mortals, still some distance away, running at the brink of exhaustion, and thanked the stars for being born a goddess.

She translocated the short distance to the entrance of the ancient Stump in order to avoid both the mud and the planet's blazing light. Not because it hurt her – no light would ever hurt her – but because she didn't like being watched. She'd only met Seth once or twice in her youth and she'd completely missed his war with Horus, too busy exploring all the Universe had to offer before settling down to write her chronicles. He'd seemed… nice. A bit gloomy and tempestuous, sure. Prone to conflict, yes. But then again, most gods were, especially those with a talent for chaos. She'd never given much thought to his fate, nor had she questioned Thoth's record of the events that shook the very foundation of her pantheon. And that might have been naïve. After all, she knew better than anyone how much more weight the written word of a god had against actual facts.

Anubis appeared right behind her, swaying slightly, as if caught off guard by gravity. For a god able to cross realms at will, he sure had a lot of trouble moving across short distances within one. Either that or… "You've been to the Underworld," she said, astonished at her own deduction. Not because he'd been to the Underworld – after all, he was a god of the dead – but that there was an Underworld to go to on this moon.

He shifted his weight and winced. "I was hoping you wouldn't notice that just yet."

"Anubis, please tell me you didn't set up a temple

here because you usurped another god's Underworld." She wouldn't put anything past him at this point.

He bristled with resentment. "I haven't usurped anything. Cats, Seshat, I'm not the Suzerain. It was abandoned, all right? Temple, world and Underworld. Whoever ruled here once left long ago."

"How can you be sure?"

"We searched – both realms. Not even Thoth has a record of this rock."

He spoke as if that was the only good thing about it. Unrecorded worlds were not known for being coveted. Quite the contrary. Anything left to oblivion was likely for a good reason. And she found it hard to believe Thoth, who had been a lunar deity in his youth, had no record of this place. Something didn't add up. Besides, Anubis looked as if he was going to be sick.

"Is anything amiss down below?" she ventured airily.

He rubbed his temples, visibly distressed. "No, actually." He paused, although he had already decided to elaborate. "They're gone, Seshat. The souls; they are all gone."

"Gone where? How?" Souls lacked initiative. Without a mind or entity to guide them, they'd remain in their underworld until the end of eternity.

He puffed his cheeks. "I have no idea." In truth, he had a few. But none worth contemplating, let alone mentioning.

"Seth?" she suggested.

He shook his head. "No. It's not his talent, and it doesn't work like that. Even if the realm had been breached – which I found no evidence of – souls are not exactly prone to wandering. They have little agency by themselves, and they can be pretty hard to catch on their own, too. That's why the Nephilim keep the bodies of the gods they link their souls to."

"Psyche, then," Seshat said. "The goddess of the soul would have no problem taking them, I reckon."

He cringed as he entertained the possibility, but decided against it. "I've already told you; I'm fairly certain I kept this place from her Reach when we met."

"She's cunning."

"So am I." His tone defied her to say otherwise. Seshat crossed her arms. Anubis rolled his eyes. "Sure, she's cunning but she's not subtle. If she found out about what we were doing here, I'd not have heard the end of it. Fortunately, she already has her hands full with both Hades' and Hel's souls to sort through."

Seshat had to agree with him there. The goddess of the soul had indeed enough to keep her busy, and she would have a few things to say about this for sure.

She expanded her Reach, searching for whatever else she might have missed. The moon was anathema to her senses: ancient, incomprehensible, and – she realised with a start – sentient. That was extremely rare and even stranger. "What about the moon itself?" she asked.

He gestured dismissively. "I doubt the moon even knows or cares we're here. We're no more relevant than fleas."

"Fleas can be a nuisance," she said, then pointed at the planet above. "Being pulled out of orbit to be used as a shield in a battle of wills and destroyed in the process is a pretty big nuisance. Mortals would call it murder, in fact. Were I a moon, I'd be pretty upset."

"And what would you do about it?" he sneered.

Anubis had a point. Moons were not known for their agency. Still, their existence was enough to influence the planets they orbited. And a moon this size could cause serious trouble.

"How's Quetish?" Anubis asked, deviating from the subject. A poor attempt, for they both knew he hated the sphinx.

Seshat pressed her lips, shifting her awareness to focus on their bond. Nothing, which was unusual. Quetish had never shielded her mind before. Seshat had begged.

"Probably enjoying herself more than we are," she said.

Anubis snorted. "Hopefully you, too, will enjoy writing about all this afterwards."

The best stories only revealed themselves in hindsight. Would this be one of them? Somehow, she doubted it. She looked at the petrified Stump, then at the sky above, sighed and said, "You still haven't told me the truth about Mnemosyne."

Anubis tilted his head like a perplexed puppy. "I think I'm having déjà vu. Haven't we had this conversation before?"

She wasn't in the mood for his quips. "You said she would be here."

"She has to be. This was where her soul was last linked to a host."

"You told me she was linked to a ship because no mortal vessel was able to contain her soul," Seshat said through clenched teeth.

He spared her a sheepish glance. "Ah, yes… well… details."

"Lies!"

"I only found out about that particular development after we last talked, and it's too late in any case. She's no longer contained..." He spread his hands in an irrelevant gesture. "You can't expect me to update you on every single development."

"Yes, I can and I do. You brought me here – practically kidnapped me – so you will tell me anything you learn, the moment you learn it. Are we clear?"

"You mistake me for Hermes."

"Anubis!"

"All right!" he snarled. "The ship got wrecked, so they had to improvise. Find a new host, flesh to tether the soul. It doesn't matter now because it didn't work. She broke the link, damaged the host, and I believe she's the reason everyone's memory is screwed. She's messing with us. I was certain that I would find her hiding in the Underworld, but..." He trailed off, head shaking.

"If she's not in the Underworld, why would she linger in this... this..." Seshat struggled to find the right adjectives to describe the colourless scenery. The place was so dismal it defied definition. It wasn't just the aesthetics of the moon itself. There was something utterly depressing about it – soul crushing. Almost as if it didn't belong in the same realm as life or joy. Cats, even Niflheim had more cheer than this place. Seshat reckoned that if she were a Titan like Mnemosyne, she'd be halfway across the Universe by now.

"She can't leave. Not the way things are now," Anubis said meekly.

Seshat followed his eyes as they darted from the

planet to linger on the petrified Stump of what had once been a World Tree. "Explain."

"There's only one way out for us – unless, of course, you're willing to board a Nephilim ship again. But I doubt there's one coming. Even if Namrive decides to betray us and manages to convince the Mentor to despatch a fleet to 'deal with this issue', they wouldn't arrive in time."

"So why are we here, really? What has Seth to do with Mnemosyne? And please, no more lies."

Anubis hesitated. Kicked a pebble. Took a deep breath. "What if I told you I'd brought you here to record the end of the Universe?"

She crossed her arms. "I'd say you're lying. The Universe didn't end when Chronos shattered Nix's soul. Not even when He merged the Aesir and Olympian Underworlds. It will not end because one chaos god gets free. Cats, there are dozens of them out there, causing entire galaxies to collide. What's this little clash in the grand scheme of things?"

"The stone that ripples the pond..." Anubis said gravely, glancing up. "Yes, Seth will get free, one way or the other... It's not his freedom I'm concerned with; it's his mental state. I need you to convince Mnemosyne to make him...er... forget some of the things that were done to him."

"Coward." Seshat scowled at him. "You try to convince her to do anything. Just apologise to her for what you did. Then ask her yourself."

"I had nothing to do with her capture," he said vehemently. "The Nephilim must have had help, but not from me. I was done, free of them and this place for good. But…" He paused and rubbed his forehead as if the next thought had just occurred to him. "Maybe I've been set up too. I never expected Hel to let me go. Let alone Hades. But now that I think about it, Olympians have been overly accommodating of us in the past age."

She chuckled. "Oh, Anubis. I hate to break it to you, but you're not that important to gods like them. The golden ages of our pantheon are long gone. No one really cares about what we do or don't do, except each other."

He bristled slightly at this but managed to maintain his reasonable tone. "Perhaps you and I are not important. But Mnemosyne still is."

Seshat tapped her lips absently. "Have you considered the possibility she's already working on the problem? After all, she does have a nasty habit of deciding what one should or should not remember. It's her talent, her purpose. And if anyone should know what's best left forgotten, it's her who remembers it all. You said it yourself. Everyone here has their memory screwed."

Anubis rubbed his jaw, unable to find fault in her argument. "Ignorance is bliss," he quoted absently. "I'm sorry, Seshat. I should not have dragged you into this."

Seshat was stunned into silence for a moment. To receive an apology from a god was a rare thing. From Anubis, practically unheard of. "Why so many lies?" she asked him earnestly. "We've had our differences, but had you asked, told me the truth from the beginning, I'd still be here."

"No, you wouldn't. If there's one thing I've learned in all my aeons, its that the truth gets you nowhere."

Seshat tsked. "Now you sound like Psyche." The goddess of the soul always had a way of mixing brutal honesty with lies to mask the truth. Much like a writer, she mused resentfully.

Anubis smiled ruefully. "Any god who deals with souls knows the value of lies."

"And any god who deals with you knows you're a terrible liar."

"What if the best lie I've ever told was to convince everyone that I'm a bad liar?"

Cats, she wanted to be furious, but annoyed was as far as her mixed feelings went. A good thing, for she hadn't even faced her father yet. If she let herself become upset now, she would be livid dealing with him. That would never do. Besides, she'd come this far, endured this much. If there was a chance, no matter how small or convoluted, to talk to Mnemosyne again, to write down her memories, to learn and apologise, even if it hadn't been her fault, then she had to see this through. After all, that is what she wanted, right?

∞

Their conversation was cut short by the approaching ragtag group of assorted mortals who had finally made it to the Stump. Apart from the strange Nephilim, they were in a pitiful state: filthy head to toe and drained to the bone. Even the Lokian looked tired and unkempt.

"How kind of you to wait for us," Lyam said sardonically as he bent at the waist, hands on his knees, panting.

"You know what would have been kinder?" Berdnard said in a strained tone. "Helping us get here faster!"

The gods exchanged awkward glances. The notion had not even occurred to them. "Yes, well, gods only help those who help themselves," said Anubis severely. Seshat raised an eyebrow at him.

'It's something I learned from an expert,' he explained telepathically.

'An expert on pretence?' she questioned dryly.

'And tyranny,' he added, trying not to smile. 'You'd be surprised how far fear, shame and guilt will get you with weak-minded mortals.'

Seshat snorted.

"You find that amusing, do you?" the dwarf asked them rhetorically, axe in hand, wisps of ash falling from his moustache as he huffed with indignation. "You'd better help us get out of this mess before it hits, for I'd bet my beard it's all happening because of you. Am I wrong?" Berdnard clearly expected an answer to this question.

Anubis leaned closer to Seshat, bemused. "How quaint. It's like watching a kitten having a tantrum."

Berdnard swung his axe with a mighty growl.

Everyone stood very still, eyes wide, their breaths held.

Anubis looked down at the blade half-buried in this chest, then to the mortal who put it there.

Seshat recovered first. "Anubis! Wait —"

Everything that had been Berdnard vanished from existence in a puff of displaced ash.

Mouths hung open. Enraged, disbelieving frowns followed. Audric's red eyes, blazing like molten metal, articulated his thoughts better than words ever would.

"What did you expect?" Anubis said defiantly, the jackal aspect overlapping his features in a menacing snarl. "He attacked a god, for cat's sake! You'd have done the same if he'd attacked you – or not, because you'd be dead. Just because I can't be killed by a mere blade doesn't mean I should let the attacker live after the attempt. Next time he might have tried to take my head off. Do you have any idea what that's like?"

"No. As you said, I am not a god," Audric replied coldly. "Otherwise, I would have offered him a fair trial. It is what we do, is it not – lord?"

Anubis puffed out an exasperated breath. "We have no more time for trials, or fairness. The dwarf's lucky to have hit me. His death was quick. Seshat here would have set him on fire."

Seshat groaned. She wanted no part of this discussion, but she couldn't deny Anubis' point either. "Only in reflex," she mumbled half apologetically. "I'd probably have put him out before he…" She fell silent upon seeing Lyam's expression.

"Don't mourn your little friend, Audric," Anubis said. "And for all it's worth, I did give him a fair trial. I can weigh souls with a thought. The scales are just for show. He was a deeply distraught creature. Torn between murderous rage and suicidal ideation. I did him a favour."

"Only gods would call killing a favour." Pandora actually sounded amused at the idea.

"That's rich coming from a Nephilim," Anubis shot back. "What do you call it?"

"Rebirth," said she in all seriousness.

"Until what hits?" Lyam murmured when he finally

found his voice. He'd no love for the dwarf. Deep down beneath the initial shock, he found himself slightly relieved, for he'd rather not be around a constant reminder of the terrible things he'd done in the past. But he'd never actually witnessed a god's true nature before. Suddenly his entire perception of the Universe shifted, and more than ever, he did not like his place in it. "Berdnard said something was about to hit. What was he talking about?"

Anubis rolled his eyes at the sky. "This moon will collide with the planet soon. When that happens, you'll die." He turned from Lyam's horrified face to Seshat's open-mouthed disapproval. "Ain't the truth great?"

Lyam remembered one elder saying something about the moon being in a decaying orbit. "But impact should not happen for centuries yet, maybe even millennia!"

"Time is not what it used to be, mortal."

"What is that supposed to mean?"

Anubis turned to Seshat. "I can't make it any clearer. Perhaps you, with your extensive experience amongst their kind, can explain?"

She gave Anubis another exasperated look, this time tainted with scorn. "A god's will is more powerful than the basic laws of physics," Seshat told Lyam. The answer only confused him further. Then again, his problem wasn't lack of intelligence or understanding, only huge amounts of denial.

"Why is that?" Audric asked her, genuinely intrigued. "Why do gods get to bend the rules and we don't?"

She stared at him for a long moment, then shrugged. "I honestly don't have that answer."

Anubis, now bored, led the way to the temple's antechamber in a whirlwind of cloth and determination. Seshat momentarily wondered why he hadn't just translocated to the temple proper and avoided the whole unfortunate scene with the mortals – for it couldn't have been for her sake – when the reason hit her in a wave of frustration.

"Oh, no, not another one. Not again," she said, walking backwards until she crashed into Pandora.

"It's all right, Seshat. This isn't like the other Stump," Anubis assured her.

"A clowder it isn't!" As she spoke, she realised he was right, though. The sensation of being abruptly smothered by her surroundings was similar, but both her powers and talents were still there, just very, very faint. She conjured a ball of light to reassure herself that she still could, then set it between her and the Nephilim, who stared at it with the innocent fascination of a moth.

The narrow passage opened into a cluttered room. Seshat kept the light going with a little extra flame, ready to unleash if necessary.

Anubis whistled in mocking appreciation. "It's like a museum of Nephilim artefacts in here."

"Anything useful?" Seshat asked, picking up a piece of shattered glass she recognised as part of a devise that functioned like a portable window to their virtual realms.

"Doubt it. Not useful to us anyway, only to the Nephilim. Crymure must have stolen this stuff in order to stall their efforts to establish communication and repairs," he said, striding down a dark passage.

Seshat bit out a curse. Anubis appeared to be right – again. Whatever wasn't broken seemed to be depleted. But there were a lot more than just broken devices lying around. Furniture, offerings, and gems glinted amongst the clutter. Lush tapestries hung from the walls. Seshat covered her mouth to muffle the ungodly sound she made deep in her throat as she recognised what she saw in them. One, fairly new and intact, depicted the birth of Athena; another, much older – the one that left her aghast – was a fairly impressive portrait of the Titans who'd once ruled the Cosmos alongside primordial deities such as Atum, Kauket and Ymir. Back when the Universe was still young, long before mortals, Olympians, the Aesir, herself or even Ra came into being. Mnemosyne had been one of them. Brought into existence when Chronos arrived. Of course, Seshat already knew that, but seeing her there, standing proud alongside deities such as Hyperion and Thea, made her tear up in wonderment.

I wish I'd been there. With the thought came the realisation of how sincere the wish was. She genuinely wanted to have been there. To have seen it all unfold instead of just recording it second hand. It was the root of her obsession with Chronos, her passion for Mnemosyne and – she had to admit – her attraction to Loki as well. The idea that Anubis might be right and they were indeed witnessing the beginning of the end depressed her, for beginnings were always so much more exciting to write than endings.

∞

"Friends of yours?" Lyam asked.

She spared him an annoyed glance before she spoke. "These eight are the primordial gods of my pantheon. And those are the twelve Titans, the Olympian ancestors, if you will. They were allies once, before… well, before we gods came along, I suppose. They set the first rules of conduct in the universe. Rules we still exist by.

"Did the rules apply to them too?" he asked.

Seshat pondered this. "Not particularly."

"Doesn't seem fair," said Lyam.

She shrugged. "Fairness is not a rule. We may have been born gods, but in order to remain so, we have to earn our place in the Universe. And even those who can break the rules must do so according to their own rules."

"Why have rules in the first place?"

She gave him a weary smile. "There's no one answering our prayers. No higher power than ourselves. We're all we've got. To us, rule and responsibility are one and the same. To break one is to abandon the other. Without them, we have no place in this universe."

"What happens if your place is taken?" Pandora asked.

The goddess turned sharply on her. "What do you mean?"

"The same way the scions of Ra replaced the Ogdoad, and the Olympians usurped the Titans, what will you do when the next generation of immortals takes your place?"

There's no next generation! she almost said, but then she thought better of it. The fact was that there was no shortage of candidates: the Nephilim, definitely, but even the Dharkan might become a threat.

"Then we fight." Seshat let her golden eyes glow slightly for emphasis. "And believe me, gods don't like to lose. Whoever messes with us will have to face dire consequences. A defeated deity can be much more dangerous than the winner."

There was no denying the menace in the features of those portrayed.

The hairs on Seshat's nape bristled, and she turned to find the Lokian close behind her studying the tapestries. "They say a picture is worth a thousand words," he said, as if speaking to the fabric.

She cleared her throat, annoyed at the mortal's wit. "I am the goddess of writing, so…" So what, you idiot? She hated that old adage because sometimes – this one included – it was true.

He lifted an eyebrow at her. "You don't agree?"

"No," she lied curtly.

A corner of his mouth lifted in a sardonic smile. There was something about the Lokian that deeply unsettled her, and it wasn't just the chosen appellation of his race – although that inevitably set off all sorts of alarming questions and unpleasant plot threads. Was Loki aware of their existence? Somehow she could not bring herself to believe he would have stayed quiet about it had he known an entire civilisation had named themselves after him.

"Why are your eyes red?" she asked out of idle curiosity and a lame attempt to justify why she was staring back at them like a young girl smitten by a pretty boy.

She wasn't. Red eyes were just extremely uncommon, even amongst gods.

He leaned in and whispered. "So I can see in the dark."

"Oh…" Not the answer she was expecting.

"And underwater," he elaborated with a wink.

"What for?!" Lyam interjected. "It's not like you can breathe underwater." He frowned. "Can you?"

The Lokian half shrugged non-committally, clearly enjoying their bewilderment.

"Where did you get them?" It was known Lokians 'borrowed' bits and pieces from many other beings, but Lyam had never heard of one with red eyes like those. And he should have. After all, studying creatures whose biology was compatible with humans had been his speciality.

"Won't tell you. Their kind are wary of Prometheans. You take too much," Audric said in rebuke.

"You took their eyes!" Lyam pointed out indignantly.

"I traded them," Audric said slowly. "Two eyes for a lung."

Lyam opened his mouth to speak. "Well, then…" he said stiffly. And that was all he had left to say on the matter just then.

Audric's triumphant expression was short-lived. "Where is – fuck!" He forced Lyam and Seshat flat against the wall as he dashed past them after the Nephilim, who had followed Anubis down the tunnel before the banter started.

Seshat watched him go, once again pondering their

relationship. Pandora – or whatever the Nephilim woman was called, the name too contrived to be real, she reckoned – was indeed very different from Namrive, whose body and mind were completely artificial. She reminded Seshat of the Suzerain, a dryad who'd managed to combine living flesh with the Nephilim's technology, turning himself not only immortal but powerful enough to match gods and Nephilim both. The notion disturbed her. But if he'd achieved that on his own, it was only natural the Nephilim would eventually learn how to improve themselves in similar ways.

One problem at a time, as Ideth would say.

"You guys had it easy," she told the deities of old. Existence had to have been better without mortals and sentient machines, she decided with a resigned exhalation before heading down the gloomy passage after them.

CHAPTER 24

The Way Downwards

Gods would rather die than be forgotten.

– Memory on Record

"So you're Thoth's daughter." Lyam spoke in the casual tone of someone beating about the bush. He'd never met a deity in such a chaotic emotional state. Seshat seemed to bounce from annoyance to apprehension, curiosity and tedium in a single breath. Her mind was a buzz of activity as she ran through several lines of thought at once, and try as he might, he could not pick up the thread to any of them. Thoth's mind was as organised as a Nephilim's in comparison, but much like with the Nephilim, Lyam had never sensed any real emotions to speak of from the god. That he sensed so many from her was both fascinating and unsettling in equal amounts.

The goddess bristled at being addressed. She'd forgotten about him. The Promethean might be easy to miss; not so much to dismiss, apparently.

"Your point?" she asked tersely. Like most scions of Ra, she hated dark confined spaces, especially those below ground, and her uneasiness showed.

"It's just that you look like you could be his twin, that's all." Gods never aged. Lyam reckoned that had to cause some issues within their family dynamics.

"Yes, you mortals all look the same to us too," said she.

Seshat had no patience for idle talk. Anubis' light remained visible a considerable distance away, bright and distant like a star in an empty black sky, and yet she couldn't Reach him or catch up to him either. How did he get so far ahead in such a short time? Sure, Anubis walked fast, but so did she when the occasion called for it. She was now all but running down the seemingly endless tunnel, getting no closer to its end. It might as well be a Mobius strip. Something's not right.

"There's no need to be rude," Lyam grumbled, catching up to her.

"It's a fact, not rudeness. I don't care enough about your feelings to be rude, mortal." She conjured more light and focused all her senses on the descent. She was definitely in a limbo of sorts – a very ancient and capricious one by the look of things, similar to those controlled by Chronodéndrons to guide travellers across forgotten realms, and nothing good ever came from travelling through them.

"What do you care about, then?" Lyam asked, fighting his exhaustion and the ever-growing sense of hopelessness that his recalled knowledge and subsequent loss of innocence brought him.

"Right now, I only care about getting to the end of this tunnel. I swear it's getting longer with each step!" Seshat admitted in exasperation.

Lyam sighed. "It was the same coming up. At least

we are walking downwards this time… Don't worry, we'll get there, eventually." Had it really only been two shifts since he left the temple? It felt more like two years… an entire lifetime, actually, now that he remembered it all. A lifetime that he was not only struggling to accept but that also might be about to end.

Eventually wasn't good enough for Seshat. She wanted to be there now. She'd only encountered this type of spatial distortion in the spaces between realms, where no god in their right mind would linger if they wished to remain sane. Mortals shouldn't even be able to survive for more than a few moments. That someone or something had found a way to adapt such a liminal space to be crossed on foot by living flesh was both impressive and deeply worrying.

"Why did Thoth bother to save us when we crashed and keep us alive in the temple if we are destined to die when the moon hits the planet?" Lyam asked, hitting that metaphorical bush dead in its centre.

"I don't know." It was true. She didn't, not exactly. But knowing her father, she suspected he wanted something from them, something besides their souls and company. Information perhaps, some obscure piece of intelligence the Prometheans themselves might not be aware they possessed. Or, more likely, he figured how to use them to gain an advantage. Against whom, though? Anubis, Seth, the Nephilim? The god of reckoning always strove for control. His endless thirst for learning and knowledge was the product of his desire to rule everything: the narrative, the stars, space and even time itself. How he went about it, however, had always left her confounded.

Lyam clicked his tongue. "I'll be dead soon, anyway. Why lie?"

Seshat gave him a narrow glance. "Believe it or not, being related to a god doesn't give you any insight or power over them. Quite the contrary. I've been deceived and dragged into this plot against my will, much as you have."

Except you'll get out of it alive. I won't, he thought bitterly, then ground his teeth and thought again. Yes, I will.

"At least tell me why he made us forget who we are." Lyam wanted to know that much. Maybe then he could also understand why the memories had returned. He had a few theories but liked none of them.

She shook her head. The way her straight hair brushed her shoulders made her look more girl than goddess. "My father can tell you a story in such a way that you would believe it, word for word. He can make you live that story, as in a daydream, make you think it actually happened to you in a way your mind can't tell the difference. But he can't make you forget anything. Only Mnemosyne can erase memories." Mnemosyne and a handful of crafty magic users, Seshat added to herself. But there was no need to further confuse the poor mortal.

He cursed. "The Nephilim's ship… of course! They sabotaged our memory stores with some sort of beam or signal or –"

"No, you idiot. I'm talking about the actual goddess of memory," she clarified, to shut him up. The Promethean was too keen on asking questions, more so on making assumptions. Seshat turned sharply, forcing him to an abrupt halt. "What do you know about Mnemosyne?"

"N-nothing," he stammered, taken aback by the question and intensity of her glare. Her eyes were the golden amber of flames – a cat's eyes – burning through thick lines of kohl. He actually felt their heat. "Only that it was their ship's name." The memory returned along with the others and was just as useless. He paused. "Wait, was Mnemosyne the one in the tapestry? The one you were admiring?" He wouldn't dare to imply anything else, although worshipping came to mind first.

Seshat pursed her lips; her gaze grew hotter. He moved on to his next question. "How can memory be a goddess?"

She chuckled despite herself. "She's not a goddess. She's one of the oldest, most important, most powerful deities in the entire Universe." It shocked her how little knowledge, not to mention respect, these post-humans had for gods. How would they ever expect to evolve without having the slightest admiration or regard for what they intended to become?

"Ah," he said, for lack of a better word. To Lyam, all gods were old and powerful – more powerful than he'd ever be, for sure – but their importance was relative and, in most cases, not particularly justified. But he had also seen the way Seshat had looked at the other entities depicted on the wall, and to hear a god speak of another with such respect and admiration certainly put a different perspective on things.

She gave him an amused half-smile upon reading his thoughts. "Not all gods were created equal."

The notion fascinated him. He had to find out more.

"All right… so why did the Nephilim have her?" How they'd got their hands on such a powerful entity had also crossed his mind, but he'd save that question for later.

Seshat puffed out a hot breath. "Because she controls memories. And since we are the product of our memories, she controls us: what we are, who we are. What we've done and all that we might still do because of what we've done."

He began to see the advantages of such a talent. "Doesn't it bother you that one god has so much power over others?"

"No. Does it bother you that I can reduce you to ash with my will?"

He grimaced. "It does now."

"But what can you do about it?"

"Nothing. That's why it bothers me." Not as much as it should, though, he reflected.

"And yet you still stand there, talking to me as if it weren't a real possibility. You have to trust me, that much at least, or you wouldn't be able to function. Sure, Mnemosyne can make me forget myself and everything I've ever done, Chronos can stop time, shatter this reality at will, making all of us redundant fixtures in a dead Universe, and the Goddess of Life and Death can send me on a one-way trip to the Underworld of her choice if she so wills it. There's no point fretting about what can happen or what others can do to you. You just have to get on with things."

Lyam was gobsmacked. "That is probably the wisest thing I've ever heard." That it had been said by a god destabilised the foundations of his beliefs.

"I have my moments," she said facetiously.

"Thank you," he said, meaning it.

Before Seshat could react, he placed his hands on her cheeks and kissed her chastely on the forehead.

Seshat couldn't remember the last time a mortal had thanked her for anything, let alone shown any devotion or appreciation. He was being sincere, in that careless, spontaneous way that made mortals so endearing to gods.

But she knew better than to confuse sincerity with honesty.

"Don't count on me to save your life, mortal. I'm not that kind of deity."

"Ah, well. I had to try." He dropped his hands and gave her his best smile. "So what kind of deity are you, then?"

Seshat eyed the end of the long tunnel wistfully and sighed.

CHAPTER 25

The Pyramid

If time leaves, memories will be all that remains.

– Memory on Record

Lyam and Seshat's voices became more distinct as they neared the exit of the tunnel.

"Finally," Anubis grumbled peevishly. He, Audric and Pandora had been waiting on the other side for a while, and the god – who clearly hated waiting – could define impatience by this point. Audric, on the other hand, was the very personification of patience while Pandora seemed fascinated by her surroundings, running her hands along the rough rock, caressing them in a way that was almost erotic.

"No, not many gods have mounts," Seshat was saying, her voice slightly distorted by the distance and its echo. "To be fair, it's not like we need them. We can pretty much will ourselves anywhere, as long as we know exactly where it is. But the practice of riding creatures of myth became fashionable amongst my pantheon when

Ra linked to a phoenix. Thoth was the first to emulate Ra by linking to a hippogryph. He rarely uses it, mind, but he always strove to be more like our scion… Personally, I had no intention of following that trend, but then I met Quetish when I was in Thebes recording the life of Oedipus – a mortal and a victim of a bizarre prophecy. I don't normally write about mortals, but humans were still a novelty back then, and wherever there's a prophecy, there's a good chance of finding a good story too. In any case, that's not relevant right now. Quetish is a sphinx. Like so many of her kind, she had been cursed to guard the entrance to the city. And the way she chose to do it…" Seshat chuckled, remembering the clever riddle. "I just knew we'd get along. So I offered to link with her. The bond broke the curse – as links often do – and to keep a long story short, we've been together ever since."

"But she appeared out of nowhere," Lyam said.

"She spends most of her time in other, more abstract realms, satiating her appetites and devising riddles. This reality is too boring, too limited for her. I have to summon her each time. She won't come of her own accord."

"Ahh." The tone of Lyam's interjection showed how little his grasp of realms was. He really wanted to learn more about them, but instead he asked, "Will she be all right?"

"Oh, yes. I'm sure Quetish's fine. I'm more concerned for the Manticore." She chuckled. Lyam did not understand why.

"Is he Anubis' mount?"

"Oh no. Anubis doesn't have a mount."

"Why not?"

"Well, rumour has it he tried to link with a harpy once – it did not go well," Seshat added in a conspiratorial whisper. "So he came up with another way to stand out amongst the rest of us. He linked to a jackal. Except, being him, he performed the ritual in the Underworld. The realms of the dead are far less substantial than those of the living, and so, instead of binding the animal's spirit to his soul, he sort of amalgamated the two. I believe this, combined with his natural talent to shape-shift and cast himself across realms, allows him to project his will as a jackal pretty much anywhere. That must take some serious amount of willpower," she had to admit.

"Why a jackal?"

"Anubis has a soft spot for the underdog – no pun intended. No one cares much about jackals, while wolves, dogs and foxes get all the attention."

"So he was the jackal?"

"In a sense. Yes."

"That means he knows about the abyss and the tower. He's seen them."

"Correct."

"He was spying on us." Lyam sounded outraged.

"Correct again."

"Bastard."

"I couldn't agree more," Seshat said, beaming at a glowering Anubis face to face.

"What took you so long?" the god of the dead asked peevishly.

"I got lost," she replied truthfully. She knew how much Anubis hated waiting, and it gave her a sort of petty satisfaction to see him seethe.

"Lost – in a straight passage?" The jackal aspect overlapped his features with a snarl. "I'm surprised you found the exit," he said sarcastically, trying very hard to remain cool. He failed. "I've been waiting for ages, Seshat! While you strolled along leisurely with a mortal, sharing our secrets like gossip. We're no longer in Niflheim. Chronos is not here, and he will not delay this end, I assure you."

Seshat stepped up to him. "The next time you have me cross a realm on foot, make sure to show me where we're going first, then you won't have to wait."

Travelling through liminal space was just a longer, more awkward method of translocation. It was all well and good when you had a clear destination in mind. Otherwise, you could end up walking the paths between realms for eternity. Seshat had never been to this temple, so she had no way of knowing how to get there. It wasn't until she'd let Lyam take the lead that they began making progress on the descent.

"You should have Reached out to me!" Anubis snapped.

"I did," she admitted. "You kept slipping away."

He gave her a sad smile. "I see. I guess I'm not as important to you as I once was."

She gave him a levelled look. "I guess not. Surprised? After everything you've done? Oh, please. Let's just get this over with." She cast about and frowned. "What is this place?"

"An artefact from when the Universe was young," Anubis said.

Seshat frowned. "Who built it?"

"We don't know." He sounded sincere. Then again,

Anubis often sounded sincere when he was annoyed. "This place is older than us."

"If it's that old, how is it still here?" Lyam asked, unable to even guess the gods' age.

"Willpower, my boy; it runs the Universe."

"It is true," Pandora interjected, without taking her gaze from the walls.

"So whose will is it to destroy it, then?"

The gods exchanged complicit glances, like parents at a loss for how to explain the complexities of adult life to a child.

Lyam had calmed down substantially during the descent, even more so now that he'd confirmed the tunnels weren't flooded. But the fact that neither Ninguém nor Nenhum were there to greet them and the whole place looked and sounded abandoned brought his anxiety back tenfold. "Right," he said, realising that whoever wanted to destroy the old moon was irrelevant compared to the need to escape before it happened. "Where is everyone?"

"I'd give you two guesses, but you'll only need one," Audric replied. On him, annoyance often turned into glibness. "But hey, at least they haven't drowned." This sounded like, "You're such an idiot" to Lyam's ears. Gods, how he despised the man.

A sudden quake nearly knocked them to the ground. Dust filled the air, and for a long moment, no one did anything but cough and curse.

"Sounds like the party's already started. Come." Anubis dashed off in the direction of the pyramid, all but dragging Seshat in tow until they were out of earshot of the mortals. And turned on her then.

"You're upset with me. I get it. But what possessed you to speak to the post-human about our ways? I can't have these mortals seeing me as anything less than a god, or worse, a weak one."

"Spare me the lecture Anubis. Your godhood was never in question. The quality of it, though…" – Anubis growled inside her mind – "Fine. I'll stop. What do you suppose Lyam is going to do with the information? Like you said, the mortals are doomed."

Sometimes it grated on Anubis how little she cared about reputation. Not every god had the luxury of editing stories to suit their character, or to write them in the first place. In his experience, who or what you were often stayed in the shadow of what others believed you to be.

"He might tell that story in the Underworld, where it would become a much greater nuisance, for example. You know how much the dead like to gossip." Anubis groaned at the thought. "Anyway, that's not the point. I'm worried about you, Seshat. I leave you alone for a few moments and you become best friends with a post-human who's only interested in gaining your favour so he can survive."

"And? You think I can't see that? I wasn't born this age."

Anubis took a deep breath. "You grew too fond of mortals back in Niflheim."

"While you're still not fond enough," she retorted. "Especially for a god who depends on them so much."

"Wrong. They depend on me." His eyes glared as he spoke.

Seshat disliked that glare almost as much as she

did his tone. All gods were a bit megalomaniacal – cats knew even she'd been guilty of it on occasion – but Anubis had always been sensible and dispassionate in his pursuits. Such an emotional reaction told her his reasons might be more personal than delusional.

"Why did you do it, Anubis?" She had no need to specify what. The question applied to pretty much everything he'd done since the fall of Midgard.

He took a moment to answer, mulling it over. "You know when you want something so badly for so long that you forget why you wanted it in the first place? All that remains is the wanting, but you can no longer explain why?"

"No," she lied. The truth was, she was beginning to feel that way in regard to finding Mnemosyne. As if she was being summoned rather than driven by her own free will.

He grinned lopsidedly at her, aware of the lie. "Yes, you do." He raised his hands as if to illustrate something, then clasp them behind his back again. "We are gods. Our will is strong, but our motivations are weak."

"Speak for yourself."

"I am. But I'm also right."

Chapter 26

The Forgotten Realm

*Once Chronos broke into this realm, it was
only a matter of time before others followed.*

– Memory on Record

A temple my arse, Seshat decided as they burrowed deeper under the petrified World Tree. Her powers remained compromised and of little use in this rarefied reality, but she perceived enough to understand this was a place set outside time and realm, where space became fluid, for lack of a better word, like a dreamscape you can visit while awake, powered not by a god's will but – "Magic," she whispered. Primordial magic. She stopped, determined to not take another step until she had a very good reason to. "Where have you dragged me, Anubis?"

"Haven't you figured it out yet?" he asked, condescendingly teasing.

She wanted to hiss but only glared.

"This" – he spread his arm in a half turn – "is where the first Underworld came to be."

"Huh?"

Anubis grinned like a child, unable to help himself, for despite everything, no god – certainly not a god of the dead – would be indifferent to such a relic. "It's the birthplace of Tartarus."

Seshat had to take a moment to fully process this statement. "Tartarus… as in the deepest realm of Hades' Underworld? The Titans' prison? That Tartarus?!"

"That's what he is now, true. He is to Hades' Underworld what the Underworld itself is to Olympus. But before… back when the Universe was young, Tartarus was a god, the god of the abyss, he was called, although his talent was not creating abysses per se, but in fact realms. And more importantly, the bridges between them. They happen to look like abysses, for some reason."

A terrible notion came to her. "Like black holes…"

Anubis blinked. "What? No. Gravity is the one responsible for black holes. Every time it kills a star. You know that, Seshat." He shuddered. "Why did you have to bring those up?"

"Apologies."

"Anyway… this temple was built in Tartarus' honour before the other Titans realised how dangerous his talents were. After he… er – never mind." He waved a hand in dismissal, having lost his enthusiasm for the narrative after her mention of dead stars. "His story is not mine to tell. Let's just say they asked Chronos to help them strip him of his talents and, in doing so, He created what would later become their prison, for only a Titan's soul is strong enough to bind another to its own. Or dozens of others, in this case. Suffice to say, no deity asked Chronos for help after that. They didn't know about Kali, you see. No one did back then. Again, that's beyond the point. The good news is, some of Tartarus' power still lingers within these walls, and we figured out how to use it."

"Are you kidding me?"

"Do I ever, Seshat?" he said in all seriousness.

Seshat shut her eyes, and "Oh, Anubis…" was all she articulated in reply to such hubris, sure he did not realise or even understand the implications of what he'd just told her. If only she'd learned about Chronos' role in the creation of the Underworlds before travelling to Niflheim. How differently that narrative would have unfolded. Regardless, she was here now, living this story. And yes, she knew many primordial deities had given their names and even their souls to the embodiment of their talents. Selene had become a moon, Oceanus a water realm, and Eos was on her way to becoming dawn itself. But this chthonic nightmare was more than the physical manifestation of a god's talent. It was a fissure in reality, the fabric of the universe itself. She looked down, past solid rock to the fathomless abyss at the centre of this moon that, she now realised, wasn't really a moon either.

"Anubis, where – exactly – does this abyss lead to?" She'd already guessed the answer, but needed to hear it, nonetheless.

He displayed his canines in a feral grin. "Another universe."

She closed her eyes tight. "Oh…" The sound was more moan than word this time. There are limits even to a god's comprehension. And one universe was quite enough for one to write about. Suddenly, everything about Chronos made sense. But he was not the villain of this story.

She wanted to skin the grinning cat. "Anubis, you said you used the power of this place to keep Seth's soul trapped within the planet."

"Yes. Yes, that was the original idea. To send souls to this Underworld and use them to power the curse, to counteract his own will. We didn't realise what we had until… well, until we used it. That's when we recognised the abyss for what it was. Not just a conduit between realms but a portal to something much larger. It has to be another universe. I mean, we can't know for sure since none of the souls we sent have returned. They just… ceased to exist. It's both fascinating and terrifying when you think about it."

"Oh, so you did think about it! Cats, Anubis. How can you even be sure Seth is still bound to the planet?"

"You saw it. That's no ordinary planet."

Seshat had no arguments there. That planet definitely had a soul and sentience. But that didn't mean it was Seth's.

"At first we feared Seth would fall through it too," Anubis explained. "Then, as the years dragged on, we kinda wished he had and saved us the trouble of keeping this place going in hopes of… I can't even tell what anymore. So much has changed… Horus was defeated. The Nephilim took over most of our worlds. And Ra… he stopped caring a long time ago." There was genuine sadness in Anubis' voice as he spoke. But for whom, Seshat had no idea. And it didn't last long, in any case. "But Seth didn't go, of course. Mightily wilful, that one.

So now the best we can do is try to convince him to join us upon his release."

"How can you be so stupid?!"

"I'm not."

"Yes, you are. Can't you see?"

He turned to face her, canines exposed, bristling while he waited for an elaboration, for clearly he did not see anything.

"You said the Nephilim chose that planet – or put it here, it doesn't matter which – because it was close to Ra," she said.

"Correct."

"And why do you think Ra chose to burn here, of all places in the Universe? Why next to this moon – the very thing Seth is now using to shield himself from his power."

"We figured Ra was keeping it safe," he said, still not getting it.

"Guarding it, more like," said she.

"Same thing."

"No, it is not." She could not believe this. He acted as if he really did not know. She took his hand, hoping the touch would help her make sense of his mind. "Ra has been purging the Universe of monsters since before we were born. What was his greatest foe? The one he's most famous for vanquishing?"

The image of a giant serpent began to form in Anubis' mind. Not Seth. This one was much larger. Truly monstrous. Its blurred silhouette shimmered like a dark flame. He could almost see it, almost recognise it, but… He squinted in an unconscious and futile attempt to sharpen the image.

"Apophis," she whispered.

The name seared through his mind like lightning. Pain lashed across his temples, so intense his legs faltered and he'd have fallen had she not steadied him. "Apo –" He did not finish the word.

"No one ever found out where Ra imprisoned him once vanquished," she said. "I guess we have now."

The ominously timed quake that followed barely compared to the shudder through Anubis' soul at the realisation that he had forgotten their pantheon's greatest enemy. He grimaced. Then snarled, "Mnemosyne!" A rage like no other burned through him. "That bitch dared to interfere with my mind?" he growled and would have howled if not for fear of looking even more stupid in Seshat's eyes. He felt violated. He could not trust his knowledge, his memories. All his plans and decisions put into question. His very self!

"How sure are you that the portal only goes one way?" she asked.

Was she mocking him? "I'm not sure of anything!" he shouted. And a truer statement had never been uttered by a god before. Already he'd again began to forget the embodiment of destructive chaos that had been Apophis. "We assume the link only goes one way, since none of the souls ever returned… but –" It was an asinine assumption at best.

"Cats! I need to write this down." Seshat conjured her notebook and pen. The moment the tip touched the page, she'd already forgotten why she'd conjured it.

∞

"Like father, like daughter, I see," Lyam said, pointing at the open volume in Seshat's hands. Last Seshat had perceived of him he had been yards behind. "What do you write about?"

She blinked at the page, unable for the life of her to remember what she'd wanted to write. The knowledge illusive like the words on the tip of her tongue, it had been clear just moments ago. Anubis scratched his forehead as if struggling to remember something himself. This fucking place, she cursed in frustration. She could not wait to leave it. "Nothing, apparently," she replied to the mortal, closing and dismissing the book belligerently.

"So how can you be sure Seth didn't go through like the others?" she asked Anubis once the moon settled, picking up their conversation.

"What…?" He looked dazed. Beads of sweat appeared at his temples. She figured the place had to be causing havoc with his talents as well, despite his nonchalant attitude. She felt no sympathy.

"How do you know he's still there? Have you seen him? Can you bring him back? I mean, you're a psychopomp for crying out loud."

There was something about his entire deal with Thoth she still didn't quite understand. Anubis had not told her the whole truth. Of that, she was certain.

Anubis shifted his gaze to her sheepishly. He felt strange, oddly anxious and embarrassed for no good reason. He willed himself to sound confident. "Taking souls to the Underworld is easy. Bringing them back… that's another thing entirely. The problem is…" He could swear he'd had this conversation before. Cats, he was tired. His head felt like mush. He longed to be done with this place. In the meantime, he indulged her foolish question. "We used mortals' souls to power the curse, to fight Seth's own will. We kept losing them by the score without understanding why. That's when we realised what we were dealing with. Now the Underworld is empty, and since I don't see any reanimated dead, I can only assume they're all gone. Perhaps to a better place, who knows?" He chuckled to himself. "Wouldn't that be just the thing? Your father and I have been purging the Universe of its most evil scum. What if they end up being the lucky ones?" He picked up the pace, not waiting for an answer. Or worse, another question. His explanations would not hold for long.

She rushed after him. "Souls are impervious to peer pressure. Without a mind to guide them, they have no will of their own. They would not simply walk into an abyss. Well, some might accidentally stumble into it, but all of them? They had to have been called or guided to it."

"Probably. Those souls were beyond redemption. Corrupted by the greed and envy of the creatures who possessed them. They would go after anything if they believed it would benefit them."

Realisation dawned on her. "You're afraid he did go to the other side. Not that he's crazy. You want him to forget what he saw there."

"Who are you talking about?" Lyam asked, trailing after them like a confused child. They were now only a few steps away from the main temple, and he had no memory of actually having walked there. Audric and Pandora walked behind him. But he could have sworn they'd been ahead of him just moments ago. His head hurt and he was tired. Probably contused as well.

Anubis ignored him. "Oh, he's crazy, all right," he said to Seshat. "But yes… we would like him to forget everything: what we did, why we did it, where he's been, who he might have met. We want him to forget this place ever existed."

Good luck with that, she thought.

She had more to say on the subject. All forgotten the moment Thoth's deep voice penetrated her mind.

'Welcome, Sunshine.'

She could have mewed.

CHAPTER 27

The Reunion

*The Underworlds were no accident but the
product of a bicameral mind. Chronos didn't
know what he was doing. Only that it needed
to be done.*

– Memory on Record

Suddenly all curiosity, worry and frustration drained from her, leaving only a sense of deep resignation.

"Oh, cats," Seshat mewed, bracing herself for the aggravation of seeing her father again. She changed into her formal attire: long golden dress emblazoned with jet-black spots and a headband sporting a seven-pointed leaf. She hadn't worn this aspect since the pantheon's golden era in ancient Midgard. The garments actually smelled old. Still, she figured the occasion called for it. Thoth was a stickler for protocol.

"This is a pyramid," she almost gasped, gazing at the chamber before her – a real pyramid, not the opulent imitations mortals built to honour the egos of their kings. Which meant the temple was not only a temple but a shrine. "Just how old is this place, Anubis?"

"I already told you. No one knows. Our best guess is older than Chronos."

"That's not possible," she said.

He smiled wolfishly. "My dear Seshat. Everything was possible before Chronos, if only because there were so few possibilities. Now…" He puffed his cheeks. "The impossible is keeping track of all of them."

She frowned at him, unsure if he was being serious or not.

"Eloin!" Lyam blurted out, shoving past the two gods without ceremony or apology, the first to enter the pyramidal room. And there he stopped, unable to take another step. The site had changed dramatically since the last time he'd stood on that very same spot, only a few shifts ago. The hatch wasn't merely open, it had vanished entirely. The ground floor around it had collapsed, revealing a chasm as dark and deep as the one they'd found in the dry riverbed, except the walls of this pit bulged with gnarled tree roots covered in reptilian scales. They weren't roots, of course. No tree root ever moved like these. They pulsed, burrowed through and wrapped around the stone as if trying to crush it. Some questing tendrils slithered above the rim, like snakes or the tentacles of some monstrous predator searching for prey.

Thoth levitated in the centre of the room, looking radiant. Behind him, Eloin, also in midair, swayed gently, her eyelids fluttering as if in a trance. There came the echoes of screams from all around them, terrible and eerie. A torrent of pleas and curses of countless souls, similar to the horror Lyam had sensed earlier from the void left by the river. Only this was louder, closer, and much more threatening. He shook his head, trying to clear it and focus his awareness. Not all the screams were coming from the depths. The loudest and most desperate seemed to be actually coming from above and behind the walls: Narrum screams, more animal than human, caused by hunger and anger rather than fear or despair.

Nenhum and Ninguém stood guard on opposite sides of the horrific pit. Their solemn expressions broke into a smile when they saw them. "Hey! You made it," they said, beckoning enthusiastically. "Come down. We're about to get started!"

The greeting was so casual and jovial and so at odds with the rest of the scene, Lyam took a step back, unsure it was real.

"Are those the gods we've been waiting for?" one twin – he could never tell which – asked the other.

"Either that or they are the strangest aliens I've seen," the other replied, smirking.

"I suppose that amounts to the same thing." His twin smirked back. Both laughed.

"Belus and Agenor...?" whispered Seshat, awe-struck with disbelief. All the possibilities, indeed.

"Who?" Lyam intoned.

Anubis shook his head, imperceptible to anyone but a god.

Seshat licked her lips. "They remind me of these characters I once wrote about, that's all," she said to Lyam, glaring at Anubis. It seemed that, impossible or not, her father had been keeping track of a plethora of possibilities. She had yet to grasp the full scope of this story.

Lyam glanced back at Audric, trying to read something in the man, for he certainly got nothing useful from the gods. They all seemed to have barricades around their thoughts and emotions thicker than the temple walls. The Lokian wasn't looking at the pit, though. He had his gaze locked on something behind Lyam's head. The hairs on his nape bristled. He turned.

"Welcome back, Anpu." The artificial voice came from the figure of a man who stepped from behind a pillar. He wore a tattered cloak stained grey with several layers of ash, and he carried himself with the detached, icy demeanour of an efficient clerk. Lyam jumped back, but the man hadn't been addressing him; his black eyes were fixed on Anubis. "What took you so long?"

"Chronos, mostly," said Anubis, matching the man's cynical tone.

"Ah… He always does." The man blinked, shifting his gaze to Pandora. His confidence and aloofness were gone in an instant. "What are you doing here? I told you to stay in the tower."

Her body language hinted at a shrug. "I got bored."

"Bored?" he scoffed. "You're not supposed to understand the meaning of the word, let alone feel it."

A shadow rippled across Pandora's features. "I feel many things: boredom, longing, amusement… and right now, looking at you" – she paused, and for a moment as she pinned him with her unnatural gaze, the light in the room seemed to dim, somewhat – "contempt."

"Yes, well, we're all familiar with that particular emotion, believe me," he told her flippantly. "Still, you shouldn't be able to feel anything, nor display such attitude. Who's responsible for this behaviour?" he demanded of the group.

"That would be me," Audric said rather proudly.

The man scanned him up and down with interest. "And who might you be?" He leaned closer, looked right into his eyes, rather too knowingly for Audric's comfort.

"I'm Lokian," Audric said, hoping to discomfort the forward Nephilim.

"You don't say…" Crymure curled his lip. "Well, Lokian. Since you broke her, you can keep her. Congratulations. But ah! Where are my manners? We've never actually met before. I'm Crymure," he added, extending his hand in greeting.

Audric opened his mouth to give the infuriating construct a piece of his mind but, upon noting the artificial hand with its exposed artificial skeletal fingers stretched out towards him, decided against it. There was as much point in arguing with a machine as greeting one.

Crymure clicked his tongue. "Ah, you Lokians and your sensibilities. There is just no right way to deal with you lot. So averse to your own ingenuity, disgusted by the very anatomy you've created. It doesn't hurt, although I doubt you even wondered. It doesn't ooze, nor is it contagious." He offered his hand again. Audric would not touch it. He'd rather cut off his own hand, but disgust had little to do with it. Caution stopped him, for the line between Lokian and Nephilim was thinner than skin, as were most lines between creator and creation.

Crymure gave him a knowing smile. "Come on! I had to literally crawl and climb my way through the innards of this accursed moon to get here, and you cringe at the sight of exposed phalanges? For the Mentor's sake! How will we ever respect each other enough to get along?" There was a hint of a threat in the rhetorical question. Audric's eyes shone redder.

"You're Crymure," Lyam blurted involuntarily, his gaze transfixed by the proffered mechanical hand.

"My reputation precedes me. How flattering." His tone was artificially cheerful, without taking his eyes from Audric.

"Berdnard mentioned you, yes," said Lyam.

This got his attention. "Ah! And how is the crabby dwarf?" There was genuine interest in his question.

"Dead," said Anubis.

"Oh, that's a shame." Crymure sounded dismayed. "I very much enjoyed our talks. Such an industrious fellow, that one. I anticipate travelling to his home world to collect the rare gemstones his kind digs out. We're always in need of gems." He tapped his bracelet for reference. One of the stones was missing.

Audric absently fingered a nearly identical bracelet beneath his sleeve.

"You're planning on leaving?" Lyam interjected.

Crymure smiled, reading his intention well enough. "Alas, the Underworld is not an option for a Nephilim. That is why we do whatever it takes to stay in reality." He spoke meaningfully to Anubis.

Seshat cleared her throat loud enough for the sound to echo off the walls.

"Ah yes," Anubis said, not without annoyance. "Crymure, allow me to introduce Seshat, the goddess of writing, storytelling, ruler of books and measurements, creator of characters and rider of sphinxes."

She fought the urge to strangle him. "Anything else?"

He tapped his chin in affectation. "Ah! Of course, how could I forget: scion of Ra and daughter of our highly esteemed god of reckoning over there, Thoth."

Crymure grinned. "You are exactly what I expected."

Seshat didn't like the sound of that. But Anubis continued before she had a chance to demand an elaboration of the comment. "Careful, Crymure. You'll find Seshat has a way of both thwarting and exceeding everyone's expectations."

I will scratch your eyes out, Anubis, she warned telepathically.

"Enchanted." The Nephilim's insidious grin widened as he took her hand in his, raising it to his lips. Seshat let him take it without frown or flinch. If he thought he could disconcert her with his skeletal touch, he clearly had underestimated her.

"My pleasure," she said, channelling Ideth, a nymph she'd met in Niflheim. She'd had a way of making any creature – man, woman, beast or machine – bewitched by her charms.

Crymure's eyes, large and completely black like Namrive's, narrowed suspiciously. First at her, then at Anubis. Clearly this was not the reaction he'd been expecting, but he adapted quickly enough. "Right, let's get down to business. Namrive briefed you on the situation, right?"

Anubis puffed his cheeks. "This particular situation? No. I had to work out most of it by myself. Tell me, was the omission of certain details due to ignorance, miscommunication or my attempted murder?"

"Likely all of the above, I'm afraid," he replied casually.

"And Mnemosyne?" Seshat prompted.

Crymure winced slightly. "Our mistake."

Seshat's eyes widened. "A Nephilim admitting to a mistake? Wait a moment. I need to record this." Papyrus and quill appeared in her hand. She pretended to write.

Crymure pressed his lips in annoyance. He hated being mocked, especially by a god. "We had only stone, ash, and wreckage available to build the soul catcher. We're the best engineers in the Universe, not sorcerers," he added in his defence.

No… thank fuck for that, she thought.

"And don't let me start on the difficulties we had adapting a host," he said.

"I couldn't care less about your difficulties," said she.

"You start by not caring about the big things, the ones you can't control or change. Then you realise the small things are not worth caring about either. And before you know it, you don't care enough to breathe," Pandora crooned.

Bemused silence followed.

"Right…" Crymure gestured the group to follow him. "Come, come! Time is of the essence, as they say. The tale of what happened after you left sounds less dramatic when told in motion."

"I care nothing for your tales." Audric turned on his heels, pulling Pandora with him.

Her hand brushed Seshat's, and the goddess gasped, immediately grasping her by the wrist. "Mnemosyne?" The mind was different, the personality even more so. But there was something familiar nonetheless. She had been her host. Seshat kicked herself for not realising it sooner.

Audric immediately manoeuvred himself between the two women, forcing Seshat to let go of Pandora's wrist. She resisted. The temptation to incinerate the bold cat was great, but then she would be no better than Anubis. Seshat wouldn't allow that.

Pandora smiled in sympathy. "The goddess of memory left an imprint in my mind, but she did not stay. She has a mind of her own, a much better mind than this one." She pointed to her temple. "But she has not forgotten you, Sunshine. She will fulfil her promise when you're ready."

"I've been ready for an age!"

"Ready to let go," Audric said through clenched teeth, tightening his own grip. There was such finality in his words, like the full stop at the end of a book.

Seshat released Pandora's wrist and swallowed, feeling as if she might suffocate as she watched them go. They were writing his own story and she had no part in it.

"If that's a Lokian, I'm an Olympian," Crymure said with an attempted snort, then turned to Anubis. "You should be more selective about your priests, Anpu."

"I am." The words were layered with annoyance and admonition "Seshat, ready?"

She nodded.

PART V

"Morality came with time."
"You mean, in time?"
"No."

– Memory on Record

CHAPTER 28

The Reckoning

A clear conscience is a sign of bad memory.

– Memory on Record

Seshat listened to Crymure's account of events with quiet scepticism. The Nephilim was too flippant to be a reliable narrator. Nephilim weren't known for their storytelling skills, true, but they valued details and objectivity to a detrimental degree in their reports. He didn't. If anyone, the goddess of writing would be able to recognise a constructed narrative. There were some elements of truth to it, of course, as all lies need a touch of truth to be believable, but for the most part, it was – for lack of a better word – bullshit.

According to him, Namrive – who, due to the nature of her agreement with the Suzerain, was keeping a close eye on Niflheim – had intercepted a message (intended for Pallas) regarding the sudden and persistent malfunction of their main teleportation ring. She'd immediately set out to investigate and, Niflheim being what it was, had requested Anubis to accompany her as an adviser on aspects related to the Underworld.

This much appeared to be mostly true. Seshat had witnessed what had caused the malfunction herself.

Apparently Anubis had jumped at the opportunity to accompany Namrive on the journey with the secret intention of saving Seshat from what he considered to be a pointless, reckless and very dangerous undertaking. Again, so far, nothing too out of character for the god of the dead, who never missed a chance to shirk his responsibilities or meddle in the affairs of other gods. But no god would leave their work unfinished by choice, certainly not Anubis. He left nothing to chance, for he knew Tyche was a bitch.

"The binding of the chaos god was pretty secure by that point," Crymure explained. "All we needed was a few more souls. We figured the Tributes collected by the Suzerain would suffice. Anubis' clandestine excursion with Namrive would solve everyone's problems."

Except, it hadn't. Nothing had gone according to Namrive's and Anubis' plans (except his efforts to convince Seshat to join him, infuriatingly). They'd brought no souls back with them, having barely escaped with their own intact.

"So that's what the Tributes were for?" she'd asked, as if disappointed by the revelation.

The Suzerain had made the most of the Narrum predisposition to breed by turning their women and children into currency. She'd figured the Tributes – as they'd called them, as if being one was an honour – provided the Nephilim with slave labour and an abundance of subjects for their experiments. Maybe even food for a few beasts. In truth, like with so many other things, she never actually gave their fate much thought.

"Not all of them, of course," Anubis explained airily. "The majority were sent to Pallas for, er… multiple purposes – we had to keep sending them or the Mentor would get suspicious, you see. But the Suzerain was so efficient in these duties, we always managed to smuggle a few hundred for ourselves."

The gods of the Underworld deal with souls the same way a farmer deals with cattle, she mused.

On Sombra, things hadn't gone according to plan either. No sooner had Anubis departed the system than Seth had called upon the moon to shield himself from Ra. When Anubis and Namrive did not return, Crymure assumed they'd been captured, trapped in Helheim or Hades' Underworld.

"We held on for as long as we could, but we needed more souls to power the curse, and we couldn't just ask Pallas to send them from other worlds," he explained.

"Why not?" Seshat asked.

"That would alert the Mentor," the Nephilim replied as if he had no need to.

"So?" she insisted.

The god of the dead and the android outcast exchanged a discreet but very complicit look. "Er… well, we'd already reported the situation as resolved. The Mentor reacts poorly to contretemps," said the latter. "You do know who she is, right?"

"Yes," she admitted. And she understood very well why the two of them would rather move entire galaxies than deal with Athena. But not her father, though. He would never shy away from a rational argument or a good fight, especially with younger goddesses from rival pantheons, for he took great pleasure in educating them. Which meant whatever they'd been up to in that temple had not been the task assigned by the Mentor – to bind Seth – but something else. Something far more ambitious and personal.

As luck would have it – and Crymure was adamant the goddess of fortune had been involved – when everything seemed lost, Mnemosyne – the ship – had appeared in orbit, closely followed by the Prometheans, who he figured had stumbled upon the moon while searching for their arch-enemies, the Lokians, who had long been on the moon, working with the scions of Ra without realising they in turn worked for their greatest mistake and adversary, the Nephilim.

Seshat was tempted to start taking notes in order to keep track of this mess of assumptions and misunderstandings.

After the ships collided, fortune had once again prevailed and most of the crew and cargo survived.

Despite her extensive and highly aggravating research aboard Namrive's ship, Seshat still did not understand enough about technology to calculate the odds of such a collision in orbit, let alone a survivable landing afterwards. Her own experience had taught her that spaceships were indeed prone to malfunction and highly susceptible to user error. And just because gods were all but powerless inside them didn't mean they wouldn't be able to exert power over them from the outside. In any case, every record on the subject seemed to contradict itself, so she just took Crymure's account with a large pinch of salt.

According to him, this turn of events solved at least one of the gods' problems: between the Prometheans and the Narrum now stranded on Sombra, they had plenty of souls at hand to subdue Seth's will, but they had no way to do it without Anubis to guide them (and certainly not to do it discreetly or without resistance from the mortals the souls belonged to). And then there was, of course, the issue of the quality of said souls.

"If it had just been Prometheans, we'd have been fine. But they brought the Narrum with them, and Narrum can be horrendous beasts when hungry or threatened. Not to mention their souls are invariably weak and rotten by their narrowmindedness. Such despicable creatures." Crymure shook his head in reproach.

"Riots broke out – for that's the only way Narrum handle grievances – and the Promethean elders perished along with most of the Lokians – their fine souls and minds lost to oblivion. The surviving Lokians deflected to the Nephilim in the aftermath, preferring to rationalise with their estranged creations rather than their irrational cousins. Thoth did his best to keep the pyramid hidden, buying time by glamouring both Narrum and Prometheans – now practically leaderless – into forgetting the gruesome details of their association and animosity long enough to cohabit underground without incident – not an easy task, even for a god, let me tell you. Meanwhile, I, who had always remained hidden on the surface to avoid further complications, set out to spy on the Nephilim survivors, making sure they did not leave or send any message out that might expose their dealings on the moon. Not my proudest moment, but there was too much at stake. Many of our kind take protocol a bit too seriously. I, myself, prefer to adapt. Especially in situations that fit no protocols."

"Hmmm," Seshat said. Things got even more far-fetched after that.

Crymure admitted to have been the one who'd modified the Lokian Dayna – with her consent – to host Mnemosyne's soul. That too had failed miserably, for the souls of Titans cannot be contained by mortal flesh no matter how enhanced. The rest, Seshat already knew or could guess at. After the vessel had failed to contain Mnemosyne's soul, the goddess of memory fled from everyone's Reach but not from their minds. Memories became unreliable. Many were entirely lost. And the moon, caught between the mighty willpower of Seth and Ra, began to tear itself apart. The structural damage to the underground had led the mortals to the temple and, true to their curiosity, they'd begun uncovering it until, finally, Anubis returned.

"And not a moment too soon!" Crymure exulted.

"That is quite the story," Seshat said circumspectly. The whole narrative had lasted long enough for them to descend to the temple floor proper and make their way slowly around the precarious rim to join Thoth and Eloin, now poised above an altar that looked an awful lot like a throne.

"Well, it was more of a summary than a story – a report, if you will. I'd never dare to claim to have told a story to the goddess of stories herself," Crymure said demurely.

Seshat smiled politely, making sure no glare escaped her heavily decorated eyes.

"So what happened to the Nephilim?" asked Lyam, who'd been listening intently to Crymure's every word.

Crymure flinched, or as Namrive would say,

glitched, before answering. "They, hm, fell into the abyss."

Lyam's eyes narrowed. "All of them? Tripped and tumbled into the abyss. Just like that? Or perhaps they were all swimming in the river when it happened."

Crymure pressed his lips. "There's no need to be snide. They all fell in of their own free will. I was there. I saw it all." He shrugged. "I can't explain it. Nephilim have more sense than that, I assure you. But that's how it happened."

"Oh, I believe you. I witnessed someone throw herself in too." Lyam pointed to his bruised face. "She gave me this before she jumped. Clearly she knew what she was doing."

The Nephilim nodded, not quite catching Lyam's meaning but not quite interested enough to care. "The god of chaos is a terrible thing. He's mad..." he said instead.

"I know. I felt his influence," Lyam admitted. "But I'm still here. This leads me to believe the madness only really has an effect on Nephilim and Lokian. Why is that?"

Crymure's thin eyebrows knitted in annoyance. "Felt it, did you? And how can you be sure that what you felt was the same thing they did? Or have you considered that perhaps the Abyss spared you because it doesn't want you?"

"Both excellent points," said Anubis diplomatically, before Lyam could react. "By all means, discuss them at length when they become pertinent again. We have more pressing matters to attend right now. Shall we?" He gestured towards the dais, where Thoth now stood recording their every word and gesture, black tome in hand, gilded quill steady in the other, forbearing as a monument to discipline. Seshat went first. Her countenance still held the beatific expression she'd held during Crymure's tale as she hesitantly, unwillingly, but inevitably faced her father.

"Seshat…" The god of reckoning scrutinised her dispassionately from headband to sandal, taking inventory of each item and judging everything he saw. "Why do you still dress like that? You should have acquired a more sensible taste by now."

"What?" Seshat blinked in incomprehension, then took stock of herself, finding nothing amiss.

"You look like a spotted cat," he said.

Seshat's eyes opened wide with outrage. "These are stars! They represent the constellations of –" She caught her reflection in the gold ankh embedded in his chest and choked down her next words. He was right. The black dots on her yellow dress did resemble those of a cheetah. I've worn this aspect for ages! she realised, mortified. She immediately eliminated the spots and replaced them with a sheen of starlight, making the fabric glow like liquid gold. Let's see if you can find fault now, Father, she grumbled to herself, standing proud.

"And you still favour hemp over papyrus, I see," Thoth said, curling his lip at her headband in reproach.

"Hemp has many applications; it's an extremely versatile plant," she stated in a dignified, matter-of-fact manner. That she would not change. In fact, her first instinct was to conjure a lit pipe of dried hemp flowers and blow the smoke in his face. But she didn't think she could fall any lower on her father's scale of disapproval. Besides, as much as she would like to soothe her frayed nerves, she'd need a clear mind to deal with whatever he threw at her next.

It'd been millennia since they last saw each other, and yet it was as if they'd spoken only yesterday. Seshat wondered if that was due to their long lives, or because no matter how long gods lived, they never really changed much.

"Well, Father. Here I am. I hope you didn't have Anubis drag me all the way from Niflheim to criticise my attire and herb choice."

Thoth's amber eyes slid from her to the god of the dead. "You didn't tell her?"

"I told her what I knew." Anubis spread his arms to take in the temple. "I had no idea what happened here after we left. Still not quite sure, to be honest. We always said that if there was ever a danger of exposure, we'd bury the temple."

"I did."

"Then why, in Ra's name, have you uncovered it again?"

"You buried it?" Lyam exclaimed sharply. "I knew there had to be a reason why you wouldn't just flick your fingers to clear it. You were stalling. Keeping us stuck in this hole. Working like peasants. You untrustworthy fuck." He pointed a finger at Eloin. "And what did you do to my sister?"

Thoth's hint of a smile was all condescension. "I have also stalled her fate. You're welcome."

"Let it go, brother," Eloin said, her voice barely

above a whisper, her eyes still fluttering, unseeing. "I am all right. And you're here now. Everything will be all right. Listen to what the gods have to say."

"I'd rather he didn't." Thoth spoke with such gravity it forestalled whatever anyone was about to say next. He beckoned the twins. "Take the mortal and the Nephilim away until we need them. I wish to talk to my daughter and Anubis alone."

"Only gods allowed, is that the way of things?" Crymure sneered.

"Precisely." Thoth glared coldly at him.

Lyam stood his ground. "I'm staying with Eloin."

Nenhum and Ninguém were suddenly behind him, each gripping an arm. "Hey!" he protested.

"You had your chance to be reasoned with." Thoth glowed like hot embers as he spoke. Lyam would bet he'd burn himself if he even dared to lean closer. "Now it's too late."

The twins pulled him back inexorably.

"Eloin!" Lyam pleaded.

"It's all right, brother," she whispered again in her trance. "Trust the gods. Everything will be all right."

Lyam's mouth went slack. "Eloin…" he whispered once more has they took him away. Crymure waved artificially as they passed him. Then he turned and followed close behind, seemingly content in his obedience.

∞

While Crymure strove to distract the goddess of writing with words, Anubis and Thoth took the opportunity to have a private word of their own.

'Thoth… what the fuck?' Anubis asked the moment he stepped into the pyramid.

Thoth didn't reply. Anubis took another step, another breath, and rephrased the question. He knew how much the old god hated mortal slang.

'Why are you still here? Why am I here? And why is Seth still… well… still! We had a plan, remember? A perfect plan. What happened?'

The god of reckoning always had impeccable posture. His face remained ethereally composed. Of the three scions of Ra present in the room, he was the one who would never pass as anything else. Not all gods are created equal, and whoever created Thoth clearly had broken the mould.

'Tyche happened,' he said in his clear orator's voice with barely a hint of distaste, as if it'd been foolish to expect anything else. 'Tyche and the Fates. Ra himself,' he added, and there was definitely some passion in there now.

'What would Ra care for our scheme? He never wanted any part in the dispute between Horus and Seth.'

Again, something monstrous slithered across Anubis' mind. He focused all his will on it and saw Ra engaged in mortal combat with a snake of galactic proportions. He remembered his conversation with Seshat earlier and this time the memory didn't fade. The trap had already closed.

'Mnemosyne set us up. Why? She can't blame us for what happened to her.'

'No, she doesn't blame us. She blames the entire Universe. However, she's alone in this.'

'Oh, cats. Thoth, please tell me Ra will help us.'

Thoth looked at Anubis the way he did when judging souls on his scales and said, 'He is Ra. What about Seshat?'

It was Anubis' turn to look critical. 'She's your daughter.'

CHAPTER 29

The Query

*Many events have been set in motion by His
arrival, and they'll only stop upon his leaving.*

– Memory on Record

Thoth, book and quill still in hand, turned on Seshat as
soon as Lyam and Crymure were out of earshot. "Will
you Reach Mnemosyne?" A demand with a question
mark.

Why, Father, how nice of you to ask how I've been
this past age. What I've done, what I've written. Or
what are my thoughts on this insane attempt to rewrite
the history of our pantheon! she almost retorted but
managed to answer him as best she dared. "I'm not the
goddess of the soul."

"And we're all thankful for that," her father said in
a way that left her wondering what he really meant.
"Now answer me. Can you Reach her or not?"

"Not."

He glowered at her the way parents have glowered
at their misbehaving children since time immemorial.
"Seshat, this isn't the time to be stubborn. And don't try

to be clever with me either. Neither wit nor lies, not even one of your characters will work on me, for I am the one who wrote every aspect of your personality. I gave you life, made you into who you are, taught you how to write. How to think! Or have you forgotten that?"

Stars, she could really use that smoke right about now. "No."

"So use your personal connection to the goddess of memory and convince her to make an appearance."

"You think I haven't tried?"

"Try harder."

"Why? You've never shown interest in memories. Only records."

"On the contrary. Memories are the measurement units of conscience. They are crucial to my records."

Seshat stilled herself, trying really hard not to say something she might regret. "I've been searching for Mnemosyne for an age. She clearly doesn't want to be found. And it's not like I can pray to her, either. So what the fuck am I supposed to do?"

Praying was for mortals, particularly humans. More than once, Seshat had envied their ability to disrupt a god's peace no matter where they were in the Universe. This boon had been the idea of Epimetheus, the god of hindsight – and Prometheus' asinine brother – to make up for their lack of Reach, the same way intellect and souls were supposed to make up for humans' lack of… well, pretty much everything else. Through prayer they were able to talk directly to a god no matter the distance or whether the god wanted to hear them or not. It took some effort to master the ability to block out all that incessant whining.

A god calling on another god, on the other hand, was easy if they were relatively close, preferably in sight. But all gods made exceptions for those they cared about, expanding their range of communication across galaxies and realms by mutual agreement and sheer will. The goddess of memory and the goddess of writing had long shared such a bond, and it was precisely because Seshat had felt that bond being severed that she'd began searching for her friend.

"Call to her," said Anubis almost patiently. "She's close. She'll hear you from here, I'm sure." He gestured at the altar. "That is her shrine."

Seshat blinked, taking in the pyramidal room in a whole new light. Shrines allowed a direct line of communication to gods. More than that, the god in question was always obliged to answer the call even if only to say "leave me alone". Shrines were rare things, the remnants of a much more civilised Cosmos, before humans and their endless demands came along.

This also confirmed Seshat's suspicion that the memory ship hadn't appeared in Sombra's orbit by chance, unless Chance was after Mnemosyne as well, of course. Seshat hated that idea. That whatever she did would be what Anubis, her father, or – stars forbid – Fate, wanted her to do. There was still much to this story she didn't know or understand. She needed to find out more before she even dared opening her mind to that ancient conduit.

"Why would she have a shrine here, of all places? I've been told memory has little to no influence in the Underworld."

Thoth lifted his eyes off the page long enough to roll

them as if he'd never heard such an idiotic question. "That is precisely why the shrine exists. She needs it."

"Actually, she doesn't. We do," Anubis said. "And still she defies us, plays with us, gives us access to only a trickle of her power. Titans…tsk. They believe they're so much better than us just because they're older. Age wasn't even a thing before Chronos arrived, for cat's sake."

The god of reckoning harrumphed at the interruption. "Pull yourself together, Anubis. Many things weren't a thing before Chronos arrived. It's tragic that we have no more control over time than it has over gravity. We simply write on the page that we are given."

"Seems to me there's a lot written on that page already," muttered Seshat.

"Another reason to turn it over, then," Anubis said.

Seshat cared little for the troubles caused by the God of Time compared to those caused by gravity, what it did to stars, for example, or how she felt about the idea that gods, her own kin, had used this obscure power to force the will of another in such a way. It made them no better than the Nephilim in her eyes.

She turned to her father and made no effort to disguise the condemnation in her tone. "So that's how you're able to glamour the mortals of their memories."

"Not just the mortals. The Nephilim as well," Anubis answered for him.

"The Nephilim can be glamoured?" she breathed disbelievingly, gaze shifting in the direction Crymure had gone. Now that she thought about it, he did seem a bit… off. Not stripped of willpower like the ensorcelled Promethean woman swaying in midair, but not exactly all there either. If there was one thing she'd learned about the Nephilim during her time with Namrive, it was that they mimicked the gods' traits all too well. Crymure was just too subservient, too nice to be genuine. He reminded her of Hermes in a weird way. She'd never been able to figure out his character, either, and she now wondered what had happened to the tricksy messenger after Psyche broke his curse.

Thoth pressed his lips, annoyed at Anubis, who had so carelessly exposed their secret. "It's an interesting fact. One they are not aware of yet," he warned. "It appears Lokians copied the human mind all too well. They are not only susceptible to illusions but completely clueless about magic as well."

"Ain't that brilliant?" Anubis sounded practically giddy, which she didn't think was pretence. What a pair they make, she thought in dismay.

She understood why Anubis, devious, lazy cat that he was, found the susceptibility useful. But her father? Thoth had always valued truth above all else. Glamour was beneath him. "Why are you doing this, Father?" she insisted earnestly, hoping to appeal to his integrity and famously infallible reason. He had his faults, all gods did, but he always played fair. Or used to… "Have you forgotten our first tenet? We don't interfere. We observe and record. We don't tell others what to think or how to act."

"That is the problem. We should have interfered long ago."

Hermes had once told her the same thing. She disagreed then and even more so now, after no good came from her interference in Niflheim.

"Problem?" she said, affecting surprise and scepticism. "I don't see a problem. I see a bloody catastrophe! I always thought it would be the Olympians or the Aesir or even the mindless followers of that self-righteous god drunk on his own piety who would bring the end to all stories. Not us, for cat's sake! We are the rational ones. The worthy. The enlightened."

"Yes. And only light can conquer darkness," Thoth said, glowing brighter to reinforce the point.

"Light is pointless without darkness. To conquer one is to invalidate the other," she replied coldly.

"This Universe once existed without light, so why can't it exist without darkness?" her father countered.

She had no rational response, just her intuition telling her it couldn't.

"It's not for us to decide how the Universe should be. We are scions of Ra!" she said when all other reasons failed her.

And the moment she uttered the words she realised she'd lost the argument. For Ra was a god of light, after all.

"Precisely," Thoth stated triumphantly, ankh burning bright on his chest.

She stiffened, fists clenched, hardly recognising him but not backing down. "If you respect him so much. Why did you let him do that to himself?"

That did not intimidate Thoth in the least. If anything, it made him more resolute. "I showed him my respect by not interfering in his decision. He'd been gone to us long before the Nephilim came for him. He just needed a reason to become what he always wanted to be – a star. Unlike the rest of us left to oblivion, his name will be remembered for eternity."

"Sounds like you're jealous."

Thoth's eyes narrowed. "I am disappointed. He revealed himself to be a true god, indeed. Selfish and vain. Unable to see beyond his own radiance. Don't talk to me about tenets, Seshat. I recorded and supported his every deed. And remained concealed in his light. Unmentioned. Uncredited. Unrewarded." His eyes darkened. "Once I asked him for the Midgard sun. He had so many stars under his control back then. And what did he do? He gave me the moon instead." The ankh on his chest turned cold. "So now, I'll use this moon to do what he never had the courage to do with all his suns. And I shall be remembered. Forever." He resumed his writing as if struck by vindictive inspiration.

"I'm remembered," she said rather petulantly, seeing how deep Ra's decision cut through Thoth's soul.

He chuckled derisively. "Sure, remembered as Homer and Herodotus or Lucan. Seshat is not a name familiar even to us gods." He paused to point his quill at her. "Why is it that you always pick male authors to write your chronicles, Seshat?" he asked as an afterthought. "It can't be just to annoy me, surely."

For a moment she considered telling him where to shove his quill, but took a deep breath instead. "Because, throughout the history of humanity, women weren't allowed to write. Even amongst gods, I struggled to leave your shadow. I reckon many still believe I'm just another one of your aspects."

He waved the offending feather dismissively. "Don't blame me for that nonsense. I'm not the one who created a race predisposed to such bias. As to you being one of my aspects –"

Anubis coughed, then tapped his foot impatiently, gesturing at the shrine. "Family issues will have to wait. We are wasting time."

Seshat clenched her jaw. Family issues always had to wait; that was why they never got resolved. "I honestly don't understand what you two expect from me," she lied. "Mnemosyne won't answer just because it's me calling. She won't risk being caught again." Still, she must answer something. The prospect made Seshat's heart flutter against her chest.

"I sincerely hope you're wrong about that too," her father said tartly. He took her by the arm and forced her to face the altar. Seshat did not resist. A few paces closer made no difference. Altars were treacherous things, used for sacrifices as well as worship. "This temple has the power to magnify a god's Reach. At the cost of diminishing their every other power," Thoth added resentfully. "That's how I've been able to track and guide the narratives of all these minds. You should be able to track at least one."

Seshat glanced at Anubis, almost pleadingly; he didn't even blink at her. The demigod twins, now returned from wherever they'd taken Lyam, smirked at her. One winked. She glanced at the mortal Eloin, whose mind was so far gone, she was hardly even there, much like her pulse. Her eyes remained closed. "Why are you keeping her alive, Father?"

"She might still be useful. Now kneel," Thoth commanded. "Gods respond well to humility, especially from other gods."

Seshat knelt. She was already humiliated. On her feet or on her knees, it made little difference.

"I have a question," she said before daring to open her mind to the shrine.

"You've had nothing but questions," Anubis quipped impatiently.

She ignored him. "Why glamour their memories? If Lokians are our allies, the Prometheans and Narrum could have been swayed to our cause, or failing that, eliminated." Her father had little patience for mortals; Anubis none at all. That they'd suffered them this long proved she hadn't been told the whole truth about that particular plot point either.

"We removed the memories in order to access the potential of the soul. See how an individual acts without the burden of their existence or our influence," Thoth said, confirming her suspicions.

"I see." And make them a lot more amiable in the process, for they'd never learn if they can't remember what they'd learnt…

Gods, especially gods like Thoth, should know better.

She sat back on her ankles, staying as far away from the altar as possible while still kneeling in front of it. She'd indeed begun to see the big picture and didn't like what she saw one bit. Still, she had to hear her father say it. There could be no assumptions or misunderstandings now. Her very soul depended on it.

"But why do you need Mnemosyne at all, then?

You seem to be doing fine with just her shrine and the talent you borrowed from it. What have you two cats really been up to, and why do you need me to find her so badly?"

Thoth and Anubis exchanged glances. "Too many questions."

"Oh, for cat's sake. I deserve to know."

Thoth immersed himself in his book, leaving Anubis to come up with the explanations.

The god of the dead bit out a curse. "It's like I told you before. There's no telling what Seth's state of mind is. But we can guess. I mean, you've seen the damned planet, right? Personally – and for the record" – he added assertively – "I was against releasing him. There are too many chaos gods already. They cause nothing but trouble. Anyway… what we're trying to do is con-vert – er… no, that's not the right word – persuade Seth to our cause. Or at the very least, make him a bit more… manageable. Like we did with the mortals, freeing them from their recollections and traumas so they are easier to control." He turned to Thoth with a pretend sigh. "It actually sounds stupid when you say it out loud, doesn't it?"

"Storms can be controlled to some degree," the god of reckoning replied casually.

"Seth's a lot more than a storm. He's chaos itself. I doubt even Loki can control him," Seshat said.

"Now there's a thought," Anubis mused, ears perk-ing up. A smirk formed on his snout as he envisioned both gods annihilating each other in a contest of wills. A god can dream… He shook himself back to the moment.

"In any case, meddling with the feeble wills of mortals is one thing. To edit a god's mind, we need the one whose entire reason for existing is doing just that."

Seshat frowned, not liking how Anubis referred to a deity's talent as a commodity. He'd spent too long amongst the Nephilim, she decided. Something still didn't add up, though. "So you were feeding him souls in order to control him better, is that it?"

Anubis shook his head, shoulders hunching in frustration. "No. Haven't you been listening? We used the souls to power the curse first. We made a ritual out of it – chanting and all. It was quite the spectacle. There's something about harmonised vocals that facilitates this sort of thing. Almost as if enough voices in unison can influence the soul or express it somehow. Magic users seem to believe it too, so maybe there's something there."

Thoth cleared his throat. "Stick to the point."

"All right. I'll keep it brief, in a language you might understand: The curse won't last. It's failing because the souls are being destroyed by something on the other side. We didn't even realise there was another side until it was too late. Now Seth will be free a lot sooner than we planned, so we need Mnemosyne to edit his memories before he returns. We fear that the poor quality of the souls we used – let's put it that way – how we used them and, of course, the abyss itself, might have had an effect on Seth's mental state."

"You think?!"

"We know." Thoth closed his book audibly. "Cats, you two kittens would argue until the stars freeze," he said, practically shimmering with annoyance. "Seshat, how many different ways do you want Anubis to repeat the same story?"

"I just want to make sure the story is true. It's my life, my very soul, that I'm putting at risk just by kneeling here."

He nodded slightly, his light shimmering. "I did not want you involved in this, Seshat. But here you are, so please play your part. The time for stories is past. Feel free to write about this unpleasant event once we're finished. You can even cast me as your villain. Just stop stalling and get the bloody Titaness here."

Thoth never cursed. *They are afraid,* she realised. She'd never thought of her father as even being capable of fear – or cursing – but she supposed the idea of unleashing a mad god of chaos with a thirst for vengeance would put any deity on edge.

You brought me here because I've always been neutral in the gods' disputes. As if that will save me from Seth's wrath. Do you even care what happens to me or Mnemosyne afterwards? she wondered, but kept silent. Some stories demand to be written; others just pull you in. Whichever type this one was, she would learn the end of it.

"I don't believe you two thought it possible to suppress Seth's will with the souls of mortals. No matter how many you throw at him, his soul would just fight them off, like a body fights a virus. Their will would not change his. He might weaken, but never be weak. The only thing you two accomplished here was making him angrier and insane."

Anubis knew she was just trying to buy time, but

time was the only thing not for sale in this deal. "Just do what we ask, Seshat."

"You bloody cat! You put the weight of the Universe on my shoulders and expect me to carry it lightly. Is there anything else I should know, Anubis?" she insisted, certain that there had to be.

He looked upwards at nothing in particular, making a show of giving the question some serious thought. "No. That's pretty much it, I think." What she doesn't know can't harm her, he assured himself half-heartedly. Then cleared his mind of doubt. "Now, you have to admit, had I told you the whole story back in Niflheim, you wouldn't have come. Or more likely you would have come alone, after leaving me tightly caged in the frozen pits of Helheim."

"I believe Tartarus would suit you better," she said tartly and sincerely before she remembered where they were.

Anubis laughed – genuinely laughed – as if that'd been the funniest thing he'd ever heard. The sound echoed through the walls and the endless depths as if a horde of Anubises laughed at her instead of just the one.

She wasn't amused. The god of reckoning even less so. But the god of the dead simply wiped merriment tears from his eyes and said, "Ah… well… Touché." He cast about, admiring the ancient temple. "Fate always has a way of giving us what we deserve."

"If only," Seshat said, the words laden with spite. Once again, the idea that fate might be the reason why she was being coerced to kneel in front of that cursed altar occurred to her. After all, how many times did she tell herself that she would give anything to find Mnemosyne?

That she deserved to find her, in fact. Of course, she never imagined it would happen under these circumstances, but that's precisely how fate works. What about how the shrine works? Would it suck her soul into the abyss to another universe or simply strip it from her body, leaving her untethered from this reality, forever lost and forgotten? No, Thoth wouldn't allow that… would he? She looked up at the two gods, thinking about what else she might ask or do to stall until the moon collided with the planet. She might survive that. But then she'd miss the chance to find out what had happened to Mnemosyne. Stars, but she was as excited as she was afraid. Fear hinders reason. And expectation distorts reality.

Focus.

She opened her mind as far as her Reach allowed, ignoring the darkness below she did not dare look into. Gods don't pray, she reminded herself. So she spoke instead. "Mina, if you're here, show yourself. Teach them a lesson."

She didn't know how long it took. It felt like centuries. She searched everywhere, with all her senses, as far as Reach would go. There were no traces of Mnemosyne anywhere. Nothing but echoes of souls long gone. She was about to call off the whole charade when there came a telepathic whisper.

'Thoth lies.'

A woman's voice. Not Mnemosyne's. Perhaps not even divine. Whoever she was, Seshat didn't want to scare her away or alert the gods that she'd made contact. She remained still and cautious.

'Tell me something I don't know…' Seshat mouthed inwardly.

'Mina's waiting for you, Sunshine.'

Seshat froze. 'Who are you? How do you know that name? No one calls her Mina but me.'

'My name is Rai. I am… was… Lokian. Now I'm the closest thing Seth has to a conscience. He defeated Apophis, just like Ra intended. But… but not how he expected. He –' A sharp, sibilant roar muffled her next words.

'Hello?' Seshat called. 'You're saying Ra is involved in this too?'

Silence.

'Hello!'

'Many of them are.'

'I don't care about them! I care about Mina. Where is she?'

'Mina told me about you and her promise to you when she restored my memories so I could tell you' – there was that roar again – 'and help you.'

'Is Mina not with you?' Seshat strained to remain civil.

'You have to learn the truth,' Rai said.

'Gladly! How?'

'This truth cannot be told. You have to live it. To witness it. To… will it.'

"Who are you talking to?" asked Thoth, all too aware she was hiding something.

"Seth's conscience," Seshat told him plainly while still mulling over those last words. "She says her name is Rai."

Thoth shot a glance at Anubis.

"On it," said the god of the dead.

CHAPTER 30

The Truth

Touch carries its own kind of memory.

– Memory on Record

When Audric returned to his alcove, the glowing ants began crawling excitedly about the walls and ceiling, shining brightly. He was happy to see them too, having grown fond of the little critters. He'd never figured out which god had put them there, for they certainly hadn't evolved on this moon. Would their creator come to rescue them before it hit the planet? Somehow, he doubted it. Everything's meant to die, he thought wearily, sitting down on a supply crate salvaged from the Eagle.

Pandora, or Sombra – or whatever name the entity animating Dayna's body went by – stood a few feet away, fascinated by the ants. She touched one gently, and the grin on her lips turned into an almost childish giggle as one ran across her fingers, its luminescence glowing brighter. If he'd had any doubt left about her not being his wife, it would have been resolved now. Dayna had always hated the nasty little bugs, as she'd called them.

He felt exhausted and wanted nothing more than a bath and sleep. Sleep in a bath would be ideal. Alas, he had no water or time for such luxuries. With a sigh, Audric took off his muddy cloak, then reached behind the crate to fetch a toolset wrapped in cloth carefully hidden inside a small recess in the wall. As hiding places went, there could hardly be a more obvious one, but anywhere out of sight was safe enough, since no one dared to enter his room. He'd made sure of it. And even if they did, few Prometheans and even fewer Narrum would understand the significance of what they'd found. He unwrapped the cloth, took out the tool he needed and began tinkering with the teleportation bracelet on his forearm. All he had to do was reset the imprint on the mechanism, reprogram it with his own genetic signature, then activate the teleportation ring in Eloin's quarters and… and what? Pray that there was a ship in range?

He groaned in frustration. Perhaps he should have left with the Lokian… Perhaps he should never have come here in the first place. Had he any sense or less pride, he would be begging Anubis for a ticket off of this rock. Except he didn't know how to beg. And he'd had enough of the god's lies. He'd always known gods were selfish and duplicitous. They would spare no means to accomplish their ends. As would he, to be fair. But working with the Nephilim, how could they? More than that, how could they expect him to work with them as well?

Maybe they know I'm not who I claim to be, he reflected.

He pushed the tool too vigorously into the device

and it slid off the metal, cutting into the skin of his forearm.

"Fuck," he said without thinking and immediately looked about for something to clean the wound before – it was too late. Pandora had already seen it.

"Blue blood," she said casually, then turned her attention back to the ants, leaving him somewhat perplexed, torn between the irrational need to give her an explanation and the rational concern about how little the sight had surprised her.

"Have you seen blue blood before?"

"These eyes have." She shrugged, speaking without looking at him as if the blood or its colour were of no consequence.

What else have they seen? he wondered. "Do you remember everything they saw?" Everything Dayna saw was what he wanted to ask.

She stood very still, staring at the ant on her palm as if it held the answer. "Dayna is no more. She's gone," she said in a tone that told him she'd heard his thoughts and found them somewhat endearing.

Broken doll my arse, he thought, straining to remain civil. "Where is she, then? Gone as in forgotten in the abyss like the others, or…" – he really didn't want to consider the possibility and had to force himself to say it – "seduced by the god of chaos, like Rai?"

"God of chaos." Pandora chuckled. "Seth is a god in chaos. True chaos has no gods or lords, only subjects."

"You didn't answer my question."

She pinned him with her silvery gaze, and although her tone remained calm and casual, he sensed she wasn't taking this conversation lightly.

"Rai was strong; she chose her fate. Dayna wasn't as strong as her ambition, so fate chose her."

Audric had had enough of her cryptic crap and was about to demand a straight answer when she lifted her hand and every single ant went dark – asleep, not dead – leaving the room illuminated solely by the silver shine of her eyes, like the cold white light of a long-dead star. "Dayna put too much effort into controlling her soul. She forgot to control her mind. A soul is futile without the mind," Pandora explained matter-of-factly.

Yes, Audric knew Dayna was dead. Knew that the entity standing in front of him only looked like her. That his wife's body had become a shell, a construct, a lie. That her soul was lost in the Underworld, or worse. And yet… getting that notion into his head and actually accepting it were very different things. "She died… yes, I know that," he said, hoping that saying the words aloud, listening to them from his own mouth, would finally let the idea sink in. The sooner he'd accepted it, the easier it would be to devise a way to bring her back. Anubis had refused, but he wasn't the only god of the dead in the Universe. He would find others more receptive to his request. But first, he had to find a way out. No matter the cost.

Pandora shook her head and chuckled, reading his thoughts again. "I feel your pain, your loss. Your anger. Cherish them, for they will serve you well in the future. Your will is stronger than most deities. Perhaps under different circumstances you might have succeeded in bringing her back. Death, after all, can be reversed – sometimes. Where there's a soul, there's hope, Nyx once told me right before she died. However, no amount of willpower can ever bring your Dayna back. Her soul doesn't exist anymore. It was obliterated when the others took her over. Nothing remains but her memories and" – she looked at herself with a smirk on her perfect lips – "me."

"Liar."

"Denial is a powerful thing. But changes nothing."

He closed his eyes, lest they betray him with tears. He believed her. Gods, he didn't want to, but he did. Anubis tried to tell him – straight to his mind. He hadn't refused to bring her back. He was unable to do it. And being a god, he'd been too proud to elaborate on his failure. Not that Audric would have listened if he had. After all he'd done. How could he?

Dayna is lost… her soul gone with no weighing, no judgement, no absolution, no chance of rebirth or apotheosis. He slammed his fist against the wall without care, welcoming the pain of cracked bone and torn flesh.

And how will you be able to hack the cursed bracelet now, you fool?

Audric buried his face in the palm of his other hand. Tired, oh so very tired. It had all been for nothing.

Pandora moved closer.

"Go away," he growled.

"Where to?"

"I don't give a fuck." It was a lie but, right then, close enough to the truth to sound believable.

Pandora cared little for his words, though. She remained where she stood. "I have nowhere to go. I'm not sure where my place in the Universe is anymore. But I'd like it to be with you."

He lifted his head to frown at her. "Why?"

"Because I understand gods and Nephilim well enough. But there's much I still don't understand about humans, or you."

"You're out of luck. I won't explain myself to you." And he pushed her away again, somewhat offended that he might just be a curiosity for her.

"It's not explanation I seek. It's… context. I have too many memories. From too many souls. I'm unsure of what is real, true, dream or imagination or simply… what do you call it? Wishful thinking. I'm overwhelmed by all these concepts. These feelings. One in particular. I cannot name it. Cannot explain it… Cannot deny it."

He saw the way she looked at him and felt himself looking back at her the same. "I suggest you try."

"Is that part of the process?"

"Process?"

She turned introspective for a moment. "Some call it flirting. Others seduction. The mating process."

He had to blink a few times. "No. No, there's no process between us." He illustrated a barrier between the two with his good hand.

"So what is?"

A foolish hope. A bad decision. "Nothing. There is nothing between us. Leave me alone."

She just stood there. Watching him intently.

"Obliterated how? Tell me how it happened," he had to ask, moving away from the subject and her piercing stare for the sake of his sanity.

"When Mnemosyne fled this body, thousands of souls tried to force their way in for a chance to live again. Drawn to an escape that never was. They fought each other. Dayna's soul too. They lost." There was no hesitation from Pandora, no pause to collect her thoughts. She just answered his question, caressing his hair gently as she spoke. He flinched at the first touch but relented soon enough as the tension and weariness began to drain away from him through her fingers. "They've all been destroyed," she assured him. "But they left something behind: memories, their most precious recollections. Their skills and desires as well." She paused, then whispered, "I wish to understand them better."

He lifted his head, studying her face in the gloom. A face so familiar and yet so alien at the same time, and he realised that earlier in the tower, when he'd asked her about her soul, she had not answered the question. "If they're all gone – destroyed as you said – whose soul animates you, Nephilim?" For something clearly did. He sensed it, strange as it was. More a presence than an essence.

She smiled as if the question was silly and kept running her fingers through his hair as she spoke. "Mine, of course."

"You have a soul?"

She cocked her head to the side, bemused. "I thought you knew about souls."

Obviously not everything. The realisation annoyed him. He didn't want her thinking him ignorant. Didn't want her to think less of him. Then he remembered her saying that the Nephilim called her Sombra, like the moon. Back then, he'd taken it as a fine example of the Nephilim's lack of imagination. Now, he wasn't so sure.

He hazarded a guess. "I've never heard of a moon with a soul." But if gods could turn into celestial bodies and use gravity to create a bond between them, well, perhaps he too lacked imagination.

He sensed rather than saw the shake of her head. "Your assumption is flawed." She touched his forehead as if checking his temperature, then, apparently satisfied, ran her fingertips down his cheek, along his jaw, and tilted his head to her.

"Do all living creatures have souls?" she asked, almost rhetorically.

"No," he admitted. The vast majority only had their spirits, in fact.

Her thumb traced the curve of his lips. "Neither do moons. You associate souls with life – the anima. But souls are older than life. Older than stars, planets or… or the beings you call gods," she added with a wicked smile. "We both know real gods are more than just immortals with souls. They can be many things. And so can I. This moon is only one of my aspects, a shell if you prefer. Like this body. Although, I admit, right now, I much prefer the body."

Her lips were on his before he could ask her exactly what she meant. Soft and familiar, the lips he'd kissed hundreds of times before but had never kissed him back the way they did now.

"Stop it!" Audric pushed her away, standing up.

"I'm not her," she repeated.

"I am aware," he strained through gritted teeth.

The fact was, Dayna and Pandora were very different indeed. Pandora had this penetrating glow. An eerie stillness and quirky wisdom hidden deep beneath an almost innocent insolence that he grudgingly liked. While Dayna's stoic personality had been a whirlwind of assertiveness in comparison. Always restless, dissatisfied, striving to achieve the next thing. Even cruel sometimes when things didn't go her way, to him and to others who hadn't met her standards. Her temper and competence were the things he'd loved about her, but still. Sometimes… Just sometimes… he wished she'd been different. Regardless, Pandora was just a bit too different. So different, in fact, she intimidated him.

His throat felt dry, his hand throbbed and his body, although exhausted, was not exhausted enough to stop him from craving more than rest and the absence of pain. What she craved was plain to see by the way she looked at him, biting her lip; by how she pressed herself closer against him, so close he could smell the sooty scent of her hair, feel the warmth of her body and her breath on his skin as she exhaled.

Nephilim don't breathe.

"What are you?" he demanded again.

"I'm old," said she. "But my origins are of no consequence. There's not enough future to dwell on the past. I exist here, now. In this place, this moment." She pushed a lock of his hair back to whisper in his ear, lips nibbling at the lobe. "And I'm as much a Nephilim as you are a Lokian, red eyes."

That gave him pause. He was trapped by her gaze, hypnotised by her voice. Heart racing, mind reeling. Body burning. "Why are you doing this?" His voice was hoarse, joining the rest of his body in its betrayal of himself.

She kept gazing at him with intense fascination, as if trying to memorise – or see through – his every expression and feature. "Mnemosyne's soul stayed just long enough to… hmmm, rouse me. It allowed me to learn, to understand the link between mind and body. My kind…" She hesitated, lifting a hand to touch her temple. "The minds of my kind, if they can be called as such, don't work like this one. We are aware: we perceive gravity and mass and souls so powerful and large they go by unseen, mistaken in the vastness of space. We feel temperature, distance, gravity, other forces and entities in the dark matter holding this reality together. But there's no thought, not exactly. No emotions as you'd describe them. We perceive the universe simultaneously as a whole, not as these tiny individual parts, these moments – like raindrops in an endless ocean, so random and insignificant to the ocean and yet utterly devastating for the drops themselves.

She took his hand and kissed it, and suddenly the pain was gone. The bone healed. He stared at it in disbelief. The skin, too, was smooth and whole. "How?" he mumbled incredulously.

"I already told you. Many left their talents behind, in me. Some are useful."

She had to be speaking the truth. Nephilim didn't have the ability to heal themselves, let alone others.

She smiled teasingly. "I'm intrigued by your anatomy and wish to explore it further." True to her intention, she reached inside his shirt. "I've already experienced pain and sadness. Pleasure seems much more interesting."

Pleasure indeed. Waves of it began running through his body as her hands ran over his skin. His own hands were on her without him realising.

"Don't do this," he heard himself say.

"Why not?" She sounded genuinely curious. "Your mouth says no. But your mind says yes and your body –"

"I don't love you." He cut her off because, yes, he knew perfectly well what his body was saying.

"Love?" The word was uttered with mocking scepticism.

"Thousands of souls, you said, and none explained love to you?"

"They have."

"Then you should have realised that whatever you think you're feeling, it's not it. It's not even real. Just lust combined with the echoes of lonely souls or… Dayna's love for me," he figured with a mix of bitterness and hope.

Pandora's smile became wicked. "I can tell the difference between love and lust better than you'll ever understand love itself."

"Oh, really?"

"Really. Love is like truth: everyone says they want it, but they fail to appreciate it or even recognise it once they have it. And if they do recognise it, then they often wish for a lie instead. The truth is, your Dayna loved power more than she loved you. The sort of power that eludes mortals like her. She dedicated her life to achieving it. That's why she volunteered to become a vessel, a host for something she'd never be on her own."

Audric began shaking his head. He tried to push her away, but she held his attention through sheer will.

"Yes, she did," Pandora continued assertively. "Dayna was tired of rituals and meditation. Tired of waiting. Tired of obeying. She'd grown bitter with the gods. She'd found out early on that Anubis was working for the Nephilim and she figured she might get what she wanted faster, directly from them. She never intended to search for survivors, let alone help anyone. Except herself. She saw an opportunity to become something more and took it, sparing no further thought for you, her kind, the gods, or her future. She was not defending humankind or the pyramid. She was abandoning both."

He made another vain attempt to push her away and did not look her in the eyes as he spoke. "No. You lie. Be silent. I don't want to hear those lies."

"Dayna knew she might die. She figured that, if she did, her soul would be sent to the Underworld and then you would find a way to convince Anubis to retrieve it – that was the extent of your role in her plans. And if that failed, she would live in your memory as this perfect being. You would remember her as she never was: kind, fair, loving. As everything she tried to be but never could. This was her way of achieving immortality. Through you. Your love for her. Your memory."

He kept shaking his head as she spoke. "No. No. That's not true." He considered punching the wall again so he wouldn't hit her.

Pandora moved closer still. "She also knew who and what you are. That's why she picked you as her consort." Her hands began unbuttoning his trousers. Audric had almost forgotten what anxiety – or was it excitement? – felt like. His hearts beat out of sync; his breath came too shallow.

"Lust is more honest than love," Pandora said as she stroked him gently. "It doesn't lie." She gripped harder. "And neither do I."

"Why not?" he rasped.

She shrugged. "I don't have to."

"That's not good enough." This time he managed to push her away and put some distance between them – which inside the small alcove was less than a couple of feet. Breathing hard and struggling to re-button his trousers, he snatched up his cloak instead, pulling it around him while straining for self-control, dignity and lucidity. "Nothing you've said makes sense. Dayna would never settle for being a memory, let alone sharing her body with another soul. We know what that does to the mind. And she prized her mind above her body."

Pandora kept watching him with that odd mix of admiration and detachment. "It's true. The human mind is not capable of sharing wills for long, but it has been designed to listen and interact with others to some degree. Her mind, enhanced as it was, may well have coped with a conflicting soul indefinitely." Her expression darkened. "One soul. Not thousands. And not one such as a Titan's. Or mine. That was her mistake." Pandora tilted her head, and her eyes lost some of their glow as she became introspective again. "Her last thought was that she wasn't as strong or clever as she'd believed. Funny how that realisation often comes too late for sentient beings." She focused intently on him. "Dayna is only a memory now. Yours and mine. Maybe the goddess of memory knows more, but… she's no longer sharing." She stood on her toes and stripped off his cloak. "So you see, both your love and your loyalty are misplaced." She placed a tantalising kiss on his neck. Others followed, trailing down. He swallowed.

The walls quivered, and the ants glowed faintly for a moment before turning dark again.

"Time is never on our side," she whispered, and in that moment she looked so sad, almost vulnerable, and so beautiful his breath caught. She began undressing herself, wriggling out of the bodysuit as a snake would peel off its skin. "We may not have another chance. Will you take my truth…?" Her lips were on his again.

His vision blurred. He inhaled in a shudder. "I can't."

"Why?"

He gazed at her then, deep into her dimming eyes, his own turned almost black. He was tired of fighting. Of denying. Of resisting the thing he'd wanted the moment he found her waiting for him in the tower. "Because when I look into your eyes, I see a realm that does not exist." He swallowed. "A realm I do not dare enter."

"Why?" she whispered again, teasing his touch, guiding him to her.

He released his breath as if holding it took too much of his strength. His voice nearly broke as he spoke his truth. "Because it's beautiful. And ugliness despises beauty; it seeks to destroy it. Through me, it might."

"You're not ugly."

He almost smiled. "I can be. I can do horrendous things. Or cause them. Dayna might still be alive if not for me."

She shook her head. "I've seen and felt all horrors the universe has to offer. They have not corrupted me. Neither will you."

Perhaps she's right, he told himself between half-coherent thoughts. After all, he was not a god, and she was… what was she? The avatar of a moon, an actual realm? A primordial goddess or just… the shadow of one? Whatever she was, he decided, it wasn't human, and it wasn't Nephilim either. And she wanted him as much as – heavens help him – he wanted her.

'Do it.' She spoke directly into his mind.

With a ruthless motion, he turned her over the crate, grabbed her by the hips and spread her legs without preamble or ceremony.

She gasped and moaned deep in her throat when he entered her. As did he, the sensation transcending every memory. Any attempt at reason failed against the uncontrollable madness of his actions and the mind-blowing pleasure of their immediate consequence.

She did not resist. Did not even try to take control. Passionate and uninhibited, she surrendered herself to pleasure: moaning, gasping, urging him deeper and faster until a scream escaped her throat, as if she'd been caught unaware of the need to release it, and she bit the thumb of the hand she'd healed, now pressing the side of her face down against the crate as she shuddered.

Already? he wondered, lost in his own violent delight. Before he could think or thrust further, she tucked her pelvis and rolled on her hip to face him. He groaned in frustration at being deprived of her for the instant, reaching haphazardly for her thighs to resume their union. She opened herself up for him again and he did not hesitate, unable to even remember a reason to, and thrust with abandon, his trousers wrapped around his ankles, her legs wrapped behind his buttocks. The cloak discarded at his feet. She ripped the shirt from his back, grabbed his hair, and pulled his face down to her breasts. He cupped the right one with his left hand;

the other hand grabbed her butt. They urged each other on as one, lips barely touching in their need to gasp for air, and this time both shuddered in unison, lost in glorious rapture.

Audric's upper body lay trembling over hers, his feet barely touching the floor. The crate creaked in protest beneath their weight.

She breathed as heavily as him, her skin tingling, wonder in her eyes, a smile on her lips. "Yes, I understand it now," she whispered. "They never stood a chance."

Her voice sounded distant, far beyond the roar of his blood and the power hidden deep within his soul, now awakened but not yet ready to be disclosed or even acknowledged.

"What will happen to the moon after impact?" he asked the moment he was able to think again.

"It'll be destroyed. Scattered across the universe. But I'll be free."

I won't, he realised, angry. This moment of weakness, this lapse in judgement, might have cost him his life, if not his soul. He pushed himself off her, stared at his healed hand, and with some considerable amount of willpower, pulled his ragged clothes back on, avoiding her gaze and nudity, in case his body betrayed him once again.

"Thank you for your… honesty," he said cruelly. "This is where we part ways." He turned his back to her so he would not see her face upon hearing his words. She said nothing. By the soft ruffle of fabric, he could tell she was dressing. "I hope you got what you wanted." The walls shook. Something loud and menacing rumbled through the tunnels. "Whatever the gods are doing, I reckon it's not good for anyone. You should be advising them or learning from them or whatever. I'm done. We're done." Her presence had become too distracting. He had to get the bracelet working and get far away from this rock in all its incarnations.

"I do not wish to be done with you." There was no resentment, bitterness, not even eagerness to her tone, just the usual assertiveness and calm. For some reason, that made him furious. He turned on her.

"Haven't you learned anything from your souls? No one gets their wish."

She eyed him levelly. "I do." Then after a pause. "And so did you. This is my place now. With you."

The huge tremor rocked them off balance and into each other's arms once again. He might as well try to be rid of his own skin. "Your place is with the rest of your pantheon, if you ever had one. Dead. Gone. Scattered across the Universe. Forgotten," he said, not letting go.

"Perhaps. But I exist here now. In this vessel. I must learn to live in this Universe as I am. You will help me."

He wanted to laugh. "Me? I'm probably the last person alive to teach you how to live in this or any other universe. Help you," he repeated to himself, resting his forehead against hers without realising. "Gods, Pandora… Living is not my forte. I've done little with my life but prepare for apotheosis and so ended up missing out on most of it."

"And yet you will."

"Will I?"

"Yes."

"Why?"

"Because you're curious. And I remind you of her."

He looked at her then. Really looked. "You think I'm that weak? That I can't tell the difference? That even now, I would ever replace her memory with you?"

She raised an eyebrow, considering him until her lips turned up slightly in amusement. "You're the strongest mortal I've ever known. Ever wondered why your kind has a tendency to cling to what is gone?" No satisfying answer came to mind. "Because in the end, only the past remains."

He sighed, almost relieved. "So you understand why this – us – can never be."

Pandora nudged his cheek tenderly with her nose. "And yet it already is. Never and Forever are absolutes too great, too alien to contemplate. They are the product of time. Before Chronos, there were no stories, no 'once upon a time', no 'what happened next'. There was only the present."

"Sounds blissful."

She stiffened, and her glow gained a certain incandescence when she spoke. "Time is cruel. Like light, it blinds us. It forces us to let go, to choose paths. To rely on memories while failing to make new ones because we are too worried about what might happen next. The past might be all that remains, but the present is where you live. And the future is what you make of it. I intend to spend eternity in the present. With you. And that means changing a few things." She kissed him one last time, walked out, and beckoned. "The past is not going anywhere. We must."

CHAPTER 31

The Enemy of My Enemy

Past and future are concepts created by Time.
And so is death.
Life is whatever you make of it.

– Memory on Record

Nenhum and Ninguém dumped Lyam unceremoniously inside a cell and blocked the exit behind them. It was one of the storerooms where they'd found the nectar and thankfully there was still some left. Lyam was more thirsty than hungry, but he figured if he had even the slightest chance of getting out of that accursed temple, he'd need a lot more strength than he had at the moment. He took the opportunity to let his mind run freely now that he was far from any empaths and the gods' cursed Reach. As he chewed the sweet protein, inevitably his mind kept wandering back to his past, to the things he'd done. He remembered them well now, but it was like watching a film, a fiction of someone else's life. The memories didn't feel his, and maybe because of that, he felt little guilt, remorse, or even shame for his actions. The only thing he felt, he realised, was resentment and a growing sense of helplessness. Two emotions often felt by mortals whose lives have been irreparably altered by the actions of gods and those they loved.

Eloin… why?

The nectar turned to ash in his dry mouth. Or maybe it was actual ash he was tasting. His face, hands, clothes and hair were still covered in it. Everything in my life turned to ash, he thought dramatically. It has all been for nothing.

He'd set out to discover what happened to the Nephilim, secretly hoping it would lead to the resolution of his own predicaments. He supposed it had, after a fashion. Funny how the Universe often fulfilled desires in the most unexpected and unwelcome of ways. His memories, for example. He'd once told Eloin he'd give anything to remember his past. Of course, it had not occurred to him that the price would be his future. Even if he appreciated the memories – which he didn't – what was the point?

'To learn, to suffer, to not let it happen again,' a harsh, hissing voice said. It was the same voice that had called to him from the abyss. The entity who'd driven Rai to madness and suicide. Likely the same voice that had lured Eloin to that damned hatch and wouldn't shut up until she too threw herself into the void.

Mortals stood no chance against gods, he decided, especially with their minds so open to them. "To learn, indeed," he grumbled. And what good would all this learning be worth in the Underworld, huh?

He covered his ears, not to shut out the voice – there was no helping that – but to muffle the actual noise around him.

Even from behind stone walls, the clatter caused by the handful of imprisoned Narrum was deafening. The men shouted and bleated, kicked at the doors, walls and each other; women screeched like banshees while their children bawled, neglected. They sounded mad, unhinged, inhuman. Like corralled livestock waiting for slaughter, they knew what was about to happen to them, for even the lowest beasts can sense their deaths. And these would die as they had lived – a nuisance.

"The prodigal brother returns."

Lyam practically jumped out of his skin. "Heavens! Jolyan, I didn't see you there." There were only a few ants glowing faintly in the corners, and the old dark-skinned woman always wore black. She sat primly on her ankles at the back of the room, arthritic hands clasped in her lap, as if she'd been praying. Although her head was in shadow, he just knew she'd been scowling at him.

"Why are you here and not with the others?" he demanded rather than asked.

"I asked to be confined alone." Her tone told him his presence had violated that request. She cast about in the dim light, scrunching her nose. "Should have asked to be alone and far away."

He understood what she meant. It wasn't just the noise the Narrum made that was unpleasant. They stank. With very few exceptions (Jolyan being one, thankfully) Narrum always stank, averse to hygiene as they were. But now, added to the usual stench of unwashed bodies and rotten teeth, there was the reek of urine, faeces, and fear. Someone or something had scared the shit out of them – quite literally. Belatedly, it occurred to Lyam she might be talking about him instead. After all, he too hadn't washed in days. He self-consciously sniffed an armpit. It was bad, but not too bad, he assured himself.

"What happened while I was away?" he asked out of curiosity and for lack of better conversation.

"They didn't tell you?"

"Would I be asking you if they had?"

Jolyan sucked her gums as if answering the question warranted some consideration. "It happened shortly after you left. I went to fetch water from the well, but all the water was gone." She spread out her hands on her skirt. "It was as if it had been drained to the moon's core. Not a single drop remained in reach." She clicked her tongue. "I should have kept quiet about it. Would have, except… it was so unexpected. And I wasn't alone. Merian saw it too, and she couldn't wait to tell the others. It was the excuse they needed."

Lyam wasn't familiar with that particular Narrum; they all looked, sounded and felt the same to him: ugly, loud and spiteful. But he could imagine how such an occurrence would become a sensation amongst a people to whom even bowel movements were worthy topics of discussion.

"The Narrum had been craving an excuse to riot and take what they wanted by force – again," said Jolyan. "This was it. But oh, they were in for a surprise. This time, things did not go their way. No, no. The god was prepared. He blinded them the moment they stormed into the room."

"With a bright light?" ventured Lyam.

The old woman snorted in derision. "Bright enough

to burn the eyes inside their sockets, aye. All of them, Narrum, Prometheans. Even the children," she added with a mix of horror and resignation as she relived the event.

So that's how they managed to lock the survivors in… Lyam mused almost appreciatively. The twins had tried to confine the Narrum after the first riots. It was the reason most cells had no doors.

"You're not blind," he pointed out.

"I was standing behind the god – not that that made much of a difference, I don't think. He spared me because I wasn't part of the mob. Never have been," she stated as a matter of pride. "I went there to warn Eloin of their rampage, but like I said, they already knew. They'd been expecting it." She shook her head. "Thoth did promise he would show us the light when he brought us here," she recalled ruefully. "He even said only the worthy would see. And gods do stick to their promises." She laughed then, the harsh laugh of a crone unaccustomed to laughter.

Lyam tried to imagine the scene. "I saw the hatch's finally open…" He trailed off, unsure of what exactly he wanted to ask. "Were you there when they opened it, too?"

The old woman bobbed her head slowly in silence. When she finally spoke, it was barely above a whisper. "Yes, fate saw it fit that I witness that too before I die, on top of everything else. I watched when Thoth broke the seal of the oubliette and most of the mob – still running around like headless chickens, mad with pain and panic, lashing out at anything and anyone – fell into the hole."

Seal… oubliette… Lyam mused. *Of course, that makes more sense.*

"Do you know… what's in the hole? I mean, the abyss? What are those root things…" *And the voices,* he almost said but decided not to mention those. *She had no empathic ability and so she wouldn't understand.*

"I believe the abyss is the manifestation of Oblivion, the endless fall into… nothingness. Thoth called it a portal to a realm before Time." She took a deep breath, closing her eyes as if unable or unwilling to imagine such a thing.

"Oblivion has roots?" was all Lyam managed to say in his effort to wrap his head around such a preposterous idea himself.

She scowled at him. "No. The roots belong to the moon's World Tree, or so Thoth said. Every world has one, apparently. Although if my world ever did, it was cut down long ago, along with all the other trees.

Lyam scratched his head, cringing at the idea and the crusted state of his scalp.

He'd heard of the magnificent World Trees, of course, with roots that not only held the worlds together but also connected them to other trees, on other worlds across space. He'd imagined them huge, magnificent and polished like marble pillars, their trunks and roots three-dimensional tunnels connecting worlds like wormholes. This one was not like that at all, but a monstrous thing of rough rock, its roots twisted and gnarled like those of a Chronodéndron. Lyam had heard of those too: capricious sentient trees able to subvert the laws of cause and consequence to send beings across time and realm. If ever there was a tree growing in Oblivion, it would be one of those, he reckoned.

Eloin probably thought she could travel back in time and heal herself somehow. And considering how they were running out of time, perhaps that was not such a bad plan. He shook his head. Back to when, you idiot? After the crash, so you can relive the last few years all over again and still wind up here? Or before the crash so you can avoid it, and knowing fate, go crash somewhere else instead? He chastised himself for thinking so small. They would go back much further, far enough to witness the temple being built at least. And he all but saw himself materialising out of nowhere in front of a primitive but dutiful people who subsequently would worship him as a deity. Lyam allowed himself a brief smile at this delusion before snapping his consciousness back to the present and unpleasant reality.

"Eloin… what have they done to her?" he asked, then rephrased the question. "What is she doing for them?"

"Eloin's gone." Jolyan exhaled. "At least her mind is. I think Thoth wants to use her empathic abilities to communicate with whatever is on the other side, beyond the abyss. He wants to channel it somehow. It will kill her – faster, I mean. She doesn't care, for she believes she'll live on as a goddess in the Underworld." The old woman tried to snort; it sounded more like a sniff. "Never have I heard such nonsense. You can't live on as anything after you're dead." Deep sadness, anger and guilt were coming off her in waves.

"You can't blame yourself."

"No. I blame Thoth." Her weary eyes shone bright in the gloom. "Gods can heal us when they want to. He's keeping her alive, but not healthy. I tried to tell her. As I tried to help her. She never listened to me and raged against any criticism of the deity."

Lyam empathised with the old woman. The idea suddenly made him want to laugh. Then he wanted to cry. He wanted to scream and kick the walls like the Narrum and not give a shit about any of it.

"Gods cannot be trusted," she concluded bitterly.

"Who told you that?"

"I can think for myself, thank you very much," she replied waspishly.

He smirked.

"What is so funny?"

"It's not really," he admitted. "I just… I met someone on the surface. You remind me of him. Well, not quite. No resemblance at all, in fact, apart from the attitude." He took a moment to evaluate the old woman properly. "How can Narrum be so…" He let the noise speak for itself. "And yet you seem so…" He let her fill in the rest of the sentence. Safer than using the wrong words.

"Everyone's different."

"Er… no. That's my point. Most of your kind is the same. It's you that is different."

"Are all Prometheans tall and arrogant?"

"… They are now. We selected for those traits." Along with intelligence, beauty, initiative, ingenuity… He went on listing all the qualities he was proud of inside his mind, for it would have been cruel to rub them in her face out loud.

"What happens to those who do not fit the criteria?" she asked, eyes narrowed.

"You know what happens…" he said, realising that it was no longer something he was proud of. "Any disruptive or inferior traits are culled out of the gene pool."

She nodded. "It's the opposite with Narrum. They can't stand independent thought, beauty or intelligence, for they don't allow leaders or tolerate anyone who might make them feel inferior in any way. They only spared me because I'm old and ugly and clever enough to appear stupid. Above all, I was useful to them. But the fact is, they hate me and I hate them." There, she'd said it. A weight lifted off her chest. She felt no shame for confessing it to him. "I hate you too," she added. The admission carried no passion, not even any actual hatred, only the cold statement of fact.

"But you love Eloin," said Lyam. He saw her eyes glistening in the darkness as she spoke.

"Like a daughter," the old woman admitted in spite of herself. Her face scrunched up, but no tears ran down the creases on her cheeks.

He wondered if she could still cry, dried up as she looked. Then he realised he, too, hadn't cried. He'd wanted to, still did, but he hadn't. Not when he found out Eloin was dying, or when he got his memories back, nor even when Rai jumped. He often felt like crying, as if it was something to aspire to rather than actually do. Come to think of it, he could not remember ever having cried. Not even once. Had they culled that ability as well? He remembered something Berdnard had said about Prometheans growing desensitised to emotions, as if they were no more than background noise in the clatter of human behaviour. Maybe that was why he could feel so much and understand so little.

"I suppose we're not so different, after all," he thought aloud. "We both hate what we've become as a species." Truth be told, Jolyan was closer to a Promethean than most. "But we were all human at some point, after all," he added when he saw her frowning at him sceptically.

She tutted. "So was Arachne."

Lyam blinked, taken aback by the example. "Oh? You're familiar with Olympian history? I thought Narrum couldn't read."

"Illiteracy is not the same as ignorance," she said dryly.

"Right, apologies… so you know Arachne didn't change until after she killed herself," he pointed out, relishing the unexpected philosophical debate. Then he thought about it for a moment. "Funny, we believe the reason Prometheus made us so mutable was because he wanted us to change, to evolve. And yet… despite our efforts to perfect ourselves so we could better resemble our creators, we've never really changed, have we?" The realisation came to him mid-sentence. He was too tired to elaborate or rephrase the conflicting statement.

"That's because change is anathema to perfection," the old woman said. "You've been going about it the wrong way. The gods never expected us to change by ourselves. They just wanted the option to change us on their own terms, for their own amusement. It was Athena's will that changed Arachne, not her own weaving skill."

"But she sure embraced the change," he snorted. "It's the thing about curses: they tend to bring out the accursed true self."

"As does revenge." He sighed. "Well, at least Arachne became immortal. The closest to godhood humans will ever get."

Jolyan clicked her tongue again. "You're missing the point, boy. Humans are changeable, just not through their own free will. And whenever gods use their power to change us, it's always for the worse. This means they only gift immortality to monsters."

"Huh…" The old woman had a point. "Then perhaps it is in our nature to be monsters," he said.

She cackled to herself. "Now you're finally thinking like a god."

Lyam had no reply to that, but he couldn't stay silent. If nothing else, he had to keep talking to drown out the noise.

"Do you remember what happened? Before we crashed here."

The old woman shook her head. "No. I remember very little from the ship. Only bits of it in dreams. Can't tell if they're real or…" if I'm going senile, she almost said but decided against it. "I remember enough of my life before and after to know I'm probably better without knowing the in between. Why?"

"I remember it now." He whispered the admission, not sure why he was telling her this. It wasn't like he wanted to tell Jolyan what he'd done. He just had this need to tell someone, to say it out loud, to understand who he'd been and what he'd become. "Some entity in the abyss 'gifted' them back to me. I think. I can see myself in those memories but not actually feel them. Does that make sense?"

Jolyan indulged him with a tired nod, barely visible in the gloom.

"If you don't remember something, does it matter if it happened or not?" he asked as an afterthought.

"It must matter to someone," she said.

"If no one remembers. Not even the person it happened to. Does it matter?"

Jolyan thought about that for a long moment. "Well… then I suppose it doesn't. Then again, very little of what we do matters. Even when it does, it doesn't matter for long. We're mortals. In a way, we can do whatever the fuck we want because we don't matter."

What a depressing notion, he thought. "Heavens… Did you say those things to Eloin?"

"No. Eloin would not take it kindly. All she ever wanted was to matter. That's why she never came to terms with her own mortality. Perhaps I should have said it, though. She would have hated me for it, but maybe she'd have listened. Maybe she'd have done the right thing."

The right thing, Lyam mused. What is that, anyway?

Everything he did, he'd done because he'd been convinced it was the right thing to do. The thing he was supposed to do, regardless of what others did or said or thought…

To Narrum, the right thing to do was always what everyone else did. Join the majority and you'll never be wrong, someone once said.

It seemed right and wrong were merely two sides of the same coin, flipping endlessly, defined by the perspective of those who'd tossed it in the air.

He took a deep breath of resignation. "I've spent the last years of my life trying to get away from this place, from that room, and whatever is hidden beneath. I was running from something I couldn't even name, towards what I believed to be freedom. I can't run anymore. Having my memories back hasn't freed me. Dying in this place won't free me, either," he realised soberly. "I have to go back. Do something. I can't stay here. Can't leave Eloin there. She always loved me. She remembers… She's clever, she'll see the truth, she –"

"She made her choice," Jolyan said

"And I'm making mine."

He stood up and rammed his shoulder against the barricaded door.

∞

Lyam sensed rather than heard movement behind the panels blocking his exit. "Hey! Get us out of here!" he shouted for the dozenth time. Try as he might – and he'd tried pretty damn hard – he could not break through the door. But he would keep trying until he died, for what else was there to do?

"Promethean, is that you in there?" came Audric's voice.

For a moment, Lyam considered staying silent. Of course, that would mean remaining still as well as trapped inside the room, and that wouldn't do. He swallowed his pride with a curse.

"Yes…" he grumbled despondently. Then he bolted upright. "How come you're not locked up?" For some reason, Audric's freedom infuriated him more than his own imprisonment.

"Why would I be? Why are you?" the Lokian asked in that insufferable way of his.

"Because I'm such a menace, the gods saw fit to put me in here," Lyam replied.

Silence. It suddenly occurred to Lyam that Lokians might not understand sarcasm. "Are you going to help us out or not?"

"Us? Who's in there with you?" Audric asked.

Jolyan raised an eyebrow at Lyam, waiting for his answer.

"Just a crone."

She showed him her middle finger. He pressed himself flat against the barricade, trying once more in vain to push it aside. He heard voices murmuring on the other side. Audric wasn't alone either.

"Have you come to free me or just annoy me until we die, Lokian?"

"Neither. I was just passing through."

Lyam had to bite his tongue to stop from saying something that'd guarantee he'd not see the outside of that storage room again. He almost succeeded. "Move along then! I don't need your help, Lokian. I'd rather owe it to the gods than to one of you."

"Haven't you heard? Gods only help those who help themselves," said Audric.

"No shit. Well, they can shove their accursed help down the abyss with the rest of your kind!" Lyam replied, his patience exhausted.

Suddenly, the crates and planks blocking the exit flew aside. Pandora stood on the other side, radiant next to Audric, her hands still lifted in a parting gesture.

"They have," she said. "And it left them helpless.

They ran. But could not hide from it… Time made it so," she told him in singsong.

"For heaven's sake! Can't you speak clearly for once, creature?" To say "thank you" would have taken a bit too much out of Lyam right at that moment. Probably the same amount it'd taken the Nephilim to say a simple "hello" or "you're welcome", he reckoned.

Pandora tilted her head in that flirtatiously quizzical way of hers. "My speech is clear. Your understanding is limited."

"Fuck you." The affront, if perceived as such, was ignored.

"Who are you talking to?" Jolyan asked when she finally managed to push herself to her feet. It had been a mistake to sit on the floor, something she realised the moment she'd sat down. But then again, she hadn't expected to get up again. She'd never quite figured out Audric, who she'd considered a troubled soul, and learning he was Lokian had not surprised her. His companion, on the other hand… Her forehead creased slightly in interest as she took in the strange woman. "You're new."

The silvery woman smiled kindly at her, and Jolyan decided she liked this creature, for she could not remember the last time anyone smiled at her, let alone kindly.

"I'll let Audric here do the introductions," Lyam said, hurrying out of the small room before Pandora blocked it again on a whim with her unnatural strength.

He took in the other man's dishevelled hair, the torn shirt and what looked suspiciously like teeth marks on his neck. Pandora had no marks on her but she looked different too: flushed and, despite her nonsense speech, more real and human than before.

He fucked her, Lyam deduced, rather appalled by it. 'So, the rational and righteous Lokian is as fallible as the common man,' he thought loud enough for Audric to hear it.

"You're in no position to judge, Promethean," Audric scorned defensively. "You took a Lokian as a lover and got yourself locked away with a Narrum. That's what you get for thinking yourself better than everyone else. Let this be a lesson in humility for you."

Lyam nearly choked on his outrage. "You dare to judge me on humility? Lokians are the ones who strive for apotheosis. You select your own as much as we do ours. You created the Nephilim, for crying out loud!" He spared a dirty glance at Pandora. "I think I'm starting to understand the purpose."

Not for the first time, Audric fantasised about purging Lyam to the abyss. If only the man knew just how right he was about the wrong things. "Yes, we've both made mistakes in the name of perfection and imitation of the gods. But we were not the ones who split humanity."

"No, you lost yours long before the split."

Audric pressed his lips, straining for patience. "We chose to isolate ourselves in order to learn and evolve without subjugation to and from others. The rift between our ancestors was never because we held different opinions. We respected your ideas, but we despised your methods. You Prometheans call us traitors, though your faction was the one who betrayed mankind, betrayed us, your sworn brothers. You stole most of our resources, leaving us for dead, lost, drifting in the emptiness between galaxies at the gods' mercy."

"And still, somehow, you found your way here," Lyam quipped, more than a bit annoyed at being accused of something that had happened centuries before he was born.

"We did. And you tracked us. After collecting samples from hundreds of unfortunate specimens, you realised we were the genetic mother lode. Too much inbreeding made you barren and sick. So you chased us here looking for fresh blood. We never hid."

"Perhaps you should have!"

"Oh, to have lived this long just so I could stand here and listen to the pot arguing with the kettle," Jolyan said.

Both men stared down at her, then at each other in bewilderment. The old woman shook her head, deciding further explanation would be pointless. How could these post-humans have learned so much and still know so little?

"Perhaps you should fight each other to find out who's the stronger male," she suggested. "No. We have no time for that. I have a better idea, take out your dicks to see who can piss the furthest. That should settle it." And she crossed her arms in expectation.

Lyam wanted to protest, but the old woman was right. This argument was a waste of time. Audric was a problem, but not the problem.

When neither of them moved, Jolyan snorted. "I thought so."

Gods, she was tired of humanity in all its forms. She could feel death calling for her through the throbbing in her head, the tightness in her chest and the brittleness of her bones. "Unless you wish to continue your argument in the Underworld, I suggest you put those enhanced brains of yours to work and find a way out of this shithole." The idea that their Underworld might be the same as hers made her cringe. But the alternative was even worse: an Underworld filled with Narrum. *Fuck that!* she thought. And, suddenly fuelled by new-found anger and intent, Jolyan decided death could wait for her a little while longer.

"I assume you have a plan, Audric?" Jolyan pointed at his bracelet. Her grandmother had told her about those. She'd never actually seen one before, but she recognised it for what it was.

"I may have an idea," he said, still keeping Lyam in the corner of his eye. "It did not include you, though."

"Well, it does now." Jolyan would see the end of this if it killed her. The idea amused her, and she grinned, showing him a mouthful of missing teeth.

"We shouldn't linger here," Lyam said rather unnecessarily, since he was the one now blocking the way down the gloomy passage to the temple proper. "Eloin needs us."

"Eloin needs no one," Audric said. And he took off in the opposite direction, Pandora right behind him.

Lyam cursed the man's soul to eternity, then decided to take his chances with the gods. He was halfway to the temple when he realised Jolyan was not with him. She'd gone with Audric – the old bitch! – which was just as well. He did not need her. And Eloin didn't need a mother. She had a brother. Together, they would show the gods what it really meant to be human.

CHAPTER 32

The Way Out

I, too, can play tricks.

– Memory on Record

"There has to be a ship in range, observing the situation. It's not like them to travel without backup," Audric explained to Jolyan as they stood outside Eloin's quarters, Pandora right behind them. The old woman had questioned no part of his plan, and he wondered if she'd even understood it. In truth, he didn't care if she did. She'd wanted to come, so she'd better trust him. He already had too much to worry about, too much on the precarious plates of fate and faith alike.

"A teleportation ring?" Jolyan said. "That's what's under her rug?" She'd known about the ring, of course. Had seen it many times. Eloin went to great lengths to keep it a secret – especially from Lyam – for fear others would take it for a bad omen or as evidence that the Nephilim had built the temple.

"No, the Nephilim did not build it," Audric told her. "They simply adapted it. It's what they do: reconfigure the gods' work to suit their needs."

He'd always known the Nephilim had found the temple long before the Lokians had. He'd just let himself believe the gods had got rid of them, rather than entertain the possibility they might have been taken over or, as it turned out to be, were working together. Proof that denial is stronger than magic.

The chances of teleporting onto an enemy ship (and the risk of whatever might come afterwards) concerned him a lot less than the state of the bracelet itself. Teleportation could go extremely wrong with faulty equipment. He and Pandora had done what they could to fix it but had no way of knowing if it would work without testing it on a portal. And, of course, it would not work if the portal itself didn't. The last time he sneaked into this room to check it, in the aftermath of the riots, it wasn't even on. The ring had been installed as an escape route of sorts, but there was no sign of it actually having been used. Pandora herself had reservations about artificial translocation and claimed that even a god would struggle to translocate out of that particular realm, unless already linked to a destination. Still, he had no other option. He had to make it work.

As it happened, someone was already working on it.

∞

Crymure knelt by the metal ring set in stone in the middle of the room, the lush quilt Eloin had used to cover the ring neatly folded under his knees as a cushion while he rearranged the crystals inside the access panel. "There, that should do it," he said to himself, pleased with his work. Then he cursed the dilapidated state of his own bracelet. How he regretted having left the spare one with Berdnard. It had seemed a good idea at the time. Berdnard couldn't use it, wouldn't even think to wear it, and more importantly, no one would dare to take it from the angry dwarf. Of course, he had not considered that the dwarf might die or exchange it for the Maker knows what. Or that the next time he himself visited the pyramid, he'd have to crawl up into it instead of teleporting in from a ship.

That's what you get for trusting a mortal, he thought. Then shook his head. No. That's what I get for trusting Namrive. The bitch had left him stranded there with the devious gods and angry mortals, with little more than a mental note claiming she had to 'fix herself'. And how am I supposed to fix this, huh? he wondered, glaring at the broken device strapped around his fleshless wrist.

The activation crystal was missing. The best he could do was use the communication stones to contact the nearest ship and hope they were willing to teleport him in. Unlikely, given his status amongst his peers, but what choice did he have? To stay and witness the scions of Ra tear a hole in the fabric of the Universe? No, thank you. He could almost see himself waking up in the resurrection ship, the Mentor looming above him, demanding a report. He'd rather die ignorant. If he had to die at all – an option he deeply did not want to contemplate just yet.

He'd just closed the access panel when he realised he was no longer alone in the room.

Audric, Pandora and Jolyan stood frozen by the entrance with blank expressions, unsure of how or even if they should announce their presence. For a long moment, no one moved. No one spoke. They just stared at each other like irreconcilable opponents, aware they might have to fight but reluctant to strike the first blow.

"Need this?" Audric asked, showing Crymure his bracelet.

Crymure automatically stretched out his skeletal hand. "Give it to me."

"It won't work on you anymore, but give us the coordinates to your ship, and we can all go together."

Crymure laughed. He'd always found that a friendly disposition put mortals at ease, so he'd programmed his laughter to sound clamorous and sincere. The truth was, he was rarely amused. "You want to bring yourself, her" – he frowned at Pandora – "and a Narrum onto our ship? Have you burned your fuses?" Is he carrying a concealed explosive device or something? his cynical mind wondered.

"This is not a discussion," said Audric.

"No. It's a joke," said Crymure, not laughing any-more. "It's bad enough to be in the same room with one of you. Do you really want to be on the same ship with hundreds of us?"

"Nephilim usually travel alone or in pairs."

"Usually, yes. Not always," Crymure admitted. He deliberately didn't point out that the smaller the crew, the larger the number of Faithful deployed to defend them. "And where do you think we'd go? Olympus? Mars? Heaven, perhaps? You'll find yourself on a one-way trip to Pallas. The Mentor would love to meet one of your kind in the flesh, but you'd not like meeting her, be-lieve me." This time Crymure did feel like laughing. Or maybe crying? It was hard to tell these human emotions apart sometimes. He should never have let Namrive convince him to install them.

"We'll decide our destination when we're on the ship," Jolyan said.

Crymure took in the old woman with a mixture of awe and revulsion. He'd never seen a human so old and he could not fathom what motivated her to keep living in that state. "Your destination is the Underworld."

She scowled at him, a true scowl, the kind only wrinkled old skin could pull off. "The Underworld is for gods and the dead. I'm neither."

"Well, you will be dead soon enough," he said.

Audric crossed the room in just a few strides, grabbed Crymure by the neck, and lifted him off his feet before he could do anything about it. It was one of the weaknesses of his kind: near invulnerability combined with a lack of self-preservation instinct made the Nephilim slow to react to danger.

Pandora rushed to take the bracelet from his arm and began fiddling with the mechanism of the ring.

Crymure's eyes bulged in an effort to convey surprise and outrage. This Lokian had nerve. Would he have some sense as well? "What exactly do you expect to achieve with this behaviour – suffocate me to death? I don't breathe, you idiot! Want to hurt me?" Crymure showed what was left of his hand again. "I feel no pain. Want to intimidate me, then? Oh, please," he scoffed. "I've faced the Mentor, the Suzerain and the god in the abyss. Nothing intimidates me anymore." He could still be annoyed, though. His lips curled in a snarl. "Go ahead, disable me, then teleport to our ship. Our scientists would love to work on you. As much as I enjoyed working on your wife," he added spitefully.

That got a reaction from the stoic Audric. He pushed Crymure against the wall hard enough to glitch. "What did you do to her?"

"What she asked me to." Crymure grinned callously.

The room – the entire mountain – shook. Audric barely felt it, overcome by outrage as he was.

"She didn't know what she was asking. You used her. You piece of scrap. You –"

"We have no time for this," Jolyan said. "Just break the bastard and move on."

Another tremor, this one much stronger, knocked the old woman to the ground. For a moment, she feared she might have broken her hip. Cracks began splitting the floor, and chunks of rock fell from the ceiling and walls; one barely missed her head. She expected the whole room to collapse at any moment. "Audric! For fuck's sake. Stop acting like a Promethean." She hoped that would snap some sense into the man.

Jolyan's right, Audric thought. He was not Lyam, and they had no time for this fight. Besides, the joy of pulling Crymure apart should be Pandora's, not his. He took a deep breath, looking around. His stomach sank. "Pandora? Pandora!"

"She left right before the quake," Jolyan told him, standing back up on unstable legs and making sure she had something to hold on to before the next tremor hit. A stupid fall like that could be fatal for a woman her age, after all.

"Pandora? Is that what you call her now?" Crymure laughed. He actually wanted to this time. "Bugs, you people really enjoy tempting fate."

Audric shook him, cutting his laughter short but doing nothing to keep him from talking.

"Your wife's dead. But if you hurry, you might still join her in the Underworld before it, too, is gone."

"I can't join her. You destroyed her soul."

He glanced in the direction Pandora had gone. "Is that what she told you?" He laughed again. "Only the goddess of the soul can destroy souls, you fool. Dayna is waiting for you. Counting on you. While you're here throttling me, snarling like a beast. And you call yourselves rational. Tsk."

"Don't listen to him," Jolyan said. "We have the bracelet." She showed the device Pandora had dropped at her feet before she left. "Let's use it. There will be others for you to, er… act your vengeance upon on the ship, I'm sure."

Jolyan knew she was wasting her breath. Audric wasn't even listening anymore. He threw Crymure to the floor, turned around and ran out into the tunnels after the ghost of his wife. His obsession. His death.

"Well," Jolyan sighed wryly, "another disappointment." These post-humans are all the same, she decided. A good thing she wasn't too prejudiced about anyone or anything anymore. She tapped the rim of the teleportation ring with one foot and raised an eyebrow at Crymure. "Just you and me, then."

The Nephilim stood up, none the worse for being strangled and tossed aside like a discarded doll. "There's no you and me, creature."

"I disagree." Standing inside the ring, she cut her palm on the ragged edge of an empty gemstone socket and let the thick blood flood into the mechanism, then slid her skinny arm inside the bracelet, all the way to her shoulder.

Crymure blinked at the old woman. This shrivelled creature was really pushing the boundary between courage and stupidity. Sure, he could rip her arm off or just kill her – which would amount to the same thing – but she defied his understanding of life and humanity and, above all, logic, so instead he just stepped inside the circle and extended to her his flesh-bare hand.

She cackled, for it was a far less revolting sight than a lot she'd seen in her life, truth be told, and she promptly shook it. Well, at least it's not coated in spit, she reflected.

Crymure smiled. Surprised but not displeased by her reaction.

They activated the ring.

∞

Audric ran down the crumbling tunnels after Pandora. Dust, dirt and chunks of rock fell in his path. It wouldn't be long before they entered the planet's atmosphere and then not even the gods' will would be enough to keep the moon intact. He ran faster, then skidded to an abrupt stop after turning a sharp corner. How are you here? The question was a fleeting thought in his troubled, tired mind.

Nenhum and Ninguém blocked the way, determined not to let anyone pass. "Sorry, private party. Your presence is unwelcome."

Audric clenched his fist, ready to fight his way through. He could take one of them, he was almost sure of it. But he did not like his chances against the two. They actually looked bigger than they had a few days ago.

"What the fuck are you?" he asked. He'd always thought the two giants were the result of some extreme genetic manipulation, but now he wondered if the manipulation had been divine rather than Promethean.

The twins looked at each other. "Here, in this realm? Nenhum and Ninguém, who else?"

"And in other realms?" Audric prompted dryly.

One of the twins, he thought it was Ninguém, but he wasn't sure, smirked. "Are you familiar with the expression 'those with boots of glass shouldn't kick stones'?"

"I don't think that's how the saying goes," the other said.

"The point is," his brother continued, "don't ask of others what you wouldn't want to answer yourself."

Audric ground his teeth. "Let me through," he said, prepared to take on the two if needs be, when they pointed behind him together. "Listen to your god." Audric turned to face the jackal. He cursed. It snarled. There was something glinting between its teeth.

∞

"For the last time," Crymure said. "I'm not a wizard! I don't know why it didn't work. Too many people messed with the mechanism is my best guess. Maybe there's no ship in range. Maybe it's this place. The fates amusing themselves at our expense. Or maybe you broke it with your fluids."

Jolyan scowled at him, then at the device. More shackle than bracelet, in her opinion. "It was the silvery woman. She took something from it." She pointed at the eye of the snake in the bracelet's motif. "Does this look right to you?"

Crymure zoomed in on the tiny detail. "Hmm." It did look like a pin was missing.

"Can you fix it?" Jolyan asked.

"No… I'm not a god. I can't conjure stuff from thin air. I would if I could, and leave you here to die."

She sucked her gums. "Yes. Of that I have no doubt. But it seems we're both stuck here until they return – if they return." And why would they?

"We can always go after them," he suggested.

"I will never set foot in that pyramid again," Jolyan declared sourly.

Sat side by side on Eloin's makeshift bench, they made quite the pair: she inspecting the expert craftsmanship of the quilt in her lap with her arthritic fingers; he doing mental permutations with the aid of his skeletal ones, to prevent his mind from unravelling while they waited. For what? He had no idea. There was nowhere to go. Nothing else to do in that place except wait for the end, and both Narrum and Nephilim seemed at a loss about how to act in these frustrating moments of forced company.

He took a good look at the old woman then. "How old are you?" he asked, unable to stop himself. She scowled at him in reply. "Apologies. I just had to ask. You look so…" He waved a hand. Never mind. He knew little of Narrum or their social etiquette, but he recognised annoyance when he saw it.

"How old are you?" she asked back.

"Last I checked, I was just over half a century old in Midgard years," he answered proudly.

She laughed despite herself. "I'm old enough to be your mother, then." The idea of being older than the machine somewhat amused her. As if it was some sort of achievement, which maybe it was, just not a very useful one.

"Amazing," he said, flickering eyes open wide in a poor attempt at expressing awe. "I don't think I've ever met a, er… Narrum human so old. No offence. I admit, I'm finding you very interesting."

Rarely had Jolyan's eyebrows raised so high up her wrinkled forehead. "Interesting, eh? I bet you'd like to strap me to one of your dissecting tables and take off my skin for inspection."

"Well… yes. Not just the skin." Upon seeing the depths of the frown this admission triggered, he added quickly, "It's a compliment! Bugs… you could out-scowl the Mentor herself. Have you some god's blood in you, perchance?"

The scowl turned into a grimace.

"Again, it was meant to be a compliment!" he said, at a loss for how to deal with the creature.

"You need to work on your compliments," she said.

"I need to work on many things," he grumbled, clicking the metallic joints of his hand. Then, after a moment's consideration, "There's something I never quite understood about humans, the Narrum, I mean. I understand the Prometheans and the Lokians, I even understand the gods, believe it or not, but the Narrum are like a completely different species – no offence."

"None taken."

"Yes, well…" he said, glad not to see that scowl this time. "Why are they always so…" – he struggled to find a nice word and ended up settling on several improper but very accurate ones – "spiteful, greedy, dirty, mean, ugly creatures. It's like they only possess the worst traits of humanity." He realised he wasn't actually including the old woman in this assessment, which was weird.

Jolyan had no more energy, nor desire to frown. She'd always imagined Nephilim to be these cold, haunting machines, assembled to perfection to embody all knowledge of the universe. Powerful enough to match the gods. This one had to be a child in what passed for their society. Either that, or slightly damaged, she supposed. Her face slackened. Too tired to express let alone explain her opinion, but at least the machine seemed eager to listen and learn, unlike Lyam, who only wanted someone to validate his own opinions. She hunched her shoulders, and it was as if she'd aged a decade before she spoke.

"There's a thin line between need and greed. The best amongst us either left or were killed trying to save those who clearly did not deserve saving. Then we, as a species, had to adapt to survive. Adapt to our environment, to our new status amongst other mortals, but most importantly, to each other. There's no room for individuality in large groups. Any deviation from the norm, disagreement with the majority, or simple uniqueness had to be culled from the herd. Tribes are like these big resentment pots, stewing away, waiting for a reason to spill over. Anything that makes you stand out makes you a target. Especially something worthy of appreciation. For they hate all the things they don't have: beauty, intelligence, integrity… virtue. You think they're too beastly, too stupid to see, to understand or appreciate these traits. The truth is much worse. They can and they do see them. They understand what they lack very well. And they hate anyone who's not the same as them because they represent everything they can never have or be. They smear ugliness on everything they touch, so it's not so obvious in themselves. They gather in mobs with the intent to harm and destroy the things that offend them, for they have the traits of a mindset that rejects excellence for the sake of the collective.

Crymure found the idea appalling. He'd never quite understood the concept of evil until now. If half what she'd said was true. The Narrum were not only a nuisance; they were a plague. A cancerous mass amongst humanity.

"Why are the Narrum still around, then? Why have the gods not put an end to such vile creatures?"

"They amuse them." The old woman snorted. "Perhaps the gods need to look at the Narrum in order to feel better about themselves. Or perhaps…" This had never occurred to her before, and she had to give it some thought. "Perhaps they keep them alive as a reminder of what can happen if they lower their own standards. After all, humans – the original ones – were created in their image."

"The Maker believed gods were only gods for as long as there were mortals," he mused.

"No argument there," she said with a derisive chuckle.

"You speak of your people as if you're not one of them. And here, speaking to you, I don't see any of those negative traits," he confessed.

"You don't see an ugly old woman?"

"I see an old woman. But not a Narrum."

She eyed him askance. "I was born a Narrum, true. It's what I am. But not who I am. I just had to live my entire life amongst them. There were others like me. In every generation, there's always a few who still possess the potential of our species. And the only way for us to survive is to blend in. Some do it so well, they end up forgetting themselves. I never have. But like you said. I'm old. I'm tired of pretending to be something I'm not. I'd rather die as I've always lived: alone and apart."

Crymure tried to imagine the old woman young and hopeful. He failed. "What would you have done had you had the chance to do anything?"

She leaned back, smiling slyly at the question. "I would have figured out the meaning of life."

He nodded to himself. "A worthy pursuit."

She took in the strange Nephilim again, eyes narrowing. "Why are you here, talking to me? Shouldn't you be helping the gods, or killing them, or whatever it is you, er… do." She stopped herself before saying people and found she had no suitable word to replace it.

He stared at his hand when he answered. "I don't fit the mould either." She huffed. Hard to tell if in amusement or derision, so he said, "Believe it or not, the gods can be as cruel, if not crueller, to their creator's creation than they are to their own. It's their nature, I suppose."

She shook her head. "Fuck, you are young." She never imagined machines could be this naïve. But then again, learning and maturity had little to do with age. "It's not in the gods' nature to be cruel. As it's not in their nature to be good or just. They're gods. They don't care about those things. Cruelty they learned from us. They simply have the means to do more damage with their cruelty, that's all. But they only do it as a last resort. Or when they are truly afraid."

The moon quaked again.

"Are they afraid?" he asked, unsure if he himself understood the concept.

"Oh, yes. I've learned to recognise fear in all its manifestations. And what happened in that temple had little to do with power or greed or vengeance." She sucked her gums. "I cannot fathom what can possibly frighten a god that way, but whatever it is. If they fear it, so should we."

They just stared at each other while stone dust fell from the cracked ceiling.

"Well, thank you," he said. "I'm now much enlightened. And afraid."

She cackled. "The two often go hand in hand, young Nephilim. Remember that when you're old."

CHAPTER 33

The Edge of Eternity

Memory lives in the mind, not the soul. But only the soul knows what is true.

– Memory on Record

Anubis curled his lip in distaste. He hated handling souls, especially when he had to guide them in the opposite direction of their natural course. It was one thing to send souls to the Underworld, quite another to channel them back from it, and Rai's soul was as wilful and slippery as an eel. "Keep it brief," he said. "We might not need the mortal's mind but we still need her soul – half of it, anyway. This transfer won't last long. Not that we have long in any case."

"Thank you for wasting time reminding us again of how short we are on time," Thoth said, straining for patience. If he didn't know better, he'd swear Chronos was in the room with them, locked in a contest of wills with Fate in a desperate attempt to stall the inevitable. "Very well, Rai. Say your piece before Eloin dies." Humans make terrible hosts. He gave the mortal an appreciative glance. "Poor Eloin, she always knew you'd be the end of her."

"I wish I'd had the privilege of knowing how I'd die beforehand," Rai replied dryly, a bit of the fiery redhead coming through Eloin's lifeless features. "We are just puppets to you and your need for control. But you cannot control Seth."

Thoth tutted. "The mortal's perspective is dull. You truly believe I'm this power-hungry deity who wants to control everything. I only wish to control time."

Seshat chuckled. "Good luck with that."

He turned sharply on her, Reaching – more like assaulting – her thoughts. "You met Chronos!"

The chuckle turned into a bitter laugh when she finally realised she'd been on this path long before she'd stepped foot on Namrive's ship. That every action and decision she'd made, every story she'd written in the past age had led her here.

"Yes, Father. We've talked back in Niflheim."

The glare from the god of reckoning dimmed. "Chronos… he… talked to you?" The God of Time was known for listening, not so much for talking.

"Indeed, he did. He wouldn't shut up, in fact."

Thoth rounded on Anubis. "Were you aware of this?"

"I was there," he said. Although, truth be told, he'd missed their entire conversation, busy as he'd been arguing about souls with the Psyche.

"You kept this from me!" Thoth shouted. If at Anubis or Seshat, neither could tell.

"There's a lot I hide from you, Father. Surely you can relate to the necessity of keeping some things private."

He flashed incandescently and would have burned Eloin's body to a crisp if not for Anubis. 'Calm. Remember, the quill is mightier than the strike. We can learn from this.'

"What did you talk about?"

"Not about this place, nor Seth, if that's what you're worried about," Seshat said, relishing the brief change in power dynamics. "Either he's not aware of what you're doing here or he doesn't think it's important. I'm not sure which option should worry you more, to be honest. Either way, there is something I can tell you: Chronos hadn't been himself for aeons." She paused for emphasis. "He is now."

Thoth's visage elongated into the beak of an ibis. He was losing control of his aspect. Of himself. It shocked Seshat, who never ever thought such a thing possible. He spared one more baleful look in her direction, then turned to Eloin-Rai.

"You said you were the closest thing to Seth's conscience. What did you mean by that?"

Eloin's eyelids fluttered as Rai spoke. "It means he no longer has one. You need to help him."

"It's what we're trying to do."

"No. You're only helping yourself. It's too late for that. You need to make things right."

"Again," Thoth strained. "It's what we're try –"

"How?" Seshat shouted over her father. "How can we make it right? I think Mnemosyne made it pretty clear she will not come to our aid. Not for me, not for Seth, not for anyone."

He snapped his beak, radiating outrage. "She would come if you truly wanted her to. You disappoint me,

Seshat. In all these aeons, I've only asked of you one thing. One simple thing! And you failed me."

She almost choked on hearing these words. But the truth was, she couldn't fault them. Indeed, he had never asked her for anything. All she'd done, for him or because of him, had been of her own choosing.

"No matter. I've planned for such disappointment," he said, suddenly much calmer. "There is more than one way to skin a cat, after all."

Sure, she thought impetuously, but you better kill it first.

"There is?" Anubis asked. Apprehension tainted his derisive tone. Whether caused by Thoth's cryptic statement or the roaring maelstrom forming inside the pit, Seshat couldn't tell. He did look somewhat distracted, though. As if he was not all there, literally. Likely due to the effort of channelling a soul into a realm it no longer belonged to. Or… more likely, he was onto something.

"Forcing everyone to adopt your point of view through sorcery won't make it true – god of wisdom," said Eloin-Rai.

"And yet it's what every entity who calls themselves a deity has been doing since time immemorial," Thoth replied rather defensively.

"Immemorial!" Seshat gasped. And it was like taking her first breath. Of course… Oh, cats!

"This is pointless," Thoth said. "Release the Lokian's soul. She's playing with us while trying to undermine Eloin's will – aren't you?" He grinned spitefully at her. "Good thing we don't need her will, or her mind. Only her life." A glance passed between the god of reckoning and the god of the dead. Anubis rolled his eyes in the most put-upon expression his canine features allowed. Eloin's body seized.

'She waits for you – Sunshine. She waits for you with the truth,' Rai sent to Seshat. Her presence fading.

'What about Seth?' Seshat urged.

'He's done waiting…'

Rai went silent. Light appeared at the bottom of the pit.

"Cats…" Anubis cursed dejectedly.

"What now?" Thoth demanded.

"The bitch used me – us – to show Seth the way through the abyss." He gave Seshat a wry smile. "Oh well. I guess we'll all become stars now."

∞

Lyam heard the power thrumming from the abyss long before he entered the pyramid. The walls, the air, his very soul hummed with it, like the echo of thunder bouncing off mountains. Its telepathy like the whistle of strong winds passing through unsealed windows.

"He's coming," Eloin cried out, her eyes wide, rigid body still floating above the bottomless pit. "I can almost see… Oh! –" Her eyes rolled up in their sockets. She began to shiver. Shivers became convulsions. One last jerking spasm and her body slumped in mid-air like a puppet with loose strings.

"Eloin!" Lyam cried out from the entrance without breaking stride.

"Have you finally accepted your fate, mortal?" Thoth called, coming down from the apex to meet him. "Come, it is not too late to redeem yourself."

Lyam ran around the pit, dodging roots and knowing looks with all the prowess righteous rage could muster. "Redeem? Who the fuck do you think you are to judge me?"

"I am the god of reckoning," Thoth said as if it were a duty rather than a title. Lyam figured it probably was. Gods are often bound to their talents. Unable to be anything else. He didn't care.

"You messed with my mind, my memory – my life! The only thing you're judging is your own work."

"You give me too much credit." Thoth's lips hinted at a smile. "I thought we understood each other."

Lyam squared up to the glowing deity, as if they were the only two beings in the room, as if the moon wasn't about the crash and the universe about to crack. "I understood you well enough. You wanted me to come to you. I refused. I'm only here now because you forced me."

"I did no such thing. I locked you away, in fact. You had to break free to be here – had to want to be here, not because of me or Eloin, but for yourself, of your own free will. Otherwise, it would be pointless." Thoth smirked triumphantly. "And here you are."

"Free will is a bitch," Anubis provided with a snarling grin.

There was no deceit there, Lyam realised, his outrage draining along with his confidence. Once again, he'd played into their game. He thought about turning around and running back up the colony to join the Lokian and Jolyan in their mad quest to teleport onto a Nephilim ship. He almost did. Almost… but deep down, he knew Thoth spoke the truth. He'd wanted to be there. For the first time since they'd taken shelter in that accursed temple, he felt like he was exactly where he was supposed to be.

Anubis was right. Free will is a bitch. But fate… Fate is a cunt.

He spared what he hoped was a good imitation of Jolyan's scowl to the canine god and, pointing at Eloin, said, "Put my sister down. I'm here now. You don't need her."

"Wrong. I need you both." Thoth moved his hand like the conductors of old. Lyam shot into the air towards his sister. He kicked and tried desperately to manoeuvre himself in a different direction, but this was not like being in free fall. Gravity still existed inside the room. It was just not particularly relevant beyond the well.

"You bastard, you piece of shit!" It was pointless to even attempt to offend a god with words, and Lyam felt as powerless as he sounded. Still, words were all he had. "The age of gods will end," he proclaimed, hoping it would come to pass. The Nephilim had been right all along. The Universe didn't need gods, just better mortals. But, of course, the gods would never allow mortals or machines to take their place. How he wished he'd done more to help the androids in their quest to rid the Universe of them.

"Perhaps," the god of reckoning conceded. "Everything must end. But not because of your say-so." He turned to Seshat, who watched in disbelieving silence as her father, scion, mentor and hero, turned into a villain. "Get your quill ready. If ever there was a story worth writing about, this is it."

"I will, trust me." After it's over, she added to herself. She didn't want to miss a thing, aware that this was a spectacle no entity had witnessed for billions of years.

Thoth and Anubis began to chant. She had no idea why. Chanting, much like praying, was for mortals.

"Do something," Lyam urged her. "Help us!"

She opened her mouth to utter an excuse, a reason not to. The truth was, she had no idea what to do that would not make things worse. Helplessness and ignorance were not something a god admitted to lightly. "I told you… I'm not that kind of goddess."

He spat on her foot. She looked at the spittle, and a part of her felt she deserved it. The rest of her, however, was too revolted to agree.

Eloin's eyes, now glazed milky white, looked in Lyam's direction. She lifted a slender arm and extended her hand to him. "It's all right, brother. We were always meant to do this together."

"Do what?" He didn't think they had anything to do together, least of all dying. "Eloin, we've done terrible things, you and I, but we don't deserve to die for them."

"Of course we do. That's why we did them. They were necessary things."

"Were they, though? For whom? For what?"

"For us. So the worthy can prevail." She lifted a limp hand to touch his cheek. It was cold. So very cold. He almost flinched away. "We are two halves of the same being, Lyam. Like the gods of old. And we used to love each other, remember?" She smiled sadly. Tears filled her eyes. "Not the same way now. Not anymore. It's all right. When you replace memory with opportunity, strange things happen. You don't always choose the same path. I would have chosen differently too, had I been given the option." Her eyes became clear again. "But some bonds cannot be broken, not by fate, will or memory. We're still connected. And only together will we make this work." She glanced at their audience. "We are the link."

There it was. The thing he could not escape from. Deep down he'd always known they were two sides of the same being: male and female, flesh and spirit, mind and soul. Now they acted as anchors at the opposite ends of a bridge made of souls and the willpower of the accursed. He lowered his head to kiss her hand and felt a tear run down his nose. He was still able to cry, after all. "You should have told me the truth, sister."

"I tried." She held his hand against her cheek and smiled. "At least one of us got to live, huh?"

"Are you finally ready to accept your role, mortal?" Thoth asked in what sounded to Lyam's ears like mockery.

"Fuck you." He almost choked the words through gritted teeth.

"Ah, well, I wish," Thoth said. "But I won't be the one doing the fucking this time."

Anubis cleared his throat. "Everyone's ready?"

Thoth nodded once. Seshat, still dazed and absorbed by both Rai's words and Thoth's character change, mimicked the gesture.

Anubis wouldn't meet her eye. He thought of Namrive, wherever she was. *I hope at least one of us gets what we want.* "So be it," he said.

Reality shattered. Time stopped. Seshat felt her soul being yanked from her body, pulled into the abyss. A thousand cats scratched at her mind, shredding her will.

"Quetish…" The word escaped her lips in an unbidden farewell.

∞

Lyam heard the word and had an idea.

'Seshat!' he prayed with all his conviction, as one would shout to a loved one amidst a battlefield.

'Get out of my head, mortal! I can't help you.'

'But you can help yourself.'

'How?'

'You told me earlier that curses and links don't mix. That a link can cancel a curse. And that the link between Seth and the Manticore was broken when he was cursed.'

'Yes. So?'

Darkness surged from the abyss at her feet, viscous like thick oil.

'So if we restore the bond between him and the Manticore, can't we free him from his curse?'

Seshat's immediate reaction was dismissal, for clearly the mortal had not understood how links worked, let alone curses. But then, as the darkness crept closer, sentient and determined to drown them in it, she considered it again. The mortal was onto something. We... no. Anyone can cast a curse, but only those involved in a link can forge it. If Seth could do it, he'd have done it by now. But... maybe... maybe the Manticore can – with a bit of help. We need to bring him here. To show him where here is. The smell of brimstone filled the air as dense mist permeated from the doom.

'If I Reach Quetish... perhaps she would bring him along... Seshat winced. 'But I can't. Cats! She won't let me in.' The rude creature had all but severed their link in an attempt to not be dragged into the abyss with her.

'Can we pray to sphinxes?' Lyam asked her.

'Sure, if you know their names…' Seshat stopped herself. 'Quetish! Her name is Quetish of Thebes.'

Lyam closed his eyes and prayed as if his life depended on it because it very much did.

Just as the darkness was about to engulf the room entirely, Quetish materialised, and with her came the Manticore. 'You betrayed me, Seshat.'

'I had to. I'm sorry…'

"You brought that thing here!" Thoth, who rarely raised his voice, shouted in shock.

It took Seshat a moment to realise he meant the Manticore, not Quetish. Then another moment to understand the reason behind his loss in control. And by then it was definitely too late. Seth's curse was broken.

CHAPTER 34

The Last Chance

Real memories are forged by experience.

– Memory on Record

"This one's serious!" Crymure said of the tremor that nearly dislocated Jolyan's vertebrae. They'd all felt pretty serious to her, but he had a point. This one didn't feel like it came from the core of the moon but from far out. A shockwave rather than a quake.

"Have we hit the planet?" A stupid question, she realised the moment she'd said it. Had it been that, she would not be asking questions.

"They breached it. The fools actually breached the abyss." Crymure rubbed his face. "The Mentor will be furious." He laughed then; not how he'd programmed himself to, but how he felt it should be done.

Jolyan scowled at what sounded like a string of hiccoughs. Likely the last sound she'd ever hear. If that wasn't proof of the cruelty of fate, she didn't know what was.

"What?" he asked, his laughter cut short by her silent vitriol.

"I can't believe I'm going to die here. With one of you." She'd had a similar thought earlier with Lyam and could not decide which offended her more.

He grinned. "At least you're dying in good company."

"Is that what you think you are?"

The grin vanished. "You should really reconsider your attitude towards other people before you die."

"Ah. But you're not people." She glared at his hand. "Only a poor imitation of it."

He glared at her. "I've met mortals like you. They think life is nothing but pain and suffering. A trial before death. Sure, I can't claim to know what it's like to be alive. To have to breathe and eat. To feel cold or old. But I know what it's like to be conscious, to be sentient, and I will defend this state with every fibre, gem, chip and circuit in my body. It might not be life as you define it. But it's still life. It will endure. It will survive."

"That's my point. Life is meant to end," she said.

He leaned in conspiratorially, lips curled into a smirk, and whispered, "Ever wondered why that is?"

Before she could even think of an answer, Audric ran into the room. "You're still here?" he sounded simultaneously disappointed and relieved. He was alone and looked like he'd been to the Underworld and back. He dashed to the ring without losing his stride.

"It doesn't work," Crymure replied, waving the useless device at the Lokian.

"It will." Audric showed him the missing pin and gemstone. Crymure stood up, eagerness and the need to survive trumping his pride and animosity towards the man. He helped Jolyan to her feet.

"Where's the strange one?" the old woman asked.

Audric paused a moment, jaw tensing, eyebrows furrowing, and said nothing as he clicked the parts into place more forcefully than necessary. The gems began to glow.

"Thank you for waiting," he told Jolyan.

"As if we had a choice," Crymure grumbled in reply.

"There's always a choice. You could have smashed the device and sealed all our fates. You did not."

It was Crymure's turn to tense his jaw. "Some choices are not worth making."

"A wise machine." Audric could have laughed.

The ring came alive. "You first," Crymure said as he gently guided Jolyan to the inner circle next to Audric.

"I – I'm not sure we'll all fit," she said, comparing the diameter of the ring with the combined width of the two men.

Crymure opened his mouth to say something muffled by another tremor. "We will." He pressed the old woman up against Audric and did his best to fit in himself.

He had only time to look up and see the ceiling collapse before a beam of pure white light took them. And…

… The next thing he knew, he was flailing on a metal deck with a leg missing, severed by a transversal cut from the knee almost to the groin. His right arm gone below the elbow – the arm he'd used to make sure Jolyan stayed safe inside the teleportation ring. The old woman looked dazed and confused, but alive and intact, supported by Audric, who was, much to Crymure's disappointment, also alive and intact.

"Thank you, young man," she said – to him! Crymure nearly glitched, but Namrive was there too, looming above him, looking as good as new and displaying little sympathy for his condition.

"Anubis is not with you." Her tone defined annoyance.

Crymure had always tried to remain pleasant, cheerful even, especially amongst his peers, but for some reason, could not bring himself to be so right now. "Excellent observation, Namrive. I thought you were going to get yourself fixed."

"I am fixed." The words were uttered from deep in her throat with strained civility. She assessed the rest of the group with flickering eyes. "Explain these two."

He did so as accurately and succinctly as he could.

"What I am to do with a Lokian and an old Narrum?"

"I don't know, Namrive. What about helping me up first?" She just kept staring at him as if unable to understand the question.

Crymure cursed and tried to stand, glad that he could feel no pain. If only he didn't feel shame either, that would be great. The attempt failed. He tried to sit up. And failed at that too. Jolyan finally came to his aid, bracing his torso against her spindly legs, trying to lift him up by the armpits. "Fuck, you're heavy. A little help would be good." Namrive just kept staring at them as if she'd never seen the like. For she had not.

Despite her best efforts, there was no way the frail woman would be able to lift, let alone support Crymure's dense body, not even in the low gravity of the ship. It never ceased to amuse Namrive how hard and how often these mortals tried to overcome forces so much greater than themselves. Audric, not wanting to help but also unwilling to stand inside the ring much longer, reluctantly obliged and single-handedly dragged Crymure to the nearest seat – an action that vexed the Nephilim as much as him.

Audric who'd been prepared to fight a horde of machines tooth and nail to the death, wasn't sure how to do deal with this turn of events. So he just stood there, feeling and looking – he had no doubt – much like a fool. Crymure's feelings were similar as he sat propped precariously, holding on to the last vestiges of his artificial dignity.

"We need to get out of here, Namrive – like, minutes ago."

"The drive's ready," she said. "The wormhole's open. We're one thought away from hyperspace."

"Think it, then!"

"Anubis is not back yet."

"Bugs to Anubis! He's a god of the dead. He'll be fine; we will not. I, for one, don't want to end up in a resurrection ship."

Namrive assessed him dispassionately. "In your condition, it might not be a bad thing. In any case, this ship is perfectly capable of withstanding a celestial event. It will enrich our records." And provide an excuse to erase many others, she added mentally with measurable relief.

"This will be a lot more than a celestial event. Remember when Marduk destroyed a solar system?"

"The entire galaxy will remember that for aeons

to come," she replied, still unconcerned, for the ship had withstood that one. Crymure had always been an alarmist.

"Yeah… well, this will be much worse."

"One more reason to witness it," said she.

The imminent catastrophe appeared on every screen. Audric picked the main display, closed his eyes, and sighed. Pandora… He regretted letting her go. Regretted bringing her out of the tower. Regretted… so many things in regard to her. But he regretted trusting the gods most of all.

As if by summons, Pandora appeared, radiant as ever. He smiled despite himself, but his happiness died a violent death the moment he noticed she had no bracelet. No gem or device of any kind, in fact. She wasn't even on the teleportation ring!

This did not go unnoticed by Namrive either, who rounded on her with an arsenal of sensors and shields.

"Crymure?" Rarely had so many questions been packed into one word.

His mouth hung agape. "It worked? It worked!" He sounded feverishly delighted and very, very pleased with himself. "How about that… I thought she was scrap."

The silvery woman looked harmless, practically brainless, by the way she just stood there, blinking expectantly. When Crymure fell silent, she shifted her attention to the screens.

Namrive looked closer at her. "You told me you were working on a new model, but this… There's so much living tissue on her. How did you…? How is she…?"

Audric, too, would love to hear the answer to those questions. All eyes fell on Crymure.

He grinned slyly. "It's something I only learned recently. Souls – proper ones – prefer living hosts. They rebel against the artificial and the inert. Even so, despite my best efforts, the host failed to contain the soul that mattered. As it turns out, living minds also rebel against foreign souls. It's good to see not all my work was in vain, though. We might still learn something useful out of this one."

Pandora seemed enthused by the prospect.

Namrive shared no such feelings. "How did she get here?!"

"Love," Crymure said, not really understanding the meaning of the word.

"For the Maker's sake. You can't possibly believe that nonsense."

Jolyan cackled at the androids arguing about love.

Crymure ignored their ridicule.

"I believe in magic, Namrive. Why not love?"

Even though she too had started to believe in magic, she had no idea how to even begin comparing the two.

He did not wait for an answer. "I found that the key to teleportation is not bending reality to your will; it's having a strong connection to someone at the destination."

Pandora shared the briefest of glances with Audric, confirming the hypothesis.

"If we can understand and master these connections, we won't need devices or rings. We can go anywhere. Whenever we want. Just like the gods."

Namrive almost glitched. "That's against the rules. The Mentor forbids it." And only now did Namrive understand why. For Athena herself could not translocate anywhere. It was the reason she inspired humans to build ships and coerced Hephaestus to create teleportation rings.

Crymure tsked. "Do you always do what the Mentor says? Namrive, it's me you're talking to and these…" – he paused, trying to come up with a term that encompassed the diversity in the room – "beings don't give a damn about our rules."

"Correct," Pandora said. She smiled at Audric. "But I care for this one a great deal. That's why I came to tell you that you must move the ship away."

"That's very sweet, but this is my ship. I'm the one who decides when and where it moves," Namrive said.

"And if you wish to continue making those decisions, you will set a course for Asgard without delay," Pandora said matter-of-factly.

Namrive took a step towards her. "What are you? How do you know about Asgard?"

"The same way I know Athena forgot to mention the Suzerain invited you specifically or that Anubis will get a lot more than he bargained for and that this vessel won't remain intact when the end begins." Pandora cocked her head as if listening to something. "Speaking of... There's one more thing I need to do. Now move the ship!"

She was gone before Namrive could articulate any sort of reply.

CHAPTER 35

The Cause

*You can't remember the future. You can't write
it either. You can only dream it.*

– Memory on Record

"You must not call upon the abyss!" Quetish said. The Manticore roared in a language not even the gods understood, but the tone bolstered the sphinx's words perfectly. "Your kind is not yet ready to grasp the full consequences of this action. The chaos god must not get free."

"What do you care?" said Thoth, the words loaded with scorn. As liminal creatures, sphinxes should have no take on the affairs of gods. He shot daggers at Seshat for indulging such relentless insubordination. "Your pet threatens more doom than an oracle. Don't worry, creature. We've prepared for this moment. Seth's singular will is of no match for the many."

"You're mistaken. He's no longer singular," Quetish said, translating the Manticore's words. "If you won't listen to me, listen to him."

Thoth frowned. The suggestion, the very notion, was beyond outrageous. He'd rather take advice from a burning bush than a lion with a scorpion's tail. "Souls don't share consciousness," he said, hoping it would put an end to the nonsense. Next the creature would suggest they'd listen to the Narrum's opinions as well.

"I didn't say he was conscious," she sneered.

"What did you say, then – riddler?"

"You fed the wills of thousands of corrupted souls into the Well of Eternity, believing you were powering a curse, but you were just keeping the balance. And now the balance is gone."

"What changed?"

"A Lokian soul is worth thousands of Narrum. Dayna gave Seth the strength he needed to fight back. Rai won him the battle."

That gave Thoth pause. Rai's soul was indeed more wilful than most. And she'd been a powerful empath, to boot. Still, two souls could not win against thousands, surely. Two post-human souls and Seth's own, he corrected himself. A quick glance at Anubis told him that the god of the dead shared his doubt. "Why has he not destroyed us, then?"

"Chaos is stormy, but not impatient. He'll wait until the last moment to regain full strength, for he does not simply want to be free. He wants to become more powerful than those who took his freedom in the first place."

"As if –" Thoth started.

"We have no intention of binding Seth again, Quetish," Anubis shouted over him. "We want him free, in fact. And we only want to talk – I promise!" He wrung his hands behind his back, straining for clarity and diplomacy. "Can we please get on with this? Time has no dominion here, but gravity still controls the fate of celestial objects, and it will not spare this moon on our account."

This seemed to please Quetish obscenely. "You know what, Anpu… You're absolutely right." The look she gave him then would haunt Anubis for the rest of his existence.

The entire pyramid began to undulate in heat haze. The abyss continued to swirl faster, darker than a singularity. The walls seemed to dissolve into smoke one moment, then turn to liquid obsidian the next. Quetish and the Manticore vanished, blending into that liminal darkness. Reality cracked.

Seshat tried desperately to remain tethered to the shattering realm. 'Quetish!' she called. There was no answer, but she could still feel her there in the gaps between realms, simultaneously close yet farther away than ever.

Thoth turned to Anubis. "What's happening now?"

The god of the dead, his mouth slightly agape, replied, "I'm not sure…" And he truly didn't. Beyond the darkness, on the other side of the abyss, lay the unknown.

"This is what happens when you play with curses," the entity that used to be Dayna echoed from atop the room.

"How did you get here?" Thoth's first realisation was that the twins were no longer guarding the threshold. The second was that this Dayna could teleport at will. And last but unfortunately not least, she was not hosting a deity.

Pandora, enveloped in a platinum aura, soared through the darkness, closing the distance with Thoth.

"Curses are the main weapons of gods," he told her, readying himself for anything.

"Weapons powered purely by will and whim, unopposed by logic," she elaborated, halting a few feet away from him. "Yes, I am familiar with the gods' arsenal. But what happens to a curse when logic ceases to be logical and the rules of reality change?"

Thoth frowned slightly but said nothing.

"So far your kind has been playing a safe game – a rigged game." She stared at the vortex below. "Open that portal and you'll be playing by a completely new set of rules. And once this moon is destroyed, you'll be left with no rules at all."

He remained silent. The ankh on his chest glowing white hot.

She tilted her head and blinked. "That is what you want." A realisation rather than a statement. She smiled, a very sad, very tired smile. "You don't know what you want, god."

"Who are you?" Thoth demanded heatedly, prickled by her tone.

Her eyes turned completely black. "I was One before the Three. And one amongst the eight. I am the thirteenth. I am…" She paused. "I was Order before Time."

Thoth seemed to flinch. His eyes narrowed and he shook his head imperceptibly in the overtures of denial. Then he clapped his beak in an ibis equivalent of a tsk. "No. You are a construct, a lifeless, soulless aberration of artificial flesh and circuitry. What you think you are is nothing but an imprint left by the echo of Mnemosyne's soul and the faulty organ mortals call a brain."

She moved even closer and squinted at him. "Is that what you think I am – truly?" She leaned forward still, pupils as dark as the void boring into his soul.

Thoth's eyes widened. He took a step back in the air. "Cats…" he breathed. Thoth never breathed. Seshat felt herself shiver. She looked at the entity they called Pandora again, really looked, but had no idea what he saw. "Father?"

With some difficulty, Thoth peeled his gaze from her to Seshat. His human face returned, ashen. The ankh's light dimmed, then extinguished. "I've been… mistaken," he said with the gravity of ages. He stared at his daughter, the part of him he didn't own. The only part of him he'd ever loved. "Seshat, you need to go. Save yourself. Warn the others. Tell them… Tell them the Fates…" He grabbed her by the shoulders. "Seshat, the Fates lied. They've been lying to us all along!"

"No," Pandora said, her tone omniscient. "They just don't remember the truth."

His eyes went wide. Like the eyes of prey caught between a predator and a precipice.

"What others? Go where, Father?" Seshat demanded, confused. She tried to move but the darkness had taken over her body if not her will. "There's no way out!"

"There is one." Pandora looked straight down, then back to Seshat.

Oh, no no, Seshat thought. "I don't understand you," she said.

"We often misunderstand what we don't want to accept," her father said. She turned to Anubis. "Do something!"

"What?" Anubis asked, genuinely dumbfounded. This new development had not featured in any of his plans.

"The night will return when Chaos meets Free Will." Pandora spoke in an oracle's voice. Then she winked at Seshat and let herself fall into the void.

∞

Lyam tried not to stare into the Stygian abyss – its darkness all around them – so he watched the gods instead. He could hear their thoughts clearly now – all their thoughts – as if there was no longer a barrier between their minds and his, no difference between body and mind, in fact. As if distinctions such as mortal and deity or matter and spirit no longer applied.

Their thoughts, he realised, were not their own. Much as Lyam's had not been really his until the abyss had restored them. Suddenly, the gravity of the situation became clear to him. Why the gods behaved as they had. Why nothing seemed to make sense. The thing he had not comprehended or ever have fathomed. For the gods were supposed to be the enemy. More than that, they were supposed to be powerful and divine and more aware of these things than mortals could ever be. But… They don't know. The gods don't remember it all either. They're being played, used like we are by forces far greater than themselves.

With the realisation, his role in this madness became

clear. He felt the darkness grip tighter, and he kicked at the air again, for all the good it did. "Kill me!" he demanded – begged of the gods. "You must kill me now."

"You'll be dead soon enough," Thoth assured him.

"You really can't see it. You've no idea what you've done. Seth's not alone in there!"

"I have seen more than you can ever imagine," Thoth said with unbearable sadness, burning cold.

"Enough of this shit." Anubis swirled his cape, and with a flick of his fingers – for show, Seshat had no doubt – he reached into the abyss, the Underworld and beyond.

The pyramid rocked violently. Cracks spread along its walls. The sound of stone grinding, shattering, collapsing upon itself was deafening. Seshat fought the urge to cower. She willed herself away – anywhere would do, even the heart of a dead star. But it was as if nothing existed beyond that room, and before she could take that realisation in properly, smoke erupted from the bottomless pit.

Seshat had never seen a soul, not really. Only the gods of the Underworld and the goddess of the soul herself possessed that ability. But she had seen primordial gods in their true form, before Gaea created life from matter, to both limit and enrich a god's experience in reality. What she witnessed now was the manifestation of that primordial, unbound state. A will so strong and wild and furious it smothered hers as it pushed itself from the abyss in a whirlwind of chaos, lightning, sand, and flame. It filled the room until it too realised it could not escape it, so it sought a host, an anchor of flesh and blood.

Lyam shuddered as the beam of light amongst the darkness – darker than the mere absence of light – came to claim him. It had substance, like a heavy blanket smothering air, light and space itself. An oppressing weight, both physical and metaphysical, pressed him from all sides, percolating into his skin and lungs. Helplessness, anger, dread and regret filled his mind, ravaging his will. His last sight was of Eloin, beatifically beaming up from the well, her soul already gone, beckoning. He fought passionately, desperately, aggressively. He fought like a man with nothing to lose but himself.

And he lost.

The god of chaos took Lyam's body and soul – the soul he shared with Eloin – into himself, moulding their flesh to his shape as one would a lump of clay, and once armed with it, he broke from his prison into this realm, materialising as the recognisable aspect of Seth: god of deserts, storms, chaos and – Seshat reminded herself – war.

He was handsome, over seven feet tall with dark red skin that shone with what at first resembled the shine on the other scions of Ra, but upon closer observation, Seshat saw it was reflecting light, not emitting it. He was covered in refracting scales, like those of a snake, had jet-black eyes, black hair and black lips, and his talons, also black, were longer than his fingers. He grinned wickedly as if he'd just remembered some particularly amazing mischief, fangs sharp like those of a viper.

Gods and monsters, Seshat realised. Two aspects of the same entity.

Anubis recovered first. He took a step forward, and Seth wrapped him in a tornado of sand. The god of the dead instinctively tried to translocate to the Underworld and realised his mistake just in time to avoid being swallowed by the abyss.

He cursed himself for his reactionary stupidity, pushed the sand away with his will and held his hands up, fingers spread out in an appeasing gesture. "Seth! I understand you are upset –"

Seth lashed out again.

"We just want to talk!" Anubis shouted through the sandstorm. He meant it. There was no way he'd risk Reaching Seth's mind, so they would have to use words to communicate.

Seth hissed. "Talk? You were never interested in what I had to say."

"I was, believe me. I truly was!" He really wasn't, but it's very hard to be honest without being rude.

"If you don't want to talk, at least listen," Thoth said.

"I'm done listening to you too." Seth flung a storm of ash and brimstone at the god of reckoning. Thoth immediately conjured a shield of light. The air shimmered inches away from his skin, untouched.

Seth's forked tongue flickered in distaste. "Only fools and cravens fight with magic."

"Not every god can be as aggressive and vile as you," Thoth replied. "Anubis, with me."

The two gods began combining their wills to counter another attack.

"Enough!" Seshat bellowed. If she had a star for every time she'd broken up a fight by shouting that word, she'd have an entire cluster by now.

Seth's burning gaze fixed on her in a mixture of surprise and curiosity. "Well, well, the young scribe has a will of her own but not much more sense than her sire if she thinks she can order me –"

"It's not an order; it's a request. I am asking you – all of you! – to stop. Just stop and think for a moment."

"I'm done thinking," Seth said, launching another attack, aimed at her.

"We can help you forget," Anubis interceded, taking the blow.

Seth's scowl broke into a vicious smile. "If I forget, how can I avoid being deceived and trapped again? No. When you forget, you don't learn."

"We won't curse you again, I promise. A god's promise is binding even if no one remembers it." After all, that is how Fate operates. Even if you don't remember the choices you've made, you're still compelled to make the decisions needed to fulfil those promises.

"I don't need your promises, dog. I have my will and the will of the thousands you sent to torment me – plus the one sent by Ra," he added meaningfully. "Quite addictive – willpower. The more you have, the more you want it." He turned to Seshat. A drop of venom dripped from a fang as he spoke. "I think I'll start with you."

"No!" Thoth shouted. Anubis shouted something too, but Seshat could not quite discern what. The impact that followed felt beyond physical or wilful. One moment Seshat stood above the altar, the next she was falling into the darkness, pushed by both gravity and Thoth's powerful will. He fell alongside her, Ankh burning hot on his chest. Its light dimmed fast, though, smothered by the blanket of darkness stretched out around them. This close to his flesh, her reach showed her what her eyes had not yet perceived and his Reach had not allowed her to see. Lines of liquid light radiated from deep within that symbol, all the way to his heart and brain. Not the flowing web of root and vein but the straight and angular matrix of circuity. She'd seen similar patterns in Namrive, Pandora, and Crymure. She gasped. 'Father, what have they done to you?'

'I did it to myself.'

'Why?'

'It's not important now. Listen to me. Only your heart's greatest desire can save you, Sunshine.' He sounded half a universe away. 'I'm sorry it had to be this way… You must—'

Seshat never heard the rest.

Seth brought down the mountainous World Tree on top of them, and along with them, it too fell into the abyss moments before the moon collided, ripping itself and the planet apart in an explosion of astronomical proportions.

The debris would eventually be trapped and burned away by the red giant that'd once been Ra. But its ripples across space would affect everything in their path.

Seshat fell and kept falling until she began to fade from existence. No, no, this can't be happening. She actually felt herself vanish, dissolved into stardust – by the violence of the event or the pull of the abyss, she couldn't tell. It didn't matter which. Time had ceased to exist, and without it, cause and consequence no longer mattered. Aeons passed in seconds; seconds lasted ages. Seshat remembered every story she'd ever written, every moment she'd ever lived, every dream she'd had, every word spoken, every feeling she'd felt and place she'd been.

And then there was nothing.

CHAPTER 36

The Consequences

*Time changes everything, but Time itself is
only changed by one thing.*

        – Memory on Record

Seshat floated in emptiness – more concept than a being. There was no sign of her father, Anubis, Seth or anyone. Outside her mind, there was nothing. No life, no light, no substance. Nothing. Is this death? Dread crawled across her conceptual being at the idea. She'd always wondered what it would be like to die, to experience the other side as mortals do. A curiosity, not a desire, mind. Certainly not a wish. And no matter how much she loved to be alone with her thoughts, she did not like this. Not one bit. She would go mad without light, or warmth, or touch, or someone else's thoughts.

Oh, cats… what's happened to me? Even her mind didn't sound like hers. Sound didn't sound like sound at all either. Of course not. There was no matter, no air in this vacuum. How could there be sound? There was something akin to it, though…

A rhythmic rustle broke the stillness now and again.

Soft at first, then louder, closer. Wings! Something winged approached from what seemed every direction at once in this three-dimensional darkness. A familiar presence tickled her mind, and Seshat's heart soared in recognition. Thank the stars! I'm not completely lost yet.

Quetish suddenly appeared in the wake of a luminous beam that pierced the nothingness, looking so majestically radiant it almost blinded her perception. Sphinxes were older than legends, born when the universe was young, before it'd been overrun by wilful gods and their troubles. Quetish fit right in with the emptiness, as it was a mere frame for her presence. Seshat had never been happier to see her.

"You really screwed up this ending, Seshat," the sphinx tutted.

"It's not over yet," Seshat heard herself say, although she had no voice. No mouth even. This will take some getting used to, she thought, annoyed.

"Oh, but it is. You need to acknowledge failure before you can understand success."

"Are you going to help me or just lecture me to death with cryptic platitudes?" retorted Seshat, whose patience had been left behind in the abyss along with what once had been herself.

Quetish smiled, tempted by the prospect. "You can't be helped, Seshat. You are like a problem that has no solution because it's already solved."

"How so?"

"You don't exist; therefore you cannot cease to exist."

"?" emoted Seshat, at a loss for words or understanding.

"I suppose it is the natural progression of the soul:

from life to death to eternity until the many will again become one."

For cat's sake… "Quetish, you're not making sense. Please, can you help me or not? At least tell me what happened!"

"No. I only came to say goodbye. This story is over. But this is only one book amongst many volumes yet to be written."

The Manticore appeared in her perception, and the sphinx took flight after him. "May the Fates see fit for us to meet again in Thebes, goddess of writing, chronicler of ages, scion of Thoth – my friend."

And before Seshat could say anything else or make sense of her words, the two legendary beings had vanished as if they'd never been there.

Moments – aeons? – later, she felt rather than heard their link break, like the snap of a delicate twig. Panic gripped her soul. She was about to unravel when she felt a touch on her shoulder. So light, so familiar, simultaneously real and unreal. A touch of the mind, of the will and of memory, not flesh. Could it be? Seshat turned, still bound to the concept of turning at such things, and sure enough, there she was, holding her golden torch – the light that defined darkness.

Mina.

∞

Anubis was dead. Or as close to it as a god of the dead came to be: bodiless, aimless, practically soulless in the timelessness of space. No amount of willpower would overcome that fact. Gods are able to heal their flesh, change aspects, size, and even regenerate their bodies indefinitely, as long as their souls remain intact and there's a body to repair in the first place, of course. Anubis' affinity with the stars meant he would survive even under extreme heat and pressure, but being caught between realms in a collision of astronomical proportions had pushed his survival abilities beyond the extreme. He was still aware, however. He still existed, somehow.

There were advantages to being ethereal. Translocation, for one, became much easier, and he had none of the usual vexations caused by physical bodies to deal with. But he liked to feel, to walk and talk, and to have the means to interfere. It would be hard to keep an eye on things without an actual hand to guide them.

That's what keeping promises does to a god.

He thought of Seshat. Had she heard what he'd said to her in that last moment? There'd been so much noise… so much happening at once. He hoped she'd willed herself to her heart's desire. If indeed the goddess of memory had been her heart's greatest desire. It would not surprise Anubis to find out Seshat had returned to Niflheim or the arms of another trickster. He ached at the possibility. Wouldn't that be just the thing to add insult to his loss…

Thoth was not with him, which was strange, but just as well. He'd had enough of the god of reckoning. He's probably with Ra. Either Ra or Chronos, Anubis decided. The god had always wanted to control the Cosmos. Anubis snorted at the idea of Thoth meeting Chronos. Who would be more disappointed? he wondered. Not that it mattered now. If they were meant to meet, they would, and it would not mean a thing to Anubis because he'd lost all meaning.

'Time is inexorable, and so are the things you work so hard to avoid; otherwise, you wouldn't feel the need to,' a Chronodéndron once said. He sighed and would have laughed if only he still had a smile.

And then, just as suddenly and disconcertingly as it had been vaporised, his body began to coalesce, bit by bit, until he was whole again, alive and utterly confused. He opened his eyes. Namrive, of all creatures, stood right in front of him, repaired and shining like polished jewellery.

'What in the name of Ra are you doing here?' he wondered, still breathless and unable to articulate speech. Of all the entities he'd expected to find in the abyss, Nephilim did not make the list. They had no soul.

"Welcome back," she said and sounded almost sincere. "We thought we'd lost you. That was a spectacular event."

His body tingled all over with new-found sensation – pain, mostly. Because of course, life is pain, even for a god. Through the haze of his resurrection, he recognised where he was. Back on Namrive's ship. That meant a whole different kind of pain. "How?" he croaked.

"New technology." She winked, and it actually looked natural. "Thanks to Crymure, we've finally figured out how to teleport across vast distances without an anchor or ring," Namrive replied in a tone that sounded almost cheerful. "Your body didn't make it, sorry. but that should not be a problem with this one from now on." She pointed at a diamond panel set on his forearm. It matched the one embedded in her own new flesh. "Really, I'm almost embarrassed that it has taken us this long, but you know how it is: necessity is the mother of invention, or so they used to say. For once, they were right."

'How?' he repeated in thought, already dreading the answer.

"Souls were the key. They're like serial numbers; each one is unique. Yours is quite large. It took me so long to input, I almost feared you wouldn't make it." Namrive smiled, and it not only looked genuine, it was actually a pleasant smile to contemplate.

"Seshat?" he mumbled. Still learning how to articulate his new body properly.

The smile on Namrive's lips wilted. "Too late for her, I'm afraid. I found no other souls, er… intact, shall we say, after I secured yours."

"Seth?" he asked.

"Like I said, you're the last survivor."

Last, not only, he noted.

Namrive shook her head gracefully. "The moon's gone. So is the planet and whatever realms existed between the two. There's nothing left but dust out there orbiting the sun. It won't be long before even that's burned out. You were lucky!" The notion disturbed him.

She patted him on the shoulder almost tenderly. He gawked at her, unsure if this Namrive was even real. He certainly hoped she wasn't for real.

"Is the star still there?"

"Ra, you mean? Yes, of course." She curled her lip, clearly not yet over her experience with Apollo.

He closed his eyes. Then opened them again and sighed. Ra must have intervened before the end, Anubis told himself. Better that than any alternative. It was a fair assumption. Otherwise, they wouldn't be here still. He sat up and looked down at himself, naked on the pod. His skin tone was wrong. Brown hair fell down his chest almost to his navel. And he looked somewhat longer, overall.

"Whose body is this?"

Namrive seemed confused by the question. "Yours, of course."

"My body was nothing like this."

"Hence, we made you this one. A much better one."

"Unless you have Gaea tucked away in one of your soul cages, I don't see how you could have designed a body fit for a god." And yet the body was flawless. As strong and receptive to will as any deity's vessel, once you got the hang of it, that is. Not a mortal's body at all. And certainly not his. Not since he'd become Anubis.

Namrive leaned in and whispered, "You think you've been with us this long and we haven't scanned every bit of you?" She showed him a wicked smile. "Come on. It wasn't just your knowledge of the Underworld that interested us. The Nephilim have been trying to build bodies fit for gods since the very beginning. Now we finally can. You're welcome."

He lifted the palms of his hands to his face, and when he saw the myriad web of circuitry hidden there, under his skin, he almost wished to be incorporeal again. Is this what they did to Thoth? He pushed the thought away.

"You look… well," Anubis said, shifting the subject from his body to hers, which now seemed to have everything a living body should except a heartbeat. Much like his own. Oh, cats…

"Thank you! I feel well too." She grinned, a seemingly genuine grin radiating joy. Anubis knew how to deal with the harsh, rational, artificial Namrive. Or even the broken, self-conscious Namrive. This new and improved, borderline omniscient one freaked him out more than a clowder of purring cats.

Movement caught his eye, drawing his attention to the far side of the room, where he spotted Audric and his strange new wife, judging him in silence. The other survivors, he reckoned. A pity, he'd rather deal with his priest in the Underworld. And with her, not at all. Whatever animated the android was unlike any soul he'd seen. Something untouched by time, bound to her body like atmosphere to a planet.

"Hey."

Anubis turned awkwardly to face the speaker.

Crymure reclined on the pod next to him with a mechanical contraption attached to his leg. What was left of it, anyway. He waved as if to show off his hand, thoroughly repaired. The other was like the leg, a work in progress. "Glad to have you back." By his side sat a very old human, scowling at him.

Anubis cleared his throat in an effort to avoid engaging in conversation before he fully understood what he'd resurrected into. He had no idea how long he'd been dead either. Judging by the state of affairs, long enough to regret it, that's for sure. He turned to Namrive again. "Right… what did I miss?"

Namrive waved her flawless hand in a smooth, almost coquettish motion, as if his ignorance was of no importance. "Oh, I have so much to tell you. It can wait, though. We have a long journey ahead, and quite an assortment of travellers, aren't they?" Her black eyes swept across the group, flickering faster when they took in the android.

Anubis swallowed. "Yes, I am impressed." Any being who was not a god recently brought back from oblivion would have said he was shocked, in fact. "You were always so against taking in strays."

"Ah, well… Things change," she said sternly.

He coughed to hide a nervous chuckle. "How was the Mentor, by the way?" He wanted to ask how it had gone between them, but judging by Namrive's restored state, he figured it must have gone pretty damn well. Perhaps a bit too well for her, which explained why nothing had gone well for him.

"The Mentor? Oh, she is…" Namrive tapped her lips. "What's the word, hmmm…. Shrewd. She's been two steps ahead of us the entire way."

"Oh... I see."

"No, you don't." Her face lip up with impish glee. "Because now, you and I are on a completely different path."

"To where?" As if he had to ask. He'd be shipped to Pallas and linked to a soul source in no time. Cursed to rust inside a dead World Tree on some forsaken world, playing god to a machine.

Namrive grinned, and never before had Anubis been so terrified by the sight of teeth.

"Asgard."

Few things surprised a god, but when they did… they did. "Wh –?" was all he managed to say.

Her vicious grin widened. "We've been invited – by the Suzerain himself."

Epilogue

The Record

The past is already written.

— Memory on Record

Thoth crossed the great palace of Pallas on foot, as all – mortal, deity or machine – must as per the Mentor's decree. Athena believed walking kept you grounded, humbled by gravity. And gods could always use some humbling – the Mentor most of all.

He now stood before her, humbled but not abashed. Defeated but not a failure. Bereaved but not grieving. He conjured his book and quill. And he waited.

Belus and Agenor, the demigods who'd modelled the upgraded Faithful Ninguém and Nenhum, stood to either side of her throne, looking dead ahead. Sturdy and imposing as the pillars themselves.

Athena was clearly not impressed with his report. She became impatient when unimpressed, so he didn't have to wait long. "God of reckoning, I expected a more favourable resolution from you, and great deal sooner."

He waved his quill languidly as if time was of no consequence. "It's resolved. That's all that matters."

I'll decide what matters, she thought, but kept her lips pressed shut. The god of reckoning always believed himself wiser than she because he was older. And male. And sure, age brought wisdom. A cock did not.

"What happened to Crymure?"

Thoth had no need to feign ignorance. He had not seen or thought about that Nephilim since he'd sent him away from the pyramid. "He hasn't resurrected yet?"

"Would I be asking if he had?"

The god shrugged. "Once he ceased to be relevant to my account, my attention turned to others."

"Hmmm." It wasn't that Athena cared for Crymure, for she did not. She did find him useful, though. And another point of view of the events on Sombra would not have gone amiss either. But gods like her learned to work with what they had. "So tell me, who did you and Anubis release from the abyss? Sekhmet, Ymir…" – her mouth twisted – "Zagreus?" Any of them would suit her purposes, to be fair. But she really disliked the latter.

Thoth was not surprised the Mentor knew what they had really been doing on Sombra despite their secrecy and subterfuge, only concerned about the extent of her knowledge. You're wiser than her, he assured himself. And, as her question suggested, the goddess knew very little of the actual abyss. "As far as I can tell, none of them," he said truthfully. Then waited for her reaction.

Athena's eyes widened to match those of her owl in a poor attempt to disguise disappointment with surprise. "Oh? Why not?"

"They were not there." He dismissed his book as one closes a matter.

The goddess stood, eyes blazing. "Then who was?"

"Seth," he said matter-of-factly. A half-truth. The Mentor could always tell when someone lied, but she was colour-blind to the truth. It had taken him centuries to learn this, and the knowledge had yet to fail him.

Her thin lips pressed tight while her jaw muscles worked hard. "I see," she said dryly. "And?"

"He will not be a problem," Thoth replied without hesitation. Another colourful truth. The god who had once been Seth no longer existed. Somewhere in the abyss, Seth's soul had amalgamated with Apophis and cats only knew how many others. Such things were not possible in this universe, but different universes meant different possibilities.

Athena smiled bitterly. "Not compared with the others, you mean."

He blinked, concerned that she might have read his mind.

"The other gods of chaos," she elaborated.

"Just so." He relaxed and resumed his notes.

"Will he join us?"

Thoth pretended to consider this. "He needs to calm down first. Let him cause some havoc. Destroy a world or two. He'll come to us once he gets bored. And when he does, we'll take control of him."

"You're very confident for someone who just lost control of the beast."

"In order to control the weather, you need to allow it to storm now and then."

"Huh." Zeus had said the same thing about Typhon. It had worked well for him, so she let it go. For now. There were more pertinent matters at hand.

She sat down and nodded to Agenor. From behind her throne he brought forth a book. It had to have been very well shielded, for it blazed like a sun, and Thoth hadn't even been aware of its presence up until that moment. The twin gave it to Athena, who held it with the caution and contempt most would hold a venomous snake, then threw it at Thoth's feet.

It looked very similar to his own book in terms of size and shape, but this one was alabaster-white. Memory on Record by Seshat shone in iridescent nacre on its cover.

"What's this?"

"You tell me. It's dedicated to you."

The volume would not come to his hand by will. Thoth had to bend to pick it up. He opened it. The dedication read: 'To Thoth, for teaching me that words can mean more than actions.'

His hands trembled. "Where did you find this?"

"On a lectern. Inside my private chamber. It appeared out of thin air." Her gaze fell on him with the intensity of a quasar. "Seshat. That is your daughter, correct?"

He nodded, trying not to choke on his own breath. "Have you read it?" he asked.

"I've read enough," she lied. The book brimmed with trillions of pages. To read them all would take centuries, and try as she might, the words just fled from her mind past that first page. She got the gist of it, though. A record of the history of the Universe – the real history – told by the goddess of memory herself. After all she'd done to keep Mnemosyne hidden and, more importantly, silent, the existence of such a book was more than a declaration of war, it was a violation of the rules Zeus imposed after the Titanomachy. "I want to know how that thing can even exist."

Thoth had a theory, although he would rather read the book before sharing it. He licked his lips. "Seshat fell into the abyss." No, that's not correct. Tell the truth, not the facts, for once. "I… pushed her."

"Why?"

"To save her. We'd been set up by Fate. It was her only way out at that point. She shouldn't have been there and I… whatever else I might have become, am still her father. Zeus would have done the same for you."

Athena tilted her head to the owl. The owl tilted back. "That still doesn't explain it," she said.

Thoth closed his eyes and exhaled. "I reckon what we thought was a World Tree was, in fact, a Chronodéndron – the very first one. Chronos must have created her as some sort of fail-safe when he helped the Titans create the first underworld."

Athena paled, then punched the armrest of her throne which such force, Pallas shuddered. "Tell me it's destroyed!" she shouted, practically foaming with rage. Few gods had done more to eliminate Chronodéndrons from the Universe than Athena.

"Yes! Nothing remains of the moon or its Tree. The abyss, too, is gone. I assure you."

This calmed the goddess somewhat. But did little to diminish her rage. "You should have been gone too," she said spitefully.

I have, he recalled. "No one should have gone through the abyss in the first place, Athena," he told her earnestly. Thoth felt like he'd woken up mid-fall in that resurrection ship, and he'd been falling ever since. Anubis had been right. They should have buried the temple the moment Fate had intervened. And left it buried. Now Anubis was lost in oblivion. And Thoth was… – he flipped through the infinite pages in Seshat's book – no longer the greatest writer in the pantheon, it seemed.

Athena stood up again and conjured her spear. "This is not how it was supposed to go!" She threw the spear across the hall. "First, we lost the Underworld." She willed the spear back to her hand and threw it at a pillar. "Then we lost Mnemosyne." She conjured it again. "And now this? Aargh!" She threw the spear a few more times at several different things before she was able ask the question. "Is that the only copy, you think?"

Thoth shook his head, for he knew his daughter well. But he said, "I hope so."

Athena dropped the spear. "There will be chaos."

He almost laughed. "Chaos – exactly – on a scale not even Chronos will be able to fix. The Fates –"

Athena cut him off. "Enough about those cunts. Skip to the end. Tell me what happens."

He did as she commanded.

The dust had long settled upon the marble floors by the time he closed the book. The twins dozed behind a broken pillar; the owl perched on his shoulder. It had taken him hours just to find the last chapter. Reading it might take years, so he'd skipped to the very last sentence.

Athena had not moved. "Tell me," she said.

Silence.

"Tell me how it ends!"

Thoth took a deep breath. Then another. "The end, goddess of wisdom, is just another beginning."

Acknowledgements

Some say it takes a village to write a book. Not mine. I work mostly alone and I can count with my fingers the number of people who genuinely helped me from draft to publication. But each one is worth a dozen in this little hamlet.

So once again, I'd like to thank my husband, Dave, who is not only my alpha reader and emotional supporter, he also took up the role of cover designer on this one.

My editor, Lisa Gilliam, for her reliability, professionalism and attention to detail.

My beta readers, especially Paromita and Jozua B., who made it to the end of a still very convoluted manuscript, riddled with typos and mistakes, and helped me sort through the mess.

To Taylor DeVayne for her meticulous proofreading and advice.

To The Fantasy Book Nerd for another cover reveal, great Wyrd Talks and thoughtful reviews.

To Sarah Kempton for giving voice to these characters and making my prose sound a lot better than it is.

A shout out to all who bought, read, rated and reviewed Timelessness over the years.

And to the lovely crowd at the Page Chewing forums for all the discussions, advice and support, especially to Frank, Varsha and Livia J. Elliot for their in-depth analysis of my work.

Last but not least, to Freya and Daemon for not letting me sit still staring at the computer for too long and reminding me that there's a world outside my imagination and I should enjoy it more often.

www.ingramcontent.com/pod-product-compliance
Lightning Source LLC
Chambersburg PA
CBHW061542190726
48289CB00004B/1138